THEY FOUGHT, TRIUMPHED, AND DIED IN A SWEEPING DRAMA OF LOVE AND REVOLT

Simon ben Eleazar: The Galilean shepherd rose to become an Emperor's best friend—and mortal enemy—as the legendary Wolf of Masada.

Vespasian: The wily peasant soldier battled his way to the Imperial throne—with the help of an ex-slave named Simon.

Claudius: Stammering but shrewd, he ruled Rome with a firm hand—and shared his wife's favors with a certain Jewish gladiator.

Shimshon Bar Giora: He was the undisputed general of the Jews' revolution—until he promoted himself to Messiah.

Andrasta: The tawny-haired princess of conquered Britannia, she swore to live for Simon's love—or die by his side.

They, and dozens more—*Nero, Caligula, Livia, Herod*—play unforgettable roles in a story of a legendary rebel and the powerful pride of an ancient people.

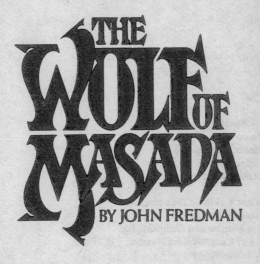

THE WOLF OF MASADA

BY JOHN FREDMAN

AVON
PUBLISHERS OF BARD, CAMELOT AND DISCUS BOOKS

Originally published in Great Britain in 1978
by W. H. Allen & Co., Ltd.

AVON BOOKS
A division of
The Hearst Corporation
959 Eighth Avenue
New York, New York 10019

First Avon Printing, March, 1980

The William Morrow edition carries the following
Library of Congress Cataloging in Publication Data:
1. Jews-History-Rebellion, 63–73—Fiction. I. Title

CONTENTS

TABLE OF DATES

In deference to Christian and Jewish beliefs both abbreviations AD and CE (Current Era) are employed in this book.

37	Petronius invades Judaea
41	Claudius succeeds Caligula
43	Britannia invaded
44–46	Vespasian reduces British hill forts
49	*Colonia* of Colchester founded
54	Nero succeeds Claudius
59–60	Boudiccan rebellion
60	Neronian games in Rome
61	The slaves of Pedanius Secundus executed
62	Nero marries Poppaea
64	Great fire of Rome Persecution of the Christians
65	Deaths of Seneca and Poppaea Nymphidus Sabinus becomes joint Imperial Guard commander with Tigellinus

PART
I

THE GALILEE
AND ROME—
WHERE THE FRIENDSHIP
WAS CONCEIVED

(37–43 CE)

"Kill him. Lash him. Burn him. Why does he meet the sword in such a cowardly way? Whip him to meet his wounds."

—SENECA, mocking the use
of prisoners in the arena

1

In 37 CE the Emperor Caligula, incensed at the Jews'
stubborn refusal to worship him as their God, ordered
his armies to march on Jerusalem and erect his statues
in the Temple.

The Roman general Petronius, in command of three
legions and a large body of Syrian auxiliaries, began a
swift march from Antioch down into Judaea and
camped at a seaside town in Galilee called Ptolemais.
Thereupon Petronius sat tight, doing nothing but make
excuses for his inactivity. The trouble was that Petronius, a devious little man who would never be distinguished for his military exploits, was nervous. His
soldiers were flabby and out of condition. He was a
garrison general with garrison soldiers, facing up to
Jews who, together with the Germans lurking in the
great northern forests, were thought to be the bravest
fighters in the ancient world. They had cut up Roman
legions before. Petronius knew that if the Jewish tribes
could ever stop their incessant quarreling and unite,
they would be able, with the fabulous tribute paid to the
Temple, to train and put into the field an army second to
none. The Roman general had a great regard for his own
skin, and while he feared Caligula in Rome, he feared the
Jews more. He preferred to listen and negotiate, rather
than fight.

His biggest problem was his Syrian auxiliaries: they
had come for booty, for women, for young boys and were
getting restless. Petronius was already uncomfortably
aware of this when Suleiman, the leader of his Syrian

3

ala of cavalry, was shown into his tent and went through the formal motions of obeisance before speaking.

"A drink?" Petronius asked nervously, indicating a pot of hot spiced wine.

Suleiman shook his head in disgust. "A fight," he said. He was a man of few words.

"I do not wish to antagonize these Jews." There was a note of pleading in the Roman general's voice.

"There are brigands in the hills that even the high priests would like killed," Suleiman said. "If I could smoke them out it would give my men"—he paused—"a little practice."

Petronius gave him a considered look. Suleiman commanded fierce and loyal fighting men, the kind who might make dependable bodyguards in the quicksand of Roman politics. It would pay to please him. "Very well," he said, "but kill as few as possible. Bring the rest back down here." He signed for the man to go, but the Syrian stood his ground. "Is there something else?" Petronius said, a trace of testiness in his voice.

"Could we have some fun with them first, Imperial Legate?"

Petronius sniggered. "Of course," he said. "Have some fun with them by all means." He waved a bejeweled finger and the Syrian quietly left the tent.

High in the mountains, the boy lay flat on his stomach and squinted into the fierce sun. Beneath him lay the well-timbered foothills of Galilee, not yet denuded of trees by the grazing of goats or the demands of shipbuilders. A kite quivered in the updraft of heated air, hardly moving as it adjusted its wings to each minute variation of wind. The boy studied the huge bird with its effortless freedom of movement, then shifted his gaze down into the valley. Haze and dust seemed to rise in distant waves. Masses of people, even a Roman army, someone had said, were maneuvering down there, but the boy was not concerned. Up in the high hills, his village had been left in peace for as long as anyone remembered. Two hundred or so of his tribe lived there, cultivating a few stony fields and harvesting their olives. They lived frugally, sharing their possessions

4

with each other and refusing to pay taxes, either to the Temple priests or the Roman procurator, in the sure knowledge that the authorities would consider the costs of collection not worth the yield.

They had not reckoned, however, with the boredom of Suleiman's men. As the boy turned and looked idly at the surrounding hills, the Syrian bowmen burst from the mountain defiles and descended on the village, riding their hardy little ponies flat out down the steep slopes, achieving maximum terror and surprise. It was early October. Harvest time. The women and children, engaged in beating and shaking the olive trees, fled at the first sight of the cavalry, screaming in fright. The men, who were turning the huge wooden olive press, exploded in all directions, reaching for their weapons, but, boxed in and unable to attain battle formation, they were picked off by the expert bowmen. A few of the older ones, excused from work because of their years, stumbled up the hill on matchstick legs toward where the boy lay. Among them was his father, Eleazar the patriarch. These men, too infirm to run or climb for long, eventually fell, to be dispatched by the short swords of the Syrians. Only Eleazar, spurred on by the boy's desperate shouts of encouragement, clawed with skinny hands at the boulders in front of him and somehow reached his side. His son grabbed him and, pulling him along behind, made for a small cave in the side of the hill.

The Syrians had been watching them and one of the bowmen pulled his pony to a halt, sighted carefully and sent an arrow right between the old man's shoulders, but the boy twisting and weaving, managed to make the cave entrance and, pulling his father after him, disappeared into the dark cave mouth.

Led by Suleiman, a detachment of Syrians walked their ponies up the stony slope and, at a sign from their leader, stopped within easy bowshot of the entrance, laughing and joking with each other. Down below, they could hear the frantic squeals of the women and girls being violated by their comrades and they were anxious to dispatch this impudent boy so that they could join the fun. One of the bowmen vaulted off his pony and went forward at a running crouch to peer into the cave, only to jackknife backward with a bubbling groan, a slim dagger stuck up to the hilt in his neck. All laughter stopped. Yet another Syrian unlimbered his bow and edged forward to get a good shot at the boy, then screamed in sudden agony as a throwing knife took him in the chest.

The smile faded from the face of Suleiman. He barked sudden orders and his men all dismounted, notched arrows and took cover. They would wait and they would watch, and sooner or later they would have the boy alive and they would make him pay.

Inside the cave Eleazar the patriarch wheezed his life away. "We grew careless," he whispered. "We should have posted lookouts. I warned them. It does not matter that we have no riches. We ourselves are the wealth."

"I do not understand you, Father."

"Slaves," the old man said, coughing up dark blood. "The Romans always need slaves."

"These are Syrians, Father."

"They work for the Romans. The Romans rule everywhere. They defile and farm humanity like cattle. They rule with the lash and the sword."

"Rest, Father," the boy said, cradling the old man's head in his arms.

"You must avenge me," the patriarch said. He lifted his eyes to the boy's, passion lending power to his voice. "You must avenge us all. You, your sons and your sons' sons, even if our people are scattered unto the four corners of the earth. Fight—until we Jews are free to live in peace."

"Yes, Father. I will do as you say."

"Make Kaddish for my departed soul," said the old man. Then his head fell to his chest and he died.

The boy sat there weeping, and at the sound of his grief-torn cries the Syrians ventured nearer.

"Come out," Suleiman cried. "Though you will be punished, I promise to spare your life."

The boy came to the opening of the cave. Suleiman, who had intended to shoot him as soon as he showed himself, lowered his bow in agreeable surprise. The boy was slim and wiry, tall although no more than sixteen. His skin under the dark tan of mountain sun was fair and soft as a girl's, his eyes gray-green; his hair, while

6

dark, was long and straight, unlike the kinked curls of the Semite. Suleiman had heard of these beautiful Galileans, their blood mixed hundreds of years before by intermarriage with Amorite tribes converted to Judaism. This was the first one he had seen.

The boy said, "I will offer prayers for my father, then I will come." He put down his cluster of throwing knives and, as the Syrians climbed up into the cave, turned toward the east in prayer. *"Yisgadal, yisgadash, shemay raboh,"* he intoned in a breaking voice. *"Yisboruch, veyistubuch, veyispoer—"* He swayed backward and forward, giving meaning and depth to the prayer, eventually finishing, *"Veyimeru amen."* He turned back toward Suleiman and said quietly, "Now I am ready."

Suleiman gave a sign and his men quickly stripped the boy of his clothes and forced him down on his knees, whereupon the Syrian, gripping the boy by the nape of his neck, did terrible, bestial things to him twice, in quick, shuddering succession.

Crouching there, his face brushing the ground, the boy, whose name was Simon, spat dust and dirt from his mouth with each cry of agony and swore there and then a great oath that he would obey his father's wishes and one day take revenge on the Romans and their lackeys.

Why, Petronius thought to himself, must this happen to me? Why are our civil governors expected to take command of armies and fight battles? The thought struck him that the Romans had become a great people because of precisely such abilities in their officials and only a few, like himself, lacked the courage to rise to the occasion. For many months now he had alternately cajoled and threatened the Jews camped on the plain of Galilee, but they had remained obdurate. They already sacrificed twice a day to the Roman Emperor but would rather die than have a graven image in their Temple.

Petronius knew he could never fight a battle and had no choice but to report failure. In the hope of buying his life, he now planned to send a present to Caligula of the two commodities of which Rome was always in short supply, captives for the arena and corn. With this in mind, he heaved his fat bulk into a shaded litter and gave orders that he be carried in easy stages to the port of Alexandria. With the prisoners following behind he set out on his journey and reached the port, accompanied by three centuries of his best troops.

The port captain, a man called Strabo—"the squinter"—was brought before him, and Petronius asked what transport he had available. Strabo knew Petronius' problem. He intended to make some money out of the situation, but the size of Petronius' escort convinced him that he would have to be careful.

"There is," Strabo said after some thought, "a large grain ship ready, owned by a consortium of influential senators, but they would only allow it to sail if the Government insured its loss. This is a bad time of year. Not only have we missed the Etesian winds, but heavy storms can be expected."

"What else?" Petronius asked.

The port captain shifted uneasily on his feet. "An army packet, my lord?" he suggested. "Very fast. It could leave today."

"Too small," Petronius said testily. "I have in mind a medium-sized galley that could carry both grain and a cargo of prisoners for the arena."

Strabo pretended to think. He said with assumed innocence, "Of course, such a cargo is particularly welcome to Caesar at this time of year..."

"You can recommend something?" Petronius said eagerly.

"Such a ship might be found," said Strabo.

"Who owns it?"

"A fat"—the port captain coughed apologetically—"a rich pig of a freedman called Eusepio, who has made several fortunes by risking his ships out of season." The two men exchanged glances. The merchant's being a freedman meant that he could probably be swindled with impunity. "I could"—there was an oily tone in Strabo's voice—"condemn his galley for nonpayment of port dues if your Excellency so desires."

"I so wish."

Strabo coughed politely. "There is a matter of—er—port dues—"

"My treasurer will call on you tonight."

"The general is most kind. May I offer one counsel?"

8

"What is that?"

"Use your strongest prisoners as galley slaves. Double-bank your oars. At this time of year a quick journey is a safer journey."

"It shall be done," said Petronius. Turning, he gave the orders.

Lined up on the quay with the other prisoners, Simon gazed with awe at the wonders around him, the huge moles constructed of pozzolana cement faced with limestone blocks and travertine marble; the great lighthouse towering into the sky continually fed with Greek fire by relays of slaves. It could be seen twenty miles at sea. What kind of people are these Romans? he thought. To survive, I must learn more. If I am to fight them I must understand them.

He was pulled from his reverie as the line of captives was led on board a nearby galley. Simon found himself sitting on a bare bench, wrists shackled to the big oar in front of him. By his side sat a man, naked except for a scrap of loincloth clinging to his spindly hips. Years of sun and exposure had dried his skin to the consistency of leather. Woefully emaciated the man was, his rib and shoulder bones protruding sharply from his half-starved body. Only on his arms had a thin cordlike layer of muscle grown as a result of constant pulling at the heavy oar. Although an occasional bucket of seawater was sluiced over them, the galley slaves were all filthy with their own excreta, and the awful barnyard smell made Simon suddenly gag.

The man watched him vomit with deep-set expressionless eyes, then said in Greek, "Do you speak my language, boy?"

"Of course," answered Simon. "My tribe is poor, but we believe in the power of learning."

"Where do you come from then?"

"We are Hebrews from the Galilean hills. We are known as the Sicarii because we fight well with the dagger and the throwing knife, which the Romans call the *sica*."

The man nodded to himself, then let his eyes droop shut, lapsing into sudden sleep as though deliberately conserving his strength. A little later a slave came round

9

with a stew of gristly meat, which, when his turn came, the boy refused. The man next to him, who had been watching with hawklike eyes, snatched the food and bolted it. "You Jews," he said, "with your strict laws, your meals without pork—you'll forget all that once you've felt the whip." He looked at Simon, his eyes feverish, sunken under his protruding cheekbones. "Now," he said, "you want to die, but when the whip comes down, you'll want to row, that's all. You'll pull your guts out to avoid the lash."

The boy shivered. He tried to be brave and said, "I will not eat their pork."

The man, whose name was Archelaus, looked at Simon for many seconds before speaking. "If you decide to live," he said at length, "perhaps I can show you a way, but I have not many days left."

"Why is that?" asked the boy.

"Down here, in the heat of the ship's hull, you strain at the oars and you sweat rivers, but they give you no drinking water to replace it. Something goes inside."

Simon watched the man's hand as he fiddled with his loincloth. He was relieving himself. With horror Simon saw that the man was not passing water, but blood.

The wind blew steadily out of the southeast, and with the big single sail bellied out amidships, the slaves sat idly at their oars. One morning, with a last freakish burst of late-summer heat, the sun beat down and the vessel wallowed, becalmed.

As the galley master uncoiled his whip and began snapping and cracking the stiffness out of the leather, Archelaus, who had been quietly sleeping, suddenly came to life and sat tensed over the oars like a nervous cat. "Now," he said, with eyes gleaming, "you can learn what hell can be like."

All through the endless day as the fierce sun arched across the sky, they were made to row, taking their time from a rhythmic drumbeat. The heat in the confined space grew insufferable and sweat poured from the bodies of the oarsmen. By afternoon, they were groaning with thirst and exhaustion, but, naked backs crawling with fear of the lash, no man dared rest for even a second. Simon, warned by Archelaus to protect his

10

hands, rowed stoutly through the day with cloth strips bound across his fingers. Apart from one warning cut of the whip that ripped across his young skin like a jet of boiling water, he avoided much torture. Archelaus though, unable to keep to the drum's beat, came in for terrible punishment by midafternoon, the lash popping and cracking across his shoulders and around his chest, the man's body jumping with agony from each convulsive explosion of leather on skin.

Only at dusk did the order come to cease rowing, and as the sound of the ship's way died to nothing, silence reigned in the bowels of the vessel. A silence of complete exhaustion, punctuated by an occasional groan and the delirious shriek of a slave gone mad who was shouting for his mother. That evening, slumped and gasping over his oar, the boy took his lump of pork gristle, washing it down with the one cup of *posca,* or vinegar wine, that each man was given, careful to swill the precious liquid around in his mouth before drinking it in small gulps.

"You are being sensible," Archelaus said, "and our Lord will forgive you for eating that meat."

"I don't want to die," said the boy.

"The strength in me is failing," said Archelaus. "I may last a day, perhaps two. Not more. I would like to teach you how to survive, because I think I have the way."

"Why do this for me?" Simon asked wonderingly.

"Because," the man paused, "you are beautiful and in better times I would have been your lover."

"Oh," said the boy, in whose tribe pederasty and perversion were unknown.

So it was that as the ship picked up a last fluky spell of easterly wind off the Asian mainland and ploughed steadily toward its first landfall off Rhodes, Archelaus explained to Simon the secret of the bulls.

He told not of the arts practiced openly on his native island of Crete, already well-known to the Romans—the graceful vaulting over a bull's horns by boy and girl ballet dancers—but of the male initiation rites handed down from the old Minoans and now performed only in secret mountain strongholds. He told how, by a close study of the bull, it was possible for a man to reduce the most powerful and dangerous fighting animal in the

11

world to gasping defeat, merely by the correct employment of a piece of red cloth. Such an art, he explained,
demanded many things from a man and few could do it.
Agility and arrogance were needed, a superb sense of
timing and ice-cold bravery to blend these things
together. One then required a bull that ran true and
straight and was, in its own way, as noble as the man
facing it. If, he said, all such things were brought
together, then a spectacle of such beauty could be
created that would bring even a jaded Roman crowd to
its feet.

Simon asked how it was that Archelaus, when first
taken as a slave, had not disclosed his secrets and thus
escaped the galley.

"Because," Archelaus said, "I thought the Romans
knew everything. It just didn't occur to me that they had
never seen this thing of the bulls. You must not make the
same mistake. When your turn comes for the arena, you
must speak up."

"What if the Master of the Games will not hear me?"

"Then you will die."

"And if the bull catches me?"

"He will either rip open your genitals or trample you.
Either way, you will die."

"And if I put up a bad spectacle?"

"The mob will see that you are slain."

"If," said the boy, with a trace of sarcasm that
surprised the Cretan, "you teach me to produce this
magnificent spectacle of emotion and beauty, will the
crowd spare my life?"

"Even then it is unlikely," Archelaus answered. "In
all the long history of captives butchered to make a
Roman holiday, none other than valuable gladiators,
has ever been pardoned."

Simon laughed suddenly, loudly—an astonishing
sound in that fetid pit of misery. He showed his white
teeth and said, "You are offering me a chance either to
live or to die like a man. Teach me your tricks."

The Cretan shot the boy a surprised look. He could
sense there was a strength in him, some indefinable
quality not given every man. For the first time in the
many years since he had been shackled to his oar like a
draft animal, he began to speak with animation and

12

spirit, and his deep-set eyes sparkled with vitality. Hour after hour, as the galley rolled and wallowed its way northwestward under its bulging single sail, he talked to the boy, instructing him in the mysteries of the bulls.

Eventually it was done and the Cretan sat back, exhausted. There was no more he could teach him. It would now depend on his athleticism, his courage and the bravery of the bull itself.

"Are you sure they have not seen this thing before?" Simon asked.

Archelaus smiled. "They have trained elephants to walk tightropes, ostriches to draw chariots, lions to hold live hares in their jaws and give them up at a word of command, but this union of man and bull they have never seen."

Such an outpouring of energy had tired the ailing Archelaus. He sat back and tried to sleep, but with the wind blowing strongly from the west, as was more usual at this time of year, the slaves were put back to the oars. Unable to keep to the rhythm of the drum, Archelaus was punished mercilessly, until at length his body gave no answering jerk to the lash and he lay lolling with the swell, sightless eyes to the sky.

They unchained the Cretan's body and threw it into the sea.

The ship continued on its way and, weeks later, the magnificent, arched breakwater of Puteoli came into view, with the huge crowd that somehow always learned of the arrival of a corn ship.

The boy still lived. Thanks to the lessons he had learned from Archelaus, he was soon restored to robust health and a burning intent to survive.

2

The carts carrying the prisoners for the arena wound
their way through the streets of Rome, creaking along in
the first rays of the rising sun toward the Statilius
Taurus amphitheater. Because of the strict enforcement
of the *lex julia municipalis* no wheeled traffic was
allowed in Rome during daylight hours, so the carts were
not impeded by other vehicles.

There was always a certain formality about the
procession. The wheels of these carts were always
spoked and the custom had not changed, despite the
success of some prisoners in wringing their necks in
these *radii* and cheating the arena of a spectacle. Behind
each cart came two members of the Praetorian Guard in
gleaming parade dress, and both this and the very
length of the convoy was enough to give the procession
the aspect of a ritual.

In the coolness of the dawn, before the sun blazed
down on the carnage in the arena and made the whole
city stink of blood, people stood around just to amuse
themselves by studying the faces of the prisoners. There
was always plenty of variation in the manner they went
to their deaths—the prisoners were only two well aware
of the host of hideous alternatives that awaited them.
Would they, for instance, be given swords and, goaded
by whips and branding irons, be made to hack each
other to pieces, or would that be too merciful a fate?
More likely they would be tied to stakes in deliberately
unnatural postures designed to make the wild beasts
hesitate and sniff at them before attacking, thereby

enhancing the suspense. Then, and only then, would the final horrific uncertainty of their end be decided. The big cats, for example, would stun or kill at the stroke of a paw, but some of the smaller beasts would kill with delicious cruelty, dragging and tearing at their victims while they quivered in protracted agony.

Some prisoners wept while others laughed hysterically in the merciful release of madness; many collapsed with fear, let their sphincter muscles go and disgraced themselves. Only Simon the Galilean remained silent and aloof, his young face set with resolve at the thought of what he must do.

To reach the amphitheater the carts needed to cross almost the entire city and, as they approached the entrances, the murmur of the crowd massing on the tiers could be clearly heard. Caught up in the maelstrom of people rushing to get in before the morning gladiatorial contests began, the carts were halted for a few minutes, and Simon, in spite of his preoccupations, couldn't help but notice the colorful scene all around him. There were senators and dignitaries, sweaty *nouveaux riches,* their fingers ablaze with rings set with precious stones, their heads shaven and their chins bearded in the current craze for the Stoic fashion, all wearing togas of a careful uniform white, since Caligula had executed his cousin for having the temerity to attend the games in a purple mantle.

Even as Simon watched, a litter arrived, carried by eight trotting Syrian slaves. A tall, statuesque blonde, half veiled in mock modesty, alighted. She was wearing a fortune in jewels and her shimmering fair hair was scaffolded on her head in the height of fashion.

As she looked around her, she caught sight of the boy in the cart, separated from the slobbering captives in an attitude of almost negligent gracefulness. Their eyes met and held for almost half a minute, hers blue, his greenish and catlike. In what looked like an impulsive gesture, she pulled her veil away and smiled at him, a smile of sympathy and encouragement; then she was gone, sweeping imperiously into the arena, her attentive slaves carving a path for her through the milling throng.

Simon could not believe it. As a simple farm boy from the mountains, he had never realized that a woman

15

could be so beautiful. She was a million years away from the ragged shepherd girls he had known. Although she was older than he by at least ten years, her poised and experienced worldliness aroused him.

A pull on his neck chain dragged him back to the horror of his predicament, and he dismounted from the cart, knowing he must survive in order to see the girl again.

The prisoners now met further tribulations. As they walked toward the passageway leading under the stands, they were fallen upon by a bunch of screaming degenerates who experienced pleasure from pawing those condemned to die in the arena. Struggle as they would, the prisoners, chained hand and foot, could not rid themselves of the fighting, kicking mob. The soldiers just stood by and did nothing while they were slowly swept under the stands until the dull clang of metal rang behind them.

The perverts began screaming and beating the bars, yelling to be let out, but when the guards merely grinned and turned away, they realized the dreadful truth—they had come up against their master, Caligula, who was going to amuse himself, in turn, by watching them die.

Inside the cage it was cool, only the roar of the crowd coming faintly to the penned captives. As the morning wore on toward noon, when the prisoners would be used as a diversion for the common people, tension grew, and each soldier who came near the cage was greeted with fearful glances. Even the perverts had ceased their frenzied screaming and now lay like the other captives, awaiting inevitable death.

The Master of the Games came down and began whispering last-minute instructions to the officer in charge of the guard.

Simon walked over to the bars and calmly crooked a finger at the Master of the Games, a man by the name of Flaminius, a burly ex-gladiator with half his nose cut away. Flaminius, amused by the liberty the boy had taken, strolled over. "You want me?" he said.

"Sir," said Simon, "if you let me go alone into the ring with a wild bull, I will show you something that will bring the crowd cheering to its feet."

"We have such acts," Flaminius said contemptuously, turning his back.

16

"Tumblers and dodgers." The boy sneered. "A clumsy baiting from the safety of horseback. How would you like to see me conquer such a bull, bring it to its knees, with nothing in my hands but a piece of red cloth?"

Somehow, the sheer arrogance of the boy's tone stopped the Master of the Games in his tracks. "You mock me, boy," he said. "It cannot be done."

"It is a mystery of the people who live in the high mountains behind Knossos," Simon said. "I am the first one who has been brought to Rome with knowledge of this art. How can you," he added convincingly, "ignore such a new spectacle? Everyone knows how jaded is the Roman mob."

"What you say is true," admitted Flaminius. He spoke with feeling. He was only too well aware of the hideous fate of his predecessor, who, for boring Caligula with the monotony of the games, had been flung into a cell and flogged daily with chains. He thought for a moment, then said, "Very well. I'll give you thirty seconds to get the crowd cheering. If you fail, you'll provide a particularly tasty final spectacle."

"What is that, sir?"

"The death of the little cuts. Caesar has a saying, when ordering such an execution—'Let him feel that he is dying.'"

The boy shuddered. "I shall do my best."

Flaminius looked at him curiously. "Boy, what can you hope to gain from this? You will die anyway."

"The crowd—perhaps they will be pleased. They could pardon me."

"It has never been known," Flaminius said shortly, and strode away to give his orders for the next event.

When his turn came, Simon took with him only the scarlet dress cloak he had borrowed from one of the Praetorian Guards. He strode out into the arena, ticking off the items one by one that Archelaus had dinned into him—details that on his slow journey to Rome he had repeated to himself time after time until they were burned into his memory, had become part of him and were proof against panic.

He let his toes bite into the green copper dust preferred to sand by the Emperor Caligula, getting the feel of its consistency, gauging his foothold. When only a few

17

yards out, he remembered to swagger and hold his head high and haughty, as if demanding respect and attention. The crowd—only those as depraved as the Emperor stayed to watch the noontime slaughter of humans by the wild beasts—was momentarily amused by his bearing.

Simon went down on his knees, facing the animal entrance, spread the scarlet cloak out in front of him and waited. He was gambling on making those first thirty seconds exciting. Again he muttered to himself those vital things he was to watch for, what he must do with absolute split-second timing when the moment arrived.

The bull, when it came out, was huge. About fifteen hundred pounds, standing six feet high. It was wide-chested, black all over, with a small snout and a wet, lustrous nose. It stood for a moment, blinking in the sudden blinding light of the arena.

When a slave laid the glowing branding iron against its rump, it's muscles rose and swelled, its eyes shone with fury and, when at that precise moment Simon shouted sharply at the animal, its ears flicked back, it let out a roar and charged him.

The boy felt the thunder of its hooves and the animal's black bulk closing in. With icy courage and timing the movement to perfection, he gripped one corner of the cloak with his right hand and leaned his body to the right while at the same time swinging his cloak around his head in a leftward direction. The bull, taking the flare of the cape at the last minute, charged past him.

The crowd cheered. The boy got up off his knees, brushed away the dust and puffed out his chest. He did a slow, lazy, almost dancing walk toward the bull. He knew now what it was like to be lucky. A man has to have luck, Archelaus had said. Without it you could draw ten kinds of bad bull and be made to look ridiculous, but if you drew a straight-running, brave bull—then there would be emotion and there would be beauty.

"Come," the boy called arrogantly. He stood stock-still, sideways to the bull. He stamped his feet, indicating to the crowd, "Here I am. Here I stay."

The crowd whistled, appreciating the courage of the

gesture. The bull lowered its head and charged hard and straight, but the boy, with a mere graceful incline of the body, took the animal safely past him, leading it away and out beyond its original path. The bull turned, boring in from the other direction, and again the boy led the bull past and away from him. Again and again the bull stopped, turned and charged in its raving fury. Man and animal seemed locked at times in some strange sinuous dance, and the crowd, taking up the rhythm of their movements, began to cheer each separate pass of the cloak.

Simon knew he had their sympathy now, that the people were on his side. Enough, he said to himself. He remembered Archelaus telling him again and again to make it short and sweet, that there was nothing more boring in this world than watching a man trying to make a tired bull charge.

The next time the bull came in, Simon brought it up short with a sharp half-movement of the cloak, then, to the amazement of the crowd, walked casually up to the animal, stroked its muzzle and rested his elbow against its forehead.

The crowd, fascinated by the boy's bravery, was not to know that his fast, abrupt movement with the cloak had been carefully calculated to turn the bull sharply in on itself, twist its back, wheel its hindquarters rapidly around, certainly wind it and, perhaps, catch its testicles painfully between its legs. The effect was that, for a few vital seconds, a man could do what he wanted with the bull and take the most incredible liberties.

Simon knew that he was doomed to die horribly in any event, and if the bull killed him then and there, it would at least be quick and clean. Accordingly, he bowed to the four corners of the arena, then shooting a last look at the animal to check that its ears were back—like most bulls it tended to attack only after putting its ears forward—he sank down on his knees, right between the bull's forelegs, and abased himself to the crowd, raising one single finger in the time-honored request for mercy by a defeated gladiator.

The crowd, not really roused by anything less than spilled blood, did not care one way or the other, but they had been amused by the novelty of his act and by his bravery. A cheer grew slowly in volume and they gave the "thumbs up." At once, war trumpets blared, signaling slaves to surge into the arena and entice the bull away so that the crowd might indulge itself in the rare spectacle of a condemned prisoner receiving an Emperor's pardon.

Simon walked toward the royal box, prepared to give thanks.

However, there was one man who did not agree that his life should be spared. A man who called himself a god.

Caligula.

The Emperor sprang to his feet on the podium, forced his way through a protesting row of white-clad Vestal Virgins, rushed down the gangway and promptly fell flat on his face to a great shout of laughter.

As Caligula had chosen to wear a woman's silk robe and slippers that day, the sight was very funny indeed.

"Hello, sweetheart," someone called.

"I couldn't resist little Bootikins today," roared a grizzled ex-centurion, his face lined and seamed from the African campaigns.

Caligula shook his fist in the general direction of the insult and screamed, "I do not spare captives and criminals." Shifting his hand and pointing at Simon, he said, "Put him to death."

A crowd has a mind of its own, each individual fusing with the other until, at length, the collective will is tripped into action. Although they had not cared particularly whether or not Simon died, these games belonged to the Romans and not to their Emperor. As the slaves moved to execute Caligula's order, a great roar of protest rose from the crowd. A thousand white handkerchiefs appeared and there was the thunder of stamping feet as the rhythmic cry was taken up, "Send him back, send him back."

"No," Caligula screamed over the top of the noise in his great foghorn voice. "He will die. You hear me? He will die."

"Still making love to all your sisters?" some wag cried.

"Go to it, baldy," someone else shouted, and there was a great gust of laughter.

Caligula, who cared little about his reputation for incest, was very sensitive about his complete baldness while still only in his twenties, and his face darkened with rage. He drew a savage finger across his neck in an unmistakable gesture and snarled, "If you had just one throat, I would cut it."

The sight of this tall, thin-necked man with his spindly, hairy limbs, his sunken-eyed, hollow-templed face and his ungainly body clad in women's robes, capering in fury as he hurled threats at them, began to annoy the mob. As the jeers turned to a storm of open insults, Caligula suddenly snapped an order to the big, blond Germans, clad in animal skins, who made up his personal bodyguard. The open menace in the way that the guard came to attention, the butts of their javelins hitting the ground at precisely the same second, quieted the crowd momentarily until one man, braver than the others, threw a piece of rotten fruit that splattered all over the Emperor's clothes.

Instantly, the air was full of flying missiles. The crowd took to this new game with relish and pelted Caligula, who, instead of ordering his men into action, now showed utter cowardice. He turned tail and fled the arena to a roar of derision. This was the time when the German guard, angry at the slight to their master, might well have cut loose and caused a massacre, but another man rose from his seat on the Emperor's podium, and the anger of the people melted the moment they recognized him.

The man was Claudius, the Emperor's middle-aged uncle. Claudius, the genial buffoon, the weak-minded imbecile, the butt of everybody's wit. The world loves a fool, and the crowd gave him a good-natured cheer. When it was plain that he intended to speak, the people granted him respect and silence, so that his quavering voice could be heard.

"He did well, didn't he?" Claudius said, pointing to the figure of the boy crouching below him in the dust.

"Yes," screamed the crowd. "Send him back. Pardon him."

"Well, I'd like to," Claudius said, "but we've annoyed the Emperor, you know. We must show our respect for him."

"Shove Priapus' symbol up him," someone shouted. There was a gust of laughter at this reference to the large appendage on the god of fertility, a figure frequently seen on Roman gateposts.

Claudius began to shake horribly and saliva dribbled from his mouth. "Oh, I don't think he'd like that at all." He scratched his head, letting the laughter subside, then said, as though suddenly struck with a bright idea, "I know what to do. I'll send him to be trained as a retiarius. We'll match him with one of the best of the Emperor's Thracians in a *sine missione*. That should be fun. You all know how much I love to watch the unhelmeted retiarii die—"

"Good old Claudius," someone yelled. "He's not such a damn fool."

"Is it a good idea, then?" Claudius said.

"Yes," screamed the crowd.

"Very well," said Claudius, "let's get on with the games." He sank back into his chair, beaming all over his good-natured face.

Simon was whisked out of the arena and put into an anteroom away from the moaning captives waiting to be sacrificed to the beasts. He was bewildered and confused, not understanding the gist of Claudius' speech, and was still standing forlornly in the middle of the room when a man was shown in.

The man waited until the door had been safely shut and bolted behind him, then said softly, "I am known as Herod Agrippa."

It never occurred to Simon to doubt him. Under the plain black cloak assumed for purposes of anonymity, he caught sight of rich cloth and the glint of jewelry. Simon took in the short, black, silky beard, waxed so as to jut out and add strength to his chin, the sensitive lips of the diplomat, ready to dissemble and flatter, or threaten with the self-assurance that comes with royal blood, and knew he must be a king.

This then was the Jew his father had told him about, who had become the friend of Rome, the confidant of emperors, to whom Caligula had awarded, first, the kingdom of Bashan, and then the tetrarchy of Galilee and Gilead, as a result of Herod's clever conspiracy against his uncle Antipas. He was now a very great man indeed and ruled over the high, barren hills where Simon's tribe, the Sicarii, lived, but the tribe had never paid tribute to anybody, neither the high priests in Jerusalem nor some bejeweled puppet king set over them by the Romans. The tribe acknowledged only one lord, their Lord, Yahweh.

A smile flitted over Herod's lips when he noted that the boy did not abase himself at his feet. He knew about these sturdy, independent outlaws from the mountains and had indeed expected nothing else.

"What does a great king like you want of me?"

"I must congratulate you first," Herod said, "on your skill and good fortune in the arena this afternoon."

"Thank you," said the boy. "Perhaps you'd explain what the Emperor's uncle meant."

"Certainly. You will be sent to the gladiator school at Pompeii and there taught to fight with net and trident. Eventually you will come back to this arena, matched against a Thracian who is *primus palus,* that is, of the first rank. The fights on that day will be *sine missione,* which means that the vanquished is always killed. You may depend on it, there's always a huge crowd on such days."

"Then where is my good fortune if I'm to die anyway?"

"You will get eighteen more months to live while you receive your training. By the time your day comes, Caligula could be dead. He is a hated man, ruling by terror, by arbitrary execution, by the informer."

The boy said coldly, "Suppose I were to repeat all this?"

Herod laughed indulgently. "Who would believe that you had been visited by Herod Agrippa? Or that you had received any visitors at all? The guard has been very well bribed."

"It doesn't matter," Simon said. "Tell me why you have come to see me."

"To give you your destiny."

"My destiny?"

"It pleases me to offer you one. By the time you fight,

23

Claudius will probably be Emperor. He is not heir to the throne, but he has two things in his favor. He will still be alive. No one ever kills the court jester. Also he is popular with the Praetorian Guard and they can make him Emperor."

The boy said patiently, "What has this to do with me?"

There is great nobility in his character, thought Herod. He behaves with me as if it is he who is king, not I. Surely he will one day become a great leader of men. He said, "I am coming to that. Claudius and I are great friends. We were brought up with the same tutor. When the rebellion against Caligula comes, I shall be here to see that Claudius receives the crown—I have more friends in high places than anyone in Rome. When Claudius reigns, he will reward me. He will add greatly to my possessions and I will become the first king of all Israel since David."

"And a slave to the Romans," Simon said, with a scornful laugh.

"Perhaps," Herod said, "but when I am king, I will rearm my people and build such fortifications that Jerusalem will become impregnable."

"You'll be a traitor to your friend Claudius," Simon said with contempt.

"But is that so important?" Herod asked with a smile. "Surely you know that it is written that a leader will come one day, who will knit the armies of Israel together and sweep the invaders from our country?"

"The Messiah, the son of David?" the boy said aghast. "The deliverer? You pretend to be he?"

Herod laughed indulgently. "How can one know until one finds out? Perhaps me, but I doubt it. I am too old and too devious. Perhaps it will be you. Either way it doesn't matter. It is only necessary that one's followers believe in the possibility."

"Very well," said the boy, with a strange and sudden calm. "Everything is explained and I am grateful to you. Would you please leave me now?"

This lad is truly amazing, thought Herod. He behaves as if it were he granting me the audience. On an impulse he took off his signet ring incised with the menorah, the seven-stemmed candelabrum. Handing it to Simon, he said, "If I die, you must take up the struggle. If not now, then in ten, even twenty years' time. A leader must be found to fight for our people's freedom. I will tell them about you when I get back to Judaea and Galilee—how you were the first prisoner condemned to the beasts to be pardoned in the arena—I will tell them that one day you will come home. I will see that they weave legends about your bravery in their songs and include you in their daily prayers. Show them that ring and they will know who you are. Will you promise to come back—if you survive?"

"I don't know," the boy said casually. "There is something about the life of a wealthy Roman that appeals to me. I find the women here more beautiful than at home."

Yes, thought Herod, they will devour you, these Roman women. You, with those green eyes and fair skin. That is our trouble. We are too pleasure-loving ourselves, too oriental to resist the lusts of the flesh. He examined the boy's mouth, straight and open, but with the hint of a quirk, the frowning pout of passion that would set into line at the first debauch. Yes, there is corruption there, he said to himself, and nobility and bravery, but first the corruption must come out and perhaps the nobility will one day win.

He nodded, then said shortly and with terrifying insight, "Do not forget your solemn oath to your father."

They waited in silence until the guard unlocked the door, then Herod left without another word.

3

Even under the brightness of a noon sun, the Pompeian school for gladiators was a grim place, the barracklike buildings standing out stark and functional against the brooding outline of Vesuvius.

The twenty men dismounted from the carts that had brought them from Rome and were paraded in the school quadrangle. They waited in a patient, thirsty line in the grilling heat, while their fetters were struck off. A burly, battered-looking slave appeared and growled, "Attention. Your master comes."

The line had hardly dragged itself into order when an enormously squat man came striding out at marching pace, snapping a cane in his hand, and stopped a few feet in front of them. Despite being in his fifties, he had not run to fat and resembled some super-fit wrestler with his enormous chest and arm muscles glistening in the sun with each movement he made. A huge white scar ran diagonally across his face, indenting his forehead, straddling a socket where his eye was now just a sightless black pulp, avoiding his nose, then splitting his lip and chin. Stripped naked as he was, except for a small loincloth, the line of the scar could be seen to continue its diagonal swathe across the man's chest, ending only at the lower rib. The effect of this man, standing legs straddled before them, marked so hideously by the scar which stood out a livid white against the dark tan of his flesh, was crushing. Something like a moan went up from the prisoners before he spoke.

"I am Centurion Flaccus," he bellowed. "Late of the Twelfth Legion, invalided honorably out of the service with my wounds. We gained the name *Fulminata* and I promise you I also am a 'lightning hurler.' I am master of this school under the Emperor, and you call me Dominus now—always." He paused, letting his voice sink to a growl so that it could gradually rise in crescendo. "I have to tell you that you are nothing. You are lower than the beasts in the field. Captives, slaves, condemned thieves, you are already dead, although you may not know it. Why do they call you the barley men? Because we feed you barley along with your beans and meat to build you up. You are just walking flesh being fattened like geese for the kill. There is no hope for you. None at all. Tonight, do me a favor. Kill yourselves and save me the trouble of teaching you how to die. Tomorrow, those of you who are mad enough to go on living will swear the oath." He laughed coarsely. "That ought to teach a few more of you to do the right thing. Believe me," he roared at the top of his voice, "there is nothing left for you in this world. You are better off in the next. I repeat, you have no hope. You are all in the same legion now, the legion of the damned." He waited for his words to sink in, then said sharply, "You'll be given food and drink and then taken to your cells. Dismiss."

The men ate thoughtfully and in silence in the huge mess hall. Simon, looking around him at the table, realized that the men were mostly the sweepings of the jails, plus a few prisoners of war—each of them picked because of his physique. After food, they were made to bathe together under the watchful eyes of more tough-looking slaves, then locked up, one man to a cell. "Sleep well, O great gladiator!" the slave said sarcastically as the key grated in the lock.

There was no window, except for a small barred slit in the stonework, and Simon's eyes took time getting accustomed to the poor light. When he could look around him, he found that he had been given a small stone cell barely twelve feet square with no more than a ledge built into the wall to serve as a bed. He heaved himself up on the thin mattress of dirty straw, put his hands behind his head and attempted to sleep, but sleep would not come.

As he lay there sweating in the tiny enclosed space, his mind went back to the days of his freedom. Most of all, he remembered the scent of thyme and eucalyptus, the overpowering perfume of the Galilean hills in spring, the bells tinkling on the necks of his goats as he brought them in from the lush pasture. He panted in the fetid heat, wishing he were out under the stars again, breathing the sharp, pure mountain air, and in spite of himself a lump formed in his throat and he wanted to cry.

He had to be brave. The past was gone now and he must try to be a man. Somehow he must survive. There was so much of the world he wished to see, so much to do, so many pleasures to enjoy. His finger drifted over the stonework and stopped at the graffiti scratched there by generations of gladiators. It was just light enough to make out what was written. "Pomponius eleven wins,"

27

he read. Pomponius was crouched, making the sign for mercy. Below him had been drawn the sign meaning "killed." He read another: that Crescens the Retiarius had been "the master and healer of girls in the night," *dominus et medicus puparum nocturnarum.* They must bring in women then, Simon thought. It would be nice to know at least one woman before I die. His finger led him to one final piece of graffiti: *"Apollinaris hic cacavit bene,"* he read unbelievingly—"Apollinaris had an excellent bowel movement here." Suddenly he burst out laughing. With humor, he thought, one can survive any misery. Feeling calmer, he turned over and slept.

In the morning only sixteen of the original twenty were left. Two had hanged themselves with their belts, the other two had smashed their chamber pots, the one eating some broken shards, the other cutting his throat.

"Right," roared Flaccus when they paraded in front of him again. "Down to sixteen, are we? Perhaps I can persuade a few more of you to 'resign.'"

Making the men squat in the yard, he now had them branded agonizingly on the thigh with the letters D A L—*damnatio ad ludum*, condemned to the games. That night three more men decided to kill themselves, and the thirteen left, with enough sheer steel in their hearts to stay alive, were put to rigorous training.

And so days turned into months as Simon absorbed his new trade, learning to cast and recast the great fisherman's net of the retiarii until he could flick a fly off the wall with its leaded tips, acquiring the quicksilver speed in offense and retreat essential to the protection of his lightly armored body in the arena.

What happened exactly three months after his arrival had been horrific and unexpected. Afterward Simon realized it had been engineered just to brutalize, to mark a phase in their training. Flaccus had assembled all the young gladiators, and was trying to teach them how to conquer their reflexes by stabbing fingers toward their eyes until they mastered the urge to blink and draw away. Only a big, clumsy Batavian could not seem to learn and kept drawing his head away at each thrust.

"Very well," said Flaccus quietly. He commanded the Batavian to assume the death position, in which a gladiator on receiving the "thumbs down" would meet his end with proper dignity. Accordingly, the man sank to the ground, gripping Simon's thigh just above the knee to steady himself and exposing his neck to the sword.

Flaccus came up and whispered into Simon's ear, "Kill him." Simon went white. He looked at Flaccus to see if he was smiling, but the centurion nodded, his face set and grim. Simon smiled into the Batavian's simple, trusting face, resting upturned on his thigh, brought the sword sharply back and thrust home. A great gout of blood burst from the man's throat. His body slid back and, with head drooping, he died like a wilting flower that had not been watered for many days.

Simon stood there shivering. At once the rough hand of Flaccus descended on his shoulder. "Why did I order that man's death?" he shouted to the assembled tyros. "For many reasons. This school has a fine reputation which it is my duty to uphold. The man was a stupid ox who would have died clumsily. He lacked the nobility to observe the proper ritual. Do you think the Roman crowd would forgive that? Also, there are other reasons. I had to prove to you that death is nothing. That obedience to orders is everything. It is my job to teach you your skills in a learned profession. Your chance to survive is tiny. You know that? You will be taken from here and matched against a *primus palus* who will slaughter you. This is how life is. That man is a big star worshiped by thousands of Romans. They like to see him win. He is worth a fortune in votes to politicians, in popularity to the Emperor if he appears. He can fill an amphitheater. You think they will risk his death? No. So they put him in with the new boys—you." His finger roved over the class. "Lambs for the slaughter." He laughed scornfully at them for a second, then dropped his voice. "But"—he paused for effect—"learn your lessons well and become skilled in your trade, then one of you—just one of you—might survive and become like Eutyches or Flamma and own estates and slaves and beautiful women by the score, and you will owe it all to your old master Flaccus, because he taught you obedience and discipline. Dismiss."

As the slaves came to carry away the Batavian's

broken body, Flaccus came up to Simon. "There is a lady of quality who wishes to visit you. Previously I have not permitted it. Now the privilege is deserved."

"Thank you, Dominus."

"Obedience has its own rewards—besides, she paid me well." Flaccus grinned coarsely, then strode away.

Safe from prying eyes in his small cell, the girl took off the cloak that had concealed her identity, the heavy yellow silk rustling as it fell to the floor. By the weak, guttering light of the cheap oil lamp, she pulled off her peacock-blue dress, and the mean little room was full of the delicious smell of perfume and Simon could see the satin sheen of her body.

She came up and nestled close to him on the ledge that served for a bed. The contrast her soft skin made with the hard stone excited him, virgin and unsure of himself. The smell of musk and rare Arabian perfume enveloped him until he felt drunk with ecstasy. For an hour they swayed and rocked together like animals, without a word being spoken, until their need for each other was satisfied. He lay exhausted beside her, the girl's blond hair shimmering in the lamplight.

"You were magnificent, standing alone and aloof in that cart," she whispered. "I had to see you again. There was just a chance, I hoped, that you might survive. Of course after you were pardoned, it was easy to find you."

"But why me?" Simon was still ingenuous enough to ask.

"Some drool with excitement over the hideous scars of battle on the old fighters," she replied, "but I wanted your youth, your innocence, to be your first woman, to suck the first excitement from your loins." She bent over and kissed him softly, and Simon, now used to the light, could make out the delicacy of her features, the powdered antimony highlighting her eyes, the rich redness of her painted, predatory mouth. She began to stroke him lightly with experienced fingers and succeeded in rousing him once again. Eagerly she took the shock of his violent thrusts until they both subsided into exhausted sleep.

Three hours later, just before dawn, she awoke, dressed quietly and kissed him awake.

"Who—who are you?" Simon mumbled. "What is your name?"

"My name is Livia," she whispered. "A noblewoman married to a pig of a commoner with more money than manners."

"I will count the days until your return."

"So soon the elegant phrases," she said lightly. "I find you amusing. Show the same passion for me when I come again, and who knows? Perhaps I can buy you a chance to live."

He watched her tall slender figure, wrapped in her cloak, let out of his cell by a respectful slave, who bowed repeatedly as he waited for his bribe.

Months passed. Slowly Simon learned how the Romans achieved the trick of making men train so gladly to die. The mystique of the gladiators enveloped and enfolded him. These were at once the lowest of the low yet adulated and worshiped, providing as they did a spectacle of steel-hard courage and noble disdain of death. The ceaseless training and fierce discipline ground the men into a macabre brotherhood and they began to exhibit a fierce pride seen only in the crack regiments of the line.

The barracks were their home and although no man had more than a mean, bare cell, there were compensations. They were fed and exercised like costly livestock, a whole village industry supporting their existence—first-class doctors, masseurs, bathing facilities, armorers to fit the golden breastplates and greaves they would wear on their pathetically brief appearance in the arena. They were made, in short, to feel elite and so the trick was done, and they would march gladly out on the sand to murder each other for the Roman mob.

As for Simon, the rich, promiscuous Livia finally tired of his youthful lovemaking, but true to her word she bought the handsome, green-eyed boy a chance to live. After a large donation by her adoring husband, Eusepio, to the imperial treasury, Claudius was persuaded to match Simon not against a Thracian of the *primus palus*, but the more usual sort of gladiator, a *mirmillo*. Claudius would not agree, however, to waive the *sine missione* because he expected the new boy to be

31

vanquished at the hands of the more experienced man and enjoyed watching the death agonies on the unprotected faces of the retiarii.

4

A feeling of electricity gripped the whole town. A white-hot heat of anticipation. There was talk of nothing else.

The new Emperor, Claudius, was sponsoring inaugural games and they would be *sine missione*. That meant everything—there would be no trickery, no rigged fights, no collusion to spare expensively trained fighting men to appear again. Of every pair of gladiators that fought, one had to die. Any friendship or brotherhood between such men would be forgotten and the encounters would be of desperate intensity.

For days now the walls and the milestones on the approaches to Rome had been covered with colored posters lettered by a special scribe, offering details of the contests. To maintain public interest, stop-press supplements announcing new pairs of fighters were added to the advertisements day by day, hour by hour. Then the lists were copied, sold in the streets and distributed in the bars, the brothels, the wineshops. Heralds did the rounds of the public squares and *fora*, crying out proudly the names of the prospective combatants. All the stars would be there—men with legendary reputations: Flamma, Astacius, Bellerophon, and for once their popularity with the crowd would not save them if, by a momentary lapse of skill, they were worsted. Beaten, they would die. Such a thought was shattering.

The town went mad.

The morbid ceremonial began the day before the fights when the Emperor, according to tradition, gave a splendid feast for the contestants. The public was admitted and allowed to circulate around the tables with gloating eyes. Some gladiators, either stupid or fatalistic, abandoned themselves to the pleasures of the moment and ate and drank gluttonously. Those fighters who were very young or lacking nerve picked at their food. The public, who usually knew what to look for, made note of those who ate with composure and would be in good shape for fight. They rushed to get their bets down.

A huge clamoring queue built up outside the stadium overnight and by morning a jam-packed crowd sweltered in the early heat. Seamen operated the huge woolen sail to provide maximum shade to the crowd; sellers of wine and soft drinks did a roaring trade.

Paegnarii came into the arena, hitting at each other in mock combat with sticks, whips and wooden swords. Dwarfs with huge, painted phalli strapped to their bodies clowned and tumbled their way across the sand. These spectacles only served to whet the appetite of the crowd for what was to come, and the amphitheater bubbled with excitement.

Complete silence descended as two priests in white robes and red scarves approached a temporary altar set up in the middle of the arena, leading a bull and a ram. With much sprinkling of incense, the two animals were sacrificed and their entrails examined to see if the gods wished the games to take place. The priests, who valued their lives, nodded to the crowd, who, not expecting any other decision, gave them a derisive cheer. The priests filed out, swinging incense burners and chanting hymns, the arena emptying as slaves removed the carcasses of the dead animals.

Music could be heard. "They're coming, they're coming," voices shouted, cracking with hysteria. Then the procession began. Led by slaves in golden armor blowing long trumpets, it filed through the Gate of Life. Floats bearing statues of gods and goddesses, pulled by gaily caparisoned horses and preceded by a band of musicians, went once around the arena, then left to great applause from the impatient crowd.

A fanfare of trumpets sounded and the Emperor

appeared, entering his box from the rear. The crowd cheered him, rising from their seats as a mark of respect. The arena was now bursting, the rows around the Emperor packed tight with senators, knights, Vestal Virgins, visiting celebrities, the pristine white of their togas and gowns clashing with the polychrome, threadbare tunics worn by the common people.

Total silence. The tableau was now complete. The crowd held its breath.

The gladiators came.

The stadium erupted into frantic applause. To the sound of martial music, the combatants swept across the arena in military formation, keeping perfect step, their golden armor and ornate, embossed parade helmets glittering in the intense light, ostrich and peacock feathers bowing and fluttering in time to the swinging bravado of their pace. Cheer after wild cheer rang out as the crowd recognized its particular favorites.

Once around the arena the fighters went, then stopped with perfect timing under the Emperor's podium. They took off their helmets and shouted as one man, *"Ave Caesar, morituri te salutamus!"* Then they broke ranks and scattered across the arena, doing limbering-up exercises and posturing to the crowd.

Meanwhile a trestle table had been erected on the sand and the gladiators' weapons were laid out for inspection. The Emperor—good old amiable Claudius—descended the steps and carried out the *probatio armorum,* testing the weapons for their sharpness to show that the games would be conducted with integrity. Dribbling saliva, Claudius pulled his finger away from a sword edge with a theatrical gesture, screwing up his lips in mock pain. The crowd, liking the joke, gave him a cheer.

Then the somber strains of a single war trumpet sounded. The deep, haunting sadness of the notes as they announced the imminence of death was in strange contrast to all the preceding gaiety. The solemnity of the moment never failed to affect the crowd emotionally and a profound silence ensued.

The first fighting pair took a stand in the middle of the arena, looking awkward and brutish. At the drop of

34

the hand of the Master of the Games, they engaged. They were dressed as a Thracian and a *hoplomachus,* their armor and weapons deliberately varied to provide contrast. Unfortunately, the match ranked as no more than a warm-up, and the two untrained slaves, pressed into armor for the mob's amusement, turned the fight into a clumsy contest that ended only when the Thracian tripped over his opponent's feet and lay stunned on the ground.

The *hoplomachus* kept stabbing his sword into the writhing Thracian while half the crowd screamed insults and the other half roared with laughter at one of the Vestal Virgins. She had become so excited by the sight of death and blood that she was openly screaming, banging her head against the stone back of her seat as she moaned with pleasure.

The victorious gladiator advanced toward the podium, where the Emperor, somewhat impatiently, handed down a palm branch in token of victory.

Several more clumsy preliminaries took place while the crowd grew impatient for the most intriguing, the most eagerly awaited of all the day's fights, the last one on the card before noon—the one in which a certain Simon ben Eleazar would be featured against a young, flamboyant *mirmillo* who had, in his short career, carried everything before him.

The crowd remembered Simon's courage and agility in the ring. Nor had any opportunity been missed to remind them of the eighteen months' tuition he had received in the art of the retiarii at the finest gladiator school in Italy.

It was, the crowd decided, going to be a great fight. The mob sighed and moaned like dust swirling in a hot, dry wind, as the opponents strode out to face each other.

They stood there in the dead center of the arena. The *mirmillo* stocky, compact, athletic, most of his face hidden by his helmet, glared at Simon. It was an old trick, often used by the Capuan school of gladiators—the look of death, to terrify you, to make your guts freeze. Simon had been warned about it and smiled back easily. The helmet of the man facing him was almost spherical, quite smooth, to offer no projections on which the net could catch, and had a fish emblem on the front. The *mirmillo,* whose name was Bellerophon, also wore a breastplate, and, although his right arm and left leg were covered, his two other limbs remained bare to give him freedom of movement. A sword and shield completed his equipment.

It was the old Roman game of weight and counterweight. Of one advantage to offset another. A lot of thought went into making Roman circuses work so well. Simon, in deliberate contrast to his adversary, was without protection except for a conspicuous armguard on his left shoulder called a *galerus* which ensured that his thrust with his three-pointed trident would be a formidable one—but only so long as he attacked, driving home with left shoulder pointing toward the enemy. Apart from this, he had only his net and dagger. One man's net play was as different from another's as the way he made love, and it was this very personal technique that made a contest with retiarii so absorbing.

A lone trumpet shrilled, silencing the arena and starting the combat. The crowd gripped their seats.

"Move around, move around." Simon could hear the hoarse voice of Flaccus braying at him. He did as he was told, circling the *mirmillo* warily, trident thrust out ahead of him, right hand balancing the net in constant menace—splitting the *mirmillo*'s vision, making him watch first one hand, then the other.

Feinting with the trident, Simon snaked the net smoothly out, settling it so that it fastened like an umbrella over the figure of Bellerophon, but at the last moment, just as he was about to jerk the cord that would tighten the net into a lethal prison, pinioning the arms of his adversary, the *mirmillo* literally cat-jumped two feet sideways and hurled himself at Simon with his sword, forcing Simon to give ground, jerking his trident into the forward position while he recovered his net. The two men met with a quick clash of steel, then retired again. The crowd admired their superb reflexes, appreciating every nuance of the tactics. As a compliment to the fighters, they called for music.

A hydraulic organ began to vibrate, wheezing out a lively ditty from one of the Atellan farces popular in Rome at the time.

"I seek you not, I seek a fish." Simon spoke the

traditional cry of his profession. "Why do you flee from me, O Gaul?"

Bellerophon laughed. His voice muffled by the long, menacing visor of his helmet, he said contemptuously, "Who flies, netman?" He came forward, tough, stocky, durable, timing superb blows with his sword. Simon lost his balance, recovered, then ran. That was expected. Unarmored as he was, once his enemy got inside his defense, behind his line of thrust and parry, there was only one thing to do. Run. Run for your life. As he ran, the *mirmillo* pelted after him, but Simon, trained for this, was faster and, outdistancing the other, suddenly turned and threw a long, wicked, raking cast with his net which wrapped around Bellerophon's legs and sent him crashing to the sand with a solid crunch as his breastplate took the heavy impact.

"Got him—finish him off," the crowd yelled. Flaccus screamed to Simon to take care, but, carried away by excitement and the prospect of victory, he rushed into the attack. Taking the trident in both hands, he stabbed savagely down, trying to spit the supine *mirmillo* right through the belly. The crowd shrieked with expectation, but Bellerophon had not been overrated as a gladiator. At exactly the right moment, he rolled to one side and, as Simon's trident plunged deep into the sand, catapulted upward with his sword arm, aiming for the boy's vitals.

Only razor-sharp reflexes enabled Simon to slide fractionally to one side, so that the sword, instead of ripping out his guts, sliced his thigh.

Blood fountained into the air. The music stopped. *"Habet!"* the crowd roared. The boy stood still, paralyzed by the slick redness pumping from his leg, and Bellerophon came for him.

Deprived of all defense, without net or trident and too deeply wounded to run, Simon seemed finished. In the tiers, bets were already being paid off when Simon, finding one last reservoir of strength and courage, threw himself on the *mirmillo*, cutting and slashing, crisscrossing the air with beautiful feinting movements of his dagger. Bellerophon was an expert swordsman but, incredibly, had to give ground.

The two men struggled arm to arm, wrestling desperately for an advantage, but it could not go on.

Simon, growing steadily weaker, slipped down the man's torso and half lay against his thigh, supine now, unable to move.

It had been a beautiful fight, at once graceful and sad, ending in a noble climax of raw courage. It appealed to the perverted aesthetics of the mob. Having spared him once, why not again? *"Mitte!"* they howled. "Send him back. Let him go."

Bellerophon paused, uncertain what to do, but the Emperor Claudius, knowing that in a *sine missione* right was on his side, would not be cheated. As was well-known, he loved watching the play of expression on the unhelmeted faces of the dying retiarii. Giggling, drooling saliva, he gave the "thumbs down."

The crowd groaned, reached for food and drinks, looked at their programs to see who was next.

Bellerophon knelt, adjusted Simon's head to the classic killing position between knee and thigh and drew back his sword for the death thrust. The billowing woolen sail stretched over the arena went shimmering colors across the pale, sweaty face of the boy held there, suspended between life and death. As he had been taught, he stretched out his throat to receive the steel.

Then something fantastic happened.

The boy arched his back and threw his knife as fast as quicksilver straight into the second row of the crowd, where it transfixed a man literally about to plunge a dagger of his own into the back of an army officer sitting in front of him. The assassin, a stupid grin of surprise on his face, toppled over the officer's shoulder and slithered down the wall of the arena onto the sand, where he lay immobile, the throwing knife embedded in his heart.

The whole stadium buzzed with confusion, and Bellerophon again stood to one side, awaiting further orders.

Claudius, saliva staining his chin from the pleasure of imminent death, pointed a finger at Simon and shouted just one word to Bellerophon. *"Jugulum!* Cut his throat!"* As the two men blended obediently again into the plastic spectacle of ritual death, the young army officer vaulted cleanly down the twenty feet into the sand, separated the gladiators with his arm, then stood looking up at the Emperor.

"I plead for his life, O Caesar!" he shouted.

"Good heavens." Claudius drooled good-naturedly, letting his head drift from side to side in the manner of an idiot. "Why on earth should you do that?"

"Because he has just saved mine."

Claudius leaned over. "Surely you're just imagining it? Let's not spoil the show!"

"I recognize the villain, sire. He is from my regiment. I condemned him to the *fustuarium* for extreme cowardice."

"Ah, yes, Colonel." For the first time Claudius appeared to take in the long military cloak, the steel cuirass, across which the soldier had stubbornly folded his muscular arms. "You are just back from service then?"

"Yes, sire. Thrace."

"And you say you made this chap run the gauntlet out there and he came back to murder you?" Claudius' nose had now begun to run and this, added to the saliva, made the Emperor look even more revolting.

"It seems so, my Caesar."

Claudius fought back a smile at the man's rustic accent and said, "Surely you do not want me to depart from the rules of the imperial games and pardon this—this retiarius?"

"Sire." The officer stood with his legs apart and gazed stubbornly at the Emperor. His intelligent brow, the strong nose, the heavy, thrusting stubbornness of the jaw were not lost on Claudius. "Sire," the officer repeated, "the boy has courage. I would like a thousand of his kind in my regiment. He must be a devil with that throwing knife, yet not once did he violate the integrity of the games by using it to save himself. Instead, he saved the life of a Roman officer. I ask you to spare him."

The crowd, which up to now had been just interested spectators, took up the officer's words and shouted, "Spare him! Spare him!" The mob started to drum their feet on the wooden planking over the stone seats, generating a thunderous noise.

Claudius stood up and silenced them with his hand. "Colonel," he said genially, "I admire the way you faced up to your Emperor, even if it was silly old Claudius who nobody takes any notice of anyway—"

"Good old Claudius," roared the crowd.

"—so I'm inclined to grant your wish," Claudius finished. He leaned back and signaled an aide, who came attentively to his shoulder. There was a short, whispered discussion before Claudius spoke again. "Congratulations, General," he said smoothly.

"Sire?"

Claudius tittered at his own joke. "Major General to be precise, my dear fellow. I'm giving you a legion to yourself. Report to the HQ of the Second Augustan in Strasbourg and take command. The lad can follow on afterward when he recovers."

"Eternal gratitude, Caesar. I shall do my best to serve with honor."

"I'm sure you will." Claudius beamed.

"There is one more thing, sire. The boy cannot serve as a regular unless he is freed and made a Roman citizen."

Claudius came close to glowering, but remembered his image just in time. "Teach me my business, would you?" He cackled. "All right, all right, I'll attend to it. Now go away."

The officer saluted, nodded to Simon and left, but Claudius was now determined to extract maximum popularity from the incident. Leaving the podium, he descended into the arena, where, to thunderous applause, he took out a large purse and counted out gold coins one by one, giving twenty to each man. Then and only then did he slowly return to his seat and indicate with a wave of the hand that the games continue.

As slaves rushed in to rake the bloody sand and carry out Simon for medical attention, Messalina, Claudius' dark-haired young wife, leaned over and whispered, "You handled that very well, darling."

"Thank you, dearest. Without you sitting at my side, I should not have been able to cope."

"Was it wise to promote that officer with such speed, dearest?"

"Did I not learn that the only real power is in Rome?" Claudius said shrewdly. "Do you forget how the Praetorian Guard made me Emperor? Both that officer and the young retiarius are heroes now, and it is best to let them dissipate their popularity defending the frontiers of the Empire."

40

"You know, darling," Messalina said, "you really are a very clever man."

"Precisely, my dear." Claudius suddenly farted heavily and, although the noise was drowned by the crowd, the unpleasant smell enveloped Messalina, who wrinkled her nose in displeasure.

"Must you do that?"

"Doctor's orders, my dove. It is particularly bad for me to allow gases to accumulate in my stomach. By the way, what was it you wished to mention to me about Seneca?"

"His behavior with your niece could one day threaten your position."

"As always, sweet Messalina, you have my interests at heart. Bring me proof and I will act."

She changed the subject, asking, "By the way—what was the name of that army officer?"

"Ves—Ves—I can't quite remember. Oh, yes—Vespasian."

"He'll go far," the girl said thoughtfully. "And the boy as well."

"Whatever you say, my love."

"Do try and stop breaking wind all the time," she said irritably.

Seneca sat waiting in his town house and wondered why he could not concentrate on his writing. Eventually he realized what it was. The quietness. The whole city was at the games and the only sound that could be heard from the streets was the click of soldiers' boots coming closer, then dying away, as one of the extra maniples drafted for patrol marched by. It was always one thing or another, he thought. Too loud or too quiet. On normal days his life was made hellish by the sounds from public baths nearby, the singing, the screams and oaths as men threw a leather ball around, the hollow, much-amplified noise that all sound makes over water, and always the sharp *slap-slap* of the masseur pummeling flesh.

As he listened, there was a huge burst of applause from the stadium, the crowd noise lifting and dropping irregularly like storm-tossed waves on a pebbly beach. He frowned, wondering why he tolerated the over-crowded city life and did not retire to his country home.

41

He was rich enough, with his banking and building interests, his farm revenues, the large sum Eusepio paid him as a secret partner in his wine import business. There was something to being a philosopher, a geographer, a successful essayist, a senator who was a master of rhetoric, he thought. These *nouveaux riches* freedmen paid you a fortune to act for them, smooth their path to success with influential people, because nobody believed that you could, by nature, be interested in money. As an ascetic intellectual, you were ascribed an honesty and saintliness beyond belief.

The thought made Seneca laugh to himself: everyone wanted power, but he, Seneca, had already achieved it, would shortly achieve much more, because he had bent his great intellect to creating an entirely false picture of his personality. How could anyone ever be jealous of a harmless writer converted to Stoicism? Half the fun, he thought, was the brazen hypocrisy of the thing. All this time, right up to his present age of forty-five, he had been a lecher and a pervert, yet no one, not even his wife, whom he was careful to keep at his country residence in Campania, had suspected a thing.

His mind turned to the two seventeen-year-old slaves he had bought at auction, the harvest of the legions' last campaign across the Rhine. He kept them here, in Rome, so that his wife would know nothing about them. They were truly delicious, with bright golden hair and pale, white skins which, since he forbade them ever to go into the sun, were impossibly soft and creamy. He used them to provide hours of deep, dreamless ecstasy.

He had sent the two girls away now and, in his lassitude, lacked the will to write creatively. He would have a couple of hours' sleep, then go for his run. The populace was used to seeing Seneca, clad only in his loincloth and sandals, pounding the streets of Rome for mile after mile, sweat bathing his lean frame. This was his facade—the need to get back to nature and away from the excesses of modern Rome. Seneca, the health fanatic. They should know, he thought. He burst into sudden laughter.

His thoughts switched to the current affair he was having with Julia Livilla. At times, the nobility of her blood frightened even him. The girl was not only the late

42

Emperor's sister, but a direct descendant of Augustus and Mark Antony! Not bad for the son of a provincial grammarian. If only he could get her to divorce her husband, then anything was possible. Anything and everything. He was playing a very dangerous game though, sleeping with the Emperor's niece, and at times he wished he could curb this terrible lust for power that drove him irresistibly closer, like some ambitious moth, to the white heat of Roman imperial command.

He clapped his hands, and his Greek secretary came running.

"Yes, master?"

"My engagement tonight."

"You dine at Eusepio's, master."

"Very well. Have my oldest senatorial toga ready."

The slave bowed and went. It would do no harm, Seneca thought, to show these vulgarians his seniority and rank. It was always a bore having to dine with Eusepio, but the man was a source of so much money. A positive gold mine. He would make an excuse and retire early. Already his fertile mind had dreamed up another tableau of sensuality involving those smooth little bodies of his girl slaves and he could not wait to get back and try out the fantasy.

5

He had his litter set down outside Eusepio's house. At the entrance, a servant knelt in front of him and murmured, "Right foot first, sir." In Rome, one had to adapt to another man's superstitions. Seneca smiled indulgently and allowed the slave to remove his sandals in the desired manner and then gently bathe his feet in rosewater.

Seneca was shown into the dining room. He always made a point of arriving late and making the entrance that befitted his senatorial rank. Being a man of great learning and charm, he was a real catch and liked to play the part expected of him.

"Everybody! Everybody! Look who's come," Eusepio shouted at the top of his voice. "Now you can't say that old Eusepio doesn't know the right people, can you?" Seneca allowed himself to nod at the assembled company with a grave, preoccupied face, as though some weighty matter were on his mind, then took the place of honor on the couch next to Eusepio's wife and sat back while two Alexandrian slave boys washed his hands and placed a crown of flowers on his head.

Seneca looked about him. The usual collection of wealthy merchants with their plump, sweaty wives. He forced himself to smile a greeting at the two tame aristocrats Eusepio had imported to give the party tone: old Marcus, a withered ancient who was senior member of the college of augurs—the job could be done by a child, but the prestige was enormous—and Habinnas, a supercilious young aristocrat who had just been elected quaestor with the help of a large bribe made in the right place by Eusepio.

It was obvious that Eusepio had spent a fortune. Tall pillars of roses had been erected around the room for the occasion, and all the tables were decorated with peacocks' feathers arranged so that the wide part trailed just over the edge. While Seneca picked at a bewildering *hors d'oeuvre* of eggs, tuna, shellfish and quail cooked in honey, he watched a troupe of acrobats going through their paces. He ate sparingly, to preserve his reputation as a noted ascetic.

Soon slaves came in and began arranging cages full of live larks. As the birds would not sing at night, a small choir of little boys assembled behind the guests of honor and sang in high, twittering notes.

"What do you think of that, eh?" Eusepio said proudly. "Larks and bird songs. That's just a beginning."

Seneca allowed himself to smile and took the

44

opportunity to steal a further glance at the boys, some of whom were quite beautiful. He decided at once to install his own choir, which would enable him to debauch slave boys without anyone's suspecting.

He watched idly as slaves came in with a basket, inside of which sat a wooden hen. They began searching through the straw in which the hen lay and dug out eggs which they distributed, two to a guest.

Seneca picked at his eggs, which turned out to be plump little figpecker birds covered with yolk, seasoned with pepper and baked in delicious pastry. As slaves distributed Falernian and Tusculum wine, he listened with boredom to the conversation going on around him.

"There I was," Eusepio was saying to the man nearest him. "I had this ship—lying at Alexandria it was, fast and seaworthy, absolutely stuffed with grain. I was all set to make a killing and then do you know what happened? The port captain condemned it for unpaid dues and I didn't owe a penny!" Eusepio was a fat little man and as he warmed to his story, his belly and double chins began to quiver with indignation. "You know why? Because he'd been bribed by that crook of a general Petronius, so that he could give my ship to Caligula in the hope that it would save his skin for giving in to the Jews. Yes, that's what happened. Well, I couldn't get it back from Caligula, could I? He wasn't the kind of man to grant favors exactly, was Gaius Caligula. The only favor Caligula ever granted anybody was removing his head. He liked doing that, cutting off heads, Caligula did. Well, if it hadn't been for my old friend Lucius Annaeus Seneca, I might never have got it back at all, but Lucius used his influence, you see—he's a full senator, you know, is Lucius."

He patted Seneca, who fought down a shudder. It amused him to see the way Eusepio aped his betters by putting broad purple stripes on his napkins and wearing gilt rings on his fingers, studded with iron—as close as he dared go to the gold rings worn by members of the equestrian orders.

"Eusepio," Habinnas said languidly, "talking about Jews, have you heard the latest from Petronius? No, no, not your general, but a poet everybody's beginning to talk about—"

"Tell us," Eusepio said.

"It goes something like this," Habinnas said.

"A Jew may adore his God in the sky
And pour out his woes to his ears on high,
But unless he locks up his scabbard, you see,
Then the tip of his penis will never hang free."

Everybody laughed loudly, except for a young man seated just along the table from Seneca, who stopped eating and gazed carefully at Habinnas with eyes that had hardened into chips of stone. Seneca was struck by their sheer hatred.

His mind was distracted by the fresh food slaves were now bringing. It consisted of a deep silver dish with the twelve signs of the Zodiac arranged around the edge, over the top of which food appropriate to each sign had been placed. A young sow's udder for Virgo, two baked mullets for Pisces, and so on. As the guests gazed at this strange offering, dancers hurled themselves forward and, in time to music from the orchestra, removed the upper part of the dish to show masses of plump fowls and hares in rich sauce underneath. Simultaneously, bottles of expensive perfume were lowered from the ceiling in front of each guest, and as everyone applauded, a slave appeared, carrying bread in a silver oven.

Seneca, thoroughly bored, found himself examining the youth again. He noticed that he wore only a simple tunic and bore no jewelry or any other mark of affectation. Apart from the momentary look that crept into his eyes when Habinnas had been making fun of the Jews, he sat with arrogant indifference to the people around him. Seneca noted his gray-green eyes, fair skin deeply tanned, the hard set of the shoulders and the economy of his movements. There is something special about him, he thought. Something strong that sets him apart from others. I must find out who he is.

Seneca's eyes switched to the next course being served, an enormous roast pig with an inordinately swollen belly.

"By Jupiter, he's forgotten to gut it," Eusepio shouted. "Bring the chef."

The chef was led in, admitting miserably that he had quite overlooked it.

"Then I'll give you something to help your memory," Eusepio screamed. "Strip him. Somebody find me a whip."

In a flash the unfortunate chef had been stripped naked and stood downcast beside Eusepio's couch. A sturdy slave brought Eusepio a cruel-looking cart whip, which he inspected and handed back. "Right," he said. "Six lashes and no shirking, or you'll get the same yourself."

"How corrupt we are," Seneca said with superb timing, raising his voice slightly so that everyone could hear, "that we do not even question our right to treat our fellow man like some draft animal." He glanced idly at the interesting boy, who, to his surprise, was actually smiling at him. His heart leapt. Seneca was always ready for a stimulating encounter with a beautiful boy or girl, if necessary intellectual, but preferably sexual. He smiled back, putting into the expression all his noted charm.

"Oh, let him off, Eusepio," Habinnas said lazily. "They will do these things, you know."

"Yes," everybody said, joining in support, "give him another chance. Accidents will happen."

"Let me show you something, master," said the chef. Seizing a knife, he slashed open the pig's belly, left and right. As the slits widened, out poured delicious food—hot sausages, blood puddings, then, incredibly, a flock of thrushes, thrumming their wings in panic, banging their heads against the walls in their efforts to escape. In a flash, the chef had waved in fowlers, who caught them with limed reeds. "There you are," the chef said proudly, "Trojan pig."

Everybody applauded the chef, who stood there naked, sweatily triumphant.

"That was a fine trick to play on me, I must say," Eusepio mumbled, his chins wobbling. "I can take a joke just as well as anybody else—you'll see." He pointed to the chef. "You. Put your clothes on and sit down here." He indicated a space next to himself on the top couch. Nervously the chef sat down.

"Who are you, anyway?" Eusepio demanded. "What's your name?"

"Publius, master. I'm your second chef."

"Where's Ascoltus then?"

47

"You had him crucified, master, for insulting the household gods."

"I did?" Eusepio looked mystified. "Are you sure?... Oh, yes, I remember now."

Somebody down at the far table laughed. Eusepio looked gratified and attacked his roast pork voraciously.

"You are against slavery then?" the young man asked Seneca in a quiet voice.

Seneca started. There was some way in which the boy managed to polarize his personality that made Seneca concentrate on every single word that he was saying. He answered diffidently, "My views on the subject are well-known."

"I would like to hear them."

"One should be kind to one's slaves. I try to set an example. I have, I believe, the reputation of a humanitarian."

"If you feel that way, why do you not free them?" Simon persisted.

Seneca said, "I believe in Stoicism, which is an exercise in mental discipline. I must therefore surround myself with every conceivable luxury in order to prove that I can do without it."

Seneca found himself wondering again who the young man was, with his open, unblinking eyes that never left one's face. Leaning across his couch, he asked Livia about him.

When he learned the secret of Simon's identity, Seneca began to appreciate for the first time the boy's true mettle. He is as hard as iron, he thought. He has looked into the gates of hell and come back a trained killer. Yet he is no stupid bruiser. This boy is a thinker. He will go far. More than ever, he was determined to start an association with him. If he could not have his body, he could at least have his mind.

Now slaves came in carrying the little household gods that they had brought from their niches in the *lararium*, and set them down on the table in front of Eusepio.

The host lit an incense candle, kissed the gods, then said drunkenly, "Let's all wish each other health and happiness."

Senece heaved a sigh of relief. Now that tribute had been paid to the lares, it was no longer rude to leave, despite the fact that the party would continue until the small hours.

Throughout the evening he had picked at his food, playing the philosopher-ascetic. Now all he wanted to do was to go to bed, enjoy a meal of plump roast chicken, then put his slave girls through some interesting maneuvers.

He was saved from having to make a formal farewell by a loud knock at the front door. A slave came back and whispered in Eusepio's ear, a worried look on his face.

"The *vigiles* are here," Eusepio bawled in a loud, drunken voice. Pointing at Seneca and Simon, he said, "It's you two they're after. What's been going on?"

Seneca rose hastily and left the room, followed by Simon. A lictor was standing at the door, clad in his formal robes of office. Beside him stood a slave carrying the rods and ax that made up the fasces, the Roman symbol of authority. A detachment of city guards stood to rigid attention in the road.

"Lucius Annaeus Seneca?" inquired the lictor, clearing his throat. His knowledge of Seneca's exalted position in society made him nervous. "I have here an edict." In a solemn voice he read: "We, Tiberius Claudius Drusus Nero Germanicus, Imperator, by virtue of our tribunicial power and the authority vested in us as consul and as father of the state and the people of Rome, do hereby banish you, Lucius Annaeus Seneca, from this city and the Italian mainland until further notice and until we, Claudius, do deem it advisable that you return."

Seneca slumped back against the wall, but recovered himself. "Very well," he said. "My wants are simple. I presume I am allowed a slave to attend my personal needs?"

"The Emperor has made no limits on your retinue. He desires to inconvenience you as little as possible, provided that you fall in with his wishes."

"Which are?"

"That you go to live on the island of Corsica."

"A pestilential place," Seneca said, "but I have my books and the peace will be welcome." Inside, he was seething with fury. Damn—damn—damn, he thought, I had everything going so well, then the fool had to find out I was making love to his niece. I bet it was that jealous bitch Messalina. I underestimated her. A quick divorce followed by a quick wedding and I would have been one of the royal family—well, a near miss. One must be resilient. My time will surely come again.

The lictor turned to face Simon. "You are known as Simon ben Eleazar, the gladiator from Galilee?"

"I am."

"I have here," the lictor said, handing over a scroll of papyrus, "papers containing your manumission, your Roman citizenship and orders drafting you into the next vexillation leaving Rome for the Second Augustan Legion at Strasbourg."

"Thank you."

The lictor saluted, said to Seneca, "By tomorrow night then?" with just a hint of threat in his voice, then stepped back. In a brisk voice he about-faced his men and marched away.

"Shall we walk a little?" Seneca said pleasantly to Simon. He had completely recovered himself. They fell into step, sauntering along the quiet street. Seneca's litter slaves followed at a discreet distance behind their master, ready to move should he be threatened by footpads.

"Do you find it odd," Seneca said, "that we should both be sent away from Rome at the same time?"

"Coincidence, perhaps," said Simon.

"No. There is design behind the whole thing. I am too influential, you are too popular. Although you may not know it, you have been exiled too. If each of us has enough power to make the Emperor nervous, imagine what we could not achieve together!"

"I don't follow you."

"A man of intellect and a man of action," Seneca said patiently. "Together we make the perfect combination. Let me tell you about this Emperor of ours—he plans to extend the realm. There will be new conquests, new campaigns. Shall I tell you what this means? Ruined economies will need to be built up. Penniless vassal kings will want large loans. This takes capital, a commodity that I and my friends have to offer. You find us the opportunities and we'll find the capital and together we'll make a fortune. Will you be my agent and my partner?"

"Yes," said Simon.

Seneca stopped walking. He pointed to a large vessel standing outside a cloth merchant's shop. "Let us seal our bargain in the fuller's pot." He grinned. "At least it will be an oath neither of us will forget." They both laughed, lifted up their clothes and pissed hard into the pot. "I often wonder," Seneca said idly, "why we do not charge these people for making them free dye." They started walking again. "Never doubt," Seneca said, "that I will be back before long. Claudius cannot do without me. He needs people of my ability."

"I am sure you are right," said Simon.

They shook hands and, after planning to exchange their new addresses, went their separate ways.

6

The camp of the Second Augustan Legion at Strasbourg was a huge place.

On arrival, Simon, with the rest of the day's inductions, lined up at the quartermaster's stores for kit issue. First, *caligatae,* elaborate boots, thonged up the leg, consisting of many thicknesses of sole studded with stout hobnails to withstand campaigning in all weathers. Then linen undergarments and short-sleeved woolen tunic to wear over the top. Also braccae, leather trousers fitting skintight to just below the knee: a special issue, this, as it was rumored that they would soon be campaigning in a cold climate.

At the armorer's he was given two seven-foot javelins, a short sword, a dagger and a large semicircular shield cleverly glued together so as to combine maximum resilience with lightness of weight. He was then provided with body protection consisting of new armor, strips that were fully articulated to give complete freedom of movement, riveted onto a leather jerkin. For his head there was a beautifully designed bronze helmet with iron skull plate and cheek- and neck- pieces for additional protection. After the issue of blankets, messtins, plus the digging, trenching and road-making equipment that he would be expected to master, it took Simon three trips to carry it all to his hut.

A Roman legion was the elite, cutting thrust of the nation's defense, and the expense of providing such fabulous equipment for each man was enormous. Only an empire that controlled most of the known world could have found the necessary resources.

With superb equipment came superb training in the person of Gaius Scribonianus.

Centurion Scribonianus, taken off the active list as a veteran of fifty, had spent his last fifteen years teaching men to be soldiers. His face was scarred by blows from the iron-studded cestus received during his reign as boxing champion of the legion, and his body was still fit and lean, despite his advanced age. He had a way of screwing up his face and scowling savagely, which impressed the raw recruits for some time, until they realized that Scribonianus was essentially kind, would use discipline only reluctantly and, despite his power of life and death over the men, was incapable of any cruelty.

"Now then," he would say, "pay attention. Don't sit there thinking about those pox-ridden camp women. I've got more important things to tell you, so pay attention. Suppose some big hairy barbarian comes rushing at you with a broadsword. What would you do then, eh? Just listen to me and I'll tell you. This"—he pointed to a *gladius*—"is a sword. 'What about it?' you might say. 'It's only a sword.' But you're wrong. It's a Roman sword and it's special. It's short—short to stop you slashing. A slash cut rarely kills because a man's vitals are protected by his weapon and his very bones—so stab 'em, men." He rolled bloodshot eyes ferociously. "Stab 'em to death, that's right. A thrust going in two inches can be mortal. Now then—" he paused, "this is a shield. Again, you might well say, 'So what? It's only a shield.'

52

And again you'd be wrong. It's a Roman shield and it's special. Why? Because of its nice color and the picture of Jupiter firing his thunderbolts? Not at all. Look at this." He ran his finger around the metal flange that had been built onto the shield's edge. Then, taking another shield, he neatly locked them together. "See that? Once locked, they won't part without a very careful movement. On the command 'Form testudo,' you lock shields over your heads and creep up toward the enemy's walls, and there's not a thing he can do to stop you getting there. Any questions? Right. Now then—pay attention. What's this?" He picked up a javelin and hefted it in his hand. "'So it's a javelin,' you might say. 'A javelin's only a javelin—there's nothing unusual about that.' But you'd be wrong, wouldn't you? Now tell me why."

"Because it's Roman and it's special," said the recruits, groaning.

"Very good." Scribonianus scowled. "You're catching on quick. I'll turn you from farmhands into fighting men yet. It's Roman and it's special and this is why." With an easy, fluid movement, he sent the javelin swishing through the air for some thirty yards before it impaled a shield standing up against a wall. "You!" He beckoned to Crixus, one of Simon's mates, a cheerful, red-faced Swiss boy with enormous thews he had developed working in a blacksmith's. "You look pretty strong. Go and pull it out!"

Crixus ran over, put the shield to his knee and pulled hard, but the javelin head, already bent on impact, broke, leaving some two feet of iron stuck in the shield.

"See what happened?" Scribonianus said. "It bends in the shield, and if you try to pull it out, it breaks. The soft iron shank does that—you can't use a shield with a ruddy great lump of iron stuck in it, can you? When we was fighting the Gauls they learned some of our tricks and come at us with interlocked shields. You know what we did? We chucked our javelins and literally locked their shields together. It was like fighting with their hands tied, so pretty soon they threw away their shields and fought without them, and after that we slaughtered them to a man. Any questions?"

"Yes, Centurion," said Aristides, a dark-haired little thief from the Roman gutters who had joined the legion one jump ahead of the *vigiles*. "What about them camp women?"

So the training went on. There was much to learn—techniques of pit building for concealed weapons, of turfing ramparts, weapon maintenance, the precise drill to the standards that would be needed to maneuver on the battlefield, the skill to build Roman roads and the stamina to march them hour after hour at "military" or the slightly increased "rapid" pace. As the hot summer ran its course, the recruits were forged into soldiers. There was tree felling, swimming, constant battle practice with wooden swords and wicker shields, the accent always on fitness. Simon, after many months of convalescence, was now completely recovered and because of his gladiatorial training shone so much at his work that he was put in charge of his *contubernium*, the group of eight men allocated by the army to each room in the barracks.

On some nights the whole legion went under canvas; they would need to perfect the technique of making proper overnight camp if the rumors were true that they were going to Britannia.

On nights like these, sitting outside their tents under the stars, they got Scribonianus talking about their commander.

"Vespasian? Now there you've got a real good 'un," he said. "D'you know he never wanted to leave his granny's farm down in Cosa, until he was shamed into standing for an aedileship after his brother was elected senator? That's what they say. Oh, yes, he's a farm boy at heart and knows what it's like to spread muck. They do say that his great-grandfather was a laborer who crossed the Po every year to help the Sabines with their harvest, and though his mother comes from a noble family, I reckon the soil's in his blood. Doesn't give a damn about rank, I can tell you that—married the daughter of some penniless quaestor's clerk, the story goes—so he hasn't got much money, though it hasn't stopped him getting on."

"But, Centurion," said Camerinus, a rather sensitive-faced, slender boy who had come from Sicily to join up, "doesn't a general usually reward his soldiers?"

"Oh, I know what you're getting at," said Scribonianus, "that Vespasian won't be giving you presents like some generals do. That's so. They say he's a bit of a tightwad anyway, but he's a soldier, and those who served under him when he was a colonel, in Thrace, swear by him. He always looks after his men and once, when they was caught in a snowstorm, he gave a month's pay out of his own pocket to buy his chaps a coat each, made of fleece. No, you mark my words, you'll be better off with him than some rich patrician."

"Well, I'll be off to bed then, Centurion," Crixus said, yawning.

Scribonianus cleared his throat. "One thing before you go, lads," he said. "I've got some news for you. Not all of it good, I'm afraid. It's Britannia for sure and the legion leaves tomorrow for the north. Now, as you know, I won't be coming with you and you'll have a new centurion, Lucilius—" He dropped his gaze, not wishing to look the recruits in the eye. "He's known as *Cedo Alteram* and you'll find out what that means for yourselves. I'm afraid he's a bit of a disciplinarian, lads, and you'll just have to put up with him as best you can." Scribonianus' description of his successor turned out to be an understatement.

Simon and the men of his *contubernium* marched out of barracks next morning as the legion headed towards its assembly area on the Dutch coast.

The Second Augustan Legion camped on the desolate mud flats at the mouth of the Rhine and waited for further orders. The long march to the north gave the men of Simon's *contubernium* a chance to get to know each other. There was Aristides, the sneak thief with all the city boy's cheeky humor, and Crixus, the blacksmith from the tribe of the Rhaeti, also Camerinus, the tall thoughtful Sicilian boy with soft eyes and slender body. The four other men were Roman citizens from the mainland, who had been lured into the army with the promise of security and a land grant on discharge. Simon kept himself apart and made no friends. Because he was their leader, ready to take on more than his share of the work load, patiently helping any man over a particularly difficult task, he was respected and his right to privacy granted. Besides, there was something in his eyes that frightened them, a kind of pain there which told of terrible things that a young man of his age should not have had to endure. Simon, remembering old comrades, and how he had watched one whipped to death and been forced to kill the other with his own sword, determined to have no more tragic friendships.

All had gone well enough until Lucilius took over as centurion and immediately began a reign of terror. Lucilius was a bully with bulging eyes and thin lips that would twist bloodlessly whenever he inflicted punishment. As bullies will, he chose a small group and concentrated on making their lives unbearable. Unluckily he picked on Simon's *contubernium*.

Early on his first morning, in a howling, lashing gale of northern wind and rain, he condemned their tent. He strode over, kicked a couple of tent pegs with his boot, put his head inside and smirked at the half-sleeping men. "Right. This tent is badly erected. Pull it down and put it up again." Slowly, unsure of what their new centurion had said, the men had tumbled out of their blankets, yawning and rubbing their eyes. "Slow, are we?" said Lucilius quietly. "I'll have to teach you to be a little faster." *Crack*—he brought his swagger stick down across the muscled back of Crixus. As the man yelped in surprised agony, he brought it down again with the full strength of his arm, and the stick broke from the force of the blow. "Bring me another," Lucilius said to little Aristides, who scampered off to the centurion's quarters for another stick.

All day in the pouring rain, precursor of the autumn storms that set in early at those latitudes, the men toiled, trying to erect the flapping leather tent to exact army specifications, but in the screaming wind it was impossible. Lucilius kept them at it. He was always careful to stay well within army regulations, and any complaint to a senior officer would have been useless. He never used his fists or boots, but only his thin swagger stick, which could cause agonizing pain when laid on to sensitive parts of the body—and he used it all the time. By the end of that first day, the men lay soaked and exhausted in their tent, their bodies covered with weals from Lucilius' stick.

Next day, in similar weather, he made them do it again; that evening the men, almost too tired to speak, held a short conference, asking Simon for advice. Lucilius had broken three swagger sticks that day, lashing their legs and backsides till they were black and blue, and the men now knew only too well how he had gained the name *Cedo Alteram*—"Bring me another."

"Be patient," Simon told them, "and I will think of something. Besides, there is always the chance that he will grow bored with tormenting us."

But next morning when they assembled, slow and tired from the constant bullying and beating, Lucilius declared their drill to be slack and ordered them to assemble carrying full kit. This was rarely done in the legions, most of the equipment issued to the men for road making and digging being very heavy and normally carried on mules. However, once again, Lucilius was within regulations.

He had the eight men form in front of him, strictly to attention. In addition to armor and weaponry, each man carried pickax, saw, sickle, rope basket and heavy tenting equipment slung from a forked pole over his shoulder. Lucilius strolled behind them, adjusted a pole at the regulation angle, gave his thin-lipped smile and said quietly, "Right. Round the camp perimeter at rapid pace. Quick march."

For two hours the men, staggering under their load, sloshed through the mud at a speed of just over five Roman miles an hour. As the men stumbled and puffed for breath, Centurion Lucilius lashed their bare legs mercilessly with his swagger stick. Only Simon, by some iron resolve of will, appeared to keep up the pace, marching erect and impassive with apparent lack of effort. This seemed to annoy Lucilius even more, and he redoubled his blows on the others.

Around and around the camp rectangle the men marched. The third circuit, Vespasian came to the front of headquarters and gazed at them intently. Simon recognized him by his obstinate jaw and the way he had of folding his arms. Not by a flicker did either man show that he had recognized the other. Half an hour later Vespasian was still standing there, impervious to the cold soaking drizzle, as the men staggered in, his

57

figure motionless as though carved from stone.

That evening, lying weary and aching, prone with exhaustion, Simon's *contubernium* was detailed by Lucilius for sentry duty. In the middle of the night, the legionary cavalry whose job it was to inspect all pickets and guards arrived to check the *tesserae*, the wooden, waxed tablets on which the passwords for the night had been written, but even after they hailed him, poor Camerinus did not appear. Worn out from beatings and from sheer exhaustion, he had fallen asleep.

For that offense, there could only be one issue. A courtmartial, followed by sentence of death. Camerinus was immediately taken to the guardhouse and put under close arrest.

"A *fustuarium*," Lucilius said, smirking, next morning, as he paced up and down in front of the assembled men. "There's nothing like a *fustuarium* for discipline, you know. When you've seen one of those, you'll remember it all your life."

Simon looked at him—a tall man, bigger, stouter than himself and tough from years of army life, the unduly thin lips, the cold eyes that seemed to glow when inflicting pain. Holding himself stiffly at attention, he listened as Lucilius described the revolting details. He came to a decision. Somehow, somewhere, he would find a way to finish Lucilius and he would have to do it soon.

7

Vespasian sat in the praetorium tent feeling ill at ease. He hated these eve-of-battle conferences. There were many reasons for the way he felt. These occasions required proper formal dress: decorations, full armor, properly polished and burnished, plumed helmet that you never wore indoors anyway but that you needed to keep resting on your knee and which was a damned nuisance. If that was not enough, his cheap, gold-plated greaves cut into his legs, and he was uncomfortably aware of the coarse stuff of his purple cloak compared to the fine silk of the other commanders of field rank.

As a newly promoted legion commander, he was looked down on as a farm boy who had gotten ahead in the world. Surrounded on every side by patrician tribunes and aides-de-camp, with superb manners, he had never felt more aware of his provincial accent and lack of formal education. A look of strain came over his face and he prayed that the conference would end quickly so that he could get back to the peace of his own tent.

There was a stir and a bustle, a jingle of accouterments, as Aulus Plautius came in, flanked by staff officers. Everybody got up and stood to attention.

"Be seated, gentlemen," Plautius said, taking in the assembly with his keen eyes.

He was one of those big, genial men, always at the center of power, so sure of themselves that they had no need to show their intellect, or bravery. They belonged. They were establishment—especially if they happened to be related to the Emperor's first wife, as Plautius was. Now in his late forties, he was a senator of note and commander-in-chief of the Claudian expedition to invade Britain.

"Good morning, gentlemen." He waited for the answering chorus of greeting to die down, then continued, "I do hope you'll pay attention and forget for a moment about the beautiful mistresses and ten-course meals you've all got waiting for you back in your quarters—" There was a roar of laughter as the officers remembered their desolate, windswept tents. "Well, gentlemen," he continued, "the invasion of Britannia is definitely on and this will be a full, prebattle briefing. First I shall give you a short sketch of the political situation, then you will receive a military and economic survey of the country from one of my aides, after which I shall conclude."

He paused. "Very well. Now the present need has arisen because of the recent death of Cunobelinus, chief of the Catuvellaunian nation, the paramount tribe in so-called civilized Britannia. Our relations with the old chief, while never friendly, were always correct, and this stability enabled trade to expand greatly. Since his death, however, his two young sons, Togidumnus and Caractacus, have been looking for trouble. Not only have they threatened our allies the Atrebates, who control a good bit of strategic coastline, but they've begun military and religious subversion among the leading Gaulish tribes which we've only recently managed to civilize—yes, those damned Druids are at it again, fanning the old customs." He paused once more, then said, "Now then, because of trade and the old chief's wise rule, the Catuvellaunian nation has become very powerful. Should they take it into their heads to form an alliance with the Gaulish and German tribes, with whom, I might remind you, they are related by close ties of kinship, there is no way, gentlemen, that the Roman legions could contain them. I am sure we all remember the fate suffered by Varus' legions." There was a short silence. "Accordingly, we're going in." He sat down, conscious that in his effortless way he had conducted a masterful summary.

Petilius Cerialis stood up. Vespasian grinned. Although Cerialis was as much a sprig of the establishment as all the others, Vespasian could not help liking him. He was a big man with a flashing and absolutely genuine smile. His success with the opposite sex was the talk of the army and if any among Plautius' young aides had managed to filch a soft-bodied young girl to grace his bed while he read up on his conference notes, Vespasian knew it would be Cerialis.

"Economic assessment," Cerialis said briskly. "Better than you might think. Julius Caesar taught them a lot. Most of the southern tribes have mixed cattle and grain economies. There is some mining and metalworking, but most of the better-made stuff's imported from the Roman Empire in exchange for hides, fine hunting dogs and slaves. Since the introduction of the iron plow they've made a lot of progress in forest clearing and cultivating the heavy valley soils. Some of the tribes are really quite rich and are now even minting their own coins, but all the money's in the hands of a few chieftains and the standard of living of the average tribesman is abysmal. Their living unit is usually a large family in clusters of wooden huts, although, as I've said, some finely worked metalware or pottery might be found inside. What else can I tell you?"

"Are these conditions uniform?" Vespasian asked. He sensed, but ignored, the smiles at his rustic accent.

"Southern and eastern Britannia, yes," Cerialis answered. "We've had a lot of contact with these people and know more or less what makes them tick. Go west and north and it gets hilly and mountainous. There you're really on the frontier—one heavily fortified hill camp after another in the uplands and trackless forests elsewhere.

"Now then, the military assessment. Their capability is poor. Singly, their men, built like the Germans, can outfight us, but they rarely move in more than family units and even to march as a tribe is beyond them for more than a few days. They have no discipline, no central command, no ability to plan more than the most elementary tactics. From the point of view of matériel, their position is pathetic. The chiefs have finely wrought armor handed down from generation to generation, but their soldiers wear nothing very much. Don't get lured into the forests—fight your battles in the open and you'll cut them down like thistles. They have some chariot formations that could cause trouble, but these are usually confined to the nobility, and are limited in size. Follow Julius Caesar's battle instructions in antichariot warfare and you won't have any real problem." Petilius Cerialis flashed his white teeth and sat down.

"Thank you," said Plautius. He beamed at a little blue-jowled man wearing naval insignia, who at once got up and started a boring technical analysis of tides and the value of flat-bottomed boats for invasion purposes.

The open brazier in the middle of the tent was giving off a lot of heat and with the monotonous voice of the naval officer droning on and on, Vespasian felt himself falling asleep. He would have to resist this terrible urge to doze off, he knew that, otherwise he might easily injure his career. Although his own staff would be taking the required notes, he forced himself to keep his eyes open and look interested.

In reality, Vespasian was thinking about a matter within his own legion: what to do about Centurion Lucilius. These men were the backbone of the army. It was only right that they should have large powers of punishment. Unfortunately, every tree had its rotten apples and when you got one in the army, it could be hell. You could not just dismiss them, or the whole disciplinary structure would be undermined—nor could you advise them in day-to-day relationships with their men. Such presumption would cause resentment in the centurions' mess. Altogether it was a difficult problem. Lucilius had reported the commission of a capital offense, and Vespasian knew that the court-martial would have to find the offender guilty and that a good man would then suffer the dreadful fate of the *fustuarium*—being clubbed to death by his comrades. What worried Vespasian particularly was that the boy was involved, the same boy who had thrown that knife with such skill and saved his life. Vespasian had seen him march, showing incredible inner strength under the wicked sting of Lucilius' vine-stick, and knew that there was fine material there. He was equally sure that if the boy's comrade were executed, the killer streak planted in Simon by the gladiator school would come out and he would turn on Lucilius and finish him. That would be bad, not only for the boy but for the legion. Morale would be strained by any further sentence of death. Vespasian was too good a soldier to let this happen and as the naval officer droned toward the end of his speech, he had already arrived at a decision.

Plautius stood up again. "And so it only remains for me to conclude." He was no longer genially casual and he became brisk, competent, to the point. "The invasion force will consist of Second Augustan, Ninth Hispana, Twentieth Valeria and Fourteenth Gemina. In addition there will be two wings of Thracian cavalry and five cohorts of Batavian infantry stiffened by elements of the Eighth Legion and a detachment of the Praetorian Guard released by special order of the Emperor. Because these northern seas can be stormy, we will anchor in the first harbors we come to, appropriate to wind and course. I do not, gentlemen, I repeat, I do *not* anticipate resistance to our landings. By going in now, in the autumn, we will achieve the element of surprise. The battles will come later. All regiments will assemble for divine service at dusk tonight, when the haruspices will take the omens. I am assured"—he smiled blandly— "that they will be found favorable. Now I wish you all the best of luck and will see you on the other side." He nodded and swept out of the tent, followed by his aides.

Back in his own quarters, Vespasian thankfully took off his parade greaves and told his orderly to prepare a hot tub. He then summoned Lucilius.

"Centurion," he said coldly to the man standing at rigid attention in front of him, "we invade Britannia tomorrow. Accordingly, the court-martial is postponed, and as it will entail an unnecessary waste of manpower to keep your prisoner in captivity, I propose to release him until a new trial can be arranged."

Lucilius thumped his hand across his chest in salute, turned on his heel and walked stiffly from the tent. Vespasian smiled ruefully. He was painfully aware that he had not canceled the court-martial, but only deferred it.

The invasion went according to plan.

The legions hit the Kentish beaches in three waves and, meeting no resistance, pulled their boats high up on the shingle, re-formed and, leaving a small corps of veterans to construct a base camp at Richborough, marched cautiously inland.

When they came to the Medway, they found the enemy massed on the far side of the riverbank, clearly intending to make a stand. While the natives capered and screamed insults under the phlegmatic gaze of the Roman veterans, the nobility, partly out of arrogance and partly for morale, put on a display with their chariots which was quite dazzling. Weaving and turning, they crisscrossed the field in the most compli-cated maneuvers. One huge man, with hair even redder and longer than the others', stood proudly erect in his shining armor while his driver urged his two powerful thoroughbreds into a mad gallop, putting them to an almost vertical slope, then turning them so sharply downward again that the sheer gravitational pull on the chariot's chassis prevented it from turning over. Some of the Romans shouted encouragement. The big nobleman instructed his driver to do the same thing again, but this time he charged out of the car, walked along the pole and balanced himself there with superb poise as the horses turned in their tracks and plunged down the hill. It was as good as the Romans had seen at the circus and they gave him a cheer. The man got out and stood on the riverbank, mouthing curses in broken Latin, casting aspersions on their mothers and challenging any of them to single combat.

Plautius, taking in the situation, had his *cornicen* blow a piercing blast on his *cornu,* a large circular instrument with an expanding mouth curving over his shoulder. The note could be heard clearly above all the tumult and indicated his wish for an immediate staff conference.

When the generals had assembled, he said, "Well, gentlemen, as you see, the enemy is badly disciplined and carelessly sited—a situation that I intend to put to advantage. At first light I am sending the Batavians across. As you know, they can swim even the most turbulent rivers in full armor. Now, if all goes well, this will put the whole enemy force onto them, and this battle will be lost or won by our ability to take them in the flank at the right time." He paused for emphasis, then went on, "My scouts report that the river narrows sharply about ten miles downstream, and although it floods with the morning tide, this is the only place where a fording is possible for our men. Vespasian, I'm relying on you. Take whatever force you want, except the Batavians who'll make the initial assault here. In order for us to get into this battle, you'll have to achieve and hold a bridgehead long enough to pass the cavalry through. Geta, are your Thracians in good heart?"

Hosidius Geta, clad in the mail cuirass and leather jerkin of the light cavalry, walked up on the bowed legs of the lifelong horseman and saluted. "Ready to go, sir." He grinned, lean and dark, incisive-looking. "They all served under General Vespasian in their homeland, sir. They trust him."

"It is only because of his contact with your men that the general has been given command of this operation," Plautius said stiffly, in a voice which suggested that he would have been far happier with someone more experienced.

There was a short silence and Vespasian, sensing Plautius' doubts, said briskly, "Don't worry, sir, we'll get 'em across."

"See that you do, General—see that you do." His voice left no doubt what would happen to Vespasian's career if the operation failed. "Remember, the cavalry has to be through your bridgehead and galloping upstream within one hour of first light." He strolled off, nodding to his officers, his superbly polished armor glinting and flashing in the sunlight.

Vespasian turned to Plautius' staff officer and said briskly, rubbing his hands, "Right. Is it true that they've got a century of Syrian bowmen with the Ninth?"

"Yes, sir."

"Fetch 'em then," Vespasian said. "Also, tell the quartermaster I want rope, twine, timber for making rafts and plenty of wineskins. I'll take some of them full. The boys'll empty them during the night."

The tribune said, "Anything else, sir?"

The old look of strain came back to Vespasian's face—the look of a man responsible for other men's lives. "Ask him if he has any mobile catapults."

"A small onager, sir?"

"Should do nicely. All right, Tribune, off you go. No excuses now. If this lot isn't delivered at Second Augustan HQ within the hour, there'll be some asses kicked."

The young officer grinned at Vespasian's well-known coarseness, saluted and dashed off.

While he waited for the men and equipment for which he had indented, Vespasian sent the first century of his legion, the most experienced men that he had, to scout the bank and select a place from which the assault could be launched in the morning.

The Second Augustan camped in a large meadow shielded from the other side of the river by a mound which rose sharply from the bank.

It was a clear, cold October night, with the stars showing in the sky and, no fires being allowed, the legionaries huddled together in their leather tents, shivering and grumbling.

Vespasian walked slowly toward the area inhabited by Lucilius' century and allowed his steps to take him toward the tent occupied by Simon and his *contubernium*. With all Roman marching camps staked out in exact reproduction of base camp, this was comparatively simple. What was difficult was to make his course seem casual so that his aide-de-camp would not realize that he was walking there deliberately. He lifted the tent flap and ducked inside.

The men shot to their feet, standing rigidly to attention half dressed in their tunics, terrified at this sudden visit by someone who, to a common ranker, was close to a god.

"Oh, sit down, for Hercules' sake," grunted Vespasian. He took off his general's purple cloak and handed it to his aide. He flapped his hands across his body and said, "It's cold enough to freeze the member off a fertility god."

The men roared in sudden, relieved laughter and sat down. Crixus, the blacksmith, bolder than the rest, had the temerity to pass the wineskin to his general.

Vespasian tilted the skin back, sliding the vinegary liquid expertly down his throat, his Adam's apple bobbing. The men nudged each other delightedly. Only a peasant knew the way of drinking wine like that without spilling a drop. "You men all right then?" Vespasian asked, smacking his lips.

"Yes, sir," they chorused.

"Then I'll tell you what I'm here for," Vespasian said. "I want someone to take a line across the river just before dawn. He'll have to be a good swimmer, I can tell you that. Once over, his job will be to haul a rope across and tie it to a stout tree. Meanwhile, the savages will be doing their best to stop him."

There was dead silence for a moment, then all the men volunteered as one. Vespasian was moved and a lump formed in his throat. He could never understand how a leathery peasant like himself managed to inspire such affection, and yet here they were, every man jack of

66

them, asking for the chance to go to almost certain death. He said softly, "Thanks, lads." Without quite looking at Camerinus, he said casually, "They tell me the Sicilians are good swimmers."

"Take me, sir," Camerinus said eagerly. "Oh, yes, let me go. I'm not much shakes as a soldier, but I can swim like a fish."

"Is that right, lad?" Vespasian said slowly in his barnyard accent. "All right then—you do this for me and maybe I can do something for you."

8

Camerinus slipped into the river as the first gray glimmering of dawn streaked the eastern sky. Although his lean, spare body was well covered with lard, he was shivering with cold. Over his shoulder he carried a spool of thin twine which he would pay out as he swam.

He raised a hand in brief farewell to the dark, huddled shapes on the bank and made strongly for the other shore. The tide was flooding now, and a fierce current tore at him with icy fingers. Battered by floating debris, he felt his strength ebbing, and there was very little left in reserve when the river spewed him up on the other side. Gasping and wheezing for breath, he slowly hauled himself out of the water.

Camerinus gave a low whistle and, when he received the faint reply, began hauling the twine until the first piece of rope to which it had been sliced came to his hand. It was light now and he backed off from the bank and began making the rope fast around a stout tree. As the first sleepy challenge came from the sentry guarding the detachment of Catuvellaunians camped in the nearby wood, Camerinus gritted his teeth and frantically endeavored to tie a knot in the rope, made heavy and awkward from its passage through the water.

With angry shouts, the natives realized what was happening; they reached for their weapons and rushed for the riverbank.

On the other shore, twenty picked Syrian bowmen intently watched Vespasian's hand. They were all armed with bows made from layers of wood, bone and horn. The bows, with their remarkable elasticity, were almost bent double and the archer's arms ached and quivered with the strain as they awaited the order to fire. Then Vespasian dropped his hand. There was a deep, thrumming whistle followed by screams of agony as the arrows went home. The first wave of advancing natives dropped in their tracks.

Vespasian now beckoned to the onager crew, who at once galloped their mule-drawn cart to the riverbank, turned around, unlimbered the piece and fed it a large boulder. At the command "Fire!" there was a great creaking and whistling, and the boulder flashed across the river as quick as lightning, knocking down an entire reinforcement in a carnage of smashed limbs and broken bodies.

With the brief respite he had been granted, Camerinus at last managed to secure the rope, but as he turned to flee to the safety of the river, a native arrow took him in the back. He fell full-length, face in the water.

Meanwhile, under cover of the broadside, picked elements of the Second Augustan Legion hauled themselves across the river on life rafts, pulling a foot at a time on Camerinus' rope which was buoyed with inflated wineskins.

When sufficient men were across to screen his cavalry and safeguard his valuable horses, Geta floated his troopers over on rafts, their horses swimming along behind them as they had been trained. Geta's forces gradually built up until two hundred of his best riders were assembled, packed tight in the small bridgehead, the horses rearing with impatience.

Geta looked at the sun. It was, he estimated, two hours from false dawn.

He was an hour late. He could wait no longer.

At the command "Advance!" his Thracians charged through the thin screen of Britons and galloped along the riverbank toward the main battle.

Plautius, watching from his vantage point, was becoming anxious. His Batavians were now being made to give ground. The native horde had recovered from the surprise of a dawn attack by two thousand wild swordsmen who had risen incredibly from the fast-flowing river and charged home.

Through sheer weight of numbers, the Batavians were slowly being pushed back into a tight knot of men who, while still fighting spiritedly, would shortly reach breaking point. When that happened, they would be slaughtered. Anxiously Plautius kept glancing up at the slightly wooded knoll, the direction from which Geta's troopers would come. As he was a Roman commander, it had not occurred to him that two or three hundred of his horsemen attacking an enemy of thousands would do anything other than rout them.

Even as he turned away in despair, the first line of horses came through the trees. The Thracians turned in their saddles and saluted the sun, low in the sky behind them, as was their custom before giving battle, and the Britons who saw them do this assumed they were an advance party waving forward their comrades massed in the woods for attack.

Undisciplined at best, they ran and panic spread through their ranks. Geta pointed at the natives spread out below in one shrinking mass between them and the river and yelled "Charge!" The Thracians swooped down the hill at a full gallop, screaming battle cries, their long, sharp swords slashing about them, the twin pennants that distinguished the Thracian wing of cavalry streaming proudly from their standards. The whole Catuvellaunian nation erupted into chaos from this murderous attack on their rear. They scattered, running for their lives, fanning out like ants in all directions.

Hours later, peering through thick forest at the pitiful little force that had worsted them, they re-formed and were about to charge back down the slope and repossess the riverbank when Vespasian's Second Legion came swinging up from the west, marching in open order against sudden ambush, their standards and their armor gleaming in the sun.

The joint commanders, Caractacus and Togidumnus, no match for Roman discipline in the open field, called their men off and melted away into the forest.

Satisfied with the disposition of his forces for the night, Vespasian strolled into the medic's tent, to which the injured were being brought from all over the battlefield. He caught sight of Camerinus, lying pale and drawn among the rows of wounded. Summoning the doctor in charge, he asked him about the man's condition.

The *medicus,* a very overworked man, came as near as he dared to shrugging his shoulders. "The arrow wound is close to his gut," he said. "Also he suffers from exposure and from swallowing too much water."

"I hear you have a Greek surgeon on your strength," said Vespasian.

"Indeed we do, sir," replied the *medicus,* "a most eminent man who has come on the campaign for the experience in treating wounds. These Greeks have evolved a technique for extracting barbs or arrowheads using an instrument they call 'the scoop of Diocles'— very effective, I believe. Naturally I'm reserving him for the officers."

"To Hades with the officers," said Vespasian. "I want this man's life saved. If he dies you'll be answerable to me."

"Yes, sir, very good, sir," the doctor said obsequiously. He went off to find the surgeon.

Vespasian bent over Camerinus. "That was well done, lad. You did a good job."

"Will—will I live, sir?"

"Of course you'll live," Vespasian said. He patted him on the shoulder and walked off. Oh, yes, he thought grimly, you'll live all right—but only until the court-martial. The thought depressed him as he walked slowly back to the commander's tent. Suddenly, he heard the sound of a harsh voice raised in anger, the sound of a stick swishing through the air, the crack as it struck flesh and the yelp of pain that followed. He looked at once over toward Simon's *contubernium* and there was Lucilius, making the weary soldiers take down their tent

70

again. As usual, he was cursing them in a thin, sadistic voice and lacing into them with his twisted stick. Vespasian came to a sudden decision, marched back to his headquarters and summoned Lucilius and Simon to come before him.

"Centurion," he said, addressing himself to Lucilius, "I need two men to go out and reconnoiter the exact positions of the enemy tonight. I have chosen you and *Miles Gregarius* Simon ben Eleazar for this task, as you both have great fighting experience and know how to move silently. Bring me your report in the morning."

The general, Simon thought, had shot him a particularly meaningful look.

The soldiers, dressed in dark tunics and with faces blackened, passed through the sentry lines.

Later, Simon came back alone, sweating heavily and bleeding from superficial sword cuts. He related how Lucilius had perished in a chance encounter with the Britons.

Vespasian folded his arms and stuck out his stubborn jaw. "Most unfortunate," he said unsmilingly. "He was a valuable man. He'll be badly missed."

"Yes, sir," said Simon.

"Won't be able to hold that court-martial now, either," mused Vespasian. "Not with the complainant dead. That's too bad—too bad."

"Yes, sir," said Simon.

"What is most inconvenient," said Vespasian, "is that your century now lacks a centurion." He paused. "I have it in mind to appoint you acting centurion—you would hold the rank of *optio ad spem ordinis* until your commission is confirmed. They're a tough bunch of campaigners, some of them quite a bit older than you. Think you can hold down the job?"

"Yes, sir."

Vespasian looked at him. There was a tough resilience about the lad, confidence in the way he held his shoulders, hardness in those gray-green eyes. I wonder what you're thinking, he said to himself, I'd hate to have you for my enemy. "Go and wash your hands, Optio," he said, with sudden harshness. "They are stained with blood."

Simon saluted and left the general's tent. He could not

help wondering how deliberately Vespasian had intended to give the phrase a double meaning.

Aulus Plautius moved his legions steadily inland, halting only at the River Thames, where the Catuvellaunians, regathered in strength, were holding the last natural defense line before their exposed capital, Colchester.

The native leaders, Togidumnus and Caractacus, had chosen well. The Thames was no swift-flowing, clearly defined stream to be crossed by sudden assault like the Medway. It was a vast estuary of marsh and treacherous bog, ideally suited to the guerrilla tactics of the leaders, who knew every inch of the secret tracks through the morass and where the firm going lay under the desolate stands of tall reeds.

Somewhere near Woolwich, Plautius' force struggled and skidded off firm ground and into cold, deep, gluey mud.

Once again Plautius split his forces, sending the Second Augustan on his wing together with Geta's cavalry, who tended to fight particularly well under their old commander. Gamely the two columns plodded forward. Progress one moment would be good, then without warning they would sink down into stinking, yielding morass, and there would be backbreaking labor as the highly bred cavalry horses were harnessed with difficulty to help pull free the wagons, the suffering pack animals and the artillery carts. The heavily armored infantry suffered a special hell, floundering waist-high in the reeds, sometimes slipping under the water and drowning from sheer exhaustion. Even the Batavians, strong swimmers though they were and unhampered by heavy armor, lost numbers of men as they scouted boldly ahead and disappeared into quicksands and bogs.

Over everything hung gray clouds, the autumn rains and deathly, damp mists that helped split up the legions and reduced them to isolated groups struggling through the vast estuary.

On top of it all, the Catuvellaunians, seizing their chance, would strike hard—swift-moving bands of horse and chariot erupting out of the dense reeds and catching the legionaries in momentary swearing confusion as they mustered, formed up, locked shields and beat the savages back. Several luckless maniples of struggling soldiers, although not more than a hundred yards away from their comrades' help, were so isolated by the terrain that they were cut to pieces.

Even Simon had his own personal experience. Pushing forward with a few men ahead of his main century, he found to his consternation that Vespasian, mounted on one of the cavalry horses, insisted on accompanying him. As they approached a dense growth of reeds, there was the sudden jingle of harness, and eight enemy chariots came speeding down a causeway toward them. The infantrymen, who by now had evolved a certain technique for dealing with these guerrilla tactics, at once threw themselves into soft mud where the chariots would be unable to follow. The armored noblemen leaped after them, sword in hand. Several man-to-man combats developed. Vespasian was unlucky. One huge redhead—Simon saw with a shock that it was the same man who had maneuvered his chariot and bawled open defiance at the legions mustered on the banks of the Medway—had burst from the reeds and, attracted by Vespasian's purple cloak, an obvious badge of field rank, had set his chariot straight for him, knocking his horse flat and pinning the general helplessly underneath.

Simon, disposing of his adversary with one solid sword thrust through his unarmored neck, rushed to Vespasian's aid. His throwing knife took the redheaded warrior right in the armpit just as he was poised, his ruddy face stretched wide in a smile of triumph, to decapitate Vespasian with a single stroke of his great broadsword. As the man screamed, clawing at the slender little knife which had found one of the spots not protected by his old-fashioned armor, Simon launched himself into a flying kick, his hobnailed boots thudding into the giant's chest and knocking him flat. In a flash, Simon was on top of him, fingers ready to gouge out his eyes, but there was no need. The knife had gone home into the upper lung. A bubble of blood burst from his mouth and he died without a sound.

Terrified by the fall of their leader, the natives fled at

once into the rushes, leaving their dead and wounded behind. Vespasian, picking himself up shakily, nodded to Simon and said, "That's the second time you've saved my life. I won't forget that." It subsequently turned out that Simon had slain Togidumnus, the natives' joint leader.

When, to their intense joy, some of the Batavian scouts burst from the marshes to firm ground on the far side of the estuary, Plautius did not allow the legions to rush and join them. Instead, he kept them shivering in the mud and reeds for one more day while he knitted together the wings of his scattered forces. When he was ready, he ordered Geta's cavalry to gallop out of the marsh and challenge the enemy, which was now lined up in force on high ground, ready to hurl back any Roman assault.

Caractacus, on seeing Geta's cavalry, assumed it to be an isolated force, as at the battle of the Medway, and immediately gave the order to attack. Only hours later, returning tired and dispirited from chasing Geta's fleet riders, did the natives see the might of the Roman legions massed on the high ground that they had vacated. Screaming their mad battle cries, they hurled themselves courageously on the legions, only to be massacred by the highly trained and superbly armored Roman infantry.

At the end of the day, their army shattered and in ruins, the natives sent emissaries to negotiate peace and the uncontested entry of the Roman army into their city of Camulodunum.

Back in Rome, the Emperor Claudius sat with his wife, Messalina, discussing the situation in the East. Although it was late at night, he was eating. He always felt the need for food when he was worried, and he was worried now. Over and over, he read through the urgent dispatch he had just received from Vibius Marsus, the governor of Syria.

The news concerned Herod Agrippa, his old friend. It appeared that he was using all the wealth of the previously splintered Jewish nation to fortify Jerusalem. The town, the dispatch said, was now almost surrounded by immense walls and would soon be

74

impregnable to siege. If that were not enough, the report went on to detail alliance after alliance, treaty after treaty, that the king had made with neighboring states which threatened to outflank the whole Roman position in Palestine. Finally, it now appeared that Herod had reembraced the orthodox Jewish religion.

"My dear," said Messalina, who, despite her youth and beauty, was even more shrewd and cunning than the Emperor himself, "the whole thing's obvious. He thinks he's their Messiah, come to lead them back to independence. They're absolutely obsessed with it, you know."

"Why on earth can't they put up with a few taxes and the odd Roman statue on the Temple walls?" Claudius said, frowning. "We don't even ask them to worship our gods—I mean, couldn't they have chosen that fellow Jeshua, whom we call Jesus, instead of crucifying him? Things would have been so much more peaceful with him."

"You yourself have given the answer, dear," said Messalina. "They are a proud nation, these Jews—do you know they even have the gall to call themselves 'the chosen people'? It's all in their religious writings. Mark my words, with them it will be war or nothing."

Claudius scowled. "As soon as Plautius conquers the Britons, I'll recall his legions. You know, I'm really worried about Herod Agrippa—really worried." He let out a long, panting burp. She just managed to hide a grimace of disgust.

As they sat nodding in their chairs, ready for bed, bonfires flared in a long line from Dover to Cape Gris Nez, then across transalpine Gaul, taking wing on the high peaks of the Alpes Maritimes and leaping the long distances to the Italian valleys. All through the night, sweating details of Roman legionaries on lonely mountaintops lit their fires and plied them with brushwood so that, flaring into brilliant flame, the message could finally be seen in Rome as a tiny red point on Mount Soraxte, thirty miles away. Rome had conquered once again and the British tribes stood ready to surrender. An excited Claudius was awakened early in the morning. He studied the semaphore messages as they came flooding in and dictated his reply.

Departing in wonderful spirits for Britannia, he took ship across the Gulf of Lyons and, using relay after relay of picked horse teams, his coach crossed Gaul at great speed. In an incredibly short time he was over the Channel, smelling the brine-laden wind of the Thames estuary, catching the bright gleam of the Roman helmets, the blare of war trumpets and the shouting of the massed ranks of the Roman legions as they yelled his name. "Imperator—Imperator—Imperator!"

King Antedios, chief of the Iceni, sat toasting his legs in front of the fire. The smell of cooking came from the other side of his spacious, circular hut, and he could see the rumps of his wife and his concubines as they crouched over the pots. The sight of his women busying themselves never failed to put him in good humor, despite certain problems which lately had become more pressing.

"I'll dine off the golden dishes," he bawled.

As his wife scuttled over and obediently placed the heavy yellow plate before him, Antedios could see nothing incongruous about this fabulous treasure gracing his simple timber hut with its wattle-and-daub roof and charred central hole which did for a chimney. His tribe was his, to do with as he saw fit, and the gold merely represented the proceeds of the sale of so many Icenian young as slaves. The Romans craved the strong thews of his tribesmen and the soft, pale-yellow skin of his women. Years of trading with them had given Antedios an insight which was to prove valuable in the present crisis.

Sitting at his feet was his coltish young daughter, Victoria, the apple of his eye. After years of trying to produce a male heir with a variety of native princesses, Antedios had, at the age of sixty, a very old age indeed, accepted failure and concentrated on grooming his daughter for royal power. He did not have the sophistication to send her to Rome to be educated, but had sent her to his relatives in Gaul, long civilized by the Romans. She had come home at the age of twenty not only able to read and speak Latin, but with considerable charm, poise and a Romanized name.

Now, with the native British armies shattered and

the Romans camped on the Thames as they waited for their Emperor, Antedios was more conscious than ever that Victoria, properly used, was his trump card.

"What will happen, Father?" she said, flicking her long red hair off her forehead. "Will the Romans kill us and burn our huts?"

The old man chuckled. "Nothing will happen. Your father has been very clever. Did I not refuse to send a contingent to join Caractacus? Have I not continued to trade with the Romans and send emissaries assuring them of our friendship? I tell you they will spare us. Not only that, they will make us their allies." He looked proudly at Victoria. "The Romans look after their friends. When they see you and realize how civilized we really are, they will make us rich."

"You are rich now, Father," said the girl quietly. "Why do you want still more?"

There was silence while Antedios lay back and thought with pleasure of his fat cattle grazing in the fields, his horses, hunting dogs, his hundreds of personal slaves all branded with the same insignia that he put on his coinage. Not many tribes in Britannia had the technology to mint and he had been producing two issues for many years now: one with his name stamped on the coin, the other with the image of a powerful, rearing horse. That is symbolic, he thought, for I am indeed a powerful man. His mind turned back to his daughter. The girl asked peculiar questions sometimes—questions to which he could find no satisfactory answer, questions which women did not normally ask for fear of the certain reward of a blow or a cuff. The Roman way, he realized, gave considerable status to the women of the family—in better houses, at least. He would have to see to it that his wife and harem of young native girls did not become stubborn or disaffected. "Go and read, girl," he said sharply. "You must be able to impress the Emperor with your learning and charm. That is all I want. Leave the governing of my people to me."

"Yes, Father." The girl rose obediently, went to a corner of the hut and began reading from one of the scrolls she had brought back from Gaul. Antedios noted with pleasure the graceful way she moved, her exceptional tallness, the strikingly classical face. I must use her well, he thought. Marry her off where it will do most good. There was only one answer—his cousin Prasutagus, to whom, in the absence of a male heir, his throne would pass on death.

Prasutagus was an amiable, plump little man of fifty, happy with farming his large estates. Just the kind of person not to offend anybody, Antedios thought, especially those arrogant Romans. What was more, Prasutagus, being of royal blood, had frequently been sent across the Channel to parley with their relatives in various Gaulish tribes and had acquired a smattering of Latin and Roman customs. In every way he was suitable as a marriage partner for Victoria. Not only was he rich and Romanized, but he would inherit the Icenian throne, which would make Antedios' daughter queen of the Iceni. Antedios did not stop to think that Victoria might actually object to marrying Prasutagus. It was always the custom in Britannia to treat women as chattels. If, for reasons of policy, he had chosen to give Victoria an education, that did not affect his parental right to dispose of her entirely as he wished. They would marry and as soon as possible.

"Victoria," he called. "Come back here."

The girl rose to her feet and walked over to Antedios, slim and lithe. She squatted at his feet, flicked her rich, silky red hair out of her eyes and said, "Yes, father?"

"I have decided to marry you off."

"To whom, Father?"

"Prasutagus. He will be king on my death and you will be queen."

For a moment her eyes flashed and her shoulders tensed in repulsion, but she knew where her duty lay. "Yes, Father."

The old man leaped from his chair, seizing a switch. "Get back to your work," he yelled suddenly to the women, who, hearing talk of marriage, had edged closer out of curiosity. "I'll teach you to neglect your duties." He laid the switch across his wife's legs until she gave a satisfactory scream and the clattering and bustling around the cooking pots resumed. He dispatched a servant at once to summon Prasutagus, then slumped back on his couch. The effort had tired him. He was not getting any younger and all these women weakened him. His head nodded forward and he dozed until the food was brought.

9

It was a cold, bright early-winter day.

Claudius sat on a special podium, flanked on either side by a maniple of the Praetorian Guard, who gleamed in the brilliantly plumed helmets and gilded greaves which they alone were allowed to wear.

The legions, drawn up in ranks, made a colorful sight with their bright armor and crimson cloaks; but the auxiliary cavalry, sweeping past at a canter, were by far the most distinctive, with yellow plumes nodding from their helmets and special parade masks which, hiding their swarthy barbarian features, gave them the uniform, classical facade of so many Greek gods.

Claudius, watching the flashing splendor of his troops, could not help but feel proud to be their Emperor. He raised his hand and the religious ceremonies began, the priests chanting at they prepared the animal sacrifices at the specially erected field altar. After five *supplicationes,* which involved a special thanksgiving ceremony for the army's recent victory, they finished with a final dedication to Jupiter Optimus Maximus. Leaving the field, they allowed the presentation of medals to begin.

Most of the troops would be granted their battle honors through normal regimental channels. The present ceremony would be only for the important field decorations which the Emperor would personally distribute.

Simon watched, his heart pumping with excitement as one by one the commanders of the legions stepped up and received their medals in the shape of *hastae purae,* small silver replicas of spears—the usual reward for distinguished military service.

Hearing his own name called, Simon at first did not believe it, but nudged forward by his comrades, he walked up to the Emperor in a kind of trance, standing stiffly to attention as the aide read laboriously from a long scroll how Simon had saved Vespasian's life in the Thames marshes. Claudius then placed the crown of oak leaves on Simon's head (a high decoration given solely for saving a fellow citizen's life under danger) while the troopers of the Second Augustan cheered lustily.

"Congratulations," Claudius leered, sniffling, putting on one of his vacuous grins.

"Thank you, sir."

"Now don't I know you from somewhere?" Claudius looked at him hard for a moment, then said, "Oh, well, nevermind." He beamed. "I'm told I've got to make you a centurion. What do you think of that?"

"Thank you, sir." Simon saluted, about-faced and returned to the ranks.

With the decorations distributed, the surrender ceremonial now began, the defeated British chiefs being paraded and put on their knees in an attitude of humility before the Emperor. Loaded with chains, crouched in submission with their families, they were either pardoned or condemned to death in accordance with Claudius' whim or political expediency as explained to him in a whisper by his trusted adviser, a eunuch by the name of Posides.

Finally, the delegation from the Iceni was brought forward. The old king had with him his new son-in-law, the heir apparent, Prasutagus, his daughter Victoria, and a small escort of picked noblemen. Mounted on fine horses, they looked picturesque and wild.

Claudius was struck by the sheer barbaric splendor of their dress, the thick skins and colorful tartans contrasting with the carefully handed-down archaic armor they wore, old King Antedios looking especially magnificent in his beautifully worked bronze helmet from which two great gleaming horns protruded.

Claudius nodded to his interpreter, who said, "The Emperor asks for your formal surrender."

To Claudius' surprise, the tall red-haired girl, sitting so gracefully erect and effortlessly handling her richly ornamented thoroughbred, set spurs to her horse and came up alongside her father in one bound. Speaking in good Latin, she said, "Sire. My father desires me to remind the Emperor that he has always had good relations with Rome—that he sent no men to fight against the legions. He asks if 'surrender' is not an incorrect word."

Claudius forgot to roll his head and behave like an idiot. He looked intently at the girl, then inclined his head and whispered to Posides. "Is this true? Did they not fight?"

"No, sire," Posides answered. "We have no record of participation by their tribesmen. Also, we have good trading relations with their nation."

Claudius turned back, smiling. "All right, and who might you be, my girl?"

"I am the Princess Victoria," the girl answered with a touch of hauteur. "And this"—she indicated a plump little man—"is my husband, Prasutagus." Digging his heels into his horse's side, Prasutagus tried to canter alongside his wife, but the animal refused to budge. Not used to riding, the little man kept flapping his heels like mad and began to sweat. Eventually, desperately, he squeaked out from where he was, "I make obeisance to you, O Caesar."

Claudius sat back and roared with laughter. "Well, well, well. A funny little fat man who speaks Latin. Fancy meeting that out here in the wilderness! I like funny little fat men—they don't make good traitors, you know. And you speak Latin—that's good. Oh, yes, I like that." He belched, resumed his idiot's expression and said, "Now why don't you get off your horses and do homage to me?"

The two of them at once dismounted and sank to their

knees, but the old man, using his lack of Latin as an excuse to keep his dignity, sat stone-faced and erect in his saddle.

"Tell your father the king," Claudius said to the girl, "that a king does not kneel before another king. That I would have him rule his nation in peace and friendship as my ally. Ask him if he will make a formal treaty."

Victoria turned to her father and translated, and the old king nodded, his craggy features lighting up in a leathery smile.

"You," cried Claudius, pointing to Prasutagus, "that's some wife you've got for a tubby, middle-aged man. Ho, ho, ho," he bawled vacuously. "We're both in the same boat, d'you know? You'll have your work cut out to manage her, I can tell you that. Ha, ha, ha!" He sniffed, wiping his running nose with his forefinger, and the legions howled with delighted laughter at their beloved fool of an Emperor.

Claudius now waved a tired arm, indicating that the audience was at an end, and after making a short speech in which he thanked the assembled troops for their loyalty, he dismissed the parade and retired to his luxurious tent.

"Well, thank the gods that's over then," he said grumpily to Posides. "These parades always irritate me." He started in on a plate of roast boar, fresh from the nearby forest, his handsome white-haired head rolling absently from side to side. Appalling smells now rose from his body, but Posides, inured to the revolting habits of his master, stood impassively by the side of his couch.

"Sire," Posides said, "with our friends the Regni securing our left flank, you have now achieved marvels in finding an ally of strength on our right. The way is now clear for your legions to march westward where the enemy still remains to be subjugated, and there is talk of much mineral wealth. Permit me to congratulate you. Only you, sire, could have done it."

Claudius said, "Save the flattery, Posides. You're the politician, not me. As for Britannia, you can keep it. It's a foul climate and I don't care about the minerals. You know why I invaded—I needed that triumph. To stay Emperor—perhaps to stay alive."

"Yes, sire."

"And let Vespasian handle those western tribes. He's too damned popular in Rome. With any luck, it'll keep him busy for years."

"Yes, sire."

"As for the Iceni, go ahead and give them a nice generous treaty. One day, when it suits us, we'll absorb 'em."

"Very well, sire."

"Tomorrow I start my journey back to Rome. I have a crisis in the East, with Herod, remember. Leave me now. I need sleep."

"Yes, sire." Posides started for the tent entrance.

"Posides—"

"Sire?"

There was hidden mischief in Claudius' eyes. "Do you think I am a complete fool?"

"Perhaps the wisest fool that ever lived, sire."

King Antedios and his family rode swiftly for home. Bad weather was spreading from the east and few words were spoken. All that could be heard was the muffled thud of the horses' hooves and the creaking of leather mixed with the jingle of bit and harness. Soon, rain turned to wet snow, as the icy wind blowing off the east coast laid cruel fingers on their averted faces. The king, tired from his exertions, swayed in the saddle, feeling dizziness come upon him. But the old warrior shrugged off his increasing weakness and told no one.

Only when they pulled him off his charger, stiff, frozen, practically mummified in his saddle, and carried him into the smoky warmth of the royal hut did they realize that the old man was in a raging fever.

From the way his women gathered around him, weeping, Antedios knew he was close to death. Quickly he dictated his will, leaving most of his wealth outright to his daughter and son-in-law, including his herds of cattle and hundreds of slaves, recommending that the brands on both be changed, as cattle could be stolen and slaves escape.

Lastly, he summoned them to his bedside. "I have done my best," he said, "I have kept my kingdom intact and given you peace with the Romans."

"Yes, Father," said Victoria.

"Honor that treaty. Give them no excuse to invade."

"As you say, Father."

Strange, Antedios thought. Her husband will be king, yet already she speaks for him. He went on, "When the Romans have no more enemies to fight, they will turn on you and you will find what kind of men they really are. They take everything and need yet more."

"What shall we do, Father?"

"Your best," the old man answered wearily. "When that is not enough—when in spite of all you can do, they abuse you and grind our land under their heel—then and only then you must act."

"What kind of action, Father?"

"You cannot beat them in open battle. Be cunning as a fox. Assemble your numbers in secret, then one dark night when they are unready for battle, fall on them and kill them all."

"Yes, Father."

"You promise?"

The girl drew herself to her full height. Her eyes glinted and her face flushed as she remembered Claudius' banter with her husband, how he had discussed her as if she were nothing. I will be no man's slave, she thought. I will be my father's daughter. "I promise," she said grimly. "It will be as you wish, Father."

Antedios died with pride on his face, for the first time not regretting that a daughter was to carry on his noble line.

Months later, in the early Roman spring, Claudius had his triumph. It was a splendid, picturesque occasion.

To the screaming approval of thousands packed into the upstairs windows of the Roman tenements and on the pavements behind the massed spears of the city *vigiles,* the procession entered the city from the northeast, by way of the triumphal gate. First came the Senate, on foot in their finest robes, followed by a band playing *tubae,* yard-long trumpets which blared out high, harsh notes which set the crowd on edge with anticipation. Then came carts bearing the spoils of war: gold and silver coins, lead ingots, metal plate beautifully incised and decorated in the La Tène curling style that

British craftsmen had made their own. After this, a line of floats rumbled through the streets, picturing the British countryside and the battles that Claudius' army had fought. Then, to the sounds of flutes, came the white bulls destined for sacrifice, followed by a trail of British chieftains and their families, walking in fetters, knowing that they would soon be put to death.

Now the pulse of the procession quickened, as the huge Germans of the Imperial Guard, resplendent in bearskins over their gleaming armor, came marching down the Via Sacra, escorting the Emperor. Cheers rose to a new pitch as Claudius came into view, driven in a simple chariot. He was wearing the rare naval crown, adorned with miniature beaks of ships and granted by the Senate only for a successful seaborne invasion. Behind Claudius, indulging in her newly granted privilege of driving through Rome in a covered carriage, came the ivory-skinned Messalina, saluting the crowd with slender, bejeweled fingers.

A contingent of auxiliary cavalry now followed, looking superb in their parade masks, tight leggings and knotted scarves, the yellow plumes of their helmets dipping and fluttering as they controlled their beautifully groomed horses. Then came a small contingent of Syrian bowmen, the archers who had laid down such a lethal covering fire at the Medway. In their conical helmets and flowing, skirtlike garments they were somehow alien and menacing.

As the long procession built to a climax, the crowd was becoming hoarse with screaming. Now, moving nearer, came the splendid sound of the massed band of the legions, drums beating, fifes and flutes trilling, tubas and *cornua* blaring away. Then the successful legion commanders came into sight, preceded by Aulus Plautius himself, glorious in full ceremonial armor. Finally—what the crowd had been waiting for—the legions, the massive core of the Roman army, their hobnailed boots crunching down on the stone with well-drilled, powerful impact. First the standard bearers, clad in leopard skins, holding high the imperial eagles and their own distinctive regimental banners— Simon's regiment proudly displaying the Capricorn standard, the personal emblem of the Emperor Augustus, who had founded the legion. Then the hard, tough veterans, arms swinging, the disciplined *corps d'élite*, the finest fighting men in the world, heads up, chests out, their scarlet cloaks making a brilliant spectacle as they swept by in perfect order, roaring their marching songs. The crowd was wild now, pelting the legion with flowers. Line after line, rank after rank, they swung past, men drawn from all over the known world, the second Augustan, Fourteenth Gemina, the dark, stocky Spaniards of the Ninth Hispana, the hard-swearing, sun-bitten veterans of the Twentieth Valeria.

Then suddenly it was over, the legions marching away into the distance, and at the tail of the procession came the inevitable clowns dressed in outrageous parody of the Emperor and his wife, the legions, the British prisoners—midgets aping the senators, prancing around with gigantic phalli strapped to their legs.

Simon had been excited by the sheer physical splendor of the parade and his young blood flowed fast at being one of the all-conquering veterans. Only a few years ago, he had been nothing but a ragged shepherd boy from an obscure Jewish tribe in the hills of Galilee, but now here he was, clad in gleaming armor, wearing the distinctive greaves and double skirt of a centurion, standing to attention in front of his men at the solemn climax of a Roman triumph.

As the legions assembled in a rigid square at the foot of the Capitoline Hill, Claudius prayed at the Temple of Jove and then, to the ruffle of drums, the condemned British chiefs were executed, one by one, along with their families. Even months ago, this might have struck a vengeful chord in Simon's mind, but now, standing shoulders back, eyes staring straight ahead under his dress helmet, Simon was a long way from remembering his massacred family, the broken bodies of his kin, the shrieks of raped women on that far-off Galilean hill, his solemn promise to his father. Simon was now thinking in only one way: like a loyal Roman.

Soon, he was to learn that loyalty was not enough, that with a Jew, his country of adoption would always be suspicious—wary of a higher loyalty to a single God and to the sacred homeland of Israel.

10

With the formal parades over, Simon was free to enjoy his leave. Not one, like so many other veterans, to get drunk in the wine shops or brothels that abounded in Rome, he was determined to spend his time exploring the city, with all the fascination it had as the hub of the civilized world.

He roomed with Camerinus at a cheap but comfortable lodging house and set out early next morning to see the sights. Jostled by the crowds who had come for Claudius' triumph, the two men marveled at the many stalls of ripe fruit, vegetables and flowers; small jewelry shops in which rows of slaves sat cross-legged, doing intricate work in gold and silver. Mixed with the rich smell of spices from the Orient, there was the beguiling music of the Indian snake charmers with their cobras swaying in their baskets. Avoiding the heavily laden mules bringing provisions through the streets, the spirited horses that would suddenly charge by, ridden by young bloods, they ambled along, drinking in the essence of Rome. Now and again they would stop and take refreshment—pickled pork, slices of melon and boiled watermelon seeds. Eventually they stopped to buy a large plate of hot roasted chestnuts from a stall run by a blind veteran, his military history shown by the various phalerae, or campaign disks, sewn to his dirty tunic.

"Psst," said the blind man, who was not sightless at all, wagging his finger for Simon to come closer. "You are being followed. Three of 'em." He paused, said nervously, "I hope you're not in trouble with the authorities—"

"Not that we know of," said Simon grimly. He gave the man a generous tip and the two went on their way, alerted, wary as cats.

Near the Forum they came to a fashionable barber's shop and Simon, hairy and unkempt from the campaign and flush with back pay, decided to have himself spruced up. He went inside, leaving Camerinus sitting on the steps, chewing pomegranate seeds.

The barber, taking his cue from Simon's apparent surliness, made no attempt at conversation and got on with the job. Soon Simon's hair, curled with tongs heated in a little charcoal fire, began to shine. After shaving him, the barber handed him the highly polished metal that served as a mirror, then said proudly, "There! Was it not Lycurgus the Spartan who said that a fine head of hair lends beauty to a good face and terror to an ugly one?"

"He has scented you a little, master," Camerinus said, wrinkling his nose, noting that his master had been transformed into an elegant male of high fashion.

"An oversight," Simon said, grinning. "It'll wear off. Are they still there?" he added, careful not to glance down the road.

"Yes, master." Camerinus jerked his head at some ruffians lounging by a flower stall. Grim-faced, they walked on farther. Noticing a crowd gathered around the Album—the official notice board kept in the Forum—they strolled over for a look. The main item read: "The sudden death is announced of Herod Agrippa, ruler under Caesar of Judaea and Galilee. These areas will now be taken under direct imperial government." There was a wealth of meaning behind the terse announcement, and Simon, who dimly remembered meeting the king, could not help wondering what was going on.

Meanwhile he had a more important matter on his mind—to try and shake off the men who had been tracking them all day. Hiring mules from a stand near the Forum and moving slowly at first along the Via Sacra, where work gangs were still engaged in clearing rubbish from the day before, they were able, once past the law courts in the Basilica Julia, to break into a trot.

Now they descended rapidly on the stone *pavé* into the slum quarters of the city.

Too late, Simon and Camerinus found they were trapped in a dead end. Their pursuers, now reinforced by others carrying cudgels and swords, closed in on them purposefully.

"Quick," Simon yelled. "Follow me." The two of them vaulted off their mules and ran into a dark, narrow alley. Halfway along it, they drew their swords and, standing back to back, determined to sell their lives dearly.

Whistles blew and there was the sound of sandals slapping on stone as the pursuers took up their positions. Then, at a word of command, men poured into the alley from both directions. With the alley so narrow, hardly more than the width of a man's shoulder, those in front hesitated, but urged on by commands from the rear, they finally attacked.

"Aarrhh!" The first man screamed in agony, collapsing with Simon's throwing knife sunk up to the hilt in his throat. Behind him, Simon could hear another give a bubbling scream and moan, "Venus, help me," as Camerinus, all whipcord from his campaigning and now fully recovered from his arrow wound, got his attacker full in the belly with a sword thrust, then prized the blade out of the body with his hobnailed boot, spilling the man's guts onto the ground in a slimy, stinking heap.

The two men, spitting and hawking saliva, waited for the next charge. Simon knew they could not hold out much longer. They were panting and sweaty, bleeding from flesh wounds, their muscles aching. Gritting their teeth, they hacked away until blood began to pour down the alleyway in dark-red streams.

Suddenly they could hear fresh shouting as a new battle started outside the alley, the men fighting Simon and Camerinus being gradually drawn off to help their surprised comrades. Finally, there was the sound of running feet. Then, as their attackers fled, a deathly quiet.

A man came running up the alley, blood streaming from a cudgel wound. He touched his forelock. "Please come, sir," he said. "It is safe now and my master awaits you."

They emerged exhausted and bloody, arms around

each other's shoulders, grinning with joy at just being alive. The road was deserted now except for a knot of panting slaves standing beside a curtained litter with ornate alabaster panels. The curtain opened and a gaunt face peered out.

"Just in time," said Seneca.

"But how on earth did you know?" asked Simon, still breathless from combat.

"I was in the Argiletum, buying books. When I saw those men following you, I put two and two together. I knew who they were, you see."

"But what are you doing back here, sir?" Simon asked, mystified.

"Oh, that," Seneca said blandly. "Claudius in his mercy has allowed certain prominent exiles a few days in Rome to see his 'triumph.'"

"And the men?" Simon demanded. "Who were they?"

Seneca paused. He said slowly, "Emperor's men. Security police seconded from the Imperial Guard."

"But I'm a loyal Roman—I bear Rome's decorations!"

"It's precisely because you are a war hero that they needed to kill you," Seneca said. "They couldn't very well award you the civic crown, then arrest you."

"Arrest me? I don't understand," Simon said. "What crime have I committed?"

"That of plotting rebellion against Caesar."

"Impossible," Simon swore.

"You are implicated, nevertheless."

"I must see the Emperor. I must prove myself innocent."

"I'm afraid that's impossible," said Seneca. "You would never get an audience."

"Then what do you suggest?"

There was a pause as Seneca, the ascetic poseur, the sophisticated degenerate, the devious schemer, practiced one of the many arts that he was so good at—procuring. "There is," he said, "a certain lady of high rank who might be interested in your problem. You could make your explanation to her. Will you come? She is—quite charming—"

Simon grinned, white teeth showing against the tan of his face. He had met ladies of high rank before and they had only wanted one thing—a favor that he was never averse to granting. "What have I got to lose?"

They moved off, Seneca discreetly out of sight in his swaying litter surrounded by slaves, Simon and Camerinus following along behind.

The woman rose as they came into the room. In the dim light of the single oil lamp, Simon could see that she was slim and graceful with flawless white skin. "Thank you, Lucius Annaeus," she said imperiously. "Perhaps you have now shortened your exile." She dismissed him with a wave of her hand and Seneca left the room, bowing.

"I would like to wash and clean up," Simon said.

She came closer and laid her cheek against his. Her skin was soft to the touch, like satin. "No," she said, "I want you fresh from battle, your cuts bleeding, the sweat not dry on your skin, the violence still showing in your muscles." She began to stroke his biceps, strained and gorged with blood from wielding the heavy steel sword. Her fingers were slender, impossibly sensitive, her scent, imported by caravan halfway across the known world, was subtle yet bold. Half-crazy with lust at the sight of his battle wounds, desperate to be bruised and savaged, she reached up, with difficulty locking petite hands around his neck, so that she floated, light and slim as gossamer, pressing against his body.

Simon, strong as a bull, knowing the strange barbaric tastes bred by a life of idleness, was aroused yet infuriated by her bold femininity.

Eventually, much later, they lay exhausted in each other's arms, Simon asleep, the girl smiling, catlike, in the semidarkness. As Simon began to snore, she sank sharp fingernails into his back, ripping his skin from shoulder to waist, bringing blood in even, red strips. He came agonizingly awake, bellowing with pain.

"People do not generally fall asleep in the presence of their Empress," she said, her voice throbbing with amusement.

Simon gritted his teeth with anger and pulled her arms over her head, clamping her tiny wrists against a cushion with a rough hand. "Whatever you may be on your feet," he said, "I know well what you are on your back. I should give you a good beating for that."

The girl tinkled with laughter, her jet-black hair

curling deliciously over her eyes. "I have," she said, "three Nubian bodyguards waiting outside the door. They would kill you at the first blow from your hand."

Simon stretched himself, feeling the strength return to his powerful body. "You think," he said, "that I have killed so many men today that I cannot kill a few more?"

She laughed, then said, "Since you are no respecter of rank, call me by my first name, Messalina. I like to hear it pronounced by a man."

As anger slowly left him, Simon released her wrists. He said in a gentler voice. "I have enjoyed making love to you, Messalina, but I did not come here for that."

"Then what did you come for?"

"Answers to questions. Why your husband the Emperor should want to kill me, a loyal centurion holding his civic crown."

"You really do not know?"

"I'm afraid not."

"You have heard that your friend Herod Agrippa is dead?"

"I have read it on the notice board. But why do you call him my friend?"

"Do you deny that you met? A slave has confessed it under torture—or that you wear his ring?"

"I deny nothing. What you say is true, although I scarcely remember him."

Messalina pulled herself up on an elbow. When she spoke, her voice was curt. "Herod Agrippa was a traitor. He used his position as overlord of Judaea and Galilee, given to him in trust by Caligula and Claudius, to conspire against Rome."

"In what way?"

"Last month in Jerusalem, he was ready with eighty thousand heavily armored men to proclaim an independent Jewish state, and with powerful allies annihilate our small garrison in Syria. Before making his proclamation he was taken ill."

"You are sure of this?"

"There can be no doubt. The governor of Syria has sent us detailed dispatches. Before he died, Herod sank into a fever. In his delirium, he renounced his claim to being the Jews' Messiah, saying that yet another, stronger, younger than he would take up the Jews' fight for freedom. He described this man in detail."

"In what way?"

"A Jewish gladiator, son of an obscure Galilean chief. A man who wore Herod's ring, who would one day come and lead his people's fight against the Romans."

"This is madness," Simon exclaimed. "I hardly met the man. I am a Roman citizen and proud to be so. I am loyal to the Emperor."

"While you wear his ring, you serve two masters."

"It means nothing to me," Simon swore. "Here, I give it to you." Pulling the ring with its menorah insigne off his finger, he laid it beside her head on the pillow. "I serve one master only. The Emperor."

"That is sensible," she said in a quieter voice.

They lay back, each thinking his own thoughts.

Eventually Simon asked, "What will happen now?"

"I will report to Claudius and he will believe me. I am his eyes and ears, you see. Worth two thousand paid agents! Naturally I will tell him that you have accepted permanent exile in Britannia"—she smiled—"just in case you might be tempted to change loyalties."

"Is it necessary?"

She sighed. "I am afraid so. It would be politic to leave tomorrow. Don't look so glum," she added. "I have saved your life, and besides, Britannia is a developing country. There should be a great future for you there."

"I suppose so."

"Come," she said softly, "let us make love again."

Simon grinned. "Your royal command?"

"My command."

"Then I cannot disobey."

They came together, the girl's slender body writhing palely in the light of the single oil lamp as they enjoyed one brief, shuddering union.

"It's late," Simon said. "What will the Emperor say?"

"He lets me come and go as I please. While I am useful to him, he puts up with my infidelities. When I grow older, less attractive, less sought after, he will execute me for all the pain I have caused him."

Simon slowly got to his feet, dressed and buckled on his sword. In a sudden, impetuous gesture which betrayed his immaturity, he went down on his knees and said, "Now it's time to go, I don't want to leave you."

She swung off the couch so that she was sitting very erectly, very upright. With her lush dark hair cascading

93

down her shoulders, a slim hand draped modestly across her breasts, the other extended, drooping and palm downward, toward Simon, she looked every inch an empress. "Good-bye, Simon ben Eleazar," she said formally. "I wish you luck. We shall never meet again."

Simon kissed her hand, rose and walked toward the door.

"You know," she said, calling after him, "that I will be giving Claudius false information, don't you?" She paused, measuring her words. "You Jews will always be a danger to Rome. Only you people have the arrogance to worship one God and one God only, refusing to enshrine the Emperor in your temples. Only you circumcise your private parts to keep yourselves separate from your fellow man. You are proud and stiff-necked with a loyalty you give only to yourselves. Only you have the cheek to call yourselves 'the chosen people' and the stubbornness to go on fighting for your independence for thousands of years, even though you know your cause is hopeless. If I were to give proper advice, I would tell the Emperor to kill you."

"Then why not do so?"

"Because, although it will be your destiny to fight Rome, it will not be my destiny to see it." She smiled roguishly, drawing her cat's tongue over her soft lips. "Besides, there is another reason."

"What is that, my Empress?"

"You make love superbly. I could not kill such a man."

The next evening, Simon went to dinner with Seneca. Glancing around the triclinium, he said he had never seen such wonderful floor mosaics and wall paintings.

"Ah, yes," Seneca conceded, "they are rather fine." He whispered briefly to a slave, who lit up an elegant candelabrum of fourteen oil lamps, so that light filled the room. "I am rather fond of that." He pointed to a hauntingly dramatic painting of the Trojan horse that covered an entire wall. "And that goes quite well in here, doesn't it?" He indicated a superbly fashioned floor mosaic depicting the River Nile with ducks, hippopotamuses and crocodiles swimming together. "A certain Dioscurides of Samos wrought the design in exchange for interest he owed me on a loan. He is quite famous now, I believe." Looking at Simon's face, he added hastily, "Of course I do not believe it is a sin to surround oneself with beautiful things. In fact I find it makes for spiritual stimulation."

The meal progressed, with Simon eating his way through a succession of rare game birds served by pretty boy and girl slaves from Seneca's retinue. Seneca just sat there, toying with a few cheese scraps, looking gaunt and almost saintly, until Simon had finished his meal.

"Now," Seneca said briskly. "Let us discuss your future. First of all, you will never be allowed back in Rome. You are aware of this?"

"Yes," Simon said bitterly. "It seems that as a Jew I am different. All other races may become good Romans, but I may not."

"That is so," Seneca said. "To be frank, you will always be under suspicion. You are lucky to have escaped with your life. Why not handle something with which your race is known to be expert, the commodity of money?"

Simon looked sharply at Seneca but saw only persuasiveness there and no intent to offend. Wearily he let the insult go. He said, "It shall be as you direct, Lucius Annaeus."

Seneca said, "I calculate that the campaigning will be over in Britannia within the next three years. With you on the spot as my agent, it should be possible to arrange loans to the allied kingdoms."

"Very well," said Simon.

"Of course," Seneca added, "although I stand to benefit, this is secondary to the contribution I shall be making toward improving the lot of those poor people."

Simon looked at Seneca's intent, thin face, but absolutely no humor showed in his eyes. "I'm sure you're right," he said. He paused. "I shall leave Rome at first light with two centuries of reinforcements for the Second Augustan."

"Just as well," said Seneca. "We have both outstayed our welcome with Claudius, I believe."

The two men discussed their business, finalizing their arrangements, taking leave of each other with embraces and handshakes.

Toward the end of their long haul back to Britannia, Camerinus insisted, "Master, master, we must

95

get that smell off you. The general will not like it."

Despite Simon's protests, Camerinus gave him a regulation army cut, then, every night for a week, washed his hair until the perfume was gone.

On his return to camp, Simon was at once summoned before the commander. At the sight of the young man standing to attention, Vespasian broke into a smile. He was becoming very fond of the boy. "I'm glad you didn't come back from Rome stinking of scent," he grunted. "The last chap who did that got demoted on the spot. I wouldn't have minded if it had been garlic."

There and then he appointed him to the post of Hastatus Posterior in the first cohort, making him effectively one of the senior centurions in the whole legion.

11

"The Durotriges," Petilius Cerialis said, rubbing the sweat off his wide mouth with the back of his hand, "a rough bunch, I can tell you that. Not like the semicivilized Belgae you've been fighting."

The assembled officers of the Second Augustan stared at him thoughtfully. Cerialis had preserved his playboy reputation right through two tough years of Britannic campaigns. He had also developed a remarkable facility for gathering intelligence. With a small group of picked, highly mobile cavalry and British scouts, he roamed with seeming impunity through the dangerous countryside, picking up information regarding the habits and fighting capability of the various tribes and their defensive readiness. No legion would now think of mounting a new campaign without asking for a briefing from Cerialis.

How does he do it? wondered Vespasian. He had heard the rumors that all the wives of the tribal princes were in love with him—that he had the pick of the chiefs' harems. Yes, he said to himself, that must be where he gets his information. He had a fleeting pang of jealousy, then dismissed the thought and listened.

"Quite different from anything you've yet encountered," Cerialis was going on. "Not whole tribes defending palisaded lowland encampments, but dozens of family groups, closely related by blood, sitting on top of high hills with all their retainers, challenging you to come and get them."

"What do you suggest?" Simon asked. "Destroy the biggest groups first?" Over the long months he had now become Vespasian's privileged aide-de-camp and was expected to make a contribution at staff conferences.

"I reckon so. By cutting off all prospect of reinforcement, it would destroy the morale of the smaller families. It won't be easy," he warned. "They've got money and a good mixed farming and cattle economy, not to speak of a thriving pottery industry derived from coastal shale beds." He shook his head. "Not to be underestimated."

"What about the country?" Vespasian asked in his broad rural accent.

"Arrh—what aboit the country," Cerialis mimicked him, with such charm that the assembled group of patrician officers roared with laughter and that old strained look came back to Vespasian's face. "Hill country. Bare windy downland, little forest, no protection for you as you advance up those damned hills toward the savages. They'll take your heads off with slingshot at forty yards." Cerialis continued, "At the first sign of danger they'll dash off to their great hill fort and sit there behind multiramparted defenses, while you starve to death outside. Huge complexes, the biggest of them—fifty, maybe sixty acres of paved streets, houses, storage pits. The two most powerful are the fortresses of Hod Hill and Mai-dun. You'll have to reduce them before you can subdue the country, and with winter coming on you haven't got all that long."

There, thought Vespasian, you are right. Every year

97

we have the same problem. For two long years now he had been campaigning farther westward, one hostile tribe after another, and just when he was getting the upper hand, appalling weather had set in and he had been forced into winter quarters, needing to do much of the same work again the following spring. In the case of the Belgae it had been pitched battles for their populated lowland encampments, but with the Durotriges it would be a fight for the strategic places, hill forts with complex defenses—difficult to conquer.

"Very well," Vespasian said briskly, "seems like a reconnaissance might be in order. Could you spare the time to have a look?" Although Cerialis was only a colonel, he was so thoroughly likeable and obviously competent that the general preferred to express his wishes by way of a request rather than a command.

"Sure—why not?" Cerialis said. A firsthand view of Vespasian planning a battle was pure gold in terms of professional experience. "Hod Hill should be nearest. No more than twenty miles from here."

Taking some of Cerialis' roving cavalry and two picked scouts, they set off across rolling downland, having first rubbed mud over their armor to dull the shine. Eventually one of the scouts reined in his horse on the top of a slight rise and held up his hand. Everyone dismounted, then crawled up for a look.

The scout, body wrapped in animal skins despite the late summer heat, had hitherto ridden in silence, but now spoke to Cerialis in a low, guttural tone. Cerialis began nodding intently.

"He says," Cerialis translated, "that visibility is extra good and you must not be deceived by the indifferent appearance of the defenses. He says I must tell you that we are still some fifteen miles away."

"I can gauge distance too," Vespasian said testily. "Ask him what else he can tell me."

While Cerialis conversed again with the scout, Simon and Vespasian studied the stronghold. Set among peaceful fields and rolling pastures, the fort, so far as they could see, occupied an almost rectangular area of some forty or fifty acres. Viewed from the east it seemed to rise up from the valley bottom fairly steeply on three flanks, the back, or western flank, being entirely hidden

98

from view. In the distance, barely distinguishable because of their uniform green color, the long defensive banks could be seen, staring at around the three-hundred-and-fifty-foot contour line with one rising higher than the other until the highest was reached, capped with formidable wooden ramparts.

"He has been there," Cerialis said, translating again. "They have at least two thousand men easily mobilized at the blast of a horn, and the women are great fighters too. Many other families would undoubtedly go into the fort once they knew of your presence. Even now, they are working desperately to strengthen their walls."

Cerialis paused, his tanned face parting in a smile of pure deviltry. "He considers," Cerialis went on, "that your infantry lacks the mobility to surmount these defenses."

Stifled laughter burst from some of Vespasian's staff. It was not often that a Roman general received a lesson in tactics from a native scout.

"Oh, he does, does he?" Vespasian said. A look of strain reappeared on his face, mixed with anger at the readiness of his officers to be amused.

Simon felt sorry for Vespasian. He had come very close to the general in the last two years of hard campaigning and knew just what must be going on in his mind. Anyone could direct lowland battles against packs of half-armed savages—these engagements more or less fought themselves, straight from the military manual—but now he was coming up against his first real tactical problem, how to subdue quickly—and quickly was the operational word—a well-armed hill fortress. Vespasian's military career was at stake. He had to show he was good enough to solve the problem, and his aristocratic staff, instead of pitching in, preferred to snigger at his manners.

"Ask him," Vespasian said stiffly, "what he knows about the chief—what kind of man is he?"

Cerialis talked again for some while and Vespasian hid his irritation at the coarse snickers that the hitherto unsmiling scout was now exchanging with his questioner.

"Apparently he is a great lover," Cerialis said, "and has recently bought three young and beautiful wives

99

from the Silures. They tend to keep him—fully occupied. Also, because of interest shown by the younger men in the settlement, he has found it necessary to fortify his own little area within the camp."

"Ask him where—to show me precisely the chief's living quarters," Vespasian broke in with sudden urgency.

Cerialis again spoke to the scout, then lifted a finger and indicated the southeastern corner of the fort. "In that area, about two hundred yards from the highest palisades, you should just make out a horseshoe-shaped wall around a large circular hut. That is where the chief lives. For convenience, the houses of his brothers—the senior commanders—are close by."

"Excellent," Vespasian said, the thin, irregular line of his mouth turning up in a smile. "Excellent." He turned to Simon. "Centurion—have your men completed those sketches?"

Simon went along the ridge, collecting hastily drawn papyrus maps. He brought the sketches to Vespasian, who studied them intently.

"There," Vespasian said, tapping a map with his swagger stick, "is where we will attack. The main legionary force will advance down that defile under cover of the trees and will assault the northern wall on my signal, following a short and very noisy diversionary attack from the south."

"But, General," Cerialis said, "how about the reinforcements? What can be done to prevent the enemy bringing up massive support groups to throw the legion back?"

Vespasian smiled. "Have you noticed anything strange about this fort?"

Cerialis considered for a moment, then shook his head. "No, sir. I should imagine it was like any other fort on high ground."

"The hill keeps rising on the other side of the defenses," Vespasian said patiently.

"And so?"

"We will be able to pinpoint their positions with complete accuracy. Does not that suggest anything to you?"

"Not particularly, sir."

"It does to me," Vespasian said quietly. "That, Colonel, is why they made me a general. Those northern walls will get no reinforcements."

There was a long silence, then Cerialis, who could not be serious for long and was entirely incapable of taking offense, said, "With your permission, sir, I think I'd like to stay around for the fight."

Vespasian said curiously, "What makes you so eager to fight my battles, Colonel?"

"Those three pretty little wives," Cerialis said with a grin. "They at least should get reinforcements."

"Well, Centurion, show me around," Vespasian said.

Back at camp, he was inspecting his artillery, rows of ballistae on carts harnessed to mules, standing in neat lines. Vespasian passed quickly along until he came to the machines which interested him. The old artilleryman, his face creased with pleasure at the general's interest, took his cue when Vespasian stopped, and began describing the huge contraptions. "These be onagers, zorr," he said in a broad Campanian accent that warmed the general's heart, "named after the wild ass, because of its kick, they say, also called scorpions because of the upright arm which be like a scorpion's sting, zorr."

He hesitated, wondering if he was boring the general, but Vespasian put his hand on the centurion's shoulder and said simply, "Carry on. I want to learn all about them."

"As you see, zorr, one big cart for each machine and four stout animals to pull it. To deploy for firing would take about two hours—can't fire it from the cart like the ballistae—the recoil be something terrific, zorr. It needs a firm base, four men to erect it and four men to fire it." He indicated the crew standing to attention by the side of the cart.

"At ease, you fellows," Vespasian said briskly, then added, "Isn't it Marcellinus? And, yes—Ostorius—I haven't spoken to you chaps since we were campaigning in Thrace."

The man's amazing, thought Simon. He does not do it through staff work. If he did, I would know. He could only wonder at Vespasian's facility for remembering the names of common soldiers in his regiment. The artillerymen, he noticed, mostly middle-aged, bald and gap-toothed, were knuckling their brows and smiling at Vespasian with love in their eyes, almost like children.

Vespasian turned to Simon. "This seems like a good time for you to learn how the artillery works."

"Yes, sir," Simon said eagerly. "Yes, indeed."

"Carry on, Centurion," said Vespasian.

"Well, there be ten onagers to a legion, zorr," the artilleryman went on. "The old tradition used to be one to the cohort and no one has ever changed it. Now, zorr, as to how it works—the hurling arm be held in a twisted skein of hair and gut." He pointed to what looked for all the world like a gigantic pigtail which ran horizontally along the lower part of the machine and into which the thick wooden arm, bound with iron for strength, was securely fastened. "Now zorr," continued the centurion, "we have two sets of handspikes to tighten one way, another two at the back where the sling be fastened at the end of the arm, to tighten the other. Oh—arr, zorr," he said, shaking his head and rolling his eyes, "there be some mighty strong torsion applied when we have the contraption fully armed. You know the arm'll be bent nearly flat? Needs real stout timbers to hold everything together."

Vespasian thought for a moment. "Give me an idea of range," he said.

"Depends on the size of shot, zorr. They can fire near a hundredweight, but 'twouldn't go very far. Now if you drops to half that, we can send it as much as four hundred and fifty yards. Halve the size again, zorr, and I'll guarantee you seven or eight hundred yards and that's still quite a lump—enough to smash in a wooden hut."

"What about accuracy?" Vespasian demanded.

"No trouble up to five hundred yards, zorr. Drop it on a Jew's nose up to that."

Simon felt his fists balling with resentment. Why will they not accept us Jews? he thought. Why must we always be different? Apart? With difficulty he fought down his fury, realizing that none had even noticed his reaction.

"And the ballistae?" said Vespasian thoughtfully. "What can they do?"

"Bless you, zorr, they fires a nine-inch bolt of solid iron on a heavy twelve-foot javelin that'll go through a line of men like butter at three hundred yards and will penetrate anything less than a stone wall. As it's light we can fire it not only from the cart but can maneuver it much closer to the enemy. There's a quick reload too."

"Very interesting," Vespasian said. "Thank you, Centurion. Very interesting indeed." He turned to the assembled crews. "I'll be needing all you lads can give, shortly."

One of the men raised his helmet and shouted, "Three cheers for the general!"

All the men cheered him to the echo.

"Come on," Vespasian said curtly to Simon, "there are things to do." Simon could always tell when the general was moved, because his voice never failed to thicken when he tried to hide his feelings.

Later that evening, Vespasian held an informal staff conference which went on for some hours. The officers listened attentively while the general outlined his overall strategy, and one by one the commanders of the various arms were given the precise part their men would have to play in the coming engagement.

As time passed and the more serious details were settled, mulled wine was served by the orderlies and drunk in some quantity by the Roman commanders, whose blood was still chilled by a late-summer evening in the English uplands. The conversation became convivial and with barriers of rank temporarily brushed aside, one man after another began to recount anecdotes of humorous mishaps. Cerialis, in particular, had been telling funny stories about senior officers.

Vespasian, tolerant to a degree and caring little about rank, listened easily enough to Cerialis' scandalous tales. But with the burden of command on his shoulders and the knowledge that the patrician Cerialis could break his career with his description of the coming battle, he sat worried and hunched. Feeling that he was not playing his part in the conviviality, he turned to Cerialis, his face racked with terrible strain, and said, "Now tell a funny story about me!"

"I will, General," Cerialis replied, with an absolutely straight face, "when you have finished relieving yourself."

Forcing a smile on his stubborn, homely face, Vespasian went to his quarters, the laughter Cerialis' joke had caused still ringing in his ears.

For days the legion sat in camp, chafing at the inactivity through what appeared to be perfect campaign weather. Vespasian sat, silent and withdrawn, in the praetorium tent, refusing to see anyone. Staff commanders took Simon to one side and asked, "Is he all right? Is he ill? Has the responsibility become too much for him?"

To all of these men, Simon made a single reply. "The general knows what he's doing."

At length, one morning, Vespasian emerged from his quarters, gazed at the sun, sniffed the air, raised his finger to the wind and went into action. Issuing sharp orders, he had the legion paraded, then moved off.

With the weather still fine, the legion, together with its whole cumbersome baggage train of supplies and artillery, moved slowly up the Stour Valley until, three days later, it halted in the cool of the evening.

Under the ramparts of Hod Hill, frowning at them from only a few miles away, Vespasian, instead of allowing his tired men to bivouac, now issued battle orders. With the wind which had providentially risen from the west to hide the sound of their passage, he sent the artillery along the riverbed of the Iwerne, a chuckling little tributary of the Stour which wound almost directly under the eastern battlements of the fort and dried to a mere trickle in the summer. The main body of the legion he sent by way of forced march over easy, undulating ground so that it would be ensconced in thickly wooded country to the north of the fort by morning.

Almost as though Vespasian were able to control the weather at will, dawn broke with a full gale blowing in from the south and heavy rain lashing down from scudding gray storm clouds. Now Vespasian showed his true genius—the transition from inexhaustible patience to quicksilver, flamboyant action, traits rarely found in the same commander.

Hosidius Geta's entire force of auxiliary cavalry, horses plunging and snorting from the sting of the rain on their flanks, suddenly roared up the gentle southern slopes of Hod Hill at a full gallop in a deliberately noisy diversionary attack. At that precise moment, as the whole enemy camp roused at frantic blasts of the *carynx,* a native war trumpet, Vespasian, his face a study in concentration as he stood next to his artillery veterans, held his hand high, then lowered it and yelled the word "Fire!"

Wheeuew-ew-ew went the missiles, tearing into the air one after another with a great creaking and groaning from the timber apparatus; then, carried clearly from the southeastern corner of the camp, came the sound of screams, the rending crunch of timber. The naked eye could now see the round wattle-and-daub structures of the chief's buildings fanning into the air under the onslaught of boulders raining down with shattering effect. The *ballistae,* lighter, less cumbersome, now joined the bombardment—*peeow-ow-ow*—the heavy javelins singing a different humming song as they lanced through the air, completing the terrifying attack on the sleeping chief and his senior commanders.

Chaos reigned in the camp, tribesmen milling around, searching for their weapons, then heading for the sounds of battle at the southern ramparts. Now, the noise of their marching carried away by the gale in their faces, the armored might of the Second Legion emerged from the woods and with shields locked over their heads in the tortoise formation, assaulted the three northern ramparts. For a short while the defenders resisted sharply, their lethal slingstones pinging off the soldiers' armor and sometimes smashing bones. But when they looked for reinforcements, there were none. As Vespasian had correctly foreseen, the main force had been pulled to the more gentle southern slopes to fight off Geta's cavalry, and with the central command paralyzed by the artillery bombardment there was no overall tactical leadership.

The defenders on the northern ramparts broke, threw down their arms and ran. Bursting over the top bank, the legion took the Britons in the rear with overwhelming force and there was not even a fight. The tribesmen surrendered.

Within the space of an hour, Vespasian had conquered one of the strongest natural fortresses in the whole southwest.

* * *

"I wouldn't have believed it," Cerialis said. He added with easy familiarity, "My dead general. Not unless I had seen it with my own eyes." He was about to take his leave with his assembled troop, his great legs sticking out on either side of a small, long-suffering cavalry nag. "Pray allow me to ask you how you knew the weather would change so providentially?"

Vespasian replied, deliberately broadening his barnyard accent, "Oh, we peasants understand these things—a freshening wind from the west plus high cloud usually means rain in this island, with the wind soon veering to the south. I'm a wind man, you see," he added, with his well-known coarseness. "Next to old Claudius, I'm probably the greatest in the Empire."

Cerialis' picked troop of cavalry chortled. Few of them stopped to realize that it was precisely because of Vespasian's contempt for the aristocratic establishment that he had been relegated to using his talents in this frontier zone.

"Tell me, General," Cerialis said, his voice sounding exceptionally genial, "you said 'usually.' Supposing you had been wrong and the weather had stayed fine?"

Vespasian put his finger to his nose as a sign of shrewdness. "I'd have had to think of something else."

"Well, good-bye, General," Cerialis said with great cordiality. "I shall certainly not neglect to tell the Imperial Legate of your proficiency. Incidentally, you have, I hope, no objection to my taking these three prisoners into protective custody?"

Again the cavalry roared its mirth. Cerialis was referring to the native chief's three young wives, none of them over fifteen, who sat demurely, each on a sturdy little pony, behind the colonel's back. Small, with the white, velvety skin of the Welsh mountain folk, they seemed delighted at exchanging their previous master for one so big and obviously virile.

In spite of himself, Vespasian burst out laughing. Cerialis never failed to amuse him. He said, "Colonel, I think you will soon have battles of your own to fight. I wish you good-bye and good luck."

"Until we meet again," Cerialis said. He saluted, then wheeling his horse, galloped off with his men.

"Now," Vespasian said with considerable irony, watching Cerialis' troop disappear into the distance, "that we are no longer in high society, we must turn our attention to Mai-dun, the last and greatest enemy stronghold in this area. It is bigger than this place. It has never been conquered and the steep banks are said to be impregnable."

"You'll need months to reduce such a place, sir," said Simon. "Yet you have only weeks."

"I intend to take it in one day."

"But, sir—such a great fortress—"

"The scouts tell me that they have built huts under their eastern ramparts," Vespasian said. "Because of this, they have probably handed it to me on a plate."

"Sir, I don't understand."

"The wind," Vespasian said craftily, tapping his nose again. "Always watch the wind."

12

Hurrying by forced marches, the Second Augustan reached the River Frome in two days. Faced with the truly mountainous ramparts of Maiden Castle, Vespasian was determined to use the one thing he had in his favor, the element of surprise. The chiefs of the Durotriges would never have expected Hod Hill to fall, let alone in the course of one hour, and Vespasian, intent on unleashing a totally unexpected assault on Maiden Castle, was determined to take the attendant risks.

"Geta," Vespasian asked, "how do your horses react to fire?"

"They have been trained, within reason, to ignore it, my general. After all, it is one of the conditions one encounters in battle, is it not?"

Vespasian nodded. Borrowing a horse, he rode with Geta up to a forward position from which the great defenses of Maiden could be seen outlined against the horizon. "See those huts just outside the ramparts, Geta? If you could burn them—if the wind was right—it would provide a perfect smoke screen."

The cavalry commander stroked his chin. "An idea, sir. And perhaps we could even improve on it. Does not the legion carry a little Greek fire?"

Vespasian looked at him with approval. "Yes—you're right. Brushwood soaked in Greek fire. Because it's wet the smoke will be thick. By Jupiter, yes. That's what we'll do."

"Unfortunately, sir, there's no wind. With the weather prevailing from the west, the wind when you get it will be adverse if you are thinking of assaulting that particular entrance."

Vespasian said thoughtfully, "We are in a series of storms, Geta. Often—not always, mind you, but often—these begin from a southeasterly point before veering and strengthening from the southwest. If we could catch the wind at the right time—" He paused. "Yes. Here's a job for a troop of horsemen, Geta. Swoop in from the southeast at full gallop, fire the huts, deposit the brushwood, ignite it and retire. Can you do it?"

"For you, General, we can do it." He hesitated. "The men think you are a god, sir, able to control the weather as you please. Can you now conjure up a southeasterly breeze before the enemy discovers our presence?"

"I will try."

All through the night, the cavalrymen stood by their horses, sweating from the oats and bran they had been fed to extract the enormous energy needed for a flat-out gallop up the long gradual slope to the eastern entrance.

Vespasian paced outside the praetorium tent, watching the stars run their courses across the crystal-clear night sky, sniffing the air. Now, more than ever, he needed a miracle. By nature, he was not religious, but as in all men, there was an awareness in him of the supernatural—of the possibility, no more, of divine intervention. Striding back into his tent, he lit incense candles and prayed, first to Epona, the goddess of horses, and to the *campestres*, deities who protected cavalrymen, in the hope that Geta's mission would succeed. Then he prayed to Mars, god of war, reserving his best and longest prayer for Jupiter Optimus Maximus. Finally he brought out replicas of his personal household gods and, placing them on a field altar in front of him, held each of them fondly, the way a child does a doll. He had done all he could. Impatiently, he strode into the open.

He put his finger to the air. A feather of wind? Yes. No more. If Maiden Castle was not reduced by sudden, overwhelming assault, it had every chance of beating off the Second Legion until spring came, and by that time it would have been made impregnable by the arrival of reinforcements from the shattered tribes. One defeat would breed another. The whole hill country would take heart and rise again. Far from subduing the area, he might be hard put to survive, might even have to call on Aulus Plautius for help. The end of his career? There was no lack of enemies to cheer the fall of an upstart peasant. The thought made him shudder. Anxiously he began to pace, his homely features racked with strain.

There it was again. A cat's-paw. Fitful. Just a woman's sweet breath of love. It reminded him of his wife, Flavia Domitilla. What a struggle she had to keep up appearances on his wretched pay! Unlike most generals he had no private means, and there was little money put by if he were sacked—disgraced by his rashness. There was no doubt, if he threw the legion at Maiden Castle and failed, that they would call it incompetence. What would become of Titus or little Domitian? His children, he thought bitterly, would be beggars.

He clenched and unclenched his fists, conscious of Simon's anxious eyes upon him. Simon, who was perhaps closer to him than any other person in the world except his wife.

"It will come, sir," Simon said.

"Will it?"

"I have prayed to my own God, sir. It will come."

Vespasian forced himself to look severe. "You, a

109

senior centurion of a Roman legion, praying to a heathen god? I should keep that quiet if I were you."

"For many years I have ignored Him," Simon answered quietly. "All that my father taught me I have forgotten in the service of Rome. Now, for you, for a man I respect above all, I invoke my Jewish God."

Vespasian said nothing. He loved this boy who had twice saved his life. Loved him as his own son. And the boy was paying him the compliment of baring his innermost thoughts.

"Walk with me," he said.

For hours they walked—ten paces forward, turning, ten paces back. There was nothing more to say.

At five in the morning, the wind came. Sudden. Like that. A slap in the face. Then more, much more—a blast roaring up from the south, unstable, then setting in as a good solid blow from the southeast.

Now, with incredible speed, Geta's cavalry galloped out and fired the native huts with brushwood, the legion following along behind, sweating under the weight of their heavy armor as they marched up the long approach slope.

And so it was that, aided by this providential wind which sent such blinding, choking smoke drifting back onto the defenders, Vespasian's soldiers, the flanges of their shields biting together in one instantaneous clash of metal as they formed testudos, assaulted and finally took the great enfilading ramparts of the eastern entrance.

By early afternoon it was all over. When the smoke had finally cleared and Vespasian, standing on the summit, surveyed the carnage, even he was struck dumb by the awful sight.

"Congratulations, sir," said Simon. "You have won a great victory."

"Half the dead are women and children," Vespasian said grimly.

"Did they not bear arms against the legion?"

"Well, you have an argument," said Vespasian. "Still, I am glad it is over and we can go into winter quarters. I'm tired of all this killing." He paused, weighing his words. "One more thing, Centurion. I've been giving some thought to your future."

"Sir?"

"Promising material should not be wasted out here in the backwoods of Britannia. You must stand for political office in Rome. You'll never have a legion, you know, unless you've been through the mill."

"I would not wish to leave you, sir."

"That is loyal of you, Centurion," Vespasian said bitterly, "but with me, you have no future. None at all. I have neither the money nor the influence to win a rich command where a young man might attract attention."

"Nevertheless, I will stay with you, sir. You see, I am banned from Rome. Forced to serve in exile."

"Exile?" Vespasian said. "What is all this about?"

"I cannot—" Simon's eye caught something moving by the flap of the tent and he never got to finish the sentence. He saw only the gaunt, red-eyed face of the Durotriges chief. Wounded in the body, he had been carried by his horse out onto the grass embankments and had rolled down the hill to come to rest near the general's tent. The chief had found a bow and arrow and now stood with bow bent, ready to send the missile straight through Vespasian's heart.

Moving like quicksilver, Simon threw his best knife, at the same time hurling himself in front of the general to protect him from the arrow. His knife took the savage in the shoulder a split second too late, because the arrow was already on its way. It struck Simon with tremendous force high in the chest, hurling him back on top of Vespasian.

By the time a shaken Vespasian had extricated himself and called the guard, Simon was unconscious and bleeding badly.

"Guard—get *capsarii*," Vespasian roared.

At the general's command, medical orderlies rushed into the tent and stanched the flow of blood. Simon's inert body, wrapped in blankets, was put in a cart and rushed down the hill to the field hospital.

In fact, the arrow had penetrated a lung and the only reason that Simon did not die there and then was because of the fortuitous presence on the legion's strength of the famous Greek surgeon Scribonius Largus, who had in turn been at Tiberius' and Claudius' courts and had stayed when the latter returned to Rome, to study battle conditions. Thoroughly cleaning the wound, he cut away little rib sections with a medical saw, then, using special scoops and forceps, extracted the arrow and its broad-barbed head. He then sewed up the wound after packing it with soil that he carried around in a glass vessel, saying to the admiring army doctors gathered around him that "Dirt fights dirt." At Vespasian's express command, he stayed with Simon day and night, fighting any change in his condition with simple botanical remedies and bringing down his violent fevers with a distillation of the leaves of a purple-flowered weed called monkshood.

At length he professed himself satisfied that the patient could travel. Simon was loaded into a covered coach with other wounded and taken to the army base hospital at Colchester.

The hospital itself was remarkably modern, with sixty wards, continuous circular corridors, its own baths, operating rooms and specially insulated walls to allow quiet and prevent extremes of temperature.

Because of skillful treatment Simon did not die either from shock or subsequent infection, and one day in the following April, Vespasian, in the course of a general tour of inspection, was able to visit him briefly.

Simon knew how glad the general was to see him by the way his stubborn, homely face kept breaking into a smile, then freezing again with embarrassment.

After discussing Simon's condition, Vespasian gave some surprising news. "They are relieving me of my command," he said bitterly.

"What?" Simon was astonished. "But you've done so well, sir, and there is much more campaigning before the island can be subdued." He paused. "Besides, the men love you."

"Well, the Emperor doesn't like a commander to get on too well with his legion," Vespasian said jokingly. "There's always cause for rebellion there. Then there's another reason for getting me out of the way. I've been making a nuisance of myself. I put in for you to get the job of senatorial tribune, expecting Aulus Plautius to rubber-stamp it, but there was a long delay, and

112

eventually he came back and said you were too young. Of course, I reminded him there were many promising soldiers who were second-in-command by your age, but he wouldn't change his mind. In the end he got quite annoyed and said the orders came from Claudius himself."

"I told you I was in exile from Rome," Simon said. "Now you can see for yourself the mark of my disfavor. It is because I'm a Jew."

Vespasian wrinkled his brow. "They certainly appear to have it against you people."

"And as a result you have blighted your career by befriending one. What will become of you now, sir?"

"Oh, perhaps I'll pick up a couple of priesthoods," Vespasian said jocularly. "If I'm lucky they might shuffle me off to the governorship of some hot, dusty province where"—he ran his hand wearily across his forehead—"there's not a penny to be made."

There was such an expression of misery on Vespasian's face that Simon had the temerity to say, "Are you short of money, sir? I have a little saved up—I know you have a position to keep—perhaps I could lend—"

"Thank you, my old friend." A look of pure warmth lit Vespasian's face. He laid his hand on Simon's arm. "Not many men would have said that. Yes, a general is expected to keep up a certain standard, and with neither my family nor my wife's family being moneyed"—he gestured—"things do sometimes get difficult. But it is not for you to solve my financial problems. I already have debts enough to you that I must somehow repay."

"I don't understand, sir."

"Have you forgotten that you saved my life no less than three times? I have at least prevailed on Plautius to award a bar to your *corona civica*. That should make you a very important man wherever you go, but it is the army's recognition, not mine."

"Thank you, sir, but I was only doing my job."

"My friend," Vespasian said gently, "there is a tale told about how careful I am accounting for my money. Have you by any chance heard it?"

"No, sir."

"Well, I was feeling a bit horny one day," Vespasian said bluntly, "and I bought the services of this woman. Next day, she presented herself to my secretary for payment. 'But how shall I enter it?' cried my secretary. 'You have always insisted that every payment be shown in the account.' 'Oh, put it in the books as "love for Vespasian,"' I told him." Vespasian laughed heartily at the reminiscence.

"Now this is the point," he went on, becoming serious. "In my books are shown three debts, all of them owing to you, and Vespasian always pays his obligations." Simon could feel the man's fingers bite into his arm. "One day, somehow, I will find a way. Depend on it."

Simon said weakly, "There is no need, sir."

"You are tired," Vespasian said gruffly. "I must leave now." He got up, buckled on his sword. "Get well soon. We will meet again."

In a burst of emotion, the two men spontaneously put their arms around each other's shoulders and embraced. Then Vespasian walked to the door, picked up his waiting staff, shook hands with the *optio valetudinarii* who was in charge of the hospital and left, shoulders square and straight.

Simon knew that he had never loved any man more.

For months, Simon stayed on his back, looking at the whitewashed ceiling of his ward. Eventually, as his wound healed, he was able to convalesce, spending that summer in a chair, brooding about his misfortunes. Despite the almost unique feat of winning two civic crowns, he had, as a Jew, been suspected of disloyalty. He remembered the prejudice, the changed look in people's eyes when they first heard his name. He remembered Habinnas' nasty little rhyme at Eusepio's dinner party, Seneca's slip of the tongue about the Jews being good with money. These thoughts rotted and festered in his mind until the boy's face became lined and bitter.

Invalided out of the army at the end of the summer, he was able, with his discharge grant, to buy a small plot of land—just enough to keep body and soul together and support one slave.

114

The size of his plot did not matter. From being a strong, handsome fellow that women had found irresistible, Simon had changed. Now he walked stoop-shouldered. A grudge-filled recluse.

PART
II

BRITANNIA—WHERE
IT WAS BORN
(43-60 CE)

"Why do you—who have everything—covet our poor tents?"

—Caractacus, conquered
British chief

13

The smartly dressed courier and his escort of five slaves looked with barely concealed contempt at the little knot of people clad in skins and furs—the gaunt man with burning, gray-green eyes, who held his shoulders in a peculiarly hunched way; his servant, with whom he was obviously on familiar terms; and a brown-eyed woman, a slave bought cheaply, he judged by the stigmata, the runaway's mark branded into her forehead.

Wrinkling his nose at the barnyard smell, the courier said with a sneer in his voice, speaking distinctly in case they did not understand Latin, "I seek an old Roman soldier. Do any of you know him? His name is Hastatus Posterior Simon ben Eleazar, late of the Second Augustan."

"I am he." Simon stepped forward.

"Then I have a dispatch for you." He did not lean forward to hand over the roll of papyrus, but made the gaunt farmer reach up to take it from him.

Wheeling his horse, the courier galloped off without a farewell. If there was one thing he could not stand, it was a Roman centurion who went native.

The farmer opened the scroll, quickly scanned its contents, then crunched it under his heel. In an embittered voice, he said, "So he still thinks we're good with money, does he?" Minutes later, the sound of spade on soil could be heard as he resumed work in a corner of the smallholding.

His man, Camerinus, and the brown-eyed woman stood looking at each other. "Can you read?" she asked him.

119

"Yes."

"Then read it."

"I dare not. The master will be annoyed."

"Read." There was such spirit and determination in the woman's voice that Camerinus picked up the scroll and did as she said.

"Seneca Simonio suo salutem," the letter began formally.

Such a wonderful thing has happened that I hasten to tell you the news. Under the patronage of the Emperor's new wife, the lady Agrippina, I am recalled from exile and made personal tutor to the Emperor's adopted son, little Nero, and for my services I am given sole concession to lend monies in Britannia. Things are exactly as I foresaw them, are they not? Enclosed are two authorities, one appointing you agent to distribute these loans throughout all settled parts of Britannia, the other directing the paymaster attached to the Ninth Legion at Camulodunum to advance you, on the personal authority of the Empress, 100,000 sesterces for your immediate needs—Seneca's agent must live and travel in style!

More good news: a large *colonia* is to be formed at Camulodunum. This *colonia* will consist of ex-veterans able to protect the rear of our advancing armies as they extend our frontiers, and whose families, with their strong army tradition, will provide future generations of Roman soldiers. Large areas of land are to be allotted in ratio to years of service or gallantry and you, with your double civic crown, rank for one of the largest grants of all! No less than five hundred acres. I have seen to that.

Write soon. Tell me you accept. *Vale!*

Your old friend,
Lucius Annaeus Seneca.

Camerinus and the woman stood looking at each other. Their master, because of some terrible agony of mind, had just turned down a great opportunity.

The woman said quietly, "Leave him to me." She marched over to where Simon was working, back bent, as he dug away at the wet soil.

"Master," she began, the papyrus in her hand.

"Go away, woman."

She stamped her foot. "I will talk to you!" As the farmer cocked an amazed eye at her, she went on, "Are you a fool or just a coward? Does an arrow wound deprive a Roman centurion of his wits or all his courage?"

"Woman," he roared, "leave me!"

"I will not," she said scornfully. "Only when you are a man again shall I obey you."

"For the last time," the farmer said, setting his teeth, "go away!"

The woman stood her ground. "There is work for you in this country," she said. "With money wisely lent, much could be done."

The farmer turned away from her, wallowing in self-pity. The woman in final desperation suddenly leaned forward and smacked him hard across the face.

Anger finally rose within him. In two bounds he caught her. The woman was no lightweight. Hard, physical work had built muscle on her and good food had filled her out, but rage had made the gaunt veteran strong again and, curiously, the woman made no attempt to struggle.

Dragging her inside the hut, he threw her on the floor. "Slut!" he shouted. "Ever since I bought you off the block, you have treated me with—disrespect. Not only have you denied me your body, but now you nag me until I'm at my wits' end. Perhaps I should chain you to the plow and work you like a beast of burden, the way your last master did."

"Why not?" The woman's voice still rang with defiance. "Be cruel or be kind! At least it will show you have a will of your own—that your mind dwells on something other than yourself!"

A red film came over the farmer's eyes. "You presume too much," he gritted. He picked up a stick from the corner of the hut, ready to beat her, but threw it away in disgust.

"Hear me, master," the woman said. Her tone had

121

changed completely and she now spoke in an odd, choked voice. "It is true you craved my body and I refused you—and yet you did not force me, as was your right. You must be the kindest of masters and all I have shown you in return is ingratitude. Now things will change. There has been a devil gnawing away at your mind for too long and only I know how to chase it away."

"I do not understand."

"We Britons know about demons of the mind," the brown-eyed woman said softly. Reaching up her arms, she held him tenderly to her. "Now let me show you something of my love and then you must go and do Rome's work. You have rotted here too long."

Hours later, they were still lying together by the smoking fire, when the man suddenly got up and dressed. "You are right," he said. His voice rang now with much of its former confidence. "I have been blind. I have been stupid. I'm still young and there's much to live for—so much to do." Then he laughed—a refreshingly unusual sound. "To think that it took an ignorant slave like you to bring me to my senses!"

Simon ben Eleazar had not laughed for almost three years.

14

Simon entered the gates of the turf-ramparted fort and waited patiently for his turn to go before the duty officer, one Marcus Ostorius Scapula.

Scapula, a man of enormous bulk, labored under the eagle eye of his father, Publius Ostorius Scapula, now governor of all Britain. Confined to staff duties, the young Scapula longed for active service and dealt slowly and wearily with his daily clerical chores. Simon's wait was a lengthy one.

Standing in the sun-filled courtyard, Simon idly watched the daily life of the camp: soldiers drilling, recruits training under hard-swearing centurions; then, as the gates of the fort were flung wide open, he looked with suddenly sharpened interest at the procession of prisoners being led inside.

Simon, with a shock, had instantly recognized the two at the head of the miserable, shuffling, chained line of captives. They were old King Antedios' daughter, Victoria, now queen of the Iceni, and her husband, Prasutagus. The queen, exceptionally tall, with long red hair reaching down to her waist, had grown into a formidable figure of a woman. On the other hand, her husband, trotting meekly at her side, still looked ridiculous.

A little girl was chained to the queen's wrist. The child could not be aged more than seven and had hair of a fine tawny color. Her half-formed features already promised an exceptional and fragile beauty and Simon was struck by her loveliness. With her hair neatly braided and still showing the ceaseless grooming it had received in the past from household slaves, the child looked every inch a princess despite her present distressed condition.

Several things now happened very quickly.

"Move," growled a centurion. He began to cuff the child back and forth across the head with senseless brutality, making the princess burst into tears of pain and terror.

"Stop. I will have you punished for that," Simon snapped. He stepped forward into a knot of grinning soldiers. In his rude farmer's skins he looked absurd.

"Out of my way, British pig," the centurion said contemptuously. He strolled up to Simon and aimed a blow at him with his leather gauntlet. Next thing he knew he was flying through the air. He hit the ground some yards away with a great rending crash of his body armor, and lay there stunned.

For one stupefied second, nobody moved, amazed at this Briton's temerity, aware that the man had almost certainly signed his death warrant; then, as one man, the soldiers drew their murderous short swords and rushed for him.

"Stop," Simon ordered. The soldiers, reacting to the tone of command, checked their stride. There was a brief whistling in the air and the leading soldier gazed incredulously at his hobnailed sandal where it had been riveted to the ground by a slim, still quivering, throwing knife. All right. So they had a fight on their hands. The men, all tough, experienced veterans of the Ninth Hispana, quietly spread out, then began to stalk him, closing in from all sides.

Simon retreated to a wall and, knowing that his back was secure at least, crouched there like a hunted animal, prepared to sell his life dearly.

Marcus Ostorius Scapula, disturbed by the jeers of the onlookers, came to his hut door and watched. Meanwhile the fallen centurion, one M. Favonius Facilis by name, a man renowned through the legion for his huge ears, had got to his feet, dusted himself off and, anxious to impress his senior officer, came crouching and weaving into the attack.

"I would come no farther, Centurion," Simon called sharply, "or I will improve your ears for you."

Facilis grinned and hurled himself forward. There was the silver flash of thrown metal, then the sight of red blood welling, as Facilis stopped and felt with disbelief the tattered remains of his ear.

Scapula came forward. Now that decisions were called for, he was a changed man. With his great size he had a formidable presence, so that when he called "That's enough," he was immediately obeyed. Without showing the slightest fear he walked toward Simon. "Right," he said. "Now tell me what's going on."

"Your soldiers were mistreating these people."

"They are rebellious barbarians. They have no rights."

"Do your soldiers, then, torture little children?"

"Explain." Scapula's amiable face hardened.

"Do you consider beating a child correct behavior by an elite legion of the line?"

The soldiers, looking sheepish, began to drift away. Scapula's face hardened still more. "Who are you? You speak Latin too well for a native."

"You would have been told by now, had I not been kept waiting in the courtyard while traders and tinkers were given priority."

Scapula thought carefully for a moment. Despite his poor clothes the man spoke with authority and could demonstrably fight like the devil. Quickly he put a whistle to his lips, and as a platoon of soldiers formed up, he said, "Escort this man to my office—and be careful with him—the dog has been known to bite." Looking at Simon, he extended his arm and said ironically, "After you, sir."

Scapula led Simon straight into the commandant's private office. He said, "Father is away, arranging details of our expedition into Wales, and will not mind my using his room." Looking at Simon's garb of skins and unshaven face, he added bleakly, "Now identify yourself."

Without a word, Simon handed over his discharge certificate. Scapula took the thin, precious sheet of copper on which Simon's military record had been inscribed, his eyebrows moving higher with astonishment as he read, "Vespasian's personal aide—Hastatus Posterior to the Second—civic crown won twice—there can't be many men with a bar to that particular decoration, I fancy. Ah, I see you were invalided out here at Camulodunum." He turned to the captain of the guard. "Get this checked at the record office at once." He glanced again at Simon, noting once more his rude clothes and bewhiskered face. "Not," he added courteously, "that I doubt you, of course."

Simon shrugged. "I was wounded. My brain became fevered. Do you know what I mean when I say that I lost the will to live?"

"Possibly."

"I have now regained my senses. The mission with which I have been entrusted by Lucius Annaeus Seneca is an important one. I would have you read these authorities."

"Very well," Scapula said. His chair groaned with protest as the tribune reached forward for the papers. Interested by the casual way Simon had dropped such an illustrious name, Scapula's face hardened again at what he read. "Yes," he said, "I can arrange an escort for you. I regret it will have to be a token force—the Roman legionary is a precious commodity in Britannia at the moment. I see you are promoted to colonel—we can kit you out for that. Now, perhaps you'd like to have a bath first? Not," he added hastily, "that I would ever make the suggestion except for the fact that we Romans have so much to discuss—old battles, old campaigns. We do tend to make such a social occasion of it, do we not?"

Simon found himself taking to Scapula immensely, and the two men went off together to enjoy the makeshift baths that the army had set up. After going through the usual routine of the tepidarium followed by the caldarium, then enduring the scraping of their bodies with strigils by earnest but clumsy orderlies, Scapula politely excused himself.

When he reported to Scapula's office, Simon looked a completely changed man. Not only was he spruce and smart in his colonel's uniform with his elaborately plumed helmet under his arm, but once again he carried himself erectly, with authority.

Scapula rose and saluted instinctively. Suddenly the two men roared with laughter. "Sit down, my friend," said Scapula. The transition from formal deference to informal condescension came naturally to the son of the governor of Britannia and a member of one of Rome's aristocratic families. The gesture was not lost on Simon, who despite his powerful backing was all too aware that without it, he would be nothing.

"Now then," Scapula said, "what else can I do for you?"

"I will need to see the paymaster."

Scapula tinkled a little bell. When the guard answered, he said, "Ask Colonel Decianus if he would be good enough to spare me a minute."

The two of them waited until Decianus came in. Catus Decianus was small, with the air of pomposity that all little men in official positions seem to find necessary. He had a shifty, dark-jowled face, and Simon disliked him from the moment he saw him.

After the official introductions had been made, Simon said to the paymaster, "Colonel, I shall require one hundred thousand sesterces. Here is an authority for you to pay out the money on behalf of Lucius Annaeus Seneca, signed by the Empress Agrippina."

Decianus read the papyrus carefully. He said in a thin voice, "What do you need the money for?"

"My own personal use."

"Very well." Decianus shrugged, handing back the document. "I'll have it made up. Is that all?"

"You will also be receiving imperial authority to make available to me several million sesterces," Simon said.

"No doubt also for your personal use?" Decianus sneered.

With difficulty Simon restrained himself. He said bleakly, "The money is to be used to stimulate trade and encourage prosperity."

"You mean Seneca's prosperity," the paymaster said with a nasty smile.

Simon's eyes blazed. "Have a care," he said softly. His hand went to the pommel of his sword. "Seneca is a man of the greatest integrity."

"You may have powerful backers," Decianus said, "but I also have influence at Rome. Britannia is too big a country for Seneca to have the whole cake." Turning his back, he marched abruptly from the room.

There was silence for a moment. "Be careful of him," Scapula said. "He's ambitious and has important friends. You know what he's after?"

"No."

"The job of procurator. That would put him in charge of tax collection for the whole province. Britannia would certainly be the loser."

"I will remember."

Scapula saw Simon into the courtyard, where his escort awaited him. Before moving off, there was something else that needed to be done. The Icenian prisoners still stood patiently in their chains, the picture of despair.

"Those," Simon said, flicking a finger at the prisoners. "What will you do with them?"

"The usual." Scapula yawned. "Hang some. Send the rest back to Rome as slaves."

"But what have they done?"

"Caused a rebellion."

"A rebellion? Why should they do that?"

"Father found them with weapons. He thought it

advisable to disarm them. In the end we had to use force."

"On what authority?"

"The *lex julia de vi publica*."

"Exceptions can be made by imperial authority. Did you not know that Claudius concluded a treaty with them? They are allies of Rome."

"Allies?"

Simon said wearily, "You must release them at once."

"I cannot do that without Father's authority."

"Then send an urgent semaphore to Rome. I suggest you treat these people well until a reply is received."

Scapula yawned again. He was hungry. It was time for his meal. With a big man like him, hunger was never far away. He said genially, "Everything shall be as you wish."

Simon walked his horse over to the little princess. Leaning low in his saddle, he took her fragile, pale little hand. "Nobody is going to hit you anymore," he said kindly. "Soon you will be going home with your mother."

"Thank you, sir, thank you very much," the child said shyly in good Latin.

Simon smiled. "Do you like dolls?" he said. "I will come and visit you soon. Shall I be your uncle Simon?"

"Oh, yes, please," the child said eagerly.

Simon turned and looked at the queen, but she showed no sign of gratitude, her aristocratic features remaining stern, full of implacable hostility. "Good-bye, then," he said. Waving his hand first at the child and then at the bulky figure of Scapula, he wheeled his horse and galloped off with his escort.

On his way home, Simon stopped at a small settlement and made a purchase, avoiding any possibility of haggling by dropping a bag of gold at the seller's feet.

When he arrived back at his farm, the brown-eyed woman was tending her cooking pots. As Simon came into the hut, she cowered and tried to push past him.

"What is the matter?" Simon asked, restraining her with his arm.

"Now that they have made you into a great man," she gasped, "what would you want with one like me?"

Simon grinned. "I am the same man I was before. As

for you—I am going to build a big house here and I want you to share it with me."

The woman kissed his hand, looking up at him with worshipful eyes.

"On your feet," said Simon. "There will be no more kneeling in this house. You will be a slave no longer than it takes to sign the official documents."

In a broken voice, the woman said, "I do not deserve this."

Simon smiled at her. "My old commander Vespasian taught me many things," he said, "and the most important of all was that a man must pay his debts. With what I have now brought you, I hope I have settled my obligation."

"What can a woman like me ever need?"

"I have brought you your son."

Unbelievingly she rushed out of the hut, then with tears of joy lifted the boy out of his saddle.

A few days later, after urgent directives had been semaphored through from Rome to Colchester, the Icenians were released and started their long trudge home, the royal family marching at their head.

The little Princess Andrasta took no interest in the journey. Her mind was too full of that man with glittering gray-green eyes, the strange smile and that wonderfully gentle hand. A man who had sprung from nowhere to save her from those terrible soldiers. With a combination of childish logic and royally feminine precocity, she was already certain of one thing. She loved him.

15

Vercingetorix, chieftain of the Dobunni nation that bordered the Bristol Channel, sat warily in his hut, listening to Simon. Although he bore the proud name of a Gallic hero who had fought the Romans with bravery, Vercingetorix was not a warrior by choice. He was a bean pole of a man, with a long face made gloomy by the continual problem of protecting his valuable lead mines. He had made the mistake of sending a contingent to fight the Romans at the Medway and had endured the ordeal of being marched in chains before Claudius, where he had successfully begged for his life.

The chief knew perfectly well why he had been spared: the Romans needed his cooperation. Not only had his tribe worked the mines for centuries, but they had also mastered the technique of producing silver by cupellation from lead. Once the Romans acquired these skills, they would take everything, he was sure of that. Even now he was uncomfortably aware of the extravagant display in which his many silver plates and ornaments gleamed before the curious eye of this Roman envoy.

Playing for time, he said courteously, "How may I help you?"

"It is I who wish to help you," said Simon. "The Emperor has made it clear that he would welcome Roman investment in your economy."

"In what way would you propose to invest?" Vercingetorix asked with gloomy foreboding.

"Your mines could be much enlarged."

"That would cost a great deal of money."

Simon smiled. "I am authorized to offer you a satisfactory loan at reasonable interest."

Vercingetorix sat up. His face, normally so full of anxiety, cracked into a slow smile. If the Romans really planned to confiscate his mine, why would they lend him money to develop it? He said eagerly, dredging up the kind of phrase one would expect of a king, "I accept. You have my assurance that the Dobunni will cooperate with your government in all respects. Together we will build prosperity for our two nations."

A month later, hundreds of miles farther north, Simon sat in audience before Cartimandua, queen of the great tribe of the Brigantes. Cartimandua, in contrast to the queen of the Iceni, was a dainty little woman. The extraordinary power she wielded—her tribe was by far the mightiest in the whole of Britannia—she owed to a single compromise of unusual sophistication. Had the Emperor known how she kept her domain so tranquil, even the worldly Claudius might have been shocked.

As the queen considered Simon's offer of a substantial loan at low interest, Simon glanced at the rows of grinning enemy skulls lining the walls of her great audience chamber. He was enchanted at the contrast between those grim trophies and the queen's consummate grace. She talked with a tinkling little voice, illustrating the points she made with the prettiest of gestures. As her hand traced patterns in the air, he found himself increasingly bemused, almost hypnotized, by the fragile delicacy of those fingers. He only half heard her say that she accepted the loan with great pleasure. Although her features were not beautiful in the accepted sense, such was her aura of sensuality, her overwhelming femininity, that Simon felt himself violently aroused at the thought of those feather-sensitive fingers touching and caressing his skin.

"Now you will please come with me?" she asked. Her voice had taken on a low, throbbing sexuality that reminded Simon of springwater sliding over shining gravel in a mountain stream of high Galilee. With a quick movement of her hand, she unfastened the gold fibula that caught a shawl at her throat and suddenly her bare shoulders glowed white, flawless.

Simon started toward her, then hesitated.

"You are thinking of the consequences?" she asked gently. For a moment Simon wondered where she had learned such perfect Latin. "I assure you there is no need."

"Your Majesty?"

"Only if you refused would it be an insult to my state. How do you think I am able to rule over a collection of robber barons? Either I bed with one or I bed with all. As one of them would rape me, sooner or later, I chose the latter course as the only way to keep my state peaceful. It has now become"—her dainty little mouth began to curl at the edges—"the custom to extend the privilege to important visitors."

Hours later, his lust satisfied with appalling competence by this dainty, blue-eyed little woman, Simon went on his way, his pack animals loaded with skins lined with the warm, fleecy wools of the Pennines—an appreciative good-bye present from Cartimandua, the Brigantian queen, who had taken considerably more from Simon than Seneca's money.

With a shock, Simon realized that she reigned over the great nation of the Brigantes not as a figurehead of purity, but as temple prostitute.

It was one way of governing a country.

Another British queen was not so generously inclined.

For some time now, Victoria, ruler of the Iceni, had been left in peace to govern East Anglia. The queen had not been fooled. She knew the Romans required a tranquil countryside in their rear while they campaigned against the obstinate Welsh. She knew as well that one day they would return and take her kingdom. Her father, Antedios, had warned her against their rapaciousness and she had not forgotten.

She kept hearing tales of her rescuer, the Roman Jew, who traveled the length and breadth of Britannia, offering large loans of Roman money at an attractive rate of interest. Already, many had succumbed to his blandishments—the Brigantes, the Dobunni, the Trinovantes—but she knew better. She had watched and waited for his coming, then as time passed had grown careless. Now, three years almost to the day after the Jew had saved her family from the brutality of the Ninth

132

Legion at Camulodunum, he had chosen the one night when she was away to sweep in with his glittering retinue and arrange a loan of several million sesterces with her husband, Prasutagus.

As she sat on her throne in the large wooden hut that served as audience chamber, she looked a picture of majestic rage. She was furious with herself for not being able to stop the loan, but part of her anger was directed at her husband. She examined the plump little man and clenched her hands at the sight of his amiable, vacillating face. Why, why did it have to be? Why was I saddled with this shiftless drunken oaf? Forced to be both king and queen of my country? She had asked the question of herself many times. The country needed a strong hand, the hand of a son of Antedios. But there had been no son, so Victoria, at her father's command, had stepped into a man's shoes and, by marrying the heir to the throne, had eventually reigned. With the patriarchal Iceni—men who treated their women like beasts of burden—she had faced the problem of her womanhood and triumphed, being stronger than the strong, cleverer than all the nobles around her, and had thus gained their respect. But in its gaining, she had lost her femininity. Now, domineering, stately, excelling in weapons of war, she had all the attributes of a man. For this—for what he had done to her—she hated her husband.

She examined him again, bored, lounging on his throne, waiting for an excuse to leave her presence. "Affairs of state," he called it. She had a better description. Hunting, wenching, drinking. For his latest stupidity, putting the whole kingdom in the gravest danger, she knew she could never forgive him. When she spoke to him, her whole being throbbed with rage.

"You fool," she said in her deep voice. "Do you know what you have done?"

"There's nothing wrong in a loan on the right terms, my dear."

"You stupid man," she raved. "Even if you do not squander it—even if you buy seed and good cattle-breeding stock—the Romans will merely wait until all the money is spent, then call in the loan."

"Then they'll have to wait." Prasutagus shrugged.

133

"Fool," she cursed him again. "The very kingdom is security for the loan and will be forfeit. It is an old ruse. A trick the Romans have used again and again."

"But this fellow Simon ben Eleazar seemed good enough to me—I'm sure he'd never do such a thing."

"I'm sure he'd never do such a thing," the Queen mimicked. "Not only is the man a Roman soldier, he's a Jew. His race are the moneylenders of the East. Even the Romans despise them. Such a man is capable of any treachery."

"Oh, come off it, you're making a mistake." Prasutagus rolled his fat bottom off his throne and stood up, stretching his legs. "Now if that's all you want me for—"

"You will stay," the queen said in an ice-cold voice. "There is the matter of our daughter, the Princess Andrasta."

Prasutagus rolled his eyes in resignation and sat heavily down. "Andrasta? What is the problem?"

"She is in love."

"What?" The little king looked astonished. "But she's only ten years old!"

"And almost a woman," the queen said. "Icenian girls mature quickly. She thinks of nobody but him. Every year he has sent her a present on her birthday—some doll or toy—but this year he brought jewelry."

"But, my dear, is that not the custom for royal princesses? Look at that beautiful golden torque around your neck. Is it not the very badge of royal rank?"

"His present was exceptional. That of a suitor courting a wife. She was bad enough before, dreaming of the hero who rescued her from the Romans. Now, I fear, the dreams will be of a different character."

"My dear," Prasutagus said, "your imagination is becoming overwrought. Andrasta is still a child. Besides, this Roman is not only married, but old enough to be her father."

The queen laughed sourly. "He lives with a native woman. Since when have the Romans not discarded them at will? And when has age stopped a man chasing a young girl?"

"Very well, dear." Prasutagus put a hand over his mouth to hide his boredom. "As always, things are in your capable hands. Now I must leave you—affairs of state, you know." Again, he half rose.

"Sit down," the Queen snapped. "I have called the girl in. You will stay and behave as a father should. Your drunken friends can wait."

"Very well, my dear," said Prasutagus.

Princess Andrasta remembered to curtsy as she entered the royal audience chamber. The queen always demanded respect appropriate to her rank, even from her own children.

The girl never failed to be impressed by the regal stateliness of her mother—her exceptional height, her great muscled body clad in glorious tartans, the priceless golden torque she wore around her neck on state occasions. Gazing up at Victoria's strong features, flashing eyes, the wild red hair that tumbled almost to her hips, Andrasta felt proud to be her daughter. She was comforted to see that her father was there. There was nothing she could not get out of him with a soft kiss on the cheek.

Andrasta rose gracefully from her curtsy. She was tall for her age. Her features had achieved that impossibly subtle blend of fragility and elegance and her pale skin was flawless. Two long pigtails of tawny hair, perfect in the smoothness of their texture, bathed her face in reflected gold. She said quietly, "You wanted me, Mother?"

"Yes. I hear you have received jewelry from the Roman. It must be given back."

The girl burst out wildly, "I love him."

"Love?" The queen's eyes flashed. "What does a girl your age know of love?"

"He saved me from those terrible soldiers. He is kind and good and I love him."

"You will see him no more. From now on, you must play with children your own age."

Andrasta stamped her foot. "I am not a child. I am a royal princess."

The queen could not help but feel fire in the girl's veins, and when she spoke again her voice was softer. "Very well. If you wish, I shall talk to you like a grown-up. This man is dangerous. Treacherous like all Romans, worse because he is a Jew—the most devious of all people, so I am told. He plans to take my kingdom, make slaves of us all."

"Mother, what does 'treacherous' mean?"

"Not to be trusted."

"Well, I trust him." She turned desperately to Prasutagus, remembering the appealing look she used to get her way. "Daddy, Daddy, surely you will not stop me from seeing Uncle Simon?"

"As you know, *I* have always given the orders in this country," the queen said in a deep, quivering voice, "and you will do as I say."

"Yes, dear, you must do as your mother says," Prasutagus echoed weakly. He rose and walked from the audience chamber, hand in hand with Andrasta. He had served his purpose and the queen would not try to stop him. Watching his ambling progress, a man not much taller than his lithe, swift-growing daughter, the queen felt only contempt. Within minutes, she knew, he would be quaffing a horn of mead, joking with his cronies. She made no attempt to call him back.

There were more important things to be done.

Summoned from his warrior training, Hengist stood indolently before the queen. He knew her to be a great ruler, much feared by many tribes, but an Icenian noble did not submit easily to a woman—a mere chattel to be used and ordered to his ways. Although not much more than a boy, he could not bring himself to bow and, instead, looked her straight in the eye with grudging respect.

For a moment the queen's iron features relaxed, the woman in her stimulated by his maleness. Blond, like most of his tribe, he was already exceptionally built, with the biceps of his upper arms showing through his skins. In a few years' time he would fill out into a magnificent animal. If only I had not been born to rule a great nation, she thought. How would it have been to be used, commanded, cuffed, ground into the earth by the lusts of such a man as this will soon be? Often she had fantasies like this, erotic, impossible to satisfy. The queen watched the boy shift his feet, grin faintly at her, as he waited for her to speak. She had an uncomfortable feeling that he could read her thoughts.

"Now then," she said, forcing herself to speak crisply, "you are fond of my daughter, the Princess Andrasta, are you not?"

"I of her, yes. But she does not notice me."

"She will learn. I have a mind to betroth you."

"It is a great honor." The boy spoke dreamily. "I will treat her well. Beat her only when she is disobedient."

"The matter is not yet settled," the queen said sternly. "There are—conditions."

"Yes, your Majesty?"

"There is a certain Roman—a man old enough to be her father. She is in love with him. First, she must be cured of this infatuation."

The boy, loose-limbed, athletic, smiled. He flexed his legs, tightened his corded biceps proudly, knowing the queen's eyes were upon him. "I am big," he said. "I will grow even bigger. Already I am the best in my class in weaponry. Soon, no man would dare take her from me."

"The Roman is a professional killer—a former gladiator. He should not be treated lightly."

"Give me six, seven years," the boy said, "and he will be an old man. I shall be twenty-two. Quick as light. Stronger than a stallion. You think he could stand against me?"

"It pleases you to boast," the queen said. "What is your weapon?"

"The two-handed battle-ax."

"Go and fetch it."

Surprised, the boy did as he was told. When he came back, the queen was waiting for him outside the hut. "Strike that tree stump," she ordered.

Hengist braced himself, balanced compactly on muscled legs, then lifted the battle-ax, designed for a fully grown man, slowly over his head. He brought it down with tremendous force. The iron blade bit inch-deep into polished, rock-hard wood.

The Queen took the ax from him. "Now watch," she said. With an incredible combination of agility and strength, she raised the ax high in the air and then, by pouring in the power of her wrists at the very last moment, slammed the ax into the wood, the blade biting twice as deep as it had with the boy.

"But that is incredible," Hengist said in awe.

"Come back," the queen said coldly, "when you can strike harder than a woman. Then, you will be betrothed to my daughter."

"I will train to be a great warrior, your Majesty."

137

"It is just as well, for there will be one more condition."

"Yes, your Majesty?"

"First, you must kill the Roman."

Two days later, the queen went into the great forest that lay to the south. The horse of one of the accompanying priests pulled a wicker hurdle on which a terrified slave had been tightly strapped.

For several hours they journeyed deep into leafy glades of elm and aspen, larch and birch, under stately oak trees where the wild stag rutted, wolves bayed to the moon, and boar, rooting for acorns, lifted suspicious red eyes at the strange procession that disturbed their feeding.

An omen of extraordinary rarity had been observed: a certain oak tree deep in a sacred grove had been seen covered with mistletoe. Now, on the sixth day of the moon, an appropriate rite would be solemnized to divine its meaning. The omen was considered to be of such significance that the high priest himself, a figure to inspire terror in the stoutest heart, had traveled all the way from the sacred island of Mona to officiate.

Noting that the queen and her retinue had arrived, he kept them waiting in silence until the sun had sunk low in the sky. "Now is the moment of prayer," he intoned, "where different worlds meet. The dawn, the twilight, the mist between sea and air, the dusk—when there is still light but no sun." He raised his hand sharply and, as if by magic, the birdsong suddenly stilled with the rushing onset of darkness.

Quickly the high priest cut the mistletoe branch off the tree with a golden sickle, allowing it to fall on a sacred white cloak that had been spread on the ground. He made a signal and the slave was lifted from the hurdle and the gag stripped from his mouth so that his spirit might more easily leave his body. The slave screamed in terror and braced himself for the agony of the knife. In one stroke the high priest drove the sacrificial blade deep into him and gave a short, expert twist that ripped the slave's stomach apart so that his guts burst forth, descending, hanging full of fluid, then trailing lower and lower before finally exploding filth and stink across his right leg. The high priest walked around the dying man, nodding to himself. The right side was the side of strength; the leg, the sign of action. Never had he seen omens that were more auspicious.

The priest moved quickly to the traveling cart on which the prayer totem lay hidden under a cloth. Normally his flock would worship a large stone phallus, swollen, bursting with power and fertility, but the priest was a man of sophistication and knew that it would be inappropriate with such a great matriarch as this. Instead, he unveiled the awful image of Sheela-na-gig, the devouring mother, the goddess of the huge genitalia, held apart by her hands to show a dark, cavernous interior ready to conquer and emasculate the strongest of warriors. The queen breathed a slow sigh when she saw it; this priest knew and understood her problem. Henceforth her loyalty to this man would be fanatical.

"My child," the high priest said somberly, "I have journeyed far to see these omens for myself."

"Yes, your Grace."

"The Romans—did they give your nation money?"

"Yes. By a trick. Now they will bend us to their customs."

"You are right, my child. With new ways come new religions and new gods. Your people will be corrupted. They will lose their ancient Celtic heritage."

"Then what am I to do?"

"Follow your father's advice."

He is all-knowing, this priest, thought the queen. She remembered old King Antedios' dying words. "Be as cunning as a fox. Assemble your numbers in secret, then one dark night when they are unready for battle, fall on them and kill them all."

"Yes," she said, "I remember."

"That time is not yet."

"When will that time be?"

"When the Roman desolates all Britannia with his greed. When the great queen of the Iceni is tortured for her treasure. When her land is ground under the invader's heel."

"Who will lead us?"

"You will be told."

"Tell me now. I do not serve under any prince."

139

The high priest stroked his chin. This queen was as brave and strong as they had said. People did not cross words with him lightly. "Very well," he said. "The omens are such that there can be no dispute. You are the one to lead the British nation and throw the Romans into the sea."

The queen's face flushed. At last she was being rewarded for her sacrifices, for her great leadership of her people. Now all her wishes were coming ture. Not only had she arranged the death of Simon ben Eleazar, the renegade Jew, but she would soon lead a great host into battle against the Romans in compliance with her vows to her father.

"You must change your name," the priest said sternly. "No more Roman corruptions can be allowed. I will give you another."

"As you wish, your Grace."

"You are called Victoria, are you not?" He thought carefully for a second. "In our Celtic tongues the word for victory varies—*bouda, boudig, buddug*. An ugly but powerful sound, and we shall retain it. Now kneel, Queen of the Iceni, and learn your new name."

The queen knelt, her great muscular, tartan-covered shoulders bending in submission before the high priest.

"You shall henceforth be called Boudicca."

Boudicca. The queen sounded the word on her tongue and found it good.

16

Britannia grew more prosperous with each year that passed, as Seneca's loans worked their way through tribal economies, stimulating trade and aiding agriculture. But the rosy light of peace and prosperity would prove to be a false dawn. There were men who envied the Jew's rise to prominence, the riches acquired as Seneca's agent, his fine villa with its private baths and hypocaust heating, all the trappings of great wealth. These men plotted his downfall, each for a different reason, bearing a different grudge.

Such men were M. Favonius Facilis and Catus Decianus.

M. Favonius Facilis, ex-centurion of the Ninth Hispana, had not gone to the *medicus* after that fight on the legion's parade ground when Simon's throwing knife had sliced one of his prominent ears. As a result, the wound became septic, poisoning his whole body. Invalided out of the Ninth, he had been awarded a smallholding by the *colonia* which had proved marshy, unproductive.

Now, almost nine years later, he blamed his misfortunes on the Jew with homicidal intensity.

This particular morning, he had discovered that half his cabbages had gone rotten in a boggy field and was about to vent his feelings by punishing one of the slaves who had planted them. Despite his rage, he had been careful to pick a man who was of no great value. The slave, tightly bound to the whipping post, shivered in the cold air of the spring morning.

Facilis hefted the belt in his hand, gave the slave fifteen good strokes, then, wiping sweat from his eyes, stood back. "Please, master," the man whined, "no more, master, please. I promise to work harder." Facilis gave the slave another half-dozen for good measure, then threw the belt to the ground and strode away toward the public baths that lay down the road on the outskirts of Camulodunum.

Facilis was pleased with his morning's workout; the slave's welted back would soon heal, but the others would remember the punishment and work better for it. Bathed, the sweat cleaned off him with strigils, his powerful body responding to skillful massage, Facilis looked forward to the appointment with Catus Decianus that afternoon. Decianus was not only a retired colonel, but highly educated, and Facilis was flattered. Decianus was an influential member of the town *ordo*. Facilis was well aware that such a man might see he was granted a better farm by the *colonia*.

The two of them had, he knew, one thing in common. A hatred of the Jew, Simon ben Eleazar.

Never very bright at the best of times, Facilis tried to clear his mind for the meeting to come. Whatever it was that Decianus wanted of him, he would lean over backward to oblige him.

Colonel Catus Decianus, former paymaster of the Roman legions in Britannia, did not believe in the necessity of frequent beatings to keep his household in order. He had a much better method. A tidy solution for a neat man. Once a year he simply crucified a slave. He liked to pick one of the older, scrawnier ones—but it was amazing how long they lasted. The endurance of the aged was twice that of the young, who could not bear the agony of the iron nails hammered into their hands and feet and died quickly. An ancient, thin one, though, would hang there for days like some yellowing strip of smoked fish and fade away so quietly that it would often be difficult to tell if he were alive or dead. During such a crucifixion the slaves would pad quietly around the house with looks of dread, and when it was all over the men would work much harder for many months and the women would submit to some of his more interesting appetites with especially meek obedience.

The former paymaster was in comfortable circumstances, but still watched with bitter fury the meteoric progress of the Jew, Simon ben Eleazar. That upstart was not only the respected leader of their local senate, but had amassed enormous wealth as a result of Seneca's patronage.

Now Decianus sought to match him with a financial coup of such proportions that even he was frightened by what he was going to do. For the operation to succeed he needed two things: the job of procurator and a strong right arm in the form of some brutal ex-veteran who had no fear of consequences. He already had the second factor in Facilis. The first requirement was the difficult one. To achieve it he would need all his brillance, all his devious subtlety.

Decianus was confident he could manage it. With the death of Claudius in AD 54 nothing had seemed to change in Rome. Young Nero was entirely under the thumb of Seneca and it was Seneca's men who still ruled the Empire and controlled its finances. However, under the surface, things were very different. Decianus' influential friends had faithfully relayed to him the latest news from court—Agrippina, mother of the Emperor, was losing her influence over her son. It was said that the wily Seneca, having climbed to power with her help, now planned to jettison her. Agrippina was no fool. If the right chance came, she would strike back and strike hard.

Now, with the aim of supplying the kind of ammunition that she needed, Decianus bent his head over the letter he was writing to her.

> ...What is the result, Imperial Majesty, of these huge sums owed to Seneca by the Britannic tribes? It is this. No revenue at all comes back to the Emperor from this flourishing economy. No taxes are paid to Rome. All surplus goes to pay interest on the philosopher's loans. The country continues to be a financial millstone around Rome's neck. Even the very temple dedicated to your revered late husband, the God Claudius, lies unfinished at Camulodunum for lack of funds. As a loyal Roman, may I offer my services to the Emperor? I have been paymaster to the legions for many years past and my skill and integrity have never been called into doubt. Your Majesty—if your son, the Emperor, will appoint me procurator, I will see that monies flow bountifully into imperial coffers and that the province is not sucked dry in payment of interest on private loans.

Decianus signed the letter with a flourish. Bearing his old army seal and with the Empire's enormously efficient courier system at his disposal, the message, he was confident, would reach Agrippina unseen by Seneca's informers.

Superbly briefed on the latest court intrigues, Decianus was backing an inspired hunch that Agrippina

143

would use the letter against Seneca, and that the Emperor Nero himself would seize this heaven-sent chance of ridding himself of his chief minister. With Seneca would go Simon ben Eleazar, his agent. Who would then be left in Britannia to fill the vacuum? The man who promised to collect the Emperor's taxes: Catus Decianus. When that happened, the first part of his plan would fall into place.

Satisfied with his work so far, Decianus rose from his desk to keep his appointment with the man necessary for the second part—Facilis.

They met in the Basilica. Only one of the many fabulous buildings that had lately risen in elegant Roman Camulodunum, the Basilica was a huge covered building with a roof seventy feet high, dominating the surrounding countryside. With its twenty stone columns and windows of greenish glass through which daylight filtered dimly, people talked softly in case the least sound penetrate the courts of justice at both ends of the hall. With the council chambers nearby, it was in all respects a perfect place for two respected members of the town *ordo* to discuss their business in whispers.

They shook hands and began strolling up and down the long hall. Decianus listened sympathetically to the ex-centurion's troubles, while Facilis, brutishly servile to a man of superior rank and breeding, waited to see what crumbs might fall his way. He did not have to wait long.

"And so, my dear Facilis"—Decianus smiled with condescension—"I have reason to believe that the province of Britannia will soon be directly taxed by the Emperor."

"Is that so, sir?" The centurion looked at him, trying to understand.

"Should that happen," Decianus went on, "there is every prospect of my being appointed procurator."

Now Facilis understood. Everyone knew that a procurator was almost as important a man as the governor, and independent of him too! Fawning like a lackey, he used his powerful body to clear a path for the colonel as they paced up and down the crowded hall.

"I need a strong right arm, Facilis," Decianus went

on. "A man who knows how to sniff out gold and silver, round up herds of cattle, take over the estates of defaulting chieftains. Think you can do the job?"

"Don't you worry," Facilis said grimly. Such an assignment would be more sport than work.

"Of course," Decianus continued blandly, "you will get a large estate from the *colonia* in recognition." He paused, relishing Facilis' look of greed. "And you will be in charge," he went on, "of confiscating all the valuables of the natives in payment of taxes, not to speak of seizing their livestock. Such things are, by their very nature, perishable and difficult to account for to the Emperor, I shouldn't wonder"—he allowed a note of studied carelessness in his voice—"if quite a lot of it didn't get lost. You know what I'm saying, of course?"

Facilis understood perfectly. His seamed face glowed at the prospect. Murder, rape, pillage, broad acres of land, countless slaves—all this would be his. "And the Jew, sir?" he asked gruffly. "What of him?"

"He will be superseded. I am dealing with it personally."

"Very good, sir."

"We will be in touch, Facilis. May I take it that I can depend on you?"

"Absolutely, sir. I only await your orders."

"Good." The two men shook hands and went their separate ways.

Decianus was glad the centurion had not seen the wolfish satisfaction on his dark, sweaty face. His plans were now set. The mules that stood ready to transport a vast treasure of British silver and gold to Rome would never get there. Instead, they would be diverted to an estate deep in southern Gaul, on which Decianus had taken an option under an assumed name. By the time the Emperor found out, it would be too late. Decianus would have disappeared into thin air. The Emperor, well known to give short shrift to rascally tax collectors, would vent his spite on one man—M. Favonius Facilis, sitting openly on his stolen estates. Facilis would be executed while Decianus lived out his life in opulent comfort. Decianus could not help smiling.

The fact that his plan could bring bloody revolution and cause the deaths of hundreds of thousands did not bother him in the least. Like all thieves, he was concerned with only one thing. Getting away with it.

Agrippina lay in bed naked, except for the beautiful copper-blond hair cascading around her, and cuddled her son. It had been her custom every morning as long as she could remember. When the boy had reached puberty she had seen no reason to change her habits. From whom better to learn the game of love than his own mother, who adored him to such distraction and schemed so ambitiously for his future?

Now it was over. She knew it. Although the boy still came to bed with her, he kissed her only perfunctorily and, with increasing impatience, barely submitted to her cuddling. Why do I love him so? she asked herself. She looked at him lying there beside her, weak-eyed, thick-necked, potbellied. I know the answer very well. He is all I have. I have made him what he is. He is part of me.

"You have a lover." The accusation burst from her. "You do not care for me anymore."

"That is not true," replied Nero. The boy had an unexpectedly deep, bass voice.

"And I know who it is." Agrippina pouted. "That slut Acte. You spend all your time with her."

"Mother," Nero chided her wearily. "Listen to me. I'm eighteen years old. You can't expect to keep me as your child forever."

"You're an ungrateful boy," nagged Agrippina. "All I ask is some consideration. Look at what I have done for you!" Nero, who remembered her so grave and stately, every inch a queen, wondered idly how she could have deteriorated like this—Seneca said that it sometimes happened when women reached a certain age. He listened reluctantly to her hectoring as she scolded on and on, rolled his eyes to the heavens and prayed that it would stop. "And what's more," she added shrewdly, "the great Seneca, who you think so much of, is getting far too powerful. It is you who are the Emperor, not he."

"Yes, Mother. But you brought him to Rome as my tutor, remember."

"I did not expect him to line his own pockets. Farm the Empire as his personal estate."

"What do you mean?"

"Do you know that the whole province of Britannia

pays no taxes except for small amounts collected locally for garrison upkeep? That there is no revenue coming to Rome? Nothing. Just a drain on the imperial treasury to build such things as monuments to my idiot husband Claudius. Shall I tell you why?"

Nero was becoming interested in spite of himself.

"Seneca has millions out on loan," Agrippina sulked. "While the native chieftains pay him interest they cannot pay Rome taxes. Meanwhile the campaigns languish in the west for lack of soldiers, lack of funds."

"What do you suggest?"

Nero lay back and listened carefully. An efficient procurator to be appointed to collect taxes to finance a final campaign of subjugation. A good general to be sent out to mop up the obstinate Welsh. After that: firm, strong rule. There was no reason why that province alone should be exempt from taxes just for Seneca's personal benefit. The old nag is really talking sense, Nero thought. He remembered with glee how he and Seneca had worked in the past year to deprive his mother of all power and prestige—even to issuing new coinage throughout the Empire showing her face eclipsed by his. Now she was fighting back with all her strength, and as she talked away Nero began to learn some simple truths about Seneca. All his youthful illusions were being shattered. Seneca was no longer the wise, austere tutor on whose advice he had always acted. Agrippina, warming to her task, was now exposing him as a ruthless financier using his position to amass riches.

Nero listened quietly. Let them fight each other, he said to himself. Bring each other down. They have controlled me for their own purposes far too long. Soon I will have absolute power.

"But my dear mother," he purred, "why have I been such a fool for so long and not listened to you before? Of course you are right in all you say and I shall take your advice."

He let his hands glide smoothly over her body, fondle her amber hair. Why is it that all my lovers must now have amber hair? he asked himself. Why do I let this damned whore of a mother possess and emasculate me? Shall I never be free of her until she is dead?

What an excellent thought! It came to him with

sudden, enormous impact. Hands already tainted with the murder of his stepbrother Britannicus could easily accomplish more ambitious undertakings.

She could die. Even Seneca could die.

Gravely he turned and kissed her. "Now, Mother," he said, "who do you suggest as procurator for Britannia?" His face was a picture of the blandest innocence.

Not all that far away, at Cosa, Vespasian, Simon's old commander, stood on the porch, watching the sunset.

When his grandmother had died, Vespasian had moved to the estate to look after his mother. The house was airy, comfortable, not too damp in the winter rains, and Vespasian, always a son of the soil, was glad to farm the land while he waited for his next assignment after his recall from Britannia.

The appointment had never come. Not only was Claudius jealous of his popularity with his troops, but Vespasian's original patron, the influential minister Narcissus, was the sworn enemy of Agrippina. While she had imperial power, Vespasian's career seemed permanently blighted.

It had been a hot day after recent spring rains and the rich earth was releasing a smell which Vespasian sniffed appreciatively. He looked at his mother. She was a small, gray-haired old woman with an alert mind. As she rocked in her chair, Vespasian knew she was thinking hard, although her little black buttons of eyes were tightly closed. She had been ambitious for her sons, prodding, then pushing, first his brother, then him, into public careers. Now, after Vespasian had languished on the farm for years after such a splendid campaign in Britannia, she said little, but he knew her to be disappointed. Flavian mothers were proud of their sons and did not like to see them passed over. Vespasian wished he could say something when she went quiet and thoughtful like this.

He had just come back from the village with provisions. He said gently, "I have wine. It is the anniversary of Grandmother's death. Shall we now drink to her memory?" The two of them drained the little silver cups.

"What has been happening in Rome?" she asked.

"Little of consequence. There is talk of another campaign in Britannia."

"They will choose you?"

"I doubt it."

"Why not? You were their best general last time."

"There are younger men as good as—better than I."

"Who? Name one."

"There is Corbulo. He has done great things in Armenia and Parthia—a fine leader."

"They will not spare him. They will use a man who knows Britannia."

"Very well. Perhaps Petilius Cerialis. Did you know they've given him the Ninth at Lincoln?"

"Bah!" The old woman opened her eyes and shot him a scornful look. "A playboy."

"There are so many others. Quintus Veranius. Suetonius Paulinus—all are able commanders and specialists in mountain warfare too. The mountains are where they'll be going."

"And for you? What is there for you?"

"The farm always needs attention."

She closed her eyes and rocked back in her chair.

Vespasian helped himself to another cup of wine. His old grannie, he knew, would not mind his draining a few more cups in her memory. He looked out at the fields. The spring rains had come just at the right time. This year, perhaps, there might be a small surplus which could be converted into cash and used to pay Titus' tutor at court. The tutor had been very good, but—as he had said—one has to live. The boy needed clothes too. It was madness, scrimping and saving to send his son to fashionable Rome, then not allowing him enough money to clothe and feed himself.

Something was moving out there. A horseman. No. A small band of cavalry. Vespasian watched with a certain morbid curiosity. With politicans and generals, the way to death was often like this. A long period of estrangement, then a curt invitation from the Emperor to fall on one's sword.

He made no attempt to rise as the courier dismounted and walked up the porch steps with a jangle of spurs. The courier saluted and handed over a letter. Vespasian noted with heavy foreboding the imperial seal. He read it, then a slow smile spread over his tough, battered face.

"What is it?" his mother demanded.

"I am made proconsul."

"What province?"

"Africa."

His mother sighed and he could not tell whether she was happy or not.

"It is a good appointment, Mother," he said. "It shows they have not forgotten me."

The old lady sniggered. "It shows something else," she said. "Agrippina reigns no longer. The Emperor must be making his own decisions at last."

"You think so?" Vespasian spoke the words automatically. His appointment raised a host of new worries. A governor was expected to kit himself out, to pay the expenses of a retinue, but Vespasian had not a penny. How could he ever handle this situation without being held up to ridicule? And money had to be found for Titus. His obstinate face knitted with thought in that look of pained concentration for which he was well-known.

"There is another letter for you, sir," the courier said.

The seal was even heavier and more ornate than the last. It could only be Seneca's.

Vespasian read: "Old friend, while I have been luckier than I ever deserved, I hear things go badly for you. Please use the enclosed draft in any way you want and make a former comrade happy. I know you will repay me in your own way in good time. *Vale*, Simon ben Eleazar."

Vespasian dismissed the courier in a gruff voice. He was ashamed that his eyes were welling with emotion. He, an old soldier, crying! It was disgraceful. Yet here he was, approaching fifty, entering the mainstream of Roman politics again at a time when other men might be thinking of retirement. And that loan had come at the right time. It was fate. Vespasian did not sneer at fate. There were other things also—astrologers had predicted when he was only a boy that he was marked for great things. Had not a stray dog picked up a human hand at the crossroads and brought it into Vespasian's room where he was breakfasting and dropped it at his feet? A hand was the emblem of power. He did not think much of omens and auguries—and yet—and yet—

Yes, he would take Simon's loan because he knew that one day he would be able to return it in full and with interest, and Vespasian, above all, paid his debts.

Although still distant, for Vespasian an illustrious future beckoned.

17

For Seneca, stark ruin beckoned. His whole world of influence and riches had crumbled around his ears. Nero, with strange impulsiveness, had appointed a procurator in Britannia who was bleeding the tribes so dry with his taxation that the Jew had warned him that he could no longer collect interest on his loans. It seemed that if the situation continued, even his very capital might be at risk as well.

If that were not enough, Nero no longer consulted him on matters of state. He had been superseded by a set of loose-living cronies drawn from worlds in which the young Emperor was more interested—horse dealers, charioteers, lyre players and ballet dancers.

He had not been summoned to the palace for some time and, treading the long corridor that linked the Imperial Gardens of Mycaenas to Nero's elegant residence on the Palatine, Seneca felt a distinct foreboding. As his footsteps echoed along the passage, the German Guard, resplendent in their parade helmets with purple plumes and golden cuirasses, snapped their javelins to attention. Seneca only half saw the beautifully dressed guardsmen, had only vague eyes for the superb, pastel-colored murals showing scenes from the Trojan wars, the painted panels of fragile, filigreed trellises that lined the walls. His mind was occupied with one consuming worry. What did the Emperor want with his erstwhile tutor and mentor?

Seneca approached Nero's private suite, walking with an air of confidence which he did not feel. He had heard that Nero had recently taken to staging displays of sexual perversion with a view to shocking his visitors, who would then be punished for showing the slightest revulsion. He allowed himself to be ushered into the Emperor's presence, bracing himself for what he might find.

He was not disappointed: jaded old voyeur that he was, he still could not quite believe his eyes. Nero had gone to a great deal of trouble to outrage his old teacher. Tied to poles, facing each other from both sides of the audience chamber, were several absolutely naked men and women, all with a high sheen of perspiration on their skins, and with wild, bloodshot, staring eyes. Standing in between the two lines of sweating, panting captives were a pair of delicately built, lithe young men, highly rouged and mascaraed, dressed in filmy tunics, who were obviously responsible for the desperately distressed condition of the naked men and women.

Suddenly, there was an extraordinary growling sound as Nero, stark naked except for a mangy lion skin, came galloping in, ferocious animal noises issuing from his throat, his flat feet making a thunderous noise as he tore around the room. Seneca, fighting the need to roar with laughter, managed a grave, statesmanlike expression which, in the circumstances, was distinctly absurd. With disbelief, he watched the Emperor prance up to the captives, subjecting them one by one, regardless of sex and in between suitably realistic growls, to what has been quaintly described as "oral outrage." Only when a victim started to scream openly did Nero then transfer his attentions to the next one.

For what must have been almost an hour, Seneca stood rooted to the spot, observing the revolting progression of this bizarre perversion, until Nero, finally bored with the thing, clambered to his feet. "Hello, Seneca," he said genially, pretending to notice the old philosopher for the first time. "Pretty clever, eh— imitating the wild beasts in the arena? Better than you ever got up to, I'm sure." He turned, indicating the two painted men standing nearby in the carefully posed relaxation of professional dancers. "Have you met Mysticus by any chance? He has an unusual distinction, that one. At least two men have died in the act of making love to him. Do you think he has a hidden set of teeth?" Nero giggled inanely and Seneca allowed an expression of amusement to play briefly across his gaunt, ascetic face. "Now Paris here," Nero went on, indicating the other, "has a different claim to fame. He once performed in a play where Mars made love to Venus, taking both parts in succession with extreme—" Nero accented the word, "realism."

Seneca inclined his head in grave acknowledgment, a gesture which made Nero roar with laughter. He is paying me off, Seneca thought. For all those years of purity and chastity, for teaching him a set of values in which I never believed, for training him so hypocritically in the Stoic ways while indulging my own private appetites. Now he intends to ruin me. I have dug my own grave.

"Seneca," Nero said, "let's leave the victims to Mysticus and Paris. Come with me." Nero picked up the black tip of the mangy lion's tail in one hand and led the way into his private chamber, his flabby white hips and protuberant stomach rolling and heaving under the lion skin. Again Seneca felt trapped between the slippery tightrope he was walking to save his life and the need to explode with laughter.

Nero slumped into a chair, breathing hard. Seneca became aware of a strong body odor the Emperor seemed to have developed lately. Nero's looks had certainly not improved, with his spots, his thick neck, his strange, writhing mouth that could change in an instant from strong and masculine to effeminate. Nero fished under a table and came up with an emerald—a recent affectation, this—which he held to one blinking, watery eye as he examined his old tutor. "Ah, Seneca," he said, "you're not looking at all well. You need a drink. Try my own personal *decocta neronis*—it consists merely of water, first boiled, then cooled in a glass vessel plunged into snow. Don't worry," he added maliciously, seeing Seneca's hesitation, "it's not poisoned."

Seneca drank the tumbler of water without comment. "Now then," Nero went on, "let's talk while I do my singing exercises." The Emperor laid himself flat on the floor and let out a long, rolling, bass note. He then instructed an attentive slave to pile one small weight after another on his chest. Seneca watched the proceedings in stony silence, convinced now that Nero, like so many Emperors before him, was becoming deranged.

"Look here, Seneca," Nero said, in between gasps, "you shouldn't have used Britannia just as a place to make money, you know."

"Your Majesty," Seneca began. His voice sounded strange. He was conscious that this was the first time he had spoken since he had come into Nero's presence. "Your Majesty, Rome has always enriched the lands it has conquered, by the infusion of private capital."

"Maybe, maybe," Nero gasped. His face was beginning to turn purple under the weights the slave was heaping on his chest. "But you were too greedy. You didn't just take the cream, you took the milk as well. You left nothing for them to pay their taxes with."

"That wasn't my intention, your Majesty," Seneca said earnestly. "Of course your taxes must come before my interest payments. Naturally, as a businessman, I must accept the risk that there is insufficient left over."

"You do accept that risk then?" puffed Nero.

"Yes, sire."

"Then there is no quarrel between us." The Emperor beamed. Struggling onto his elbows, Nero berated the frightened slave for loading him too heavily, and the slave promptly took some weights off his heaving chest. "That's better," Nero said. "Now listen to this." He pursed his mouth and took off up the scale with his deep bass voice. Even Seneca had to admit that the Emperor had a powerful set of vocal cords, the notes vibrating around the chamber like rolling, sonorous thunder.

"Congratulations, your Majesty," Seneca said.

Nero beamed again at Seneca through his weak, watery eyes. "You know I would rather have been a singer, a musician, than an Emperor?"

"I have heard you say as much, your Majesty."

"Praise for my talents as a dancer, a player of the lyre,

as a tragic singer, is more important to me than conquering any province."

"Your Majesty indeed has a remarkable voice," Seneca said. Realizing that the sentence might be considered two-edged, he added quickly, "Remarkably fine."

"Did you know that I am founding a festival in Rome modeled on Greek tradition? There will be prizes for oratory, poetry and singing."

"Your Majesty has always been a patron of the arts."

"The Senate have kindly decided to name them after me. They will be called the Neronian games. Do you think I will be allowed to compete?"

"Without your Majesty's talent the games could not take place."

"You are too kind, Seneca. Too kind." Nero picked himself off the floor and allowed his slave to dress him in a diaphanous tunic patterned with gold thread. When he was comfortably seated in an upright chair, his barber, Thalamus, came in, bowed respectfully and began to arrange Nero's coiffure, first washing his hair, then intermittently pulling at a lever in the wall which allowed a jet of rare perfume to squirt from the fretted ivory ceiling onto the imperial locks. Seneca watched in silence while Thalamus arranged Nero's hair in a series of parallel curls along his forehead, crimping the rest of his hair into steeply rising waves that stood up stiffly on his head, like a row of steps set into a high cliff.

"Seneca," Nero said suddenly, "they tell me that your Jewish agent serves you well. How about him doing some work for me?"

"I would be honored to assist your Majesty in any way I can," Seneca said guardedly.

"I'm told he can fight. That not only was he a gladiator, but twice winner of the civic crown."

"That is so, your Majesty."

"Well, I'm planning a big push against the Welsh and I'm at my wit's end to find a general who's neither senile nor dishonest. Perhaps your fellow could do the job? After all, he's a colonel now, isn't he?"

Here it was. A straw for a drowning man. The last chance of saving his capital. With Simon ben Eleazar commanding the Roman army, Decianus could be disposed of quickly and Seneca's star would rise again. Trying to hide the excitement of his voice, Seneca said casually, "They say he's a fine soldier and has kept himself in good physical condition."

"You would have no objection to his being detached on military service?"

"None at all, your Majesty."

"Very well, then. However"—Nero's voice had suddenly taken on a smug tone—"I think, on reconsideration, that he may be too young for overall command. But I'll tell you what I'll do. I'll give him command of the cavalry. That's not too bad a job, is it?"

"He would be honored, Majesty." Somehow, apart from the merest tremble, Seneca did not betray his rage, his impotent fury, his utter misery at the way Nero had tricked him so neatly.

He saw it all now; realized just how much the Emperor hated him. Instead of ordering his execution, he had taken the more subtle revenge of a sophisticated man. Not content to outdo his old tutor in sexual activities, Nero had determined to match him in deviousness, in all the wiles of statecraft Seneca had taught him as a little boy. He had succeeded beautifully. Masking his intentions by a controlled display of eccentricity bordering on madness, he had made Seneca drop his defenses. As a result, Seneca had come blundering in with both feet and had dropped neatly into the trap his former pupil had set.

It really was superb. With Simon ben Eleazar dispatched to Wales and serving under the orders of another general, he would be impotent to prevent the worst excesses of Procurator Decianus. There would be unrest in Britannia, seething and bubbling into rebellion, then exploding into terrible war. Seneca could see the future clearly.

With a shock he realized that Nero knew it as well as he; that Nero did not really care in the slightest. He was interested in one thing only: revenge on Seneca.

And he had succeeded brilliantly! Nero had done nothing. It was Seneca who had offered his agent Simon voluntarily, and thus by his own efforts completely ruined himself.

As Seneca backed away from the royal presence, he was conscious of Nero's watery little eyes gleaming in open triumph. At everything, the pupil had now shown himself to be the superior of his master. It was not that he had taught him badly, Seneca reflected, it was that he had taught him too well.

Back at home, Seneca took up pen and papyrus and wrote a desperate letter to Simon, informing him of his imminent posting to Wales, and imploring him to make one last effort to collect the money the British tribes owed him.

Then he did a thoroughly cynical thing. Showing a treachery worthy of the Emperor himself, he wrote a second letter to his sworn enemy and chief destroyer, Procurator Catus Decianus.

For Simon ben Eleazar, after so many years of peace and prosperity, the pace of life was quickening. Now, on a sunny late-spring afternoon, he had gone for a walk by himself. Above all, he needed to think.

Strolling through the elegant temples of Camulodunum with their colonnaded walks, quiet gardens with their fountained peristyles, it was difficult to believe that the civilized tranquility of Romanized Britain was coming to an end. Yet Simon, from his travels through Britannia, was convinced of one thing. Rebellion was inevitable. Any Roman official would have pooh-poohed the idea as absurd. But Simon knew. As an old soldier, he felt it in his bones. There would be rebellion.

For months now, Procurator Decianus had been slapping one imperial tax after another on the groaning Britons. First land tax *(tributum soli)*, then property tax *(tributum capitis)*, followed by two further taxes which, with the help of his Roman claque led by Favonius Facilis, he had pushed through the local *ordo* to bite with special savagery on the two East Anglian tribes, the Trinovantes and Queen Boudicca's Iceni. These were the hated *annona*, the forced requisitioning of wheat to feed the entire Roman garrison in Britannia, and a huge impost to help pay the cost of finishing the extravagant Temple of Divine Claudius.

On top of this, he had now been ordered by Seneca to call in his loan to the Iceni, collect outstanding interest.

157

He knew that Queen Boudicca, proud, intractable at the best of times, would not stand for it. There would be bloodshed. It was even possible that he would not get back alive.

Death was no stranger to him. He was a fighting man, bred from a tribe of warlike Jewish brigands on the Galilean hills, yet here he was no more than an Oriental doing Roman work. More and more, as he advanced toward the age of forty, he remembered the words of Herod Agrippa—of the legend of his bravery the tribes of Judaea and Galilee were keeping alive, of how, trodden under the iron heel of the Roman legions in the same fashion as the British, they rallied to one false Messiah after another in a vain struggle for liberty. Yet he had ignored these things; he was devoted to the brown-eyed woman who had been such a wonderful wife, but it was her very solicitude, her anticipation of his every want, that had corrupted him, softened him—made him a traitor to his own people.

He came to a halt by the Temple of Claudius, depressed by his thoughts. Even now, he never failed to be amazed by its breathtaking magnificence—the vista of snow-white steps, the high podium surrounded by majestic pillars made of the finest marble: *africano* from Asia Minor, rosso antico from Cape Matapan, pavonazzetto from Phrygia, giallo antico from Algeria, Carrara from Italy, porphyry from Greece. The list was endless and so was the cost. Now the whole load was to be shifted to the groaning backs of the Britons, and, on top of that, he had to collect Seneca's money!

He grimaced at the towering elegance of the temple, then turned and walked swiftly back to his horse. He had to organize an expedition into the Iceni country at once. He owed a lot to Seneca and he would do his duty by him. But there was no time to lose. Like all veterans technically in the Roman army, he had heard that he would soon be given command of a fighting unit. If he ever got back from the Iceni country alive, then the dangerous, ambush-infested wilderness of North Wales beckoned.

The chances of Simon ben Eleazar's surviving over the next few months looked slim, but as he galloped back to his palatial villa, Simon was exhilarated. An old feeling long forgotten, the quick surge of blood in the veins of a fighting man.

No longer did he feel that it was too late. That his bolt was shot. For Simon, as for Vespasian, the finger of destiny summoned. A destiny that had made them as close as brothers, then sent them on their separate ways for so many years, but which slowly and inexorably would bring them back together in one final, cataclysmic union.

18

"But we cannot pay," Prasutagus stretched out plump arms to emphasize his tribe's inability to find Seneca's money.

A growl of fury rose from the crowd of Iceni ringing the small retinue of soldiers Simon had brought with him. Simon could feel the tension in the air as taut as twisted gut: one that could break at any moment—and end in their massacre.

"You are well known to be a rich nation," Simon said quietly. "In particular, you have vast lands and a treasure-house full of gold. Pay something on account and I will explain your difficulties to my master, Seneca."

"But—but—" Prasutagus held out his arms again. "The treasure-house is sacred. Consecrated to our religion—protected by our priests."

"Nevertheless, you will pay something," Simon insisted. He shot a warning look to his men, who tightened their hands on their swords.

"We pay nothing, Roman pig." There was a sudden hush in the crowd. Simon turned his head to see whence this insult, spoken loudly and in bad Latin, had come.

A squat, powerfully built young warrior was shouldering his way through the crowd. From his fine armor he was obviously a noble, and Simon could only guess at the enormous strength of the boy's veined biceps and trunklike thighs.

"You addressed me?" Simon's eyes had gone hard and cold.

"Who else, Roman pig?" The boy walked forward insolently. Simon put him at twenty-three—in the first flush of manhood. In his hand swung a long-hafted, enormously heavy, iron-bladed battle-ax, which the boy carried as if it were light as a feather. Suddenly, taking a two-handed grip that made the magnificent muscles of his biceps quiver and ripple, he aimed the ax at the side of a nearby hut. The blade sliced into the wood with such colossal force that the whole structure shuddered, then collapsed, with a great rending and cracking of timbers. The tribesmen laughed, nudged each other. This was apt to be Hengist's party trick on nights of drunken wassailing, when he would rampage through the streets, senses inflamed and fighting mad on the fiery mead of the Iceni. Only Hengist had the sheer, bull-like strength to do it. The blond warrior wiped one hand against the other, spat on the ground, then said savagely, "Roman! Your taxes grind our people. The king may be a coward but I am not. We pay you nothing."

"What we are owed, we will take," Simon said flatly.

The crowd of gesticulating people pressed closer, the men shouting insults, but Hengist raised his hand and cried, "Enough. Let me speak." The crowd subsided and Hengist swaggered confidently through until he stood almost at touching distance of Simon's horse.

The men looked at each other, examining the eyes as trained fighters will do, searching for any signs of weakness, but finding no flaw in the steel of the other's gaze. Now was the moment for which Hengist had sweated and strained for seven years. Conscious of the queen's instructions and her promise of Princess Andrasta's hand, he had honed and ground himself into a fine physical specimen. Now, proudly and at the top of his voice, he issued his challenge.

"Roman," he roared, "I have an idea. You against me

at the coming games. A fight to the death. If you win, take everything. If you lose, your master gets nothing. What do you say?"

Simon looked at the boy, conscious of the formidable threat his oxlike strength would make married to razor-sharp youthful reflexes. "Single combat?" he asked.

"That's right, Roman."

"With armor?"

"Whatever you wish, Roman." The boy shrugged his massive shoulders, casting a wolfish glance down at his battle-ax as if to indicate that it would slice through any body armor like butter.

"Very well," said Simon.

A great sigh escaped from the crowd. Hengist nodded, smiled at Simon and began to turn away. But Simon called after him, "Tell me something before you go. It was in your power to massacre us without risk. Why did you then offer single combat?"

Hengist remembered his years of clumsy courting and Princess Andrasta's imperious rejection. The look of scorn in her ice-blue eyes that had made him go out and get himself mad, fighting drunk. The queen had been very wise. Only by appearing as champion of his people and defeating Simon in single combat would he win the princess's hand. All these things coursed through his brain but he was incapable of putting them into words. Instead and by way of an answer, he turned to the royal hut.

Simon's eyes, following the boy's glance, rested only briefly on the great, brooding figure of the queen. It was on the girl standing next to her that they became riveted. She was every bit as tall as the queen, but slender, with small, hard breasts already thrusting through her loosely worn tartans in the first bloom of womanhood. If it had not been for her distinctive tawny hair, braided in long pigtails, Simon would scarcely have recognized her. In the seven long years since he had last seen the princess, she had grown into an achingly beautiful girl.

He walked his horse slowly over to where she was standing. "Little Princess," he said softly. "It is many years since I have seen you. How beautiful you have become."

The girl looked at him calmly, her face in repose, saying nothing.

"Do you not then recognize your uncle Simon?"

Hengist shouldered his way through the crowd until he stood again by Simon's saddle. "She is promised to me," he said. "You must not talk to her again without my permission."

"Let her be the judge of that," said Simon calmly. He looked at the young princess standing there so erect. At close quarters there should, as in any jewel, have been some flaw, but there was none. He took in her slim neck, the fragile, finely set bones of her face, the slightly elongated nose and imperious eyes that she had inherited from her mother, which gave power and personality to her face and saved it from being merely pretty. "Little Princess," he repeated. Over the years he had always called her that. "We have been the best of friends ever since you were a small child. Do not throw it all away now."

"Roman pig!" The girl's voice was cold. "It is because of you my people live in poverty. You are no longer my friend."

Simon's eyes glittered at her with strange intensity for one long moment, then he shrugged and snapped a command to his escort. Wheeling his horse around, he tore out of the village at full gallop.

The girl followed him with her eyes for a moment, then dashed into her hut, threw herself on some straw in a corner and sobbed her heart out. She could not forget Simon's fine-chiseled features, his clear skin, those strange gray-green eyes that seemed to burn with such power. He had been her hero for as long as she could remember. Now he must be her enemy. She had done her duty, obeyed the queen's stern instructions. She was no longer a child, but a beautiful, desirable girl and was herself experiencing a flood of new and tempestuous emotions. She hated the Roman for coming back to the village. He disturbed her life. She lay there weeping violently, and when Hengist came into the hut and tried awkwardly to comfort her, she screamed at him to go away.

Some two thousand Romans came to see the death combat—just part of the games in dedication of the

Temple of Divine Claudius, now complete in all its white-marble, pristine beauty. The Romans sat in the best places, oblivious to the sullen hate shimmering down at them from the massive block of ten thousand Britons in the upper seats. Only Queen Boudicca and the Princess Andrasta had reluctantly been given places of honor among the white-robed *duoviri* and aediles. The queen sat there waiting for her champion to hack Simon into a bloody pulp, while beside her the princess gazed straight ahead with remote, unseeing eyes, her porcelain-smooth, fragile-boned face absorbed in some deep agony of mind.

Simon had known that it would be like this: a matter of prestige. As a result, he had withstood the temptation to don the heavy armor of a Samnite or of a *hoplomachus* and now stood in the center of the arena, naked except for a small body belt supporting his genitals, disdaining even greaves, thigh protectors or the smallest shield. For two long, agonizing weeks he had pounded the roads, exercised, trained, gone to bed early, his mind sick with the fever the girl had given him. He hated himself for betraying the love of the brown-eyed woman, but she just said nothing, massaged away his aches and pains and loved him as tenderly as she had always loved him.

Now, stripped for action, he looked like a lithe, rangy cat. Experienced, dangerous. Although scarred by old wounds, his skin was clear and healthy, his eyes bright and watchful. By reason of some time clock that beats slower in one man than another, Simon still had the fine, slim body of a boy and the years had not left their sign on him.

"Which god do you pray to?" Hengist called out contemptuously. "Jewish or Roman? Now is your last chance to do it."

"I need no prayers, axman," Simon answered. He flexed his knees, gripped the short, curved Thracian sword he had chosen. Light, razor-sharp, wickedly lethal in the right hands, the sword would be useless to parry Hengist's huge, iron-bladed ax. Simon, approaching forty, was defying his age, putting his trust once again in agility and speed as he had done in the arena, so many years before.

As Hengist approached, Simon smiled to himself. To

fight again revived old memories and old skills. It was as if his youth were reborn. He felt the vital juices course through his body and his gray-green eyes glittered at the huge, rippling thews of the bull-like Icenian, now coming closer and closer.

"Are you ready, Roman pig?" shouted Hengist.

Simon, calm, ignoring the insult, said quietly, "I am ready."

The ax whistled through the air with unbelievable propulsion. Only a cat-leap backward, drawn from an old armory of gladiator's reflexes, saved Simon from being literally split in two. The axman had won many fights like this, by pretending to be slow and deliberate, then striking with such unsuspected speed.

Hengist recovered the ax from the sand, hefted it like a feather, then tried the same stroke again. Once more Simon leaped backward, allowing the axhead to thunk down solidly into the sand. It could not be a long fight. Both men had scorned wearing shields. The first to be caught by the other's weapon would be badly maimed, that was a certainty. The crowd knew it. As two thousand Romans tried to encourage Simon, they were submerged by a huge bellow of triumph as the natives, repressed and bullied for so long, implored the axman to turn Simon into a bloody corpse.

Inspired by the screams and cheers, Hengist now made the ax whistle almost continuously through the air, its great iron blade carving a glistening circle in the sun, inside which there was certain death. Effortlessly, Hengist wielded the long-handled weapon, slicing first one side, then the other. Simon leaned back. Then, as the ax whistled straight across to take his legs off at the knees, leaped for his life, giving more and more ground against this ferocious onslaught. Not one thrust had he made, not a single slash with his razor-edged sword. Yet back he went. Anything to stay out of range of that death-dealing ax blade. As he retreated to the wall, the crowd leaped to their feet, victory thick and loud in their throats as they sensed the kill.

Simon's back thumped solidly against wood. The wall. Nowhere to go. The ax rose high over Hengist's shoulder, ready to accelerate into one final blow that would brush aside all opposition and turn a man into a smoking heap. The axman's blow was fast, but speed is a relative thing. Against the lightning reflexes of a trained gladiator, it was slow. It was the amateur against the professional again, and as always, the professional would prove superior. Once more, the ability to make a wide-eyed, unblinking assessment of the oncoming threat, the superb, linked timing that only a gladiator ever mastered, paid off. Simon moved. Not far. A foot, But forward, not back! His sword entered the axman horizontally, the wicked, curved, cutting edge taking him high in the thigh, cutting him to the ground like a tree, the ax leaving Hengist's hands, hurtling into the wooden barrier, biting deep, sticking there. A great sigh rose from the crowd.

Simon looked at Hengist, blood welling from the half-severed leg, the sword still stuck deep in bone. He had aimed to cripple, preferring to cut Hengist off his feet and alter the flight of his great, heavy ax rather than go right in with a killing stab and die himself under the ax's follow-through. He put his foot against Hengist's leg and heaved his sword out brutally, bits of blood and sinew sticking to the blade. Even though his eyes bulged with agony, and blood spurted in the air, staining the sand crimson, the Icenian nobleman did not make a cry. "Finish it, Roman," he whispered.

Simon took the axman by the roots of his blond hair, ready to put his sword to the sweaty, pulsating bull neck. He was amazed at the terrible hate that he had for him. Gladiators killed or spared dispassionately. But Simon, for one bloodthirsty moment, wanted to see the axman's head rolling in the dust, eyes glazing in the finality of death. Then he looked at Andrasta and knew why, and also, at the same time, realized that he must not do it—kill the girl's fiancé.

He threw away his sword and bawled, "Save this man. Take him to the doctors." Such was his authority that soldiers ran to collect the writhing Hengist and rushed him out of the arena.

Simon walked over to where Queen Boudicca sat with her daughter. The queen said with contempt in her voice, "One blow? You were lucky, Roman."

Simon said mockingly, "Madam, when a man fighting in hot blood meets another fighting in cold

165

blood, the latter will always win."

"I did not want you to spare him." The queen spat. "It deceives nobody."

"Mother," the girl burst out, "how can you say that?"

"It is just an empty gesture," the queen said savagely, "while they still grind us down to poverty. Do you imagine that this Roman will not be around tomorrow to fill up his money bags?"

Simon, the slightly mocking look still on his face, turned to the girl. For a moment their eyes held. He drank in her lovely skin, gossamer hair, fragile, arrogant mouth, and knew she was the most beautiful girl he had ever seen. He ached to take her in his arms and kiss her hungrily, tell her how much he loved her. No other woman he had ever known had stirred him as she did. Fighting down his impulses, he managed to force the emotion out of his voice. "Do not weep, Princess Andrasta, because I have saved your man for you. Is this not what you want?"

To his surprise the girl bowed her head and burst into a storm of angry tears. "Go away," she said bitterly. "Go away! Anywhere from here, but just go away. I do not wish to see you again, ever. I hate you, I hate you—I hate you!"

Within days, Simon received the imperial summons ordering him to Wales to take command of the auxiliary cavalry. Now, sitting in his formal garden, he was reluctant to go. It was beautiful at this time of year. Planned by one of Rome's finest nurserymen, blooms and shrubs were everywhere in riotous profusion. One by one, he had coped with the problems of leave-taking—his foreman of slaves had been given a program of work to be done on his vast estate, his wife given explicit directions about where he had hidden several million sesterces, and a gift of money made to his old servant Camerinus, who was getting married and who planned to set up a bakery in the thriving new city of Verulamium.

The brown-eyed woman was walking up the path toward him. Recently she had become very plump, prematurely middle-aged, as if the body were now demanding payment for the way it had been abused when she was a slave. Although no love match, the marriage had been successful—two people caring for each other, drawing closer as the years went by, never missing the absence of sexual passion. Now, about to leave her for what might be lengthy military service, Simon was more conscious than ever of the tenderness of his feelings.

"When will you go?" she asked him.

"Within the hour."

He could see tears start. "I will be back before you know it, dearest," he said, trying to comfort her.

"Hold me close," she whispered. As Simon's arms folded around her, he felt her give a sudden uncontrollable shiver, despite the warmth of the day.

"What is the matter?"

"These flowers do not smell of scent. They smell of death. A smell so thick in my nose that I can scarcely breath."

"What nonsense," said Simon.

"Is it nonsense that you love a young girl? We Britons have second sight, you know."

Simon felt his senses reeling. Not for anything would he have wanted to harm the brown-eyed woman.

She kissed him softly on the cheek. "You would have stayed faithful to me," she said. "I know that. A man like you does not desert an aging woman for a young girl. Now it does not matter anymore."

Simon tried to speak, explain that he could never possibly leave her—that Andrasta had indeed been promised to another man, but no words came forth.

"Go now," she whispered. "Whatever happens, I shall love you till the day I die."

Simon left, riding his best horse, taking the Roman road that led like an arrow toward the west, accompanied by only one orderly to look after his personal baggage. Each time he turned around the brown-eyed woman was still there, shrinking to a small black figure on the horizon, immobile, as though squeezing one last aching look at the man she had loved more than life itself.

With his right to use army way stations, his journey was not uncomfortable, but a sense of impending tragedy stayed with him all of the way. Worse was another feeling that had been coming upon him insidiously for many months. The feeling that he was fighting on the wrong side.

Procurator Catus Decianus stroked the blue-jowled chin of his unpleasant little face and sweated with triumph at what he read in Seneca's letter. Imagine such a prominent statesman abasing himself like this. He had heard rumors that Seneca would do anything for money, but until now had never quite believed them.

He still could not realize the completeness of his victory. Seneca, in his letter, had appointed him his agent instead of the Jew, with absolute discretion to recover his monies. Only when he thought about it did he realize that Seneca had no other choice than to recognize the new center of power in Britannia—and beg for a few crumbs from Decianus' table.

For Decianus, the last restraint was now removed. With Simon gone, the governor away in Wales with the army, he had absolute license to plunder.

Summoning his crony, the ex-centurion Favonius Facilis, he dispatched him to pillage a broad swathe of southern Britannia.

Certain easier, less fatiguing, more pleasurable tasks he was reserving for himself. Only just to the north, the lush treasure-house of the Iceni beckoned.

Only three days before, plump little Prasutagus, king of the Iceni, had succumbed to drink, dissipation and the strain of keeping the insatiable Romans out of his treasure hut.

In one last effort to assuage the Romans' greed, he left half his vast estates to Nero outright and the other half to his daughters as coheirs. At first glance, the idea had much to commend it. He hoped that the Emperor would be placated by such a large gift and allow the kingdom to remain independent, despite the Roman custom of annexing provinces after the death of an ally. He also dared to hope that with Seneca out of favor, a sympathetic Emperor might consider the loan from the statesman terminated.

Prasutagus might well have achieved in death the diplomatic triumph that had eluded him in life, had it not been for the ambitions of one man: Catus Decianus. Accompanied by hardened ex-veterans, Decianus lit out at a gallop for Caister-by-Norwich and the treasure he had so long coveted—the fabulous wealth of the Iceni.

19

The troop of horsemen thundered into the rutted streets of the Icenian capital at first dawn. The tribesmen, paralyzed with surprise, made little attempt to reach for their arms and were herded into captivity.

Catus Decianus rode up to the queen's hut with two of his cronies. The queen came out and stood resolutely on the wooden porch.

The men dragged her back inside and bolted the door behind them. They tied her to a chair and asked her where the treasure was kept. When the queen made it plain she would not tell them, they tore the clothes from her body and whipped her cruelly.

"That's enough," Decianus said at length. "We don't want to kill her." He took the queen's head and wrenched it forcibly up. "Woman," he said between his teeth, "for the last time, where's the treasure?"

The queen, defiant as a lioness, cursed him, then said with formidable insult, "For Mistress Domitia Nero, there is nothing."

"Fetch her daughters," Decianus commanded.

The two girls, Andrasta and Brigantia, were dragged into the hut, weeping with terror. Decianus had them stripped naked, while the veterans moaned with lust.

"Leave them alone," pleaded the queen, all arrogance now gone from her voice. "I will tell you everything. Only let them go unharmed."

169

"I promise," said Decianus.

In a broken, pain-racked voice, the queen revealed where Prasutagus had stored his huge wealth, and her torturer waited until it was verified that a fantastic golden hoard gleamed dully in the darkness of a hut.

"Now my daughters may go?" asked the queen. She was in agony, blood seeping from the raised purple welts the whip had raised on her flesh.

"Of course," Decianus said nastily, "after we have also taught them who are the masters."

The queen's face twisted with terrible rage and she strained impotently at her ropes in one last effort to reach Decianus. The procurator grinned and, together with his cronies, laid hold of the two girls.

A day later, having thoroughly sacked the Icenian capital, the Romans loaded up their treasure and carted it back to Camulodunum.

Eventually, some of the tribesmen escaped from the compound in which they had been imprisoned and timidly ventured into the queen's hut. Appalled, not believing at first what they saw, they gazed at the three royal women lying naked on the wooden floor.

A great howl of outrage, a cry of vengeance, burst from the throats of the Iceni people.

While Procurator Decianus and his men plundered the Iceni, Favonius Facilis had been carrying out his orders with cruel efficiency.

Riding for two days and nights with his own band of disaffected veterans, Facilis let his men rest only when he saw the snakelike glisten of water broadening away into the distance far below him. He had reached the Bristol Channel and knew himself to be in the country of the Dobunni.

Decianus had told him about the Dobunni. Not only did they own valuable lead mines, but they knew the secret of how to turn lead into silver, by cupellation. The huts of all the noblemen would contain silver ornaments, and that of Vercingetorix was reputed to be stacked from floor to ceiling with objects made from the precious metal.

His men rested, eager for booty, Facilis brought them

charging into the Dobunni village at full gallop, their old legionary cuirasses glittering brilliantly in the morning sun.

No sound came from the chief's hut. Just a thin sliver of smoke spiraled into the air through the central hole in the roof. Facilis pulled his one good ear and grinned. This was going to be fun. He gave a sharp order and his troopers dismounted and crashed through the door, waking Vercingetorix. The dark-haired little native girl who had been warming his bed scuttled into a corner, shrieking with fright, a shawl pulled around her.

A trooper yanked the long-faced chief upright. He sat there, bewildered, shivering with fear.

"Your mines are confiscated for nonpayment of taxes," bawled Facilis.

"But—but—there are no taxes. The government has lent me money instead, to enlarge the mines. There must be some mistake," Vercingetorix stammered.

"There is no mistake," Facilis said harshly. "Your mine workers are hereby made slaves of the Emperor." Turning to his centurion, he snapped, "Get the valuables."

Vercingetorix watched fearfully as Facilis' men collected his beautiful silver ornaments. The soldiers then transferred their attentions to the nobles' huts, piling several hundredweight of precious loot into the carts they had seized.

Next, Facilis galloped off with some of his riders to find the officer in charge of the small garrison that had been left by the Second Augustan to guard the mines.

"Your job," Facilis told him, "is to see, personally, that these mines are efficiently worked, and to send the entire produce of silver once a month to Camulodunum."

"Who are you? What is your authority, sir?" the flabbergasted centurion asked.

"This is my authority," Facilis growled. He produced a formal papyrus, heavily embossed with imperial seals and bearing the signature of Catus Decianus, procurator of all Britannia.

The centurion saluted, and a maniple of his own soldiers, assisted by Facilis' men, chained the sullen mine workers one after another to the rock face.

"Double shifts," Facilis roared. "Work them until they drop. Silver is urgently needed for the treasury. Don't be afraid to use the whip."

"Yes, sir." The centurion saluted again.

Facilis went back to the chief's hut. "Fetch me the native girl," he said to his men. "I have room for her in my household."

He grinned coarsely at her wild screams as she was dragged out, still half-naked, and tied across a horse. Facilis barked an order and the troop trotted away, followed by the laden carts drawn by teams of horses.

Facilis hurried south across the swampy, heavily forested Blackmoor Vale. Ahead of him was another tribe to ravage.

Not far away, the Durotriges farmed peacefully, unaware of the catastrophe that awaited them.

At Maiden Castle, Hod Hill, Badbury Rings, along a line of conquered hill forts that stretched across the Wessex uplands all the way to Salisbury Plain, the Durotriges had been slowly rebuilding their shattered economy ever since Vespasian and his Second Augustan Legion had smashed them into submission.

Left in peace by the Romans as long as they did not attempt to fortify their old strongholds, they found it a time of recovery, of real hope for the future. Once again, fat cattle roamed their bleak hills, their barns were full of hay, their storage pits brimming with feed—until Facilis and his ruffians swooped down from the north and confiscated their best beasts, their seed bulls, all the grain and fodder before vanishing as quickly as they had come.

With rage and despair the natives watched Facilis disappear. That autumn they would have no winter stores laid by.

From Dorest, right across the exposed windy hills of Wiltshire, the whole of the Durotriges tribe would, in only a few months, face certain starvation.

Unless something were done.

Something could be done, the high priest decided. It was a singularly opportune moment, with the might of the

Roman army pointing the wrong way, like an iron fist, at his sacred Druid sanctuary of Mona.

Never again would there be a chance like this. Normally the British tribes would not have fought to save the island of the priests, but now, with their wealth stolen, their lands pillaged, their women raped, the invasion of Mona could be a rallying point. Internal dissensions, their failure to unite, had always been a handicap. But with the legions off-balance in distant Wales, the vengeful might of the British nations would rise in their rear and swamp them with their numbers.

It could be done. The high priest would supply the overall direction, and in Queen Boudicca he had an awesome general, her sense of purpose fanned into a white heat by her recent degradation. It was just a question of gathering together the strands. In a terrible bloodbath, the Romans would be exterminated with appropriate Druid ritual. The old religion would rise again. Let the Romans attack Mona, even conquer the sacred groves. He would plan a terrible retribution in their rear!

Now was the time. The pendulum, swinging too far one way, would now begin to swing back.

Before the Roman legions had time to close an iron trap around the sacred island of Mona, the high priest and his band of acolytes, in heavy disguise, were galloping across Britannia and fanning out over hidden, prehistoric tracks unknown to the invaders.

The high priest had begun to spin a deadly web of vengeance.

20

General of the Army Gaius Suetonius Paulinus was holding a staff conference that evening, at dusk.

Resting after the blood-glut of Anglesey, where the legions had slaughtered the occupants of the Druid stronghold of Mona to the last man, woman and child, Paulinus' officers were conscious of ugly rumors from the rear and wanted some real news. They assembled in the big command tent, their parade regalia spotlessly polished. Their commander was a formidable ascetic, a law unto himself, and tended to be hard on his officers.

When Paulinus strode in, a ripple of amusement ran through the ranks of officers at the eccentricity of his dress—quickly stifled by a savage glance from his fierce gray eyes. As usual, he wore the plain armor of the legionary, which, with the scarf at the neck of his cuirass and the two distinctive phalerae attached to his helmet, was in breach of army regulations and consequently greatly approved by his men. He was small, thin, with a habit of walking in a slightly hunched, shoulders-forward manner with his swagger stick held jauntily behind his back. "Now then," he barked. His voice, although rather high, had the usual clipped patrician accent of the upper-class Roman. "For the next five minutes you will all clear your throats, cough and blow your noses, after which you will remain quiet for the rest of this conference."

Biting back their guffaws, they did as they were told and the tent rang to a wheezy symphony of trumpetings and snuffles before finally falling quiet.

"Thank you," Paulinus said. He resumed his walk, pacing backward and forward, his long, inquiring nose—held slightly to one side—giving him the aspect of an old lion stalking its prey. "Now I'll tell you what this is about. These natives have revolted somewhere in our rear. Somehow, they've got together a big army. Now it's up to us to stop them before they take over the whole province." The general tended to talk in short sentences, each ending in a rising inflection, injecting a strange charm into the sharpness of his phrases by his almost schoolboyish choice of words. "This is what seems to have happened." Paulinus went on to convey what he had learned from those of Cerialis' messengers who had gotten through.

He paused to cauterize with a glance a senior centurion who had found the courage to let out a stifled cough, then took charcoal and went over to a large map of the province. "Cerialis had a go at them," he barked, "but bumped into their best cavalry. Maybe we'll have more luck. First thing tomorrow, I'll head for Londinium with our Thracians. A looting army doesn't march fast and there's a good chance we'll be there before the enemy. Now you fellows with the Fourteenth and Twentieth will march at best speed after me, stopping—here." His charcoal bit blackly into the map at High Cross. Paulinus had at once realized the supreme importance of the semaphore station that stood exactly at the junction of Watling Street and the Fosse Way and could not understand why the Britons had not garrisoned the place. "Take it. Fortify it," Paulinus said. "Hold it. As long as we hold the interior lines of communication, we have the advantage. I've sent messengers to Postumus and you can expect the Second Augustan to march out from Gloucester and meet you there"—he slashed savagely at High Cross again with the charcoal—"within two days. By then, we'll know a little more about what these natives are up to. Now then. Is that understood? Are there any questions?" He turned his sharp nose toward his staff officers, daring someone to question him. "Very well," he bawled. "Dimiss. Good-bye and good luck." He turned and fixed Simon with a glare. "Thracian cavalry commander to stay here."

The room emptied, leaving Simon standing alone. "Follow me," Paulinus said. Simon found himself in the general's sleeping quarters—just a small tent with a straw paillasse that did for a bed and a jug of cold water for ablutions. Simple, monastic, functional.

"Colonel," Paulinus began briskly, "your slowness in exterminating those heathens on the Isle of Mona was noticed. Just how loyal are you?"

How did one answer a question like that? Simon knew the general had observed his reluctance to slaughter natives who, more and more, reminded him of the innocent hill folk in his native Galilean village. Vividly, he remembered Herod Agrippa's assurance that the Jews were waiting for him. He remembered his solemn oath to his father, still unfulfilled. Standing there stiffly to attention, he felt the need to return to his own people rise strongly within him, and he could make no reply.

"To the natives, you will always be a Roman," Paulinus said shrewdly, his fierce gray eyes burning into him.

Simon understood exactly what he meant: as one of Rome's chief agents, he was already a marked man with the Britons. His only chance to stay alive, to get back home and lead the oppressed Jews, lay in fighting with Paulinus and his tiny army against the overwhelming odds stacked against them. Yes, the decision was simple—made for him. "Sir," he said stiffly, "I promise you my complete loyalty."

"Good."

"I would ask to be allowed one condition—"

"What is that?" The general's eyebrows knitted aggressively.

"That when the battle is over, I will be discharged. I do not wish to remain in the Roman army one moment longer than is necessary."

"Granted," Suetonius Paulinus said. He thrust out his hand and Simon shook it. "It is not that I don't understand," the general said. Just for a second his face seemed to flood with compassion. "For a Jew serving Romans, things can never be easy."

Simon, at that moment, felt he would do anything for the elderly, terrierlike eccentric who now commanded his fate.

Riding flat out went Simon with his regiment of Thracians, as they escorted the distinguished person of Suetonius Paulinus, Governor of all Britannia, General of the Roman Army. Pausing only briefly, they urged on their horses until they were able to obtain fresh mounts from the way stations that clustered more thickly in the southeast corner of the province.

After three days and nights of hard driving, they entered the bustling little port of Londinium, to the relieved acclaim of the populace.

It took Paulinus only hours to realize that this fast-growing settlement of some twenty thousand people was doomed. Situated as it was on flat, low-lying ground on the riverbank, only the distant hills offering fortifiable strongpoints, Paulinus knew that if he stayed there, his men would be caught like rats in a trap.

Accordingly, he took the agonizing decision to leave. He issued an edict that all able-bodied men with their own horses could join him and told his cavalry to saddle up and prepare to fall back on High Cross. Already the sky to the northeast was bright as Boudicca's horde fired all the villages and settlements that lay in its path. Even after twenty-four hours, Paulinus could see that the enemy had moved perceptibly closer. What had previously been a bright glow on the horizon was now clearly identifiable as the sparks and cinders of burning timber, their roaring and crackling carrying easily to the ear, the great exploding paroxysms of white heat lighting the Londinium night.

Saddled up, fending off the weeping, hysterical women who ran alongside their horses, pathetically offering their babies to be taken to safety, the troopers rode out of Londinium and retraced their steps to the northwest.

Hours later, with the tumult of the city left behind and only the creak of leather to disturb the silence of the Thracian cavalrymen, Paulinus spurred his horse alongside Simon's at the head of the column.

"Sorry we had to leave those poor devils," the general said briskly. Even now there was this extraordinarily jaunty lift to the way he spoke. Simon wondered how much of it was forced.

"I think you had no other choice."

"To lose a city and save a province?" Paulinus mused. "I wonder how history will judge us."

There was silence again as the men rode side by side, each alone with his thoughts.

"Postumus should have come with the Second by now, sir," said Simon thoughtfully.

"You're right," Paulinus barked. "Then we'll give those Britons a taste of their own medicine."

But Postumus had not come up. With the same abject cowardice that had stopped him from venturing out of Gloucester earlier, he was certainly not leaving the safety of the fortress now and risking total destruction.

When Paulinus rode into High Cross and, surveying the pitifully small camp of his tiny army, finally learned the hard fact of Postumus' treason, he called a short staff conference to spell out the position the army was now in.

As Paulinus finished explaining the situation to his officers, Simon saw an amazing thing. A wolfish smile now marked the sharp-nosed ascetic features of the general. At first he could not credit it, but there was no mistaking the bright, eager look in the man's eyes. The way his whole face was lit up. Unbelievably, the eccentric old war-horse was relishing the situation, actually looking forward to the coming battle.

Everywhere in Britannia it was time to die. In Camulodunum, Verulamium, Londinium and the rich settlements of the southeast the ravening, vengeful horde had no mercy, paying back old scores.

With the victims, the manner of their dying, as with their living, varied. Some died neatly, hanging upside-down from a butcher's hook with throats cut, others died from mere sword thrusts. Still others, in terrible imitation of Roman methods of punishing slave rebellion, were crucified. Some died almost amusingly, like Camerinus, Simon's faithful old servant, wedged up to his shoulders in the oven of his Verulamium bakery while the natives baked his head instead of his bread. Those killed under the high priest's orders and accord-

178

ing to religious ritual died hard. The lucky ones had their guts ripped out and were flung headlong into mass votive shafts to the accompaniment of much chanting; others were first disemboweled and then hung up in sacred oaks, their limbs contorting like Cretan dancers. For Facilis and his predatory veterans, the high priest had reserved a special fate. He piled them into a huge wickerwork edifice of a man that had been set up outside the Temple of Claudius, then set the structure on fire so that the agonized screams of the veterans and their families as they burned alive seemed carried into the very air by the flames that licked high into the heavens.

The brown-eyed woman, Simon's companion for so many years, had, at the start of the rebellion, tried to get into Camulodunum for the dubious protection of Facilis and his veterans but had been turned away. Slowly she had gone back to Simon's estate and, dismissing the servants, had calmly awaited her end. As wife of a hated Roman agent and as a British collaborator, she knew it would be made as horrible as the Britons could devise.

She was not mistaken. First they ritually raped her. That formality out of the way, they tortured her in an effort to find Simon's hidden gold, but without result. Stolidly she told them nothing. Eventually they killed her in a particularly appalling fashion.

So, while the Romans and their friends suffered, the great mass of Boudicca's army, surfeited with loot, women and ridiculously easy victories, slowly ground to a halt.

Now Boudicca called in the high priest. When he came to her tent, the Druid was glad to see that the great tawny-haired queen was rational. No longer did hate seem to ooze from every pore, and the fire had gone from her eyes.

"What shall we do now?" she asked him almost pathetically.

The high priest, made to take a back place, his knowledge of strategy ignored, proceeded to assert himself and in none too respectful a tone. "You must fight," he said flatly.

"Is this not what we have been doing?"

"No," the priest sneered. "All you have done is kill a

179

few farmers, destroy some forts and way stations. If you wish to keep the territory you have conquered, you must defeat the Roman army in battle."

"And I suppose," said the queen, with a touch of sarcasm, "you can tell me where it is?"

"I can guess," the high priest said grimly. "When they retired from Londinium they will have fallen back on High Cross and fortified the position there."

"Why there?"

"It is the key to Britannia. I told you before to garrison it and you would not listen to me. Now the Romans will have done so. From there, they have good communications in all directions. You have no time to lose."

"Explain," Boudicca snapped.

"You must destroy them before they link up with the other legions. For all I know this may already have happened."

"Priest," the queen said arrogantly, flinging back her great mass of tawny hair, "why are you always so frightened? We outman the Romans almost twenty to one. What does it matter what they do? We will submerge them in a sea of numbers."

"There are other reasons why you have no time to waste that are even more important. You do not have an army. What you have is rabble of tribal levies gathered in search of loot. Now that they have what they came for, they will want to go home before winter. Remember, you have no supplies. By mobilizing in the spring, you forwent the spring planting. There will be no harvest this year. Your army will starve. March now, or you will never march at all."

The queen dismissed the high priest with a chill in her heart. She knew he was right. Calling her chiefs together, she gave the order to engage Paulinus and his army. She had no time to rest on her laurels. Only continuous action would keep her army intact. She must take the initiative—before the army starved, before the tribal levies slunk away in the first cold of winter. If the Romans had fortified a position, she must reduce it.

The natives had looted and plundered for too long. Now they must fight.

Face Roman steel.

* * *

Suetonius Paulinus, the grim old wolf of the High Atlas Mountains, knew the position as well as Boudicca. His army was minute. So tiny in contrast to the British horde as not to be worth counting, but it was highly disciplined, superbly trained and would stand its ground.

It did not take Paulinus long to find exactly what he was looking for. A defile near Mancetter, just to the north of High Cross—heavily wooded on both sides and with a steep escarpment rising seven hundred feet behind him. A perfect defensive position. With his flanks and rear secure, the British would have to compress their men into that corridor in order to attack him.

Having found his spot, Paulinus proceeded to fortify it.

Now the old general showed what a canny judge of human nature he really was. Keeping unsociably to himself in times of tranquillity, he frequented his officers and men, his disposition ever cheerful, his eyes confident and smiling. As his troops labored at the fortifications, he rumbled around in a cart, stopping here and there, saying in his distinctively sharp voice, "Right. Gather round, fellows." The men, seeing the small, hunch-shouldered old ascetic, the two distinctive phalerae on his helmet, dropped their shovels and rushed to him with a cheer. Paulinus would then deliver a short lecture, coming out with a typical phrase such as, "We've got to teach these boys a lesson they won't forget," then, in extraordinary contrast to his own severe method of living, he would distribute free bottles of wine that had been secreted in his private store. Morale ran high.

"But how do you know they will come, sir?" Simon asked, catching the general in a rare idle moment.

"They will come," he said, his gray eyes sparkling fiercely.

In their tens they came. In their thousands. In their tens of thousands. One wave after the other, whooping their strange war cries as they milled and eddied out of range of the Roman javelins.

181

Paulinus had his men drawn up, then rode with his staff officers on a swift tour of inspection to see that his dispositions were exactly as he wanted them. He had needed to extend his front right across the defile—everywhere the line must hold or they would be swallowed up, encircled. On the flanks he had placed his Thracian cavalry, splitting them so as to give mobility at both ends of the line. In the middle he placed the flower of his army, the battle-hardened, superbly trained and equipped veterans of the Fourteenth and Twentieth legions, in three lines stretching back into the neck of the defile. Whatever happened on the flanks, they would hold there, rocklike until the end, and take a lot of savages with them. In between them and the Thracians—corseted therefore on either side by experienced troops—Paulinus placed his foot auxiliaries, cooks, engineers, normally noncombatant personnel, together with the few hundred volunteers that had ridden with him out of Londinium. In accordance with ancient tradition, the three lines of each legion were formed with the best men in front, the older, tough, mature campaigners next, to stop a rout, give encouragement and support, and the remaining troops behind to plug the gaps.

Satisfied with the deployment, Paulinus now asked searching questions of the senior centurions who had supervised the fatigue parties. "Are the lilies dug?"

"Yes, sir," his officers chorused.

"Properly covered up with twigs and grass?" the old general snapped.

"Yes, sir."

Try as he might, Paulinus could not see anything suspicious about the ground that lay between him and the enemy. "Very well. To your places. I'll address the men."

As he paraded on a white horse in front of his assembled troops, a look of fierce pride came into his eyes. He surveyed the beautifully straight line, the gleaming armor, the weaponry in the hands of his old veterans, the purple-cloaked staff officers, the Aquilifers and Significers carrying their standards of pure gold, the centurions in their double skirts and distinctive, transverse-crested helmets spaced out in rigid formation at the head of their men. The whole, brave, colorful panoply of the Roman army about to do battle. It never failed to move him.

He cleared his throat. "Men," he barked, his sharp voice carrying easily to his small force, "not going to lecture you. Just remind you of a few facts. Look behind the enemy cavalry. What do you see? I'll tell you. A lot of naked savages." Nervous laughter rose from the ranks. The dry-throated soldiers, although ready to fight the vast enemy to the death, were convinced that they themselves would not survive. "Go ahead and laugh," Paulinus said, "but just look at yourselves in contrast. Examine your equipment. What did we do when we found your bronze helmets didn't give adequate protection? We gave you iron ones with specially polished surfaces to deflect sword cuts. Your body armor—what was wrong with the old Mark One stuff? It was still better than anything owned by some native chieftain, yet we replaced it, equipped you with articulated cuirasses that cost a fortune. Have you noticed how much lighter your swords are than the old ones? How your javelins have had lead weights added to increase range and penetration? All this has happened in thirty years. Have you thought how many provinces have been bled dry with taxes to provide you with such superb equipment? And your training. Years of it. Only the best men recruited, taught by the finest instructors. Does it matter how many savages prance and caper out there? I tell you they'll go down like grass before a sickle."

A great roar burst from the ranks, the soldiers nodding, realizing the wonderful sense of his words. Even Simon, skittering on his beautiful army thorough-bred at the head of his fierce Thracians, had to acknowledge the old general's eloquence.

"You fellows just throw your javelins," Paulinus went on. "Strike with your short swords and shield bosses, carry on from there and you'll mow them down. Remember the other fellow has no discipline, no centurions to punish him for laziness." The soldiers, with a lot of mock groans, responded to the joke. Paulinus waited for the laughter to die down, then said, "All I ask of you is this. Listen for the *cornua*. Watch your Aquilifers carefully. I've given very specific orders

183

about how to deal with these beggars. Obey your standards. Don't think of booty and you'll have everything. Do your duty, and I won't say I think you'll win, I guarantee it."

A great lusty cheer went up from the ranks, a cheer that rolled across the no-man's-land, clutching at the high priest's heart like an iron fist. All that he dreaded was now coming true, but he still could not bring himself to believe that the picked Silurian and Icenian cavalry, themselves almost equal in numbers to the whole Roman army, would not sweep away the legions at the first charge, leaving the woad-colored savages to finish them off.

Slowly the natives took their stations, contingent by contingent, each chief insisting on his place of honor. Facing Simon—both men at the head of their cavalry—Hengist sat, blond-haired, thick-necked, eyes bulging with hate, his leg stump bound tight in a special sling to stop him falling off. He could see the Jew clearly—that hated representative of the Romans, the man who had severed his leg, worsted him in combat, and who loved Andrasta. His eyes never left Simon. He would be happy to die as long as he took the Jew with him. Simon suddenly raised his mailed hand in acknowledgment and for some reason Hengist, despite his terrible rage, found himself nodding back.

In the last few minutes before battle, Simon's thoughts were for Andrasta, the tall young Icenian princess. She would, he knew, be somewhere out there with the women and children in that mass of loot-filled wagons that the Britons had arranged in a crescent immediately behind their army. He wondered how she was, hoped she was safe, hoped that somehow she at least could survive the coming carnage. He kept switching his mind back to his wife, wondering if she were still alive, but his thoughts kept returning to the beautiful Andrasta. He felt ashamed, conscious of treachery toward the brown-eyed woman, despising himself, but it could not be helped. He knew he was madly in love with the princess, wanting her more than life itself, achingly, continually. Nothing could be more wonderful than to be able to spend the rest of his life with her, but with a feeling of utter hopelessness he knew that such a thing could never be.

The emergence of Queen Boudicca drew his mind back to the coming battle. The queen drove her chariot out in front of her troops. With her flaming red hair, her imposing tartan-covered figure with the great golden torque around her neck was plainly visible to the Romans and the whole battlefield fell silent.

The queen raised her hand, then brought it down. "Charge," she shrieked.

The Silurian and Icenian cavalry, formidable in full armor, tore forward, Hengist waving his huge battle-ax, mouthing savage curses.

This was it: the moment that would decide the fate of Britannia, govern its customs, its precepts, its very language. A moment that would decide the course of history.

The battle was joined.

Lances at the ready, the necks of their fleet horses stretching forward as they extended into full gallop, the native cavalry raced down on the waiting Romans.

As the gleaming, yard-long *tubae*—one for each legion—shrilled a single, urgent note, the front line of the Roman legions went to one knee, the second crouched and the third remained standing, thus enabling three ranks of bristling sharp javelins to face unwaveringly the oncoming horsemen.

Just when the impact was seconds away, down went the cavalry amid the terrified screams of the fast moving animals, describing fearful somersaults in the air. Behind them, the rest of the force piled at full speed in a fantastic jumble of terrified horses, their heavily armored riders flying in all directions before settling in a welter of writhing bodies among their screaming, whinnying mounts.

The "lilies" had done it. Some of the Britons even knew about lilies. They had seen the murderous three-foot-deep holes, in which fire-hardened stakes, tapering from the thickness of a man's thigh to needle sharpness, had been planted, stakes which looked like the stamen of a lily. What the Britons had not realized—could never take in—was the training of a Roman legionary which made him a skilled woodworker and carpenter accustomed, after a day's heavy route-marching, to the backbreaking labor of building a fortified camp. They had not suspected—no one could have imagined—that in only a few days the two legions had been able to make deep holes lined with timber revetments, sink sharp, lethal stakes and then cover them with turf, leaves and twigs. The effect on the cavalry charge was catastrophic. Of the flower of the Icenian and Silurian nobility, only a trickle of brave, half-stunned warriors reached the Roman line, to be promptly dispatched by javelin and sword.

A great cry burst from the tens of thousands of Britons at the awful ruin of their cavalry. To the accompaniment of blood-curdling blasts on their *carynges* to keep up their spirits, the natives surged forward, picking their way over the fallen horses and warriors, a flood of manpower ready to overwhelm the tiny Roman army.

Now the deeper blast of the great circular Roman *cornua* belled out and the men looked to the three gleaming standards proudly held by the first cohort—the imperial eagle, the image of the Emperor and the regimental badge which, in the case of the fighting Twentieth, was a charging boar. At once the standards made an up-and-down movement, then dipped sharply before returning to the upright position. With the signal given, the Roman army, showing incredible discipline and élan, did precisely the opposite of what the natives expected. Outnumbered twenty to one, down secret paths through the lilies known to their centurions, in two tight wedges—they charged.

A maniple of Roman legionaries, superbly fit and disciplined, moving at a fast jog trot into the attack, was a formidable sight. Physically, the impact on half-clad, unarmored natives was akin to a great iron fist being punched into a naked gut.

Those Britons in the front rank who had not gone down under the first lethal hail of Roman javelins had survived only by catching the wicked missiles on their shields. Now, with the soft iron points held fast in the shields and making them useless, the natives were helpless as the Roman heavy infantry slammed into them.

Incredibly, as they hit, they shoved. Stab-shove, stab-shove—the centurians intoned the rhythm. To the Roman assault teams it was literally no more than an exercise out of a training manual. As the natives recoiled in shock and horror, the whole of the Fourteenth and Twentieth legions debouched through the narrow lanes in the lilies and, deploying on the ground won by their assault forces, formed into fresh attack formations. Breaking into that fearsome jog trot, they now rammed into the panic-stricken natives all along the line.

Normally such bold tactics by a tiny force so inferior in numbers would be effective only so long as the element of surprise lasted. After that would come fatigue, encirclement, annihilation. When you were outnumbered twenty to one, such a fate was inevitable unless your leader was brilliant enough to find a way of equalizing such terrible odds.

Paulinus was such a general and that was why he had ordered the attack. The Britons had brought their women along to watch the battle. Now, drawn up in a tight crescent, the heavy wagons blocked both freedom to retreat and room to maneuver. What happened now was appalling. Mass execution in slow motion. As the front ranks of the Britons shrank from the murderous short swords of the legions and turned to run, they pressed inexorably back on those behind them. Their sword arms pinioned by their own fighting men, the Britons now found themselves defenseless. Stab-shove, stab-shove. The Romans were bloodied to the elbows. Stab-shove—forward they went, pushing with their cruel shield bosses until by sheer weight of terrified, retreating numbers the natives overturned some of the wagons at the rear and fanned out across the country-side like water breaking through a dam.

Once again Paulinus timed his move superbly. The *cornua* blasted two sudden, harsh notes and Simon's Thracians, unleashed like missiles from a catapult, fell on the fleeing horde. This time he would show no mercy. You did not trifle with such an enormously superior force. Once you let them regroup, you died. Simon knew that. He had also given his word to Paulinus about the part he would play in the battle. He saw to it that his Thracians hacked down the screaming, running Britons with their wicked, curved swords, sparing no one.

Victory was complete. The murderous flicking short swords of the Roman legions had been incredibly efficient. Eighty thousand Britons fell that day. Even the Romans, recalled toward dusk by concerted blasts of the *cornua,* went silent at the sight of the bodies lying in the dust as far as the eye could see. Of that great army, not one leader was left; somewhere in those mounds of corpses lay the high priest who had planned a revolution but failed to control it; the horse-faced, miserable Vercingetorix, who would never see his ornaments or his young wife again. No trace was ever found of Boudicca.

The old fox Suetonius Paulinus had chosen his time and place, then turned on his pursuers and clawed back for Rome the province of Britannia when all had seemed lost. He had gained for the Romans one of the greatest victories of all time. Such was the glory and the triumph that his Fourteenth and Twentieth legions became two of the only three legions in the Roman army ever to be allowed to incorporate into their names the word Victrix.

Victorious in battle.

Later that evening, in the quiet darkness of the autumn night, a mist came up. It lay over the thousands of dead in a cold, miasmic stench, hiding from sight the raw carnage that lay underneath, muffling the groans and cries of the wounded.

The Romans sent out search parties to strip the beautiful antique armor off the Icenian and Silurian cavalrymen who lay among their horses in the lilies. They also had other duties—to take prisoner any of the nobles only lightly wounded. Such men would make valuable slaves—might even be ransomable. At the very worst, they were proof to the Emperor of the greatness of their victory and a hint to him of the generosity they now expected.

Simon had taken out a patrol. With the complete absence of medical facilities and the enormous numbers of the mutilated and wounded, he had given additional instructions that men badly maimed or shrieking in agony should be dispatched as an act of mercy. The work in that damp, cold mist was appalling. Simon's thoughts, however, were elsewhere. He was sickened at the part he had played in the Roman victory. The natives had rebelled because of Roman cruelty and he had been part of that system which had made them rebel. Now he had been forced into fighting on the Roman side and slaughtering natives, merely to survive. He felt guilty, ashamed. He remembered the solemn promise of revenge he had made to his father. Its nonfulfillment racked him. He remembered Herod Agrippa and his pledge to keep the legend of the fighting Jewish gladiator alive in the Galilean hills, the ring given him which Simon had handed over to Messalina. The memory of that inglorious act still brought him screaming out of his sleep. Yes, he was a renegade. All he had done in his life was grow fat on Roman money, to end up as unloved by the Romans as the Romans were by the Jews. More and more a sense of mission grew in him. The need to atone.

Also, the two women confused him. Before he did anything else, he must work out his life with them. If the brown-eyed woman still lived, his place was with her. He had made up his mind. Whether Andrasta was alive or dead, he would do the right thing. He was brought back to the present by a sharp call from one of his men. "Colonel—come here," a Thracian shouted. "A man asks for you."

The mist had now lifted slightly, allowing moonlight to play over the terrible battlefield. Simon walked over to where his men had been working methodically, stripping the ornately worked bronze armor off the corpses and the beautiful Icenian horse trappings from their dead mounts. There, lying grotesquely impaled on one of the lily stakes, was Hengist. The Thracians, looking at the powerful body, the stump of his severed leg which had not prevented him from riding into battle, murmured among themselves. They appreciated bravery and did not want to kill him.

Simon looked down on Hengist and said sharply to his men, "Leave us."

As the troopers drifted away, Hengist spoke. "Hello, Roman," he whispered. Simon could see the trickle of blood at the corner of his mouth and knew he did not have long to live.

"Are you in pain?"

"There is no pain, Roman."

"I am glad of that."

"You have won a great victory."

189

"The Romans, not I."

"But you fight for the Romans."

"For the last time. Soon, I go home to fight for my own people."

Hengist's eyes burned feverishly. "You will carry on the struggle, lead them against Rome? You swear it?"

"I swear it. By my Hebrew God."

Hengist slumped into Simon's arms, exhausted by the intensity of his emotions. "I have heard your God is a great God," he said feebly, "and I think your oath to be true."

"It is true."

"Listen." The dying nobleman coughed, allowing bright-red blood to well from his mouth, then, finding fresh energy, said, "Do you love the Princess Andrasta? The one promised to me?"

"With all my heart—but my own wife still lives. I cannot desert her."

"She lives no longer."

An icy chill gripped Simon's heart.

"She was killed—by my comrades. When she would not tell where your treasure was, they tortured her, did terrible things. This I did not know. Had I been there I would have stopped them. Do you believe that?"

"Does it matter?"

"The weight of it is terrible. I would like to face the great journey free of burden. Can you forgive me?"

"It was not your fault. I forgive you."

"That is good." Simon could feel the man's body relax, grow calmer. "Hold me tight," Hengist whispered, "for I have no one and am frightened."

Tears welled in Simon's eyes at the warrior's pathetic words. Stripped of his arrogance and his armor, Hengist was just a lonely young man, away from his tribe and his family, coughing out his life on a damp field as he watched the black mystery of death move closer. "I will stay with you, Hengist," he said gently. "Look—I am holding you now."

The man's breathing went easier. "Andrasta lives," he whispered. "I sent her away. Her mother was against it, but the girl obeyed my wishes. I knew we would die today. I took omens. They foretold death and destruction for the Britons."

"Will you give her to me? Let me take care of her?" Simon asked. He shivered, waiting for the man's reply, knowing he would not take the girl without Hengist's permission.

"Truly, you will fight the Romans? Lead a rebellion of the Jews?"

"Until death. You have my solemn oath."

"Then I give her to you." Rid, at last, of so many guilts, so many responsibilities, a look of peace now came over Hengist's face, and with a great rush of blood from his mouth, he slumped back into Simon's arms and he died.

At that moment, peace also came to Simon. He had made a second, solemn promise on his Hebrew God to go home and lead his people against the Romans. He would not break it.

First he must hold Suetonius Paulinus to his word to release him, then he must take the Princess Andrasta as his wife.

If she would go. If she would have him. If he could find her.

He would set out tomorrow. At last, the way ahead was clear.

21

Simon, with a courtesy escort of ten Thracian cavalrymen provided by Suetonius Paulinus, galloped quickly off toward the east.

He knew he must give the brown-eyed woman a reverent, decent burial. Then, and only then, could he look for Andrasta. Passion for the girl was tearing at his very soul.

As they crossed the Thames Valley and approached Camulodunum, the signs of Boudicca's passing grew starkly evident. Every farmhouse in their path had been burned to the ground with smoke still rising from the ashes, its inhabitants either crucified or lying with their throats cut. The stench of dissolution was everywhere, hanging over the countryside like a rich, rotting, pungent, sickly pall, curling the nostrils and affronting the senses.

When they came to the area of Simon's villa, he rode on ahead with two of his troopers. It was plain that Boudicca's horde had destroyed the place as efficiently as any other structure that lay in its path. Little now remained of the great villa forming a rectangle around a central courtyard with its workshops, tanning yard, barns, stables and slave quarters. Simon walked disconsolately through the ruins, all that he had built in the years of prosperity as Seneca's agent.

Brushing aside the powdery, charred beams that had fallen everywhere, climbing over the debris, Simon made his way into the dining room. He had been particularly proud of its elegant wall paintings; the almost unique eight-sided mosaic represented the latest in Roman technology. Now it was all ruined.

Eventually, he found his wife; the brown-eyed woman lay on a couch in their bedroom. Her face bore the sunken, waxy look of old death, with flies clustering on her battered, tortured features. The natives had killed her in an unspeakably horrible fashion reserved only for the women of important enemies. Simon, a hardened old soldier, could take only one look before having to rush out and vomit on the grass. Eventually he summoned the courage to go back. The breasts of the brown-eyed woman had been crudely hacked off and stuffed in her mouth. Through them, caked with dried blood, protruded the sharpened end of a wooden stake which had been hammered up between her legs, skewering her.

Almost beside himself with grief, Simon found words forming—words strange from disuse, the same words that he had last spoken over his dead father. Facing to the east, beating his breast, Simon sang the slow chant of the Hebrew Kaddish in memory of the woman who had been his wife. He finished in a breaking voice, the long-forgotten, awkwardly spoken prayer bringing back sudden, vivid memories of his homeland. The brown-eyed woman had been loving and kind and, in his way, he had been happy with her. But as he finished praying to Jehovah, he knew even more certainly that his destiny now lay in the burning plains of Judaea, the lush plains of Galilee, and that Andrasta would somehow play a part.

No sooner had his men remounted than they ran headlong into a small *eques* of Roman calvary. The *optio* in command told him that he was from the Ninth Legion at Lincoln, which had been engaged for many days now in rounding up all known British ringleaders together with the chief of their nobility, prior to shipping them to Roman slave markets. The Princess Andrasta, he informed Simon, was already in captivity.

Now Simon's heart beat fast with excitement. The commander of the Ninth Legion was a man with whom he had once campaigned—a man he liked.

At top speed he headed deep into East Anglia. At Lincoln, he would find his friend Petilius Cerialis.

"By all the gods," cried Cerialis, "welcome!" He rushed up to Simon and gave him a huge bear hug that left him breathless. "Bring wine!"

An orderly produced a bottle of Falernian, then obsequiously retired. Cerialis listened quietly as Simon told him the long story of his relationship with Princess Andrasta, his white teeth gleaming when Simon started to describe his all-consuming love for the girl. "If it were me, you could take her, Simon," he said, chuckling. "Only the gods know how much of my life I have wasted chasing women. Unfortunately she is an important Icenian princess and my fate would not be a pretty one should our revered Emperor learn what I'd done."

Suddenly, he raised his voice. "Come here, woman," he bawled. There was a rustle of bedclothes and his dark-haired Brigantian princess appeared out of the bedroom. Her eyes were sleepy but Simon had never seen such red, passionate lips set in such pale, creamy skin. "Pour wine," Cerialis said, giving the girl a sharp slap on her bottom. The girl frowned, then, moving like a hungry cat, walked around the table and did as she was told. "You see?" Cerialis said, stretching his gangling frame. "Treat the sluts like princesses and the princesses like sluts and you can't go far wrong."

"But what shall I do?" Simon asked.

"Do?" Cerialis said. "My dear friend, that's obvious to anybody. You must go to Rome, that's all. Now!" He shouted, "Enough of these problems. Let's get drunk and toast old comrades. They say Farmer Vespasian is doing well as legate in Africa, and do you remember bowlegged Hosidius Geta, the fellow who commanded your Thracians? He took over the whole High Atlas command when Paulinus came to Britannia." The two men settled down to drink and gossip until, at length, the wine overcame them and they slept where they were until cock's crow, when Simon, waking with a start and realizing that his host would have official duties to perform, stumbled back to his own quarters.

It was a gray-faced Cerialis to whom Simon reported at noon. This was an official occasion and both men would be careful to observe strict protocol. But Cerialis was unable to disguise his monumental hangover. "Now, Colonel," he said in a shaky voice, "I am appointing you my official courier to advise the Emperor of the latest position here. You will receive documents entitling you and your escort to the highest priority for accommodation and remounts at all way stations."

This was kindness indeed. Cerialis was really being very good to him. "Thank you, General—most grateful to you, sir," Simon murmured, standing to attention.

"I understand you wish to interview one of the prisoners." Cerialis managed to leer faintly. "Very well. Permission is granted. Follow the *optio* and he will take you to their quarters." Having given one last proof of his goodwill, Cerialis shot Simon a heavy, bleary, red-eyed, secretive wink, then bent back to his papers.

Simon went with the staff officer to the slave quarters, where he found the Icenian women bedded down on straw in a stable. Slaves waiting to be sold could expect no better.

Simon saw Andrasta at once. Despite the starkly primitive conditions, she was sitting, straight-backed and dignified, while serving women groomed her magnificent tawny plaits. The effect of her beauty numbed him. He went over and said quietly, "Andrasta, I am sorry we should have to meet again like this."

When the girl ignored him, looking straight through him, he said, "Surely you know that this is none of my doing? I am your uncle Simon who has watched you grow up—who has loved you since you were a little girl."

She tossed her head. "If that is so, give me back my mother."

"That I cannot do. She is lost."

"My betrothed, Hengist?"

"Dead."

"My family and friends—the whole Iceni tribe?"

He was silent for a moment. "Dead or prisoners," he whispered at length.

She raised her head. "Roman," she said, "wherever you go, you bring murder, pain and slavery." With cold precision, she spat full in his face.

Slowly, Simon wiped it away. In the flickering darkness of the candlelit stable, he found himself searching in vain for a trace of regret, perhaps even a glint of emotion, but her features showed only implacable enmity.

"Very well," he said, with a touch of disdain in his voice that he certainly did not feel, "I shall still go to Rome and petition the Emperor for your freedom." He turned and stalked away without looking back.

Concealing the misery that lay so heavily on his heart, Simon set out for Rome, stopping at his wrecked villa to dig up his accumulated wealth, which the brown-eyed woman had not betrayed to Boudicca's men despite the most terrible tortures. Soon he would be in France and then Rome, and Rome itself would only be a stop on the way home.

Judaea. Galilee. He spoke the words softly and they were like a song in his heart.

Moving steadily down through France, he reached Lugudunum, and taking the Aurelian Way via Aix, Frejus, Antibes, Ventimiglia and Pisa (which, after the repairs carried out by Nero in AD 58, had been fully restored), Simon had a speedy and safe journey and in the first week of October reached the capital.

PART
III

ROME—
WHERE IT GREW
(60-64 CE)

"You might suppose it thundered 'neath the earth."

—LUCAN, flatulent in a public lavatory, quoting from one of Nero's poems

22

Nero, Emperor of the civilized world, stirred on his couch and stretched himself. It was almost noon. He loved the coolness of October. The torrid summer heat was over and a man could disport himself in all the things he liked to do.

If ever there is a man who loves life, it is I, thought Nero—but not merely my own but everybody else's as well! Am I not a man, yet cannot I play the woman exquisitely? Not only a charioteer with iron wrists to take a four-in-hand around the spine of the Circus Maximus, but also a sensitive singer of Greek tragedy— and who else can play the lyre as prettily as I, while flexing my biceps? I can also hold my own with any dirty ruffian of a wrestler on the bloody sand of a Roman arena. I am unique. More god than man!

He rolled off his couch, and his slaves, who had been waiting attentively for the first sound of movement, rushed in. One sprayed his throat so that his master might be in good voice that day. Another massaged his muscled shoulders, while a third painted his lips and dressed him in a flower-patterned minitunic with a muslin collar, designed at once to show off his strong legs yet hide his unsightly neck. Thalamus, the barber, finished off the Emperor's careful grooming by resetting his hair in the series of waved steps that his master loved so much.

When his slaves had left him, Nero gazed into the mirror despondently. Despite all their efforts he was still squat, with a blotched complexion, and suffered from smelly armpits. Overactive glands, Xenophon of Cos, the master physician, had said. There was nothing to be done. It was the price of supreme health, the constitution of an ox and a satyr's appetite that could survive a full day's imperial business followed by a night of appalling dissipation, then do the whole thing over again. Yet what he wanted most in this world had been denied him: physical beauty. Deep down in his heart, he knew what he looked like. A depraved, muscled woman.

He sat himself down in the audience chamber and made ready for the day's work. He hated playing the Emperor. It was all too easy: the decisions, the flattery, the courting of popularity with the mob. The reins of power, which made foreign policy such a superb instrument in his hands, could be held with so little effort. There was far more artistry in singing Greek tragedy or a poem recited to the lyre—Nero's reverie was suddenly shattered by the sound of his chamberlain throwing open the doors.

"The freedman Polyclitus," the chamberlain intoned.

Nero beckoned over a slave to spray his throat, cocking a jaundiced eye at the man who had come in. Another civil servant—one of those damned Greeks who ran the country. Immensely rich, perhaps as rich as Seneca, but you could not do without them and their careful, dedicated industry. He eyed the man's tunic, the glittering finger jewelry, the shrewd eyes in the expressionless face, and recognized competence when he saw it.

"You're off to Britannia?"

"Yes, sire. I leave tomorrow."

"No doubt you'll be taking your usual palatial retinue." Nero sneered. "Well, I don't suppose it'll do those natives any harm to see how wealthy Rome is."

"As you wish, sire." Polyclitus bowed impassively.

"Now I want a full report. Suetonius Paulinus isn't the type to forgive and forget. Perhaps a little more reconciliation might be the thing. Let me have your opinion on this."

"Sire."

"Who's next?" Nero demanded, as the Greek bowed himself out.

"Lucius Annaeus Seneca," the chamberlain said, "craves urgent audience."

Nero sniggered openly. The aging statesman and former tutor of the Emperor was now an object of contempt—a contempt mixed with jealousy. Having thought he had ruined him, Nero was enraged to see once again signs of Seneca's growing affluence. Long bored with taking his revenge, Nero would have ordered the old man's death except that he was so useful. What was more, there was tremendous pleasure in seeing Seneca's terror every time Nero so much as hinted at the fate he had in store for him.

"Well, Seneca," he bawled at the gaunt-faced man kneeling before him, "what brings you here? Come to lend me some money?"

"Alas, sire, after my venture in Britannia, there is little left to lend."

"Two big houses—vast farms in Campania—and I only found out the other day how much of Egypt you own. It doesn't do to be wealthier than the Emperor, you know. A lot of people have had—well—their careers cut short, for such a thing."

Seneca blanched. He had heard terrible rumors of what the Emperor could do when pressed for money. Nero had killed his old aunt Domitia just to get his hands on her vast estates. Quickly, he changed the subject. "Sire, you will recall that the Neronian games start next week and that I am in charge of arrangements?"

"Of course. How do things proceed?"

"Up to a point, well, sire. The new gymnasium and stadium are built."

"Up to a point?" Nero said ferociously. "There'd better be no delays. I look forward to performing."

"That is the problem, sire. We have a—withdrawal of labor."

Nero looked incredulous. "How can there be a withdrawal of labor? What on earth are you talking about?"

"The Guild of Olympic Athletes, sire. They are free men, much respected and honored. None of their members will appear."

201

"And, pray, why is that?"

"They say, sire, that you are so outstanding that you will carry off all the prizes and it is not worth their entering. In fact, half of them have returned to Greece already."

"What are you saying?" Nero glared at him. "That I must not compete?"

"That is for you to decide, sire."

"Oh, go away, Seneca," Nero said testily. "I will consider the matter."

Seneca bowed himself out.

"Is that all?" Nero asked the chamberlain.

"Apart from dispatches that have just arrived from Brittania."

"That cold, damp province gives me more trouble than the rest of the Empire put together." Nero groaned. "Very well. Show the messenger in."

Nero gazed at the man who entered. A colonel, from his rank insignia; he put him in his thirties. He had a certain feline grace in his walk and his face was clear-skinned and bronzed. Nero noted the aquiline nose and distinctive gray-green eyes, and a pang of envy swept through him at the man's good looks. "Have you dispatches for me, Colonel?"

Simon bowed and handed them over. Nero read them, then questioned Simon expertly, although it was plain to see that the whole subject bored him. He appeared interested only when Simon came to the subject of the slaves Cerialis was sending him.

"Noblewomen of the Iceni tribe, eh? Should fetch good money at auction."

"I have a favor to ask of you, sire."

"Ask it."

"Among the prisoners is a young girl. The daughter of Queen Boudicca. I wish to buy her from your Majesty before she reaches the auction block."

"And cheaply, I suppose. Why should I grant you this?"

"I have served Rome well, sire. I hold two civic crowns. In the recent insurrection I commanded your Thracian auxiliaries."

"Ah"—Nero smirked—"now I know who you are. I well remember giving you that appointment. Seneca

202

was most disturbed, as I recall—but surely, Colonel, a man should not brag about his medals?"

"I have no choice, sire, because there is no other way to plead my case. I am in love with this girl and beg you to let me have her."

Nero roared with laughter. "A refreshing request at least," he mused. "Tell me something—aren't you the ex-gladiator who was pardoned twice in the arena?"

"Yes, sire."

"Well, an old fighter like you should be familiar with unarmed contests—"

"We did a small amount in training—of course that was long ago—"

"Of course," Nero purred. "Tell me, Colonel, how old are you?"

"Thirty-nine, sire."

"Well, that's no age for a man in good condition! Some of these Olympic wrestlers go on forever. I'll make you a bargain, Colonel."

"Sire?"

"Quite frankly, I'm short of contestants for my games. Enter the"—he thought for a moment—"pancratium—put up a good fight and you won't have to buy the girl, I'll give her to you. What do you say, Colonel?"

Simon felt a numbness grip him. He was conscious, like an old cat in his ninth life, that he was tempting Providence once too often. For the inexperienced, he knew, the pancratium meant death or mutilation. For him, however, there could be only one answer.

"Sire—I accept."

"The pancratium," said Seneca. "So Nero's made you fight, has he?"

He had seen Simon go in for his royal audience and, intrigued to know what had brought him to Rome, had waited for him. After some persuasion Simon had accepted Seneca's invitation to dinner, if only to wind up outstanding business.

"There's no doubt," Seneca went on, "that your situation is precarious, to say the least. In the pancratium, serious injury is common and death not infrequent."

"I had little choice." Simon went on to explain his burning need to free the Princess Andrasta and the bargain he had struck with Nero.

"Well," Seneca said, after some thought, "I'm still in charge of the games and my voice may carry some weight. I'll call the chief of the athletic guild to see me. Perhaps I can ensure that none of the disabling fouls will be used against you."

Simon nodded, then changed the subject. "I have brought you earnings."

A sudden warmth suffused the features of the old philosopher at the mention of his favorite subject. He said, with careful unconcern, "My wants are always simple, as you know. I run my estates only to give employment and proper food to common working people. They lose me a great deal of money and I can't deny that funds will be welcome."

Simon said politely, "I'm sure."

"From where has this money come?"

"It is my own accumulated savings, gained mainly through your patronage and your commissions. When you lost your fortune in Britannia I felt it only fair that you should share half my earnings."

"That is very good of you," Seneca said, looking fondly at the dull gold bars that Simon's Thracians, careful not to spoil the priceless mosaic underneath, were laying at his feet. "Very good of you indeed."

"It was my duty."

A short, embarrassed silence followed, as Seneca, glossing over the matter of his recent treachery with Catus Decianus, tried to regain Simon's confidence. "Of course, what happened in Britannia," he began, "was out of my hands. Once you were posted to Wales, I had no choice but to use the—authorities in charge."

"The matter is closed," Simon said stiffly. "I'm sure we have both learned lessons."

"No doubt you have friends with whom to stay," said Seneca, glad to change the subject.

"I will find lodgings."

"No. You must live here. There are baths, exercising rooms, slaves learned in the art of massage to tone your muscles. You do not fight for ten days. In that time we must prepare you for the contest as best we can."

"You are too kind."

"It is nothing. And as regards your own treasure," he went on with studied unconcern, "nothing is safe from the Emperor in Rome. Why not place it in my vaults for safekeeping?"

"Thank you."

With the relationship between them slowly thawing, the two men ate dinner on fairly good terms, although Simon had never found himself able to relax in Seneca's home. Simon had heard that, under his mask of asceticism, the old man was a debaucher of the cruelest kind, but slowly his dislike faded under the philosopher's insidious charm.

True to his promise, Seneca summoned the president of the Guild of Olympic Athletes to his house next morning.

The man, a Greek called Ophides, an old boxer with a blinded eye and the marks of combat all over his face, showed Seneca scant respect. "Well?" He grunted. "Why am I brought here? Perhaps your Emperor has had a change of mind?"

"That is indeed so. The Emperor has decided not to compete. He values the athletes of your association so highly that he bows to your wishes in order to make the games a success."

"He would need to," said the Greek sarcastically. With his awful maimed eye, his face was twisted in a permanent leer. Since the proliferation around the Mediterranean of Greek-style events, his band of highly trained athletes—professional boxers and wrestlers— had a stranglehold on the games. "In the circumstances my men will not compete." He rose to go.

"There is another matter."

"Yes?"

"This man, a friend of mine"—he indicated Simon— "is entered in the pancratium—"

"The right to fight is no longer willingly allowed, except to members of our association—you know that—"

"Since the games are short of contestants, you must make an exception. It is by the Emperor's command."

The Greek eyed him with contempt. "For nearly a thousand years we have celebrated the games of Hellas. Who is your Emperor to change our rules?"

205

"Nevertheless, I ask for your cooperation. If only as a personal favor to me."

A look of weary patience came over the Greek's battered face. "Roman," he said, "do you not understand why we athletes had to unite? We tour the civilized world, competing in a difficult and dangerous art, boxing with wicked thongs bound around our fingers, wrestling with few holds barred. Who will help a beginner to see that he is not crippled? How can an aging athlete, down on his luck, be given a chance to win convincingly? Who is to pay those of us"—he indicated the awful white monstrosity of his eye—"who are injured or blinded? No one cares about them. Only our guild sees they receive a proper pension. So I tell you this—if your man fights, my men will be—angry."

"What does that mean?" Seneca asked.

A slightly mocking look came over the Greek's lumpy features. "Rules can be broken," he said. "Accidents can happen." His finger strayed as if by accident to his eye, set as it was in its opaque glare. "Retire," he said to Simon in a soft, almost caressing voice, "while you still have legs with which to walk, eyes with which to see, genitals with which to procreate."

Simon's eyes glowed an unholy gray-green. "Asked and I am biddable," he whispered. "Told and I am stubborn. Tell your man to prepare well for combat."

In the few days that remained, Simon went into dedicated training. He put himself on a meat diet, as did most of the body athletes, and ran for an hour each day through the streets and alleys of Rome, alongside the gaunt, stringy old statesman. Each afternoon he submitted to a strict regime of massage and muscle-toning at the hands of Seneca's slaves, and an old pancratiast was summoned to give him instruction in the secret arts.

As the games drew close, Simon, although an amateur unprotected by sword or knife, was at least fit and not completely untutored.

23

On October 13, AD 60, in the eight hundred and twelfth year of the city, a special ceremony took place in Rome to honor the Neronian games, especially arranged as they were to begin on the sixth anniversary of the Emperor's accession to the throne.

With a view to propitiating the gods and taking auspices, a procession formed with the Emperor Nero at the front preceded only by lictors carrying ceremonial rods and axes. Behind the Emperor followed senators in pure white woolen togas, patricians in scarlet cross-gartered shoes, the equestrian knights in their togas bearing the distinctive purple stripe. In the rear came the panoply of religious protocol—priests, heralds, flute players, lumbering white oxen from the Faluscan heights with horns gilded in preparation for their sacrifice. The procession moved slowly northwestward toward the Capitol, past Julius' basilica, the Temple of Saturn and up the steep face of the Capitoline Hill, before squeezing into position among the columns fronting the Temple of Jupiter. Now, with Nero seated on the simple carved ivory stool of a Roman magistrate and facing outward to the altar and the people of Rome, the solemnities began.

As the *pullarius* threw pulse cakes into the cage of sacred chickens, the whole assembly held its breath. The chickens, however, kept hungry, pecked greedily at the food. The priest now offered prayers for the Emperor and the success of his games, the altar fire crackling and flaring with each handful of saffron he threw on the flames. Finally, with solemn chanting, the oxen were sacrificed, disemboweled, their entrails laid upon the altar for the priest's inspection.

The priest now went to the temple steps and, theatrically throwing his arms wide, announced in a solemn rolling voice that the gods favored the holding of the games. His voice was drowned by a great roar from the multitude on the Capitoline Hill, as all Rome rushed to obtain the best seats in the Circus Maximus for the inaugural chariot racing.

And so the games proceeded until, delayed deliberately to build the suspense, came what everybody had waited so patiently for, the body sports that appealed so much more to the Roman mob than the Greek tragedy they had been forced to endure for so many days. Crowded into the wonderful new gymnasium built by Nero in the Field of Mars, the mob howled their way through the blood and agony of the boxing, the sweaty grunts of the herculean wrestlers, until, in a final climactic orgy of blood and violence, they came at last to the pancratium.

The pancratium. Merciless—few rules—frequent fatalities. A brutal combination of kicking, punching, catch-as-catch-can, gouging, flesh ripping, genital crunching and bone breaking. Unarmed combat.

The low October sun, still hot, seared the eyes of the two men as they strode onto the sand of the gymnasium. Melancomas—magnificent, the best-known fighter in the civilized world, with "the bull neck and iron shoulders of Atlas, the hair and beard of Heracles, the eyes of a lion"—that was how the fulsome herald described him. Others called him by different names: murderer, a man who knew more fouls than the Emperor knew ballet dancers, "Mr. Fingertips"—because when he was feeling playful, unhurried, he broke your fingers one by one, nicely measuring the intervals at which the appalling crack of bone would echo around the arena.

Against him was Simon, untrained, aging, not one-half but one-third his size, his graceful, lithe, lightly oiled body with not an inch of fat on his belly, a sight of glistening beauty compared to the hirsute, menacing, bulky killer who glared blackly at him. There was no hope, no chance. Even the cruel Roman crowd recognized that they were watching a mere sacrifice for Nero's amusement, and a scatter of protests went up, only to be stilled by the chilling, spellbinding anticipation of rent flesh, spraying blood.

Simon knew this was the end; that in a moment's rashness he had ruined himself. His guts turned to water, but deep down inside him there was the iron streak of a ruthless fighter from the Galilean hills. He would be killed, at the least badly crippled, but he would try and take the murderous Melancomas with him.

They circled, the sun honing their shadows razor-sharp in the sand. Simon went in fast, gut-punching with both fists. The two tree-thick arms of the crouching Melancomas picked him up effortlessly in full flight and flicked him high in the air, Simon's body arching, contorting, before thumping down in the sand. The crowd sighed as Melancomas made no move to straddle him. It would be cruel; the cat was playing with the mouse. Simon's fate would be as appalling as it would be agonizing.

Again Simon rose, his oiled body quivering with summoned energy. He came in slanting, feinting, then smashed a great scything, arching blow at Melancomas' bull neck. The smack of flesh meeting flesh, sweet and true, echoed around the gymnasium, but the big man did not even grunt. Catching Simon's hand, he broke his first three fingers, the separate cracks of breaking bone and Simon's awful scream bringing the bestial crowd to its feet in roaring excitement.

Simon, his left hand hanging useless, went in again. Attack. Attack until you die. He closed with Melancomas, feeling the mother-warmth of the huge man against his flesh, almost comforting, gentle. Too late, he saw those wicked, scythelike claws of fingernails creep around his thigh, aiming to rip out his liver. Blood sprayed everywhere as Simon stiffened in agony. His lips closed on Melancomas' neck, his teeth catching and holding the hot, pulsating windpipe. Nothing would make him let go—nothing. He bit, deeper and deeper until his jaws ached, then he broke skin and the blood—oh, the sweet, hot blood. Melancomas grabbed his genitals and twisted—hard. Simon's throat bulged with the gut scream of bursting, ruined manhood, but his teeth went deeper, even deeper. Now, Melancomas, roaring like a terrified bull, fearing for his life, shifted one hand and his nails dug like hammer claws into Simon's eyeball, ripping out his eye in one appalling movement, the eyeball spinning crazily by its fleshy attachments, twisting under their flailing bodies before bursting into blood and formless flesh. The two men writhed in the sand in their crazy death dance while those teeth sank deeper and deeper until they met. A deluge of blood sprayed a yard high as Melancomas' windpipe severed. Simon knew only relief, the release of tension, the end of all effort, the way it was after making love when, exhausted, you spiraled down into black unconsciousness as he now did.

With Simon's body lying prone in the sand beside the dead Melancomas, now came the ultimate Roman treachery. Seneca, annoyed at the Jew's survival, which meant he could soon be back to claim the money the old senator had in safekeeping, sidled up to Nero and whispered in the Emperor's ear.

"Exiled, was he?" Nero said. The reappearance in Rome of the corps of ballet dancers competing in the games had brought out his homosexuality. He was wearing a flowered diaphanous tunic and his lips were painted prettily. Now they parted as he made a move of simulated anger. "A Jewish troublemaker, eh?" He turned to Tigellinus, captain of the guard. "No reward for him except prison for not asking my permission to return. That is," he said, looking at the racked, twisted body of the once handsome man, lying in the sand with blood pouring from the back of his haunch, one cavernous, moist, black eye socket glaring sightlessly at the sky, "if he lives long enough to get there!"

There was no consciousness. Only a dark, endless tunnel through which occasional, misty rays of light penetrated, always accompanied by tearing pain. The mind knew nothing—but instinct still took hold and prayed for the tunnel to return. In the deep silent blackness there was only peace, but the darkness would not stay forever and the fever-tossed, pain-racked body of Simon ben Eleazar surfaced, shuddered and screamed for release from the agony of ballooning testicles, broken bones and the sharp, searing pain of an empty eye socket still weeping black blood.

At times there were hands—careful, skilled hands that cauterized wounds, spread healing ointments, bound up the seeping blood and stroked the agonized face of the crippled athlete. At first, Simon was not aware of them, not caring, not thinking of anything, secure in his eternal tunnel of darkness which he never wanted to leave, but when those rays of light brought back the appalling agony of semiconsciousness—then there were those hands again to bring peace, to massage, to infuse liquids and secret juices skillfully prepared by the great *medicus* who had discovered them.

One day, weeks later, the one burning eye in his matted, bewhiskered face lost some of its madness and shone into the warder's face with a look of intelligence— the indefinable spark that distinguishes man from animal. The warder knew at once that Simon was at last able to think, to speak. Heavily bribed, he hastened to report the fact, which brought the venerable old *medicus,* together with a bald little man, hurrying to the dark dungeon, carrying out faithfully the orders they had been given, to sustain and help the crippled Jew back to life. Carefully, tenderly, they spoke to him, asking how he felt—with this wound—that wound— feeling, prodding, stroking.

"Water," the man croaked. He was little more, now, than an emaciated shadow. "Who are you? Where am I?"

The doctor rose, gathering his toga around him. "I will return tomorrow and see how he is." The redoubtable Xenophon of Cos had not survived the whims of so many despotic masters without learning a certain agility in avoiding palace intrigues. That he had been given no choice but to attend Simon—and by someone other than Nero whose commands he did not dare disobey—made him especially anxious.

"My name is Alityrus." The fat, bald man had a jolly, red face, cheering to anyone who was with him. "I am a comic actor, although sometimes I am not as comic as I should be."

Simon made no answer. Still hovering between life

and death, he had become exhausted by the effort to talk.

"Take a little bread," the fat man said kindly. He wedged a moistened wafer between Simon's lips, at the same time intoning, *"Boruch utoh Adonoi elohenu melach hoowlom, humoutzie lechem min ho eretz."*

A look of wonderment came into Simon's face. "That prayer," he whispered. "How do you know it?"

"I am a Hebrew like yourself."

"Jewish?" said Simon, then his head fell back. For the first time he slept quietly, with a look of peace on his face as he dreamed of the green hills of Galilee.

It was many days before Simon was ready to talk again, but the fat man was soon there by his side. Simon, a little stronger now, dragged himself to an elbow. "The blessing on taking bread," he croaked, "it was you who said it?"

"Yes."

"Repeat the blessing."

"But there is no bread."

"It does not matter. Repeat the blessing. I want to hear it again." His voice was feverish.

Alityrus shrugged, then said, *"Boruch utoh adowshem—"*

"Enough." Simon's hand shot out, clawlike, gripping his arm with sudden strength. "I know now that you are a friend—that I am among my own."

Alityrus had refused to take the name of the Lord in vain, since the bread had not been eaten, and had employed instead the sound *shem* to neuter the second half of the holy word *Adonoi.* Such a thing was not likely to be known to any impostor. Simon was sure that the man was a Jew. Terribly wounded as he was, with his life in the balance, he no longer felt abandoned. He was back with his own people who cared about him, were willing to nurse him.

The necessary steps back to health were not maintained. With Simon chained to the wall, deprived of fresh air, sunshine and exercise, it could not have been otherwise. Only by constantly increasing bribery was his cell kept clean and his food made reasonably palatable. There was no doubt that despite the secret ministrations of Xenophon of Cos, Simon should have been dead weeks ago. That he was still alive was due to Alityrus.

Only courage would determine whether he lived or died. To every man in middle age, there comes a crossroad, a moment when his juices begin to run slower. Then he either gives in, grows a paunch and spirals downward, or, ignoring the time clock, fights on. A question of spirit.

Alityrus now supplied that spirit. Always, he seemed to be there, wiping Simon's brow, attentive, never impatient. When the fever came back, sending streams of sweat down the wasted limbs of the agonized man on the straw pallet, Alityrus was by his side, murmuring words of encouragement and tenderness in Aramaic. The crazed wreck clutched at him with skeletal hands, weeping from his one mad, staring eye, dreaming in his delirium of the spring flowers of his youth, the goats feeding on the sweet green grass of the Galilee hills. Slowly, through the pain of his shattered hand, swollen genitals, mutilated in body and blind of one eye, he regained the will to live.

To fuel and sustain it, Alityrus told him of the plight of the Jews, of how the Greek communities in Judaea, Syria and Egypt were everywhere preferred to them, of indignity after indignity suffered by the Jew in his own land at the hands of priests manipulated by the foreign puppets of their Roman masters.

"Why do you tell me all this?" Simon asked one day.

"Because it has long been foretold that you will be a great leader of the Jews."

"Foretold?"

"There is a legend of a Jewish gladiator who will return to his homeland from Rome—a great soldier who knows military tactics. Such a man will be known by the ring he carries. It is said that Herod Agrippa, knowing himself not to be a true Jew, parted with this ring more than twenty years ago, and when this gladiator returns to his homeland bearing such a ring, then the guerrilla bands hiding in the wilderness will unite and with his help deal the Romans great blows."

"I no longer have this ring," said Simon.

For an answer, Alityrus fished inside his tunic, and when his hand appeared again, it bore the glint of gold. Simon, with astonishment, realized that it was none other than the ring he had given to Messalina—Herod's own personal ring, reputed once to have belonged to King David himself and carrying the menorah sign. "We have a friend in high places," the little fat man said smilingly, as he fitted the ring to Simon's finger. "Poppaea, shortly to be Empress, has the run of the imperial wardrobe. She is a staunch patron of the Jews. Now will you help us fulfill the legend, lead us home to fight? Rome is no place for Jews. Only our patron Poppaea protects us from the madman Nero."

"So this is why you have nursed me back to health, protected me so well?"

"It has long been foretold," Alityrus repeated stubbornly.

"To lead you home," Simon said, "I must first be free. Perhaps your patron—"

"No," Alityrus cut in. "Hide you—that she can do, but to engineer your escape is a job for the strong arms of powerful friends."

"Of which I have none."

"Think." There was real urgency in Alityrus' voice. "Think again. In Rome, much store is set on personal obligations between men—on the returning of favors received in the past."

"I have no such friends on whom I can call."

"There must be someone," Alityrus persisted, "one man in all your army career, perhaps now promoted, in a position of power—who is in your debt—"

"One man," Simon whispered. "Perhaps one man, but the debt is an old one and he is far away."

"Tell me." Alityrus, sensing the other's feebleness, put his face close to Simon's mouth. "Tell me his name. I must know now."

Simon, before lapsing into unconsciousness, told him.

24

For Princess Andrasta of the royal house of the Iceni, the fight was not to survive but, in her servitude, to prevent that precious kernel of free will and intelligent thought from being extinguished.

Soft-skinned, almost fragile, she could be made to do anything physical, however disgusting. There seemed little point in resisting; her body could suffer nothing worse than it had already at the hands of Catus Decianus and his thugs in her mother's hut at Caister-by-Norwich—but her soul, that tiny spark of freedom, the light of her own being, she would let nobody have that.

As it happened, conditions in the house of her master, Pedanius Secundus, had not been too bad at first. Since Secundus was an important man—he was city prefect and chief of internal security—his house was a handsome one and even the living quarters for slaves more than adequate. But when his wife had taken Andrasta as a lady's maid—that was when her troubles had really begun. The cruelty of Roman matrons was notorious and Cornelia, Pedanius Secundus' vain, middle-aged wife, was no exception.

Every morning, it would begin: Andrasta with two other lady's maids having to attend their mistress, rushing hither and thither, never daring to collide with each other, fear in their faces as they piled Cornelia's dyed blond hair on top of her head, curling it with tongs into a big, soft mass—and God help them if any of the curls so carefully tucked in should come adrift during the day. After touching the hair delicately all over with slightly oily hands to secure it in place, then came the long job, as they crouched by the side of Cornelia's seated figure, of painting on the white makeup intended to make her resemble a marble statue in complexion, the illusion being completed by powdering over with a mixture of chalk and white lead. Then, after shaving her eyebrows and daubing her eyelashes with a layer of black kohl, would come the laborious job of fitting the beautiful silk dress—the *stola matronalis*—that reached down to her ankles, and pray no stain, no blemish would suddenly appear, no stitch somehow come loose, or the girls would be kicked and beaten like dogs with all the strength at the stout woman's command.

There came a day when, with a sudden excess of rage, Cornelia grabbed hold of one of the slim arms of the youngest slave girl and, with a sudden jerk, broke it.

Her brother happened to be passing at the time—they had been bought as a pair—and out of his mind with grief at the crack of bone and the agonized cry that followed, he hastened to Pedanius Secundus, asking him to save the girl further pain. When Secundus refused, there and then he wrung his master's neck.

Strangely enough, there was no terrible retribution, no *furca*, no hangings or crucifixions, no scourging. And there was a very good reason. The law, only just strengthened by the Senate to deal with such cases, decreed that every single slave of a murdered owner must be put to death. At the thought of four hundred men and women being encased in wax, then ceremoniously burned to a cinder, even jaded Rome drew back—and rioted.

It was strange how the Roman mob, perhaps the cruelest ever known, could by some quirk of mercy take up a cause. It had allowed Simon life in the arena, forcing first Caligula and then Claudius to bow to its will, and in the same way it now demanded life for the slaves of Pedanius Secundus. A constitutional crisis took place with Rome simmering, Nero vacillating and a howling mob besieging the Senate House, while inside the eminent jurist Gaius Cassius Longinus demanded the death penalty, using such elegant humanist phrases as "The only way to keep down this scum is by intimidation."

216

For the slaves, cooped up in jail, time hung heavily, and Andrasta found her thoughts returning more and more to the man who had run like a line of obstinate thread through the disturbed fabric of her life.

How many times had he rescued her from danger—from imminent death? Yet he had always seemed to be one of them, the accursed, ruling Romans. She had heard that he had come to Rome and fought a wrestling contest, with her as the prize to the victor—well, she was no plaything to be fought over as a trophy. Sitting on the floor, aloof from the other slaves, instinctively receiving respect from them as a princess of royal blood, she tossed her tawny hair with indignation at the very thought. But there was more to it than that. It was rumored that he had somehow incurred the Emperor's displeasure and was, like her, now languishing in prison. The thought of that whipcord body, those glowing gray-green eyes, that fair skin always so deeply tanned by the sun, rotting in some dungeon, disturbed her. Hating him for his quiet superiority, animal beauty, his Roman uniform, she now found conflicting emotions of tenderness and sympathy. Suddenly she remembered good things, how eagerly she had looked forward to the visits of her uncle Simon as a young girl, and those presents that he had always brought with him; his voice, never raised, always patient; and his gentleness.

Now he too was experiencing misfortune, with perhaps death imminent at the Emperor's hands, and she wept, not for herself, because she was nothing more than a slave with a burned-out husk of a seventeen-year-old body and it was not in her nature to weep over personal misfortune—she wept instead for an arrogant, Romanized Jew.

Unknown to her, the object of her thoughts fought on for life, not at the hands of the Emperor Nero, but in a desperate battle against the effects of his wounds.

Somehow the hard steel core of the man triumphed. Comforted and supported by Alityrus, his body knitted itself together, the single eye taking on a burning, feverish brightness to compensate for the other. He would not, Simon knew, ever have a woman again. The sac between his legs had been thoroughly crushed by the expert hands of the pancratiast, but life still had other compensations. He had a country to fight for. A cause. If only he could get out, walk, run, breathe fresh air, feel the sun on his emaciated flesh and his muscles hardening from physical work, then he would live to fight again. All he lacked was his freedom and this was not long in coming.

One night, as he lay restlessly dozing, the gloomy dungeon was suddenly full of men dressed identically in black masks—soldiers, by their uniforms.

With the burly guard gagged, blindfolded and trussed, one of the soldiers gave a signal and another, responding instantly to the order, sprang forward with a hammer and spike and with a single, massive blow freed Simon's thin neck from the iron collar.

Simon tried to rise to his feet, but his legs crumpled and he sank dizzily to the ground. Gently, effortlessly, the soldiers lifted his frail body erect.

The man who had been standing in a corner of the cell, arms akimbo, giving the orders, now moved swiftly across to Simon and embraced him in a huge bear hug. Setting his mouth close to Simon's ear, he murmured, "Three debts to pay, old friend. I intend to honor them all and hang the consequences."

Quickly the man released him and, nodding to his companions to go first, reluctantly followed, leaving Simon in the gloom alongside the trussed, blindfolded figure of the guard.

Seconds later Alityrus, who had been provided with a fast chaise pulled by two good horses, burst in and carried Simon's wasted body from the prison. As Alityrus urged the horses to a gallop, Simon lay back, heart pounding, quivering with excitement, unbelieving. Yet there was no doubt. No doubt at all. Over the years, you did not easily forget that smell of peasant, garlic breath, the broad barnyard voice, the burly set of shoulder. Simon had identified his rescuer at once. His old friend, the best friend he had ever had, who, risking his life, career and future, had returned from Africa just to free a stray Jew from the Emperor's dungeon.

At last he was no longer chained like an animal to a damp wall, able once again to gaze at the black vault of the heavens. He opened his mouth wide, breathing the sharp, clear nectar of the stars. A warm glow of comfort stayed with him from that parting bear hug of his old commander. Vespasian.

The snorting horses galloped along at top speed, foam flecking their jaws. It would not take long for news of the escape to spread to the *vigiles,* and by use of the semaphore a cordon could be thrown across all main roads leading out of Rome.

There was only one place to go: Poppaea's mountain retreat, a large tract of wild country set high in the Apennines. The first two hours would be all-important. After that, one would be safe.

They tore along through the warm spring night, with Alityrus driving the horses until they could barely manage a droop-headed walk, but it was enough. They were now nearly thirty miles out of Rome and turning off the arrow-straight, poplar-lined highway. The greenly fertile fields of the valleys had already given way to soft, round, forested hills as they followed a narrow serpentine track that wound endlessly back on itself as they climbed higher and higher into the mountains.

As the sun rose, the frail, white-faced invalid screwed up his one eye at the unaccustomed brightness, then slowly, painfully uncoiled himself, taking in great gulps of the morning freshness. He listened to the song of the goldfinches and serins, the shrill cry of the wryneck, the birdsong of choughs, thrushes, alpine warblers, not believing that anything could be so lovely as that Apennine dawn. While the plodding, sweat-stained horses climbed, he gazed at the herds of red deer that crossed the track in front of them, the friendly brown bears lolloping alongside the chaise, their cubs quite unaware of the danger presented by man. That night, in a hut set in a densely wooded beech forest, Simon lay panting and fatigued, and strangely at peace. Nero, Alityrus had assured him, would not send troops to Poppaea's estate in search of one runaway Jew, or even give voice to his suspicion that she was hiding him, for fear of losing the affection of the amber-haired beauty with whom he was known to be wildly in love.

Simon stayed free, nursing his wounds, his body growing stronger, his flesh healing. By November that year he was walking in the forests, tanned, wiry, his muscles beginning to ripple with strength once again. With his youth now gone, the pancratium had also deprived him of his looks. He resembled more and more one of the shaggy, fierce old wolves which often gathered outside his hut at night to bay at the full moon. Despite the new spring in his step, the sac between his legs still lay swollen and uselessly twisted, and the hate Simon stored up for Rome grew into a pervading obsession.

Also in November of that year, the fate of the slaves belonging to the murdered Pedanius Secundus was hideously resolved, the Senate voting in favor of mass execution and Nero approving their verdict. Rome rioted and Nero rebuked the city by edict and lined the whole execution route to the Forum with *vigiles* and Praetorian Guards. For Andrasta, as she marched into the killing ground, the end would be almost welcome. The tall, slim princess had known little in her young life except cruelty and the most foul bodily abuse. Death would come as a reward, rather than a punishment. Now, she stood erect and defiant. Her hands were tied to a stake and the slave began smearing the incendiary wax on her smooth, fine skin. She would die like a princess, ignoring the agony, head up, tawny hair tossing with defiance, the way her mother would have wished.

Her eyes ranging haughtily over the slaves tying the victims with rough indifference, she saw a sudden disturbance at the back of the Forum. A white stallion ridden by a curiously masked man had burst in and the plunging, rearing beast was scything a path with its sharp, ironshod hooves straight toward her. Two city guards threw themselves at the man, trying to pull him from the saddle. *Slash—slash*—went the horseman's sword and two decapitated corpses rolled in their own blood. A centurion, leaping for the bridle, had a dagger driven with amazing precision right through a crack in his articulated armor. In no time the horseman was at her side. *Slash*—went his sword again as he severed her bonds in one sharp stroke. She found herself being lifted unceremoniously across the man's knee. With a snarl, he dug spurs into the stallion's sides and took off in a huge bound, carving a bloody trail through the soldiers and slaves who tried to bar his way, until he was out of the

Forum, galloping fast as light through Rome's narrow streets until he reached open country. Now, with no sign of pursuit, he slackened his pace, allowing his horse to rest as he took the road southeast toward his lair in the Apennines.

A little later, he allowed the girl to arrange herself in a more dignified position. She had time to study the lower, unmasked portion of her rescuer's face, particularly the scarred mouth which caused his lips to droop. She also noticed the three deformed fingers on his hand.

"I do not know you," she said, "but I thank you, whoever you are."

The man nodded and pushed the stallion into a canter, keeping his face pointed straight ahead so that she could not see the hurt in his eye.

Later that evening, the Emperor Nero took part in a most enjoyable orgy. His cronies had conceived the idea of a mock wedding night and Nero entered the spirit of the thing.

Wearing a fishnet robe of pure spun gold, he was conducted to the wedding couch and found there waiting for him a delicious slave boy by the name of Sporus, castrated many weeks earlier in preparation for this very occasion. The depraved Emperor's pleasure knew no bounds. Lying in bed, his fat, made-up face simpering at his drunken, dissolute courtiers, he pinched and stroked the boy, wondering if his satin skin was finer and smoother than that of Poppaea, reputed as it was to be bathed in the milk of five hundred she-asses each day.

Even after a breathless messenger brought news of the Princess Andrasta's rescue from the Forum, Nero was in a sufficiently good mood to laugh it off. Remembering his conversation with Simon ben Eleazar, he knew at once who the rescuer was and found himself admiring the daring of the man. In any event there was nothing he could do if he still wished to keep the affections of Poppaea.

Dismissing the matter from his mind, Nero ordered his friends from his bedchamber so that he might devote his attention fully to the slave boy. Nero would never make a bigger error than to discount Simon so casually. The Jew would live to cause him, the Roman army, the whole Roman Empire, endless trouble.

Later that night, Nero's carousing friends heard a peculiar braying sound. Clustering around the door of his bedchamber, one of them peeked through the keyhole, then recounted what he saw in disbelief. With the aid of his powerful trained voice, the Emperor was lying on his back, plump legs in the air, imitating the groans of a virgin being deflowered.

25

Andrasta lay in her bunk, listening to the moaning of the icy wind. The long Apennine winter had begun and outside the hut snow lay thick upon the forest. Inside—under suitable conditions—it might have been warm and snug.

The girl had to admit she was puzzled. She was grateful to this man who had once again proved her protector, her heart thoroughly softened toward him by reason of his bravery and self-sacrifice. With a little encouragement, she was almost ready—to love him.

Strangely, he gave her no such encouragement. Not only did he wear this large black mask over his face day and night, but made not the slightest effort to come near her, lying silent and withdrawn, on his pallet.

It was as if he were made of stone. The girl was truly puzzled.

One night, Andrasta made a point of feeding Simon too much of the local, strong wine, and when he lay snoring on his pallet, she crept over to him and, by the light of the brilliantly flickering fire, gently peeled off his mask and gazed upon his face.

When Simon awoke and found his mask gone, he moaned desperately and twisted to the wall.

Patiently, her fingers pursued him, massaging the back of his neck, kneading his mass of thick, black hair. With gentle coaxing she managed to turn Simon's face back to her, but instead of shrinking with revulsion at the sight of his distorted features as he had expected, the girl laid her head against his, the haughty proudness of her mouth softened into infinite tenderness.

"Are you not—revolted?" he asked.

"By this?" She kissed the empty, blackened monstrosity of his eye socket. "Or this?" She ran a slim finger down the livid scar incised from eyelid to mouth by the cruel nails of the pancratiast. "Surely not this?" Taking his mutilated hand softly in her own, she gently kissed the twisted remains of his fingers.

"I—I do not understand."

"When you were a handsome colonel, I hated you. Now your scars, inflicted by Rome, do you honor. Henceforth I shall be your woman." She climbed into his arms.

So, for all the following year—the spring, when the sound of rushing streams reminded Simon of his native Galilee, the hot, dusty Italian summer, relieved only by the champagne coolness of the alpine nights—they tended their few cattle, their small vegetable patch, a son of a village chief and a princess of royal blood, content to live simply as peasants, happy with each other's company. Lovers they were, but only of the soul, not of the body—and it was strong, enduring, in talk, in laughter, in silence and in sleep.

Soon enough, the early mountain winter was upon them again and the whole cycle of one, then another year, followed, until at length spring came to them a third time, finding Simon refreshed, teaklike in body, strong in spirit, his mask now discarded in favor of a menacing black eye patch which made the permanent leer on his face even more sinister. Vengefully, impatiently, Simon waited for Alityrus' summons.

When the time for action arrived there was no warning, the chance for the Jews to leave Rome coming almost as a miracle.

"Fire," Alityrus said hoarsely. His eyes were red and staring and there were black daubs of smut and charcoal

223

all over his face. "Rome burns! Now, while the city is in flames, comes our chance to go home."

Simon gripped the little actor by the shoulder. "Explain."

"Normally," Alityrus said, "Jews cannot leave Rome without a permit, but the guards cannot stop refugees fleeing the capital."

"How many will volunteer to go?" Simon asked.

"Well, it's dangerous. Fifty—perhaps seventy of us will face the risk. Possibly a hundred, with children."

"We'll need a ship," Simon said, pacing up and down, thinking. "Fast, seaworthy for a long trip, yet big enough for the numbers."

"Where?" Alityrus spread his hands. "Ravenna, Puteoli, Ostia?"

"None of those," Simon said decisively. Suddenly he snapped his fingers. "I have it. Misenum."

"Misenum?" Alityrus blanched. "The imperial naval base? Are you mad? We'll be walking into a death-trap—"

Simon's one eye went cold. He placed his bronzed, muscled hand in front of Alityrus' face so that his golden ring sparkled in the sun. "If I am to be your leader, obey me. Otherwise, get someone else."

Alityrus thought for a full minute before replying. "I will obey you," he said.

As the light chaise with its three occupants bucketed and lurched toward Rome, a livid, pink light in the sky could be seen from many miles away. It had indeed been an enormous conflagration. Starting in the Circus where it adjoined the Palatine and Caelian hills, it reached shops selling inflammable goods and had quickly sped the whole length of the Circus. With no walled mansions or temples to obstruct it, the fire swept violently over the level spaces. Feeding on itself, it had outstripped any countermeasure and, trapped and choking in the city's narrow winding streets, the population had panicked. Even two days after the worst of the fire, with only odd corners of smoking buildings and red-hot cinders to be dealt with, hysterical, shrieking people ran in all directions. With the whole city in turmoil and masses of refugees on the move,

Alityrus and his two companions were not interfered with by soldiers or the city guard. Indeed, Nero had found other, more specific uses for the *vigiles* and the Praetorian cohort.

His own popularity in jeopardy as a result of the fire, Nero had looked for a scapegoat, and found one: the Christians.

Now, as Simon, Andrasta and Alityrus rumbled across the Roman pavé, crossing the city before reaching the Appian Way, they did so in a night made hideous by the screaming, writhing Christians, crucified at intervals, their wax-covered bodies aflame, making the Roman night as bright as day. Nero, amused by the spectacle provided by the deaths of Pedanius Secundus' slaves, had decided to improve on the idea, and was now using the Christians as streetlighting.

Alityrus shuddered, trying to calm the nervous horses, who could smell the burning flesh. "You are right," he said to Simon. "We must use courage and endeavor, leave this country at any cost, even to seizing that warship."

"You have suffered a change of heart, old friend."

"Today," replied Alityrus thoughtfully, "the Jews would have burned instead of the Christians, had it not been for Poppaea—but it is said that Nero now grows tired of her. Her days are numbered and so are the Jews in this city." As if to emphasize his point, he clicked his tongue at the horses, urging them to a tired trot.

For a long time they were silent, until they had left the appalling stench of burning bodies behind them and Rome was no more than a distant glow in the darkness. Turning to Alityrus, Simon told him, "When we reach Campania, I must leave you for a day. Assemble the Jews outside Misenum and wait there for my return."

"Where will you go?" Andrasta said, a catch in her voice. The girl sat, silent and withdrawn, through the macabre horrors, but the thought of losing the man she loved more than life itself, even for a day, brought her to tears.

"Do not concern yourself," said Simon grimly.

There was such a menacing note in his voice that conversation fell silent. They moved ever southward until, halting the team at a quiet spot where only the

225

bullfrogs croaked and the cicadas buzzed in the hot summer night, all of them—men, woman and beasts— slept.

The bright red and yellow terra-cotta tiles that roofed Seneca's villa were almost hidden in the profusion of trees, bushes and wild flowers that grew so lushly in the fertile Campanian soil. Cut into a southwest-facing cliff near Herculaneum, the villa was open to the sea, sun and fresh air of a particularly favored climate, while affording complete shelter from the chill northerly winds of winter. By building on two levels, the old philosopher had created the privacy he needed for writing and could sit in his peristyle in complete solitude, admiring his idyllic surroundings yet needing only to tinkle a bell for his slaves to come running.

The garden was truly delightful. The soil could nurture and sustain any manner of exotic blooms. Wild pear, fig, pomegranate and chestnut trees grew with abandon next to vines, roses and honeysuckle, carefully planted to harmonize with nature by Greeks learned in the art. No sound could be heard except for the lazy drone of bees, the tinkle of many fountains cascading into pools of water lilies. From an aviary set in a shaded corner the song of rare birds contributed to the impression of paradise on earth.

Seneca bent in concentration as he finished one of his letters to his friend Lucilius Secundus. As he read it back, his withered old mouth quirked in amusement at the philosophy that railed so eloquently against the amassing of money and counseled a strict regime of poverty for the better discipline of the mind. What a pleasantly enjoyable joke his life had been. He had achieved every success, sampled every pleasure, experienced every delight while advising the whole of the civilized world how to be miserable for its own good!

Only two years ago he had seemed as good as dead. Had not that immoral pimp, that villainous scoundrel Tigellinus, finally obtained his coveted promotion to chief of the Praetorian Guard and, ruling Rome with a reign of terror, set out to destroy Nero's former adviser? Whispered against, plotted against, awaiting Nero's death sentence at any moment, Seneca had acted quickly. Presenting himself at the palace, resignation in hand, he had asked Nero to accept most of his wealth. Nero, with just the right amount of persuasion, had taken the gift, still leaving Seneca in comfortable circumstances and free to retire to the country and write his essays. Yes, he had been very fortunate. Now, ensconced in his bacchic heaven, he was still not too old to enjoy the sun, the scent of lovely flowers, the occasional velvety comfort of a young boy or girl held against his gnarled body. Yes, he thought, I am indeed a lucky man.

A noise made him lift his head, a movement from the lush undergrowth. Perhaps an intruder lurked there. Fear showing on his gaunt features, he reached for the slave bell, but a rough hand with three twisted fingers clamped on top of his own, pinning it to the table.

Seneca looked at the man who now stood at his side, a mocking smile on his face, a curved dagger balanced idly in his fingers. That face—Seneca had seen it before; it reminded him of someone he knew, but could not recall. A black patch covered one eye and a scar ran diagonally across the face, kinking both the upper and lower lips in a decided droop. An ugly, menacing face. And that hand, that distorted, mutilated hand—Seneca shuddered. An ex-gladiator? Then, as Simon spoke to him, he knew, he remembered and shuddered once more. "Old man," Simon said. "Twice you have betrayed me. Are you ready to die?"

"Kill me and you will never leave here alive."

"Then we will travel to Hades together. Do you not say in your essays that one should associate with people who are likely to improve you?"

As Seneca smiled, trying to nod acknowledgment of Simon's sally, despite the fingers that gripped his throat, Simon had the sudden feeling that this was not the way, that he should not murder the old man. "All right, Seneca," he whispered, "live a little longer. Why should I kill you now when Nero will soon do it for me? First retirement, then the order to kill yourself, out of the blue. There's no escape. That's the way of life, isn't it, Seneca? As a philosopher you ought to know something about that. How long have you got?" He leered into the old man's face, noting how white it had become. "How

227

long? Nero grows more savage all the time. A month? Maybe three. Perhaps a year? He won't let you last longer than that. So why should I give you a quick death when the Emperor has awarded you the lingering one you deserve? So live on, old man. Watch the road for messengers, for the imperial post, for a maniple of soldiers. Remember—it can come from so many directions."

Quickly, in one lithe bound, Simon was gone, merging into the thick undergrowth before Seneca could gather his wits and call for help. For one brief second, Simon had experienced the satisfaction of seeing mortal terror on the old man's face.

From now on, Seneca would live every single hour of his life in expectation of Nero's death sentence. The thought of it would sap his health and attack his reason until he would come to beg for the cold bite of the sword through his vitals as a merciful release. For some the threat would mean nothing, but a mind as sensitive as his would find the agony of waiting a drawn-out hellish torture.

Simon had discovered a fundamental truth: those who live by the sword die by the sword, and those who live by words die by words. He had exacted a fitting revenge.

First thing in the morning, Simon made his rendezvous with the Jews on the southern outskirts of Misenum. The people that Alityrus had managed to assemble were a mixed bunch. Although Simon was disturbed at the number of young children and nursing mothers, they would at least, as refugees from fire-torn Rome, be received sympathetically in the town.

Soon, as the procession wound down the hill, the glittering sweep of the finest natural harbor on the west coast of Italy came into view. Once the crater of an extinct volcano, the bay was linked to a previously landlocked lagoon, inside which the Roman western fleet could moor and use the dockyard facilities in perfect safety whatever the season.

As Simon had expected, the ragged procession was met with expressions of sympathy and evoked no suspicion. Thus enabled to look over the ships in harbor,

Simon halted the Jews and conferred with Alityrus. "That one," Alityrus said, excitement in his voice. "She looks perfect." He pointed to a large bireme complete with fighting turret that appeared to be in the last stages of provisioning.

Simon was just about to agree when he noticed the rakish war galley moored to the quay immediately behind the bireme. "No," he said. "We take the galley."

"But it will sink," Alityrus said wildly. "The first rough sea and down it will go. It is built for speed in calm coastal waters only."

"Precisely," Simon said, "and at this moment, the sea is flat calm. So what would happen, do you think, if we took that heavy bireme?"

"The galley will catch it," Alityrus said, as understanding suddenly dawned.

"And if we take the galley?"

"It will not be caught."

"Precisely."

Alityrus, always ready to admit when he was in the wrong, put his arm around Simon's shoulder. "As always you are quite right," he said, "and we are privileged to have you leading us. What now?"

"A little piece of bluff," said Simon grimly. "Detach the strongest young men we have and form them into a party. Wait for my signal."

Striding boldly on board the galley, Simon was suddenly aware of the deafening sound of hammering as slaves made good the wooden cover protecting a small enclosure underneath the vessel's high, incurving stem. A young ensign of marines strode up and saluted Simon, then, silencing the carpenters with a sweep of his gauntleted hand, said, "Yes? What do you want?"

"Where is your captain?"

"Down below. May I inquire as to your business?"

"I am Quinctus Torpilius, senator." Before the ensign could ask for identification, Simon went on, "I have come direct from Rome to ask for marines to help fight the great fire."

"Then you are too late, sir. The marines have already left for that very purpose, and most of the crew has been given shore leave. We are profiting from the delay by effecting small repairs."

Simon, unable to believe his good fortune, said, "Please ask the captain to come up."

The ensign saluted and turned to go below. Now was the time when Simon would have to act with lightning speed. He looked at Alityrus and let out a sharp whistle. In a flash twenty young Jews had rushed up the gangway and, with the advantage of surprise, over-powered the unsuspecting carpenters, pinioning their arms behind them.

"What's going on?" the captain raged, emerging through the hatch. He had heard the thunder of feet and the scuffle with the carpenters. For an answer he got Simon's boot in his face and hurtled back down the steps, half stunned. The ensign, light and slim, threw himself at Simon, only to bend like an inverted bow, snarling in agony as a throwing knife buried itself to the hilt in his throat. He was already dead before he hit the bottom step.

"Quickly," Simon shouted. "Get everyone aboard."

No time to pause, no time to think. He leaped down through the hatch, blinking in the unaccustomed gloom. The smell hit him, giving instant recall of old agonies, old tragedies, the smell of animals in captivity, the mixture of feces and urine that was impossible to eradicate. He could see the galley slaves, white-bodied, hunch-shouldered from rowing, crouched in listless torpor over their oars, uninterested in the fighting that had taken place. He remembered how it was; when, at one curt command, you could be made to row for hours in insufferable, blinding heat, muscles screaming for respite from the slave master's lash, then you rested when you could. You slept. Nothing else mattered. Nothing at all.

All this he took in. There was only one way to catch their attention. Snatching up the whip, he let it whistle through the air and, as one, their backs straightened, tensing and crouching over the oars. "I bring you freedom," he roared. "Only row us out of harbor and you are free." The slaves made no move. Reduced to the level of beasts of burden, their senses were too dulled to understand. "Look," Simon shouted. "No more of this." He pitched the whip out of an oar hole. "Do you not understand? You have the fastest ship in the harbor.

Row clear of the quay and you are free." Still the slaves made no move.

Suddenly, Simon heard sharp commands being given on the bireme close by and the menacing patter of feet as her crew swarmed down the gangway.

Cursing with frustration, he rushed up on deck. He was just in time to see a naval officer give a detachment of sailors the order to board. Teeth bared, he unshipped his last three throwing knives and sent them whistling home with enormous accuracy into the chests of the sailors while still in midair, so that they came down heavily on the gunwale or tumbled into the water between galley and quay. "Fight," he yelled in a cracked voice. "Show them how Jews can fight." But it was too late. Hindered by the mass of women and children gathered in the bow and stern, the Jewish fighting men could do nothing. One by one the sailors hit the deck and advanced, swords at the ready, prepared to scythe down the terror-stricken refugees. Then Simon happened to look at the water. At first he could not believe it. He looked again. It was true! They were away from the dock, the precious gap widening with every rhythmic stroke of the oars.

The six or seven sailors who had gotten on board took in the situation at a glance. Without further ado, they leaped off the galley and swam for their lives.

Grinning at each other, watching the shoreline recede, hardly able to believe their good fortune, the Jews let out a great cheer that was echoed by the slaves below, sweating and straining at the great sweeps.

Simon immediately went to them. He personally removed their manacles and promised them a new life in Judaea.

And so in the high summer of AD 64 a heavily laden war galley, riding deep in the water with the men, women and children it carried, passed through the Straits of Messina and headed across the Adriatic toward Greece.

Before long, a howling gale sprang up, and after three days of storm the galley was a mess of filth. Only the former slaves, used to terrible conditions, rowed their hearts out to maintain steerage way. Simon could see that they were nearing exhaustion and must rest soon.

With no replacements, the galley, designed for use in calm waters, would founder the moment the waves put her broadside to the wind. Accordingly he went around the merchants, shopkeepers and factors who made up most of the male Jews, organizing their stints at the oars on a shift basis. Everything went well enough until he approached a group who, by their long white robes, were obviously Hasidim—holy men belonging to an ultrareligious sect of the Hebrew faith.

They had, right from the outset of the journey, kept up an almost continuous chanting, careful even in the most fearsome weather to place their phylacteries on fingers and forehead. Left to themselves, they had been troubled by nobody—until Simon asked their leader to spare the seven able-bodied men in their group for the oars.

"They cannot do such work," the leader said flatly. "These are holy men."

"That is no excuse."

"You do not understand. They are not frightened of work, but they may do no other than pray, grow food and give to the poor."

"Are you not giving to the poor, if by helping at the oars you save life?"

The leader scratched his aged, shrewd face and smiled. There was nothing he liked better than a debate—to construe God's holy word. Arguments into the small hours on the minutiae of the Jewish faith were meat and drink to him. "My men could perhaps row," he said, after minutes of careful thought, "for the purpose of doing a good deed, but not when matters of survival are involved. At such a time, we can only pray to the Almighty."

"Some of you may pray, but your men will row," Simon said angrily.

Jeremiah shook his head, his face wreathed in a saintly smile. He had met obstinate men before and had always bettered them.

"Very well," Simon snapped. "If you will not do your bit, you will receive no rations." He strode away, furious, marshaling such other passengers as he could find.

The storm screaming down from the mountains grew rather than diminished in strength, and Simon and Alityrus joined the relief shift, working at the huge timber sweeps until their muscles groaned with fatigue.

With the Hasidim refused food or drink, the rest of the ship benefited by the increase in rations, but the next day Andrasta, who had hitherto been content to allow Simon a free hand, approached him. "You must give them sustenance."

"I will give them nothing."

"The children at least. For them, hunger is terrible."

"Nothing."

"Worry sits heavily on your shoulders and has affected your judgment," she said. She strode off, leaving Simon red-eyed and gray with fatigue, staring after her, as she went to prepare food for the Hasidim.

To Andrasta's amazement the refreshment she offered Jeremiah he refused, even for the smallest children. It was only after considerable persuasion that he consented to allow a few sips of water for the youngest of the babies. "It is no new thing for the Jews to suffer for their beliefs," he told her. "For us it is a privilege."

Three days later, the storm still blew and the Hasidim now lay hunched and shivering, holding each other for warmth, only their eyes shining in the refinement of their suffering. Simon walked over to them. "You have won and I have lost," he told Jeremiah. "Your beliefs will be respected." Turning to Andrasta, he asked her to distribute food and water. The beautiful girl stood on her toes, kissed him lightly and murmured, "I love you," then disappeared to make the arrangements.

"Where will you go when we reach Judaea?" Simon asked Jeremiah.

"To join our brethren at Qumran. There is a monastery there where we can live our lives simply and in the worship of God, copying scrolls."

Glancing out at the stormy sea, Simon asked, amusement showing on his face, "And you will live to see Qumran?"

"We have prayed for the safety of the ship," came the answer.

Simon was on the verge of making some sarcastic reply when he noticed that the continuous roar of the wind had suddenly diminished and that for the first time in almost a week the sun shone through the clouds. The change in the weather seemed to have come at the moment he had conceded victory to Jeremiah. A look of beatific smugness was now spreading over the old man's shrewd, Semitic face that made Simon go cold with rage. Controlling himself with difficulty, he turned away to deal with the ever-changing problems of setting course.

Simon, in experiencing the stiff-necked attitude of the chosen race, their obstinacy, their separatism, their perverseness, their courage, was seeing the Jews as the Gentiles saw them. He had begun to learn why his people tried the patience of the civilized world. They were not at all, he conceded wryly, an easy people to deal with.

They closed with the coast of Judaea in fine, hot summer weather in the month of September, the port of Caesarea slowly coming into view through the morning mist. When Simon saw the six colossal statues lining the handsome two-hundred-foot mole, the sun reflecting off the huge white marble Temple of Augustus that dominated the harbor, his face, instead of expressing awe, parted in a snarl. Those great Roman monstrosities were symbols—symbols of grinding taxation, of foreign domination which must end soon.

Now, twenty-seven years later, at the age of forty-three, he was returning to make good his oath to his father, to see that Rome suffered for its cruelty.

An experienced soldier, trained in the intricacies of total war as fought by the Romans, Simon knew he had much to offer. He would take volunteers and head for the hills of Galilee that he had known in his youth. There, somewhere, he would make contact with the guerrillas— the insurgents—the mad, brave, Jewish freedom-fighters who, from their lairs in the hills, had never ceased to harry the power of Rome.

Together, they would reap a whirlwind.

PART
IV

JUDAEA
(64–70 CE)

"Their drills bloodless battles,
their battles blood drills."

—Josephus, on the
Roman army

26

It had been a hot summer in Galilee, the wind from the vast, ovenlike interior of Asia blowing more often than usual, turning the green hills around Mount Tabor a rusty brown.

John of Gishala squinted out across the dusty plain and scowled with boredom. His men were getting restless. Once there had been good pickings—caravan after caravan laden with fine wines, spices and incense, plodding from Jerusalem to Caesarea, or following the endless trade routes that fanned out from Ptolemais to Parthia or the kingdoms lying to the east of the Sea of Galilee. John was a bandit, a brigand, and so had been his father before him. He and his men could never remember a time when it had not been a pleasure to relieve rich Jews, thriving on Roman protection, of their money—and there once had been plenty for all. He remembered with glee how he had intercepted a caravan escorting a great treasure chest for the Temple—all those half-shekels that every single Jew in the world was made to pay for the price of religious peace; that had been fun, stripping those priests of their robes and their jewelry. Even now he remembered how they had fallen on their knees and begged him not to take their money, as if it were they who were taxed into near-starvation and not the peasants! Galilee had everything—fruit, superb wines, fat cattle, carp in the lakes longer than a man's arm, yet every year the farmers had grown poorer as they gave more and more in taxes for Rome, taxes for the Temple, taxes for one Herodian extravagance after another. They were all the same, the Romans and the priests—each needed the other to survive in this rebellious, seething outpost of the Empire. The villagers of the High Galilee feared John of Gishala, who took their food and impressed their men into his band. They even hated him, but they hated the Romans and the priests more. John was a pirate, but he always paid back what he took, and when times were good they saw the taxes they had paid for so many years coming back to them fourfold. There would be feasting and dancing and the lovely fair-skinned girls would dally with the brigands for one night in a way that their parents would have been shocked to discover.

Now things were different. With the countryside on the edge of open revolt, the trade routes had dried up. And John of Gishala was bored. His job was to kill Romans and collaborating Jews, but they all skulked in the big cities under the protection of the legions. His men were restless, the villagers from whom he was drawing supplies, sullen. The situation was desperate. Morosely he gazed into the distance.

Suddenly he saw something—a trail of dust hanging in the hot air, then dispersing in the haze. He looked again. There it was, more of it. A procession of people was passing, winding through the foothills—going perhaps, to that nasty, craven little collaborator who ruled the petty kingdoms on the other side of the Sea of Galilee. Agrippa II they called him—as devious as the first, but without the courage. A small-minded king, who danced to the Romans' tune with an army built by Rome. Often enough, John had wondered why they had not mounted a pincer movement to finish him off, the Romans moving in by way of Ptolemais and Syria, and Agrippa leading in his forces from Gaulonitis and Auranitis. What a grand battle it would be, his fierce Galileans coming from nowhere to fall on their unsuspecting rear guards, harrying them remorselessly through the high mountains until, exhausted and starving, they trailed sullenly back to their garrisons. Well, it had not happened, but perhaps there might be a little fun now.

John of Gishala got to his feet. Standing, he made a fine figure. A large, fair man with a ruddy face, a huge blonde beard and bright, staring blue eyes. He looked again at the approaching dust cloud. Yes, here was something, at last. Quickly he gave his orders, his men mounting their ponies and galloping off to intercept the travelers, who appeared to be headed into the interior. At the prospect of action, of plunder, John stretched himself and laughed. His laugh was enormous, like his muscular frame, and when a man heard it, he shivered and urged his mule faster toward his destination.

The first hint the travelers had of trouble was when a large group of tanned, villainous-looking outlaws rose from nowhere and surrounded them.

"Well, Romans, what brings you here?" roared John in broken Latin, addressing his words to a gaunt, battered-looking man with drooping lips, wearing a black eye patch, and apparently their leader.

"We are not Romans. All of us here are Jews."

John of Gishala sneered his disbelief. "Yet your Latin is faultless. Jews you may be, but friends of Rome all the same. I smell money."

A little fat man now stepped forward and addressed John earnestly in his own language, Aramaic, explaining that they were Jews who had fled from Rome and had come into the hills to join one of the guerrilla groups they had heard about. The big blond robber listened suspiciously, then pointed suddenly at Simon and said, "And he—the mutilated one who speaks Latin like a Roman. Who is he?"

Alityrus explained about the famous Jewish gladiator, his extraordinary career in the Roman army and his return now to fulfill his oath to his father and kill Romans.

In spite of himself, John of Gishala was intrigued by the story, but it could be, he knew, just a cunning fable to let merchants pass his roadblock and reap a rich haul from trade with Agrippa. Also, he was hungry for loot—in the form of money or women—and there was a woman calmly sitting on a mule who was beautiful. The girl sat straight in the saddle, looking at him with a kind of remote, pale-skinned arrogance, and a need for her rose strongly inside him. Tugging his great fair-haired beard, he decided to test this pardoned gladiator, this so-called fighting Jew who had risen to high military rank with the Romans, by making him fight—for his woman.

Grinning widely, John said to Simon, "Your woman. I want her."

"You cannot have her," Simon said calmly. "She is my wife."

"And if I choose to take her?" John shouted. "Who is to stop me? With one word I could have you all killed."

Tension gripped the refugees with Simon. They could, they knew, be massacred and nobody would be the wiser. "Do you, then, kill fugitives from the Romans, poor people who are your kinfolk?" Simon asked. "This is not what I have heard of John of Gishala."

"You have heard of me then?" Pleasure showed momentarily in the bright-blue eyes, his vanity tickled.

"Your name is mentioned in Caesarea with some—emotion."

"Emotion, eh?" The big man held his belly and roared with laughter. Rapidly he relayed the joke in Aramaic to his ragged band, who began to laugh as well. "I'll tell you what I'll do," John said. "I'll fight you for her."

The look of scorn and contempt on Andrasta's serene face infuriated at the same time as it excited him.

"Very well. If there is no other way." There was a weariness in Simon's voice, such an all-pervading sadness that spoke of so many fights, of spilled blood, of too many injuries suffered, too many deaths seen, that it did not escape even John of Gishala.

In a flash the guerrilla leader had stripped himself to the waist, his oxlike shoulders clumsy and strong, his fair skin, where it showed under a layer of sweat and grime, shining in the sun.

Simon also stripped down, his body marked and welted from a hundred battles. He looked at the guerrilla, sniffed the air and grinned. "Has anybody ever told you that you stink like a dog?" he asked suddenly. "Don't you ever wash?"

The remark was meant to infuriate and it succeeded. With a bellow of rage the big blond man threw himself at Simon, making no attempt to use science or guile, his single gold earring sparkling with his movement—and over he went. Simon's vast experience in unarmed combat easily handled the guerrilla leader's ill-timed

240

rush. John of Gishala landed with a crash, winded. Cursing, he was up again and came in more deliberately this time, but the result was the same. As he launched a huge kick, he felt his foot gripped almost tenderly and he described a curve through the air, smashing into the ground.

As his men reached for their weapons, Simon locked an arm around John's throat and shouted, "One step forward and I throttle him." They fell back.

Simon now felt himself flung through the air. He had forgotten the brute strength of the guerrilla leader, who had waited for Simon's attention to be distracted.

"You should have killed me when you had the chance." John sneered. "Now prove you are not Roman lackeys or die."

In answer, Simon smilingly extended his hand, allowing the golden menorah ring to shine brilliantly in the bright sun.

John of Gishala bent to study the ring, casually at first and then, brows knitted with thought, intently. "Yes," he muttered. "There is a legend about a man such as you." He drew back, indicating with a sweep of his arm that his men should examine the ring.

Excitedly, the brigands clustered around Simon, pushing and jostling each other for a view.

"It is agreed," John said at last. "Your people may dwell in one of my villages, but first you must prove that you are the man in the legend. Therefore I give you something worthy of your mettle. Go to Jerusalem and kidnap me Ananus, son of the High Priest."

Simon thought for a long time, then said slowly, "And if I were to go to Jerusalem, my wife—you would not molest her?"

"She will be well treated. Respected as your wife."

"Very well. Now why do you wish this man kidnapped?"

"Last month, ten of my best men, skilled Sicarii, were captured by the High Priest and handed over to the Romans for trial. They rot in the Antonia. For a man of the importance of Ananus, they will undoubtedly agree to an exchange."

"Perhaps you would prefer me to kidnap the High Priest himself?" Simon's gray-green eyes flashed in dangerous mockery. "My chances of success would be about equal."

"There you are wrong," John boomed. "When you are inside the Temple, ask for Eleazar, captain of the Temple Guard—mention you are from the district of Gishala and he will help you."

"But he is son of the High Priest, brother to Ananus," Simon exclaimed.

"Nevertheless," he said with a chuckle, "he is one of us."

There was a silence for a moment before a slow smile spread across Simon's battered features. "John of Gishala," he said, "you are indeed a pig of enormous proportions, a despoiler of other men's wives and you stink like a randy camel, but I trust you. Give me a few good men and I will do my best."

Far from being offended, the blue-eyed robber held his sides with uncontrolled laughter. "Already you talk like a mountain fighter."

The road winding up through the limestone hills of Judaea toward Jerusalem is narrow and tortuous, with thick forests covering ground too steep to cultivate, and any reasonably level piece of earth terraced for the cultivation of olives, vines or vegetables.

With the Day of Atonement only another sunset away, the road was jammed with pilgrims, holy men in white robes, merchants, vendors of fresh vegetables, the whole panorama of population on the move. When, around a bend in the road, the Temple Mount came into view, Simon, with many others, stopped in his tracks, overcome at what he saw. Set high on a plateau to the northeast of the city, a double colonnade of Corinthian columns spanned by cedar beams enclosed the vast Court of Gentiles, within which other courts rose majestically one inside the other. Each colonnade seemed more beautiful than the last, until, at the highest point, the Sanctuary, made of finest white marble, reared a further hundred and fifty feet into the sky, topped only by its solid gold spires seemingly set ablaze by the first rays of the sun. In the clear, translucent light of a Jerusalem dawn, the Temple Mount resembled a peak capped by snow, and filled with awe the most sophisticated traveler.

As they came into the old city Simon and the four men he had brought with him split up, walking singly through the teeming, filthy streets of the slum quarter. They picked their way over beggars, cripples and half-starved children, aware that they could be arrested at any second by the hard-faced Temple agents on the lookout for Sicarii—the rebels who slipped into the city and knifed to death the friends of the Romans and even, when they got the chance, the priests themselves.

Because the priests ran Judaea. Under Roman rule the Sanhedrin controlled its own affairs. Although submitting to different degrees of discipline from the cohort of legionaries who looked down on the Temple from the sullen fortress of Antonia on its northwest buttress, the priests bled the nation in God's name and the Romans took tribute from the priests. Before, it had been only the Romans the people hated; there had always been priests; was not the Jewish tradition of an independent state that of government by a priest-king? David had been one and Solomon after him. Had not the great Maccabees been priests? It did not matter how badly treated they were by their own kind. But the thought of tribute extorted from the poor then handed over to Rome had now made the priests the enemies of the people. Insurgency and terror stalked the city of Jerusalem—guerrilla daggermen moving with lightning speed and killing the invaders of God's holy soil and the collaborators that nurtured them.

With danger lurking for every prosperous visitor, the only way to prevent a catastrophic drop in Temple revenues was to have an efficient Temple Guard, and they were everywhere—keen-eyed men drawn mostly from the priestly caste and commanded by Eleazar, son of Ananias, the High Priest. This then was the position as Simon and his men, singly to avoid suspicion, went through the massive Hulda Gates at the southern base of the Temple Mount and climbed the long series of underground steps leading to the Temple complex. Now the first check—questions, always questions, hands searching for concealed weapons—by burly guards clad in old Greek armor, then out into the vast Court of Gentiles. After the coolness of the underground tunnel— a hot, searing, blinding light, a sea of indescribable noise. Enclosed by the huge double colonnades, money

243

changers sat in booth after booth turning foreign currency into shekels, so that pilgrims, Gentiles come to see the great wonder of the world, could make a gift offering, buy a goat or some other animal at six times the normal price to donate as a sacrifice to Yahweh. For those too poor to buy a large animal, Ananias, the High Priest, bred thousands of pigeons on his large estates, offering them for sale through discreet nominees. The priests ran it all—a vast, plundering marketplace from which they lined their pockets. Where such a fortune was at stake, they could see nothing sacrilegious in hundreds of animals defecating on the priceless marble floor, braying their thirst and discomfort as they awaited the sacrificial knife, their rank smell lying thick in the poorly ventilated court and mixing with the burning incense that drifted down from the high altar.

As Simon, eyes streaming from the cloying smoke, took in the blasphemous sight, a maniple of Roman soldiers came marching rapidly toward him, reinforcements for the Antonia garrison to help cope with the crowd. He signed sharply to his men, lounging near the southern colonnade, to draw back out of the way. The legionaries went swinging by in their red undertunics and gleaming *loricae segmentatae,* the disciplined slap of their boots ringing on the fine marble pavements. Simon, casting about for a way to penetrate the Temple proper, got an inspired idea. The colonel, he noticed, had stayed behind after his men had marched up into the Antonia and was gazing around with intense interest.

With a flick of his head Simon beckoned to Dov, the most experienced of the guerrillas, and the two edged over until they were standing close by the colonel.

"You!" The colonel turned roughly to Simon. "Is this where that fellow Jeshua or Jesus—whatever you call him—knocked over the booths and threw the money changers out?"

"That is so, sir."

"And we crucified him for you?"

"Yes, sir."

"If you ask me," the colonel said, looking disgustedly around him, "we should have crucified every last one of them." He drew a wineskin from the pack that swung from his hand and took a long swig.

Before the conversation could continue further, there was a series of great crashes—the sound coming nearer until the enormous Nicanor Gates opened with a noise like thunder, the sun flaring on the beautiful burnished copper from which they were made. Two robed men stepped forward and blasted a fanfare on long silver trumpets, then withdrew, leaving the Nicanor Gates open.

"What does it mean?" the colonel demanded.

Simon spoke to Dov; then, translating from Aramaic back into Latin, he said, "The trumpets signal the morning sacrifice. They are used only for important occasions, but as we are in holy days all the time from New Year to Yom Kippur, it is permitted."

"There will be much sacrificing?" asked the colonel.

Again Simon referred to Dov, then translated, "At festival times, always. Morning, evening and special *musaf*, or extra sacrifices."

"I suppose the priests have to make their money." The colonel sneered. "How much of this nonsense is one permitted to inspect?"

"Beyond the next court, neither woman nor Gentile may go, under pain of death."

"Then you Jews deserve neither wives nor friends," the colonel said with a guffaw. He reached for the wineskin again and took an even longer pull, his face a study of moody boredom. Suddenly, a thought struck him. "How do you speak our language so well?"

"I have served throughout the Empire, sir. Britannia under Vespasian—"

"Of course, of course, a fine general," the colonel cut in irritably, sorry now that he had stirred up the endless reminiscences of an old veteran. "Tell me, is there nothing to do in this town except pray?"

In answer, Simon motioned the colonel to follow him under the huge Royal Portico spanning the southern entrance, where it was dark and almost deserted. "Do you like beautiful things?" Simon asked.

In the dimness, the colonel could vaguely make out the rich gold leaf covering the cedarwood ceiling, the fine carvings of grape clusters. "Not this stuff," he said shortly, and turned to leave.

"Sir." Simon put a finger to his lips, metamorphosing

245

in a flash from an innocent guide to a furtive pimp touting for custom. "I know a place close to here—girls with breasts like small melons—boys with lips as luscious as Tyrrhenian grapes—whatever you fancy."

"Now you're talking," the colonel began, but got no further. One smash of Dov's hand rendered him unconscious. In the gloom, screened by four guerrillas, Simon changed quickly into the colonel's clothes, to emerge from the Royal Portico dressed, as he had been for so long, as the colonel of a regular legion of the line. Swaggering with all his old confidence, he marched up to a temple guard and asked to see Eleazar, the commanding officer.

"Whom shall I announce, sir?"

"Never mind who I am. Tell him I have information from"—Simon remembered the vital code words—"the district of Gishala."

"The district of Gishala, sir," the guard repeated. Soon he was back. "Follow me, sir." He conducted Simon and his men to a garrison room in the cool of the cellars of the Temple Mount, saluted and withdrew.

There were two men seated at a table, inspecting plans and documents. They lifted their heads and looked at him. One, Simon dismissed in a moment. A weak face, spoiled, petulant—a nonentity. "What can I do for you, Colonel?" the other man said in excellent Latin. Simon took in his broad, domed forehead, the strong, thin mouth. The look of a thinker and a man of action too. Here was character, someone to be reckoned with, thought Simon.

Sweeping his hand across his chest in a smart guard's salute, Simon said, "I bring intelligence reports from—the district of Gishala." He gave just the faintest emphasis to the code phrase. "For Eleazar."

"I am Eleazar." The man smiled. "And this is my brother Ananus. You will take wine?" He rose from his seat, indicating that Simon might join him in a corner where a pitcher of wine stood on a small table.

Simon walked down the narrow room to the far end, where Eleazar said, "Try this, Colonel. It is the finest that Galilee can produce." A split second later he whispered sharply in Simon's ear, "Guards—behind the curtain."

"It is indeed an excellent wine," Simon purred. "You must tell me where I may buy some." He walked back up the room until he came level with a thick red curtain, then with a sudden roar threw himself, sword in hand, between the drapes, yelling at his men to follow. It was all over in seconds, the guards disarmed.

"You are no colonel." Eleazar forced contempt into his voice. "You are brigands. What do you want?"

"One of you as a hostage," said Simon. "You," he went on, pointing at the shivering Ananus, "might do. You don't look the type to cause much trouble." He turned back to his men. "Secure and blindfold him," he ordered.

Simon waited until the frightened, pleading Ananus was safely trussed and blindfolded, then said to Eleazar with a heavy wink, "Show me a way out of here, O pig of a priest, or have your throat slit like a sacrificial goat."

"You would not kill me!" Eleazar played out the game for the benefit of his brother.

Simon drew his lethal Roman short sword, the steel making an ugly grating sound as it left the scabbard. "You think so?" he said, his voice sinking to a murderous whisper. "Let us see." He walked deliberately over to Eleazar.

"That way," Eleazar said, putting fear into his voice. "Through that door and you will come out on the western wall. There are steps there leading clear across to the new quarter of Bezetha." He pointed to a door immediately behind him. "You will be safe that way as it is only for the use of the military."

"A likely story."

"It is true," Eleazar said complacently. "Don't you know the history of this place? Herod, who built it, was obsessed with the idea of escape. The place is honeycombed with tunnels and secret passages—some leading to the city, some direct to the Antonia."

"Very well," Simon said grimly. He turned to his men. "Tie and gag him."

When it was done, Simon said, "Farewell, Eleazar. I shall tell my master, John of Gishala, how you have cooperated." The two men looked at each other, then Simon disappeared through the door, dragging Ananus down the steep steps that ran endlessly through the

247

western wall into Bezetha, as if he were just another unfortunate suspect being returned from rigorous interrogation.

No one even attempted to stop a Roman colonel, and Simon, with his guerrillas, had no trouble leaving the city.

Eleazar watched with satisfaction as they dragged his brother Ananus with them. His face burned with a fanaticism that was neither the fervor of religion nor the nationalistic patriotism that sustained the outlying guerrillas. It was something infinitely more dangerous, more powerful. The theory of mass equality, the creed that says that no man may work for himself but only for the state, which owns all the wealth. In Judaea, with every fourth man a merchant, an entrepreneur, a capitalist, Eleazar planned a savage tyranny of the mind far stricter than the Roman and priestly tyranny over the body. With a Temple Guard so greatly expanded to deal with the Sicarii, peasant boys were now being conscripted to join the ranks of a previously aristocratic corps. The result was that Eleazar had found fertile ground in which to sow his political credo. Now several highly efficient revolutionary cells existed, waiting only for the word to seize control, first of the Guard, then of the city.

Eleazar's position was basically simple: to rule, he needed the help of all the insurgent armies of Judaea and the Galilee. They were opportunists, religious zealots and nationalists. But he would need their help, John's in particular. That was why he had engineered the kidnapping of his own brother. With the ten Sicarii saved from crucifixion through Eleazar's plot, John would come with a large army when the time arrived to seize Jerusalem.

After a reasonable wait, Eleazar tore off his gag and his bonds, then rang the alarm bell to summon the soldiers. His broad, intellectual forehead creased with thought as he went over his future plans. When, with the guerrillas' help, he had taken Jerusalem, there was one thing his men would have to do immediately. Destroy the guerrillas. No undisciplined deviationism could be permitted.

248

27

In the spring of 66 CE, Governor Cestius Gallus, ruler of the Roman province of Syria, awaited the coming of Gessius Florus with misgivings.

The weather had upset him. A cold wind blew from Asia Minor, and driving rain beat down on the courtyard outside his palace at Antioch. These Syrian springs could be freezing. If that were not enough, his ulcerated leg, always painful, ached abominably in the all-pervading damp. He spoke sharply to the half-naked slave boy to massage his leg more gently, and moved his body, flabby from lack of exercise, as he sought vainly a more comfortable position on his cushions. He would have liked to have had a nice hot, dusty assignment like Nubia or Lower Egypt—no one else wanted those damned provinces anyway, but the wheels of Roman foreign policy had awarded him Syria, which, above all, needed a young and active man instead of an invalid with a bad leg.

The rain suddenly stopped and for a few minutes there was peace—but not for long. There was the heavy, crunching sound of military hobnailed boots and a succession of hoarse shouts as the guard of honor drawn from the Twelfth Legion was put through its interminable drill. Every time the soldiers crashed to a halt under his window, Gallus winced as pain coursed up his bad leg.

A page announced the coming of Gessius Florus. The procurator, upright and athletic in his military armor, crested helmet under his arm, stamped to a halt in front of him and swept his clenched fist across his breastplate in military salute. The pain in his leg started up again—how he wished he could be left in peace to study philosophy, the rival merits of Stoicism and Epicureanism. He would give anything to be away from this noisy, sophisticated city with its two and a half miles of marbled pavements, colonnades and streetlighting, the ceaseless worry of this turbulent cockpit of rival populations that he had been made to govern.

"Sire," Florus said, breaking protocol by speaking before permission was given, "I have come to give you a report on the state of unrest in Judaea."

"Could it not have come through normal channels?"

"The situation is urgent. It requires your authorization for instant action."

"When has there not been unrest?" Gallus said. "When the Jews do not fight the Greeks, they fight us or they fight each other. What is so different?"

"They scream for independence. They riot in the cities."

"You are new here," Gallus said tolerantly. "You do not understand the nature of these people. They rioted eighteen years ago when one of our soldiers bared his behind and broke wind on the battlements on their holy day of Passover. They rioted when we impounded the priests' vestments in the Antonia as a guarantee of good order. Now and again we send in a cohort of legionaires, kill a few Jews and all is quiet again."

"I am well enough briefed about the past, sire," Florus said. "My researches go back to the days of Pompey. The Jews have never forgiven us for entering their Holy of Holies and gazing upon the face of their God. The stability and prosperity we have given them through strong kings they ignore, because the kings to them are Roman lackeys. The way we pander to them is unbelievable—do you know that they are exempt from conscription in the army? That they alone do not have to put images of the Emperor in their holy places? In spite of all this, they hate us. They only want independence."

"Independence." Gallus snorted. "What is it? A word. An idea. Which of us is not subject to the will of the other? What a stiff-necked people they are, but do you come all the way here to debate these things? They are well known."

"We no longer control the countryside. Guerrillas and insurgents are everywhere. The talk is of the Messiah coming."

"Which has always been the case," Gallus interrupted testily. "My dear Florus, you must learn to tolerate these conditions of unrest which vary only in their severity. The common people will never dare attack the legions and as long as the priests pay the tribute, what do we care?"

"That is just the point," Florus said, "the reason I have come personally to see you. They no longer pay the tribute."

"What?" Gallus jerked himself upright on his cushions, irritably pushing the little slave boy away. "What did you say?"

"They owe seventeen talents on this year's assessment."

"Seventeen talents?" In spite of the pain from his leg, Gallus guffawed. "You come here to tell me this? The sum is a bauble."

"It is nevertheless significant. My information is that they have withheld it to see what we will do. They think we will not march across hostile country. If we do not act, they will then refuse the whole of next year's tribute."

"But why?" Gallus demanded. "Do they not thrive under our protection? Are they not pocketing fortunes from the Temple revenues? Have we not always dealt firmly with this Messiah business which affects them like a running sore?" He grimaced briefly at his leg. It was an apt smile. "Did not Pilate crucify that fellow Jesus? Or Fadus not deal with Theudas back in forty-six? Or even Felix kill that mad Egyptian who tried to take Jerusalem two or three years ago? There has been no lack of these silver-tongued mendicants preaching poverty and humility, and each one was dealt with as the priests saw fit."

"You ask many questions, sire," Florus said smoothly, "and to each one I can only say you are right. The priests owe us much, but now it is not a matter of loyalties. It is merely a question of whom they are most scared."

"Explain." Gallus glared.

"As I said, sire, the guerrillas hold more and more of

251

the country and the priests go in fear of their lives. You will recall that the last High Priest, Jonathan, was killed by Sicarii. Only two years ago they kidnapped Ananus, the High Priest's son, forcing us to exchange ten of their best men for him."

"I know, I know," Gallus said testily. "What do you suggest?"

"A punitive expedition, sire, but not against the peasants or the bandits, but those who are normally our friends—the priests, the rich—"

"In other words you wish to reverse their order of fear?" Gallus said. In spite of his infirmities he was no fool and could see the way Florus' mind was working.

"Exactly, sire. A quick thrust into Jerusalem. Reinforce our small garrison in the Antonia fortress. Punish a few prominent citizens and take what is owed to us from the Temple treasury."

"You would touch the *corban?* The Temple treasure?"

"It has been done before." Florus shrugged. "Crassus sacked the place. Pilate took money to build aqueducts. It will teach the priests a good lesson. Teach them to keep their house in order."

"Very well," Gallus said wearily, "but take care not to provoke a full-scale war. So many careers have been ruined out here in Judaea—you know how they send deputations to the Emperor—always the first and loudest to whine at any infringements of their rights."

"Just a good sharp lesson," Florus said. "Rome will be more angry if we do not collect the tribute."

Cestius Gallus shot a frightened look at Florus. The point was indeed a telling one. His career, perhaps even his life, would not be worth a fig if the yearly tribute failed to reach Rome. Nevertheless he had misgivings. He would have preferred the procurator to have been a little more venal, more sophisticated, more ready to line his own pockets. But this one had the set, determined features of the perfectionist—the kind that caused revolutions.

"Just collect what is owed," he said slowly. "Execute a few rich citizens, whip a few more, then retire. Firmness but not provocation. Use your element of surprise. You understand?"

"Very well, sire." Florus saluted and retired, his step

springy with purpose, eyes shining at the thought of
Roman power to be unleashed.

Irritably, Gallus beckoned to the slave boy to
massage his leg again. He liked watching the interplay
of muscles on the boy's silky back, but there was no lust
in his eyes. All he wanted was peace and quiet. And for
that, he was in the wrong place entirely.

"Florus come himself?" Ananias, the High Priest, was
appalled. "To collect seventeen talents? There must be
some mistake."

"No," the tribune said. He was bewildered by these
exotic, bearded priests who wielded so much power. His
confusion tended to make his normally patrician
manner even more overbearing. "I'll take the money
now."

"An insult," Ananias said, flushing. "Had Caesar
demanded several thousand, he would have had it as a
mark of respect and cooperation. To demand seventeen
talents is a gratuitous insult."

"It's all the same to me." The tribune shrugged. "Give
me the money or I'll break down the treasury doors and
take it myself."

Eleazar had stood silently until now. In full armor,
the obsolete, heavy bronze plate modeled on the old
Greek pattern that the Jews had absorbed through
centuries of Hellenization, the broad, squat figure of the
captain of the Temple Guard would have looked heroic
had it not been for his domed thinker's forehead and
thin, wide lips.

"Tribune," said Eleazar, "you will have to get past my
Temple Guard."

"Your rebellious attitude is noted," the tribune
replied, "and I go now to call out the Antonia garrison."

The moment of confrontation disturbed the High
Priest, who had always been content to pay public
tribute or private bribes in order to keep control of his
lucrative Temple enterprises. "Sir," he said, "there has
been some mistake. Naturally, you shall have your
money." Turning, he gave an order to a treasury
assistant, then, bowing to the tribune, drawing his rich
robes around him, he walked away, indicating that the
audience was over.

Now, quickly, Eleazar and his radical activists went out into the city and began to spread the word. In the marketplaces, the teeming bazaars, the festering, over-crowded slums of the old city, the news traveled fast: "Florus insults us again. Florus threatens to break open the Temple treasury for seventeen talents." The mob, quick to anger, soon, with its Jewish sense of humor, saw the funny side of the whole thing. As the arrogant tribune, sitting straight in the saddle and looking neither to left nor to right of him, left the city with his small escort, he was beset by crowds lining the route, holding out begging bowls, jeering, "A few shekels for poor Nero—he's saving up to buy himself another little boy—charity for the Emperor, he can't pay his debts."

When a few hours later the tribune, still purple in the face, related his humiliating ordeal to Florus, who had camped his army just outside the city, a smile of sheer pleasure crossed the procurator's face. He had always hated the Jews with the unreasoning passion of the true Jew-baiter, managing to keep his prejudices hidden from the shrewd eyes of his superiors. At last he had the chance he needed to vent his feelings.

"Right," he said crisply. "The Emperor has been insulted. Now we'll teach them a lesson they'll never forget."

Reacting with savage speed, Florus entered Jerusa-lem behind an advance guard of fifty cavalry under a man called Capito, as master of horse. The cavalrymen made no effort to avoid the crowds of people in the streets and those who did not get out of the way in time were ridden down.

Next morning, seated on a dais outside the palatial Hasmonean fortress which he had taken over, Florus peremptorily summoned the priests and nobles to appear before him.

Looking at the priests in their finery, with little golden pomegranates dancing and tinkling on their robes, Florus remembered the endless trouble Rome had taken to protect the Jews from jealous neighbors, the respect so assiduously granted to their religion, the wealth they had been allowed to amass, and how Rome was now rewarded with a country on the edge of rebellion. A short, sharp lesson, he thought. A lesson in Roman discipline. Then perhaps they will come to heel and set their house in order.

He stood up and addressed the patient lines of notables, waiting silently with their women and children. "I send for arrears of tribute," he shouted, "and what do I get? Ragamuffins holding begging bowls and insulting the Emperor. From now on there will be order. There will be respect for Rome."

Fury gripped him. "Strip every tenth person," he shouted. "Man, woman or child. We'll scourge them by decimation."

With sickening brutality, Florus' small force obeyed. Even Eleazar, who hated these rich parasites who had long battened off the peasants, was shocked at venerable and honored old men, members of the equestrian orders, being stripped, their thin, age-spotted limbs being pinioned to receive the lash; smooth, sleek Jewesses and little children screaming with terror at what was in store for them.

As the burly cavalrymen laid on with their terrible lead-tipped scourges, Eleazar kept his face bland and expressionless. His fight was not for these pigs of priests and nobles. His time would come soon, but it was not now. When Florus began massacring the common people of Jerusalem, then and only then would Eleazar appear as leader of the popular resistance. That was how revolutions were made.

"Very well," roared Florus, at length. Having nicely bloodied the backs of the Jewish nobility, he strolled away for a late breakfast in the Hasmonean Palace. He looked out a window, satisfaction showing on his face. Several of the old men lay where they had been bound, the victims of strokes and heart attacks. Naked, moaning women and children were bustled away for treatment by their families. It had been an excellent demonstration of Roman power, and if he had left it at that, he would have done everything Cestius Gallus had required of him.

But Florus had not left it there. Even now, two cohorts of foot were marching up the steep, winding road that led to Jerusalem, with orders to seize the Temple treasure.

With the largest single fortune in the world in Roman possession, the Jews would finally come to order. Money talked with them. It always did.

Florus could not have been more wrong. In pitting himself against the whole Jewish nation, he had, instead of punishing a few priests, started a war.

At dawn, entering the city from the northwest, the Caesarea cohorts tramped in, their hobnailed boots thundering down in awful precision as they passed through the undefended gate on the outer of Jerusalem's three great walls. Instructed to be "severe" and utilize to the utmost their element of surprise, they cut a bloody swathe through the crowds lining, jamming, blocking the streets of Bezetha, the new quarter.

The mass of people, alternately furious and panic-stricken, could offer no real resistance against a thousand well-armed, well-trained and well-armored regulars other than to buy time at the cost of their own lives. The two cohorts marched stolidly on toward Antonia, the fort on the northwest point of the Temple Mount, where a small Roman garrison looked down on the Temple, emphasizing the overlordship of the Roman state.

When the colonnaded Temple Mount came into view, topped by the incredible, white marble magnificence of the Sanctuary with its soaring, golden towers, the troopers stopped, rested their sweating bodies, cleaned their bloodied swords and made ready to cut through the last line of shrieking, defiant Jews barring their way into the grim Antonia. There, reinforced by the garrison, they would spread out over the thirty-five acres of the Temple precinct, subdue the pitiful Guard and collect the uncountable, fabulous treasure of the Jews—the Temple *corban*. Every single Jew in the world contributed to it, a levy collected with the backing of Jehovah, a far greater spur than the threats of any tax farmer—innumerable bars of gold and silver, ornaments and vestments: enough money to run the whole Roman economy for five years, some said. Florus, looking down from the height of the Hasmonean Palace balcony, smiled with satisfaction. The thing appeared to be going like clockwork.

With the treasure in Roman hands, the Jews would learn to behave themselves.

Then, as if like thunder, he heard several distinct crashes. The doors of the various courts leading to the Sanctuary were being shut, the huge bolts slamming home. That was strange, because they had only been opened an hour before, at the crack of dawn. It could mean only one thing. The Jews intended to defend themselves. Behind them would be the Temple Guard. Florus sneered at the thought of those half-trained bumpkins in their old, heavy Greek armor—they would be overwhelmed in minutes. He drank sparingly from a glass of iced wine mixed with water to combat the heat of the morning and watched his plan inexorably develop. Suddenly the two colonnaded staircases leading down from the Antonia into the Temple precinct collapsed in a cloud of dust. As the air cleared, Florus could not believe his eyes: thousands of men could now be seen, the sun winking on their shovels and picks, gleaming on the sweat of their backs. All night the Jews had been laboring to break the colonnades, the only access from the Antonia into the Temple. Now, even if his cohorts reached the Antonia, they could go no farther. Another thought struck him—unless he did reach the Antonia, the fortress was isolated, possibly doomed. Cestius Gallus would not thank him for the extermination of the Antonia garrison. Florus bit his lip with concern.

Worse was to come. Even as he looked, twin trumpets blasted to the sky, not from the Nicanor Gates, where they announced services and sacrifices, but from the highest pinnacle of the Sanctuary among the soaring, golden spires. The fanfare was aggressive, utterly different from the tekiah and teruah, the strictly formalized note clusters they normally played. As the trumpets switched into a minor key, harmonizing emotionally in a slow, grave song that the Jews, it was said, regarded as their anthem, a tattered white flag, with a crude seven-branched menorah emblazoned on it, fluttered out into the wind. The squat, armored figure of Eleazar appeared on the sanctuary heights and began speaking. As his words were relayed to the huge crowds milling around him, they began to cheer hysterically, the sound rolling like doom around the walls of the Hasmonean Palace.

"Go down and see what he is saying," Florus told an aide.

Half an hour later the aide came back, ashen-faced.

"Well?" Florus was sweating. "Come on. Speak up. Out with it, man."

"He says he has taken the city in the name of the people. That is, for the Jews, not for the priests or the nobles who profiteer behind Roman swords. He has a message for you."

"Oh, he has, has he?"

"Go now, or be exterminated."

Florus smiled in an attempt at bravado which he did not feel. "Talk is easy," he said, "but it is we who have the cohorts."

"Sire," the aide said, "we have quietened Bezetha, but even now the Temple Guard arms the upper and lower quarters of the old city. Unless we move quickly, we shall be swamped by sheer weight of numbers."

Florus dismissed the aide and paced around the room, thinking. All right, he had failed to take the Temple treasure by *coup de main*. That was all. It was not so important. He had lost a skirmish, but there was little doubt that the Romans would win the battle. He would go back and tell Cestius Gallus about the open revolt of the Jews and ask the governor himself to restore order.

He grinned at the thought of Gallus crunching down through Galilee with the iron Twelfth Legion, one of the best fighting units in the eastern Mediterranean.

These obstinate Jews would soon be taught to obey.

28

John of Gishala, the dirty, blue-eyed brigand of Galilee, sat in his lair high up in the Golan mountains and contemplated the future. Recently he had found life more amusing. The strange Jew Simon of the mutilated face, icy courage and stony strength of purpose had impressed him mightily by his brilliant kidnap of Ananus, the High Priest's son. John had been grateful for the return of ten of his best assault daggermen and had shown his gratitude by the hospitality he had lavished on Simon's people through the cold, wet Galilee winter.

Simon, on his part, knowing the brigand's craving for Andrasta, did not trust the man one inch, but still, they hunted together, fought the Romans in minor skirmishes and developed a healthy respect for each other's talents. Now, John had just returned from a reconnaissance, his burly, unkempt frame positively radiating excitement, and Simon knew there was important news.

"It is war. Do you hear? Eleazar has turned out Procurator Florus with a flea in his ear and fortifies Jerusalem."

Simon said, "Are you going to help Eleazar?"

"I'll send a contingent. Whether I follow with the whole army depends on what chance there is of grabbing some of that Temple loot."

"You old reprobate," Simon said. "You don't mean that."

"You think not?" John said. "A man has to live." He suddenly burst into laughter, clapping Simon on the shoulder. "Incidentally, you're worth money. I've sold you to the rebels for two bars of Temple gold and the price of a young girl."

Simon humored him. "Explain, John."

"Thousands wish to fight, yet lack weapons. So, with the help of a certain holy man named Menahem, a group of insurgents will try to take Masada from the Romans, with Herod's armory as the prize. Now they need your military skills down there. You know more about fighting Romans than anyone in Judaea—they say you can even read their minds. That is why I have sold your services for two bars of gold and the price of a Circassian belly dancer off the next slave caravan from Arabia."

"What do I get out of it?" Simon asked.

"A chance to fight the Romans. A chance to honor your oath to your father. Isn't that what you want?"

"You may stink of goat's dung and cheap wine, but your brain still functions, I see. If I go—will you keep your hands off my wife?"

The blue eyes congealed, froze to ice chips for a second, then relaxed. "I want her all right," John growled. "I'll admit that, but I won't take her behind your back. She'll be safe here."

Both men faced each other, the tension only breaking when John passed the jug of wine.

"To whom shall I report?" Simon asked.

"A great fighter. A man as famous in the south as I am in the north."

"His name?"

"The Lion of Wrath—Shimshon Bar Giora."

Ten miles north of the fortress of Masada, at Bar Giora's camp pitched in the Dead Sea valley, Simon waited for the junction with Menahem. These were not his men and he was content to remain quietly in the background until his advice was called for.

Bar Giora was nervous as a cat. He had left his cavalry behind to come down into this arid hell of stone and rock to try and wrest a mighty fortress from a Roman garrison. No guerrilla chief wishes to rely on the skills of a stranger and here was the redoubtable Bar Giora having to depend not only on Simon's knowledge, but also on the competence of Menahem, who, famous as a thinker and a rabbi, could be expected to know little about the art of fighting. Yet without Menahem, he could get nowhere. Menahem was the only man with the key to Masada and afterward, with his spiritual following, to raise an army to come from the south and relieve Jerusalem.

Simon ticked off in his mind what he knew about them.

Menahem—his spiritual qualifications to lead a great Jewish army were impeccable. Three generations of his family had fought the Romans and died for their beliefs: Hezekiah, his grandfather, who overran large areas near the Syrian frontier before being hunted down and executed by Herod the Great, arch Roman lackey, in 47 BCE; then his father, Judas the Galilean, who led revolts in 6 BCE and again, fighting Roman tax censuses, in 6 CE, for which he paid with his life; then Menahem's two brothers headed revolts against Rome, both being crucified as rebels in 46 CE. Menahem had retired to the ultra-Orthodox monastery of Qumran to spend his life in the study of God's works and now, raising the banner of rebellion to help beleaguered Jerusalem, was bound to develop great support.

Then there was Bar Giora, young, fearless, his skill in battle ranging over the flat, marginal scrub of southwest Judaea as formidable as John's was in the north. He had a sensitive face with long eyelashes and thoughtful, rather graceful eyes. This touch of girlishness in his looks was offset by a beautifully muscled body, strong as a lion. There were many facets to Bar Giora that reminded Simon of himself as a young man.

These were the leaders who planned to capture mighty Masada, plunder Herod's armory, then raise an army to march to the relief of Jerusalem. Strange bedfellows, Simon decided. His thoughts were interrupted by the shout of a sentry. In the dry, eddying dust of the hot valley wind, Menahem's host could be seen approaching.

Even when they came in, they were praying; most in plain, white robes with shawls on their heads to shield them from the southern heat, Menahem at their head, holding a staff of honor like some patriarchal Moses out of the wilderness. "Peace be unto you," Menahem intoned. Raising his hands, he began blessing Bar Giora

in the purest of biblical Hebrew. The guerrillas, lean and
bronzed by the hot southern sun, stood around and
fidgeted uncomfortably. They distrusted these articu-
late men of religion. For too long they had done the
fighting and the dying while the fat priests tyrannized
Judaea, ransacking their own country to amass fortunes. Looking at the man's leonine head, with its thick,
iron-gray hair flowing down his neck in true biblical
appearance, Bar Giora could not help thinking that a
sixty-year-old sage like Menahem might one day want to
assume the mantle of the high priesthood, given half a
chance.

Shifting impatiently, Bar Giora waited until Menahem had finished his benediction, then as soon as
possible said, "So what is your plan, old man?"

"It is simple," Menahem said. "Once a week we are
permitted to bring fresh fruit and vegetables from the
oasis of EinGedi, to the garrison. You see the snake
path?" He pointed. Even ten miles away in the dry heat
of the Dead Sea wilderness, the path could be plainly
made out against the reds and chromes of the arid rocks.
"There is no other way to the top of the fortress and that
is where we shall go. Normally we come in daylight, but
on this occasion we shall arrive after dusk—with many
apologies, of course."

"And they will let you up?" Bar Giora asked.

"To halfway, at least."

"That is surprising," said Bar Giora, his long
eyelashes flicking in anxious thought.

"They are lazy," Menahem said disparagingly, "and
prefer us to carry the burdens. Also, they know us to be
Hasidim, holy men forbidden to take up arms. So they do
not bother too much about security. By keeping our ears
open, we have therefore learned a great deal over the
past months."

"Explain."

"They have a password that alters with each sentry
the higher you go. The whole system changes at the end
of each week. This is done on a fixed rota and they have
not considered us a sufficient threat to warrant
changing this order."

Bar Giora looked closely at Menahem and smiled,
showing even white teeth against his dusky complexion.

For a religious man, this Menahem seemed to know enough about military matters. His opinion of him rose considerably. "Let us sum up," he said. "In the darkness, our knowledge of the passwords will be enough to take us halfway up the path?"

"Exactly so—but no farther. Beyond that point we do not know the codes."

"And then?"

By way of answer, Menahem gazed around him. "You have some renegade Roman?"

Simon, who had rapidly regained his knowledge of Aramaic, pushed his way forward. "You are talking of me?" he said coldly. "Well, I'm no Roman. I am a Galilean. Son of the chief of my village."

"Well, we all have good blood in our veins," Menahem said.

"How is your Latin?" demanded Bar Giora.

"Perfect."

"You think you can bluff your way to the top?"

"Why not?" Simon said. "I was a colonel of regulars and have with me full uniform, armor and accouterments. What can they suspect if I lead the Hasidim after dark, for fear of bandits?"

The three men were silent for a moment. "Well, it is worth trying," Bar Giora said.

"You won't find a better plan," said Simon.

"Very well. It is nearly dusk. Let us go now."

"First I must say evening service," interrupted Menahem.

All his followers, turning to the north, toward the Temple of Jerusalem, began to pray, swaying in their fervor. Some of the guerrillas sheepishly joined in, but Bar Giora and Simon ben Eleazar stood apart.

It was a time for fighting. They had seen enough priests.

Masada: a stark, bare plateau, rearing fifteen hundred feet straight out of the desolate Dead Sea valley. To the west, the tawny-brown desolation of the Judaean desert, to the east, the pale-blue, lifeless salt pans of the Dead Sea, and beyond—the bare mountains of Moab, rising endlessly to the oven-heated sky. How does one describe Masada unless one sees it? A magnificence that only

263

nature can build, falling sheer on all sides. The summit accessible only by backbreaking toil up a narrow path negotiable by no more than one person at a time. Yet Herod the Great had seen its potential. Obsessed by fear of assassination, he had fortified this fantastic rock and built both a palace and a villa, hanging on the north cliff in three incredible layers, from which he could gaze out across the empty heights at his kingdom, rolling away into the haze. The Romans also had seen the value of Masada. Great caravans wound up from the south close to here, merchants trading in perfumes, slaves, and silks. High in their fortress the Romans in the crystal, dry, rainless air could dominate everything.

Masada—majestic, unconquerable. But the Jews would have to take it somehow, because far to the north, the Temple captain, Eleazar, though without any weapons, held Jerusalem in the name of the people and snarled defiance at the Romans. Here, in Herod's lair, forgotten even by the Romans, lay a huge store of weaponry, obsolescent perhaps, but usable in courageous hands. Now the Jews must take Masada, or their revolt would wither into nothing.

The very unassailability of Masada had given the Roman garrison its problems. How to prevent invaders from creeping up the path in darkness at dead of night? How to control an overconfident attitude, the peril of slack soldiering born of safety? Ten, twenty men could rush the guard post at the top of the path. Did one therefore have to pack the room with twenty soldiers all at the ready? How could one stop them from sleeping or getting drunk in the awful monotony? One was asking the impossible. Accordingly, other methods were devised. Let into appropriate spots up the path, where the narrow track turned and twisted upon itself, small niches for sentries had been constructed. During the night, these sentries would call out code words at regular intervals, a new word at different levels. The whole system changed at the end of each week.

The Jews knew everything—but to the halfway point only. The success and the lives of the guerrillas crouched at the base of the plateau, disguised in the robes of holy men, would thereafter depend entirely on the ability to bluff and the iron courage of one man. An ex-Roman soldier by the name of Simon ben Eleazar.

Bar Giora gave the command to move; in the darkness they bumped the sentries, one after another. A challenge—the right password—then a quick knife in the belly. Progress was easy, the procession winding smoothly up the path, then coming to an uncertain halt at the halfway mark, beyond which lay the unknown.

Now, Simon moved to the front and without any warning loomed suddenly out of the darkness before the next surprised sentry. "Atten*shun!*" he barked. "Half-asleep, were you? We'll soon cure any sloppiness." The sentry, confronted out of nowhere by a colonel on a line regiment, jerked himself stiffly erect while Simon adjusted his helmet to the correct parade angle. Before the man had time to struggle, Simon's hands moved smoothly down his neck and choked him senseless before laying him quietly on the ground. Quickly, his dagger pricking the man's bulging, pulsating throat, Simon rasped, "The password or you die."

The argument was convincing. "Flamma," croaked the sentry.

So they were using the names of famous gladiators. Simon smiled at the memories they stirred. Moving upward, the guerrillas crawling silently after him, Simon was, with the benefit of the password, able to dispose of the next sentry easily enough, and there now seemed little to stop him from reaching the top and attaining complete surprise. When the path kinked around a small hill and he saw, for the first time, the brilliant torches clamped into iron brackets on the rock face, Simon knew how stupid it had been to underestimate the Romans. From the guardhouse they had given themselves a clear view, day or night, of any attackers intrepid enough to have penetrated that far up the path.

Every fiber in his body rebelled, but he had not climbed all this way for nothing. It was now or never, and he signed to the disguised guerrillas to follow him closely, displaying their baskets of food as they went. Getting to his feet, flesh shrinking at the thought of the first arrow that might pin him to the rock face, he walked boldly out into the brilliant light.

"Halt," shouted the sentry on guard at the blockhouse. "The password."

"Let them through, dolt," Simon snapped. "Can't you see they're carrying food?"

"Stay where you are."

"How dare you question my authority?" Simon roared. "I'll have you whipped round the regiment for this."

"I'm sorry, sir." The sentry, miserable, bravely stood his ground. "I'm only obeying orders. One step more and I shall have to sound the alarm."

"What's going on down there?" A new voice, bleary from drunken sleep, joined in. "This is Centurion Pomponius Felix. Why don't you have the password?"

"I am P. Marcus Cornelius. Colonel in the Twelfth Legion at Caesarea," Simon shouted. As if to give authenticity, he brandished identification papyri. "Due to the operation of bandits in the EinGedi area, I have had to escort these good men"—he indicated the disguised guerrillas—"with your supplies. Don't you want them?"

"You alone may advance and present your papers." The centurion's voice was thick with wine, but he had not forgotten his ten years of training.

"I did not climb here to be insulted," Simon roared. "We are coming up." With a wave of his hand he ordered the hooded and robed guerrillas to follow him. With the sight of wine flagons and hampers of food so enticingly near, the centurion shrugged his shoulders and did nothing. Sent to this lonely desert outpost, a festering dung-hole for layabouts, ne'er-do-wells, troublemakers, he was not about to antagonize a colonel of a line regiment. Rather, he would try to use his influence to get him a home posting. As the hooded figures approached, he did not even bother to kick the sleeping guards to their feet.

Simon's throwing knife, a light, lethal, accurate weapon, took the centurion in the throat. Collapsing where he stood, he died without a sound. With a swing of Simon's arm, the sentry, mouth still open from surprise, went over the side into fifteen hundred feet of fresh air. Now, through the open doors of the guardroom, jumping through the windows, the heavily robed invaders flitted like so many ghosts. Most of the Roman soldiers, drunken cast-outs doing duty in this desolate, lonely hell where nothing ever happened, were killed where they lay, never coming out of their bibulous last sleep. The rest of the scattered garrison, no more than half a cohort in all, were caught playing dice or knucklebones, sleeping, drinking, and never stood a chance as the guerrillas fell upon them, dispatching them group by group, sparing no one, putting every single Roman to the sword.

In the morning, Simon and Bar Giora stood side by side, looking at the heaped-up dead. Their thoughts were too powerful for words; they were conscious that they had struck a great blow—that all over Judaea and Galilee the people would rise against the Romans. Silently, each man contemplated the future. It was not a moment for idle speech.

Menahem, on the contrary, was full of himself. He stalked about the plateau, hair flowing in the wind, his presence awe-inspiring in his snow-white robe: a figure carrying a plain wooden staff, right out of the days of the Prophets. Walking to a promontory on the northwestern corner of Masada, his followers shuffling obediently after him, Menahem planted his staff down sharply and said, "Here we shall build a synagogue and give thanks to the Lord."

"Amen, amen," cried his minions.

Raising his voice, Menahem cried, "The Lord has given us a great victory. Everyone must come to pray, to give thanks. Bring the soldiers." All over Masada dashed the Hasidim, whispering, "Come to pray. Menahem wishes to thank the Lord for victory—all must come to pray."

Sheepishly, tolerantly, the sunburned freedom-fighters, themselves uplifted by their tremendous success, drifted off to the place of the synagogue, curious to hear Menahem; Simon and Bar Giora went with them.

As Menahem prayed, his voice impassioned, his leonine head lifted to the heavens, his eyes lashing the sky, the two men looked at each other uneasily. "The Lord has appointed me your leader," Menahem intoned. "I will go with you unto Jerusalem and together we will purge the Kittim from the holy places."

"Amen," said the rapturous followers.

Pulling a scroll from his ample robes—one of the many scrolls his sect occupied their time at Qumran preparing from sacred writings—Menahem read: "A

267

star shall come forth out of Jacob and a comet shall rise out of Israel. The comet is the prince of all the congregation and when he appears, he will smite all the sons of Seth."

"Amen, amen," cried the Hasidim.

"Now receive the blessing of God."

Arms spread wide, as though encompassing the bowed heads of all the guerrillas who had fought for Masada, the grim mountains of Judaea a fantastic backdrop for his powerful figure, Menahem, his voice strong with his faith, blessed them. "*Yivorecho Adonoi veyishmorecho. Yoer Adonoi ponor ayrecho vechonaycho.* The Lord bless thee and keep thee. The Lord make His face to shine upon thee and be gracious unto thee; the Lord turn His face unto thee and give thee peace."

After the service, Simon and Bar Giora strolled away, both men deep in thought. "Were we right to take Masada the way we did?" Bar Giora said. "Using holy men as a cover?"

"War is war," Simon said indifferently. In the quiet demeanor and sensitivity of Bar Giora, he detected more and more of himself so long ago, an echo of his own youth. Now, an old alley cat, scarred in a hundred battles, he found that the end always justified the means.

"I suppose you are right." Bar Giora sighed. "Still, I would have preferred to have done it in some other fashion."

The men lapsed into silence. Somehow the high, lonely plateau that reared its head amid the Dead Sea wilderness, the opulent mosaics and paintings, the hypocausts, the swimming pool, the elegant villa standing untouched, unused, evoked some of the brooding misery of Herod the Great, the darkness of his murdering soul, his fury, when, having labored so long for the greatness of the Jews, they had spurned him for his lack of Jewishness. A place for grand designs, for a great monarch. By its very nearness to God, able to turn a man's head.

"What now?" Simon asked of Bar Giora. "What will you do?"

"There is armor, weaponry, artillery here. My people will convey it to Jerusalem to help the insurgents. Afterward I will take my men away."

"You will not fight for Jerusalem?"

"I will fight to throw out the Romans, yes, but afterward, when the real war comes, we will do what we do best, ride the plains of Judaea, cut supply lines. We are not city rats to fight in sewers, or a regular army to face a Roman legion."

"Yet somebody will have to build an army to use all this equipment," Simon said thoughtfully.

"Perhaps," Bar Giora said, shrugging. "And you, my friend? What will you do now?"

"John of Gishala sends volunteers to Jerusalem. I am to go there and take charge of them. May I accompany you?"

"It would be a pleasure," Bar Giora said, his long lashes lowering over his eyes as his face creased in a frank smile. He had taken to this tough, mutilated Galilean.

It would require several weeks to collect the mass of equipment, get it down the path and convoy it to Jerusalem. They both knew that. It was possible that the uprising might collapse and a Roman strike force appear over the next rugged hill at any moment, ready to annihilate them. Accordingly, there was much to do in little time. Scouts were sent out to reconnoiter and to scour the countryside for volunteers willing to reinforce the small numbers of guerrillas. Even if no more than a rabble, a small army would soon go to the help of the embattled Eleazar.

The one thing that Simon and Bar Giora did not discuss was the strange demeanor of Menahem. Each knew in his own heart that Menahem had become possessed by that ancient Jewish dream, a dream that had at once been both the hope and the scourge of their race for so long. It was something that they did not even dare talk about.

Menahem was not merely hoping to be the next High Priest. His ambitions lay far beyond that.

Menahem thought he was the Messiah.

29

In Jerusalem, paralysis gripped the city, with Eleazar overwhelmed by the responsibility of having to organize and feed thousands of poor townsfolk.

Careful to feel his way, he did not at once abolish the priestly caste and strip the nobility of money and power. To provoke an internal civil war might topple both him and his cadre of revolutionary officers. He moved slowly, broadening his power base by distributing such limited arms as he could find to the ragged, underprivileged occupants of the lower city who would be most loyal to him. His main concern was to provide himself with a stronghold—strategically placed so that he could stand against the Romans until the insurgent armies of Judaea came to help him.

Accordingly, he fortified those parts of the city with the most favorable natural features. The boundaries would be the eastern side of the Temple Mount, where it plunged down a dizzy five hundred feet into the Kidron valley, and the wall following the line of the old city around into the Valley of the Cheese Makers, so that with the exception of the northerly approaches to the Temple, he was protected on all sides by steep hills or escarpments.

Within only days of taking control, Eleazar was sleeping fitfully at the campaign headquarters he had set up in the Court of Gentiles, when his second-in-command burst in on him. "Comrade General," he called—such terms come naturally to the officers of Eleazar's staff—"Comrade General, come quickly."

"What is it?" Eleazar grabbed for his ornate Greek armor, squeezing the helmet on his head.

"They have seized the upper city."

"The Romans? They are back already?"

"No, Comrade General. The priests and nobles with the help of two thousand cavalry sent by Agrippa. They must have come through Bezetha during the night."

Eleazar cursed himself for not stationing sentries on the outer wall at Bezetha—for being too occupied creating defenses. With the arrival of two thousand men of Agrippa II, regulars trained and equipped by the Romans, his position was now perilous. That crafty Agrippa from across the Sea of Galilee had seized his chance and was bidding for Roman gratitude, hoping to acquire another kingdom. That was how the Herod family had always operated. Like chess players, with Judaea the board for the game, and the poor, blind and crippled, the pawns. A great anger shook Eleazar. Somehow they would hold. Morale must make up for lack of men and materiel.

"All Temple guards to the lower city," he ordered. "Find out who can use slings, swords, bows. Destroy all the houses on the western slope."

For days, bloody fighting raged, the nobles, aided by Agrippa's regulars, pushing Eleazar and his desperate revolutionaries farther and farther into the lower city, with Eleazar having to look over his shoulder in case of a sudden attack from the Roman garrison marooned in the Antonia.

Now, running short of supplies, fighting almost with their bare hands, the brave defenders of Jerusalem gave up more and more ground. Worst of all, the Romans, as Eleazar well knew, were coming. Unless help arrived and soon, Jerusalem would be lost.

For once in his life, Cestius Gallus of the ulcerated leg moved quickly. Putting together a formidable strike force, he punched south through Galilee ten thousand bronzed, disciplined veterans of the iron Twelfth Legion, screened by many thousands of auxiliary cavalry and supplemented by an elite contingent of the lethal Syrian bowmen.

But Jews knew how to die. In the villages, the farms,

271

the hills, the towns, they rose as one against their Greek, Syrian and Roman tormentors. In Tyre, Caesarea, Ptolemais, Gadara, a hundred towns, a thousand towns, they fought with their bare hands—and they perished: 2,500 in Ascalon, 2,000 in Ptolemais, 13,000 in Scythopolis. Even in faraway, civilized Alexandria they revolted, an incredible 20,000 being slaughtered as they tied down two terrible Roman legions. So the Jews placed their naked bodies between the Romans and Jerusalem, while guerrillas, waiting until the main force had gone through, would swoop on the supply wagons at the rear, bringing the whole army to a halt until the cavalry chased them off.

The machinelike, inexorable Roman marching pace of five miles an hour slowed, ground to a crawl.

In Jerusalem, Agrippa's trained regulars now mounted an all-out assault from the upper city. But only the night before, John of Gishala had managed to sneak in two thousand of his elite Sicarii under cover of the thousands of pilgrims thronging the streets on the feast of wood-carrying. Stiffened just in time, the Temple Guard somehow held. Then, only two days later, they came—at first just a few dusty scouts appearing out of the heat haze, swelling into a great disorderly rabble moving up from the south and pulling carts laden with armor, spears, pila and heavy siege apparatus that the Jews had somehow brought down the path and ingeniously pieced together.

Eleazar the revolutionary, watching them come in, did not bother about the niceties of command—which men were Menahem's?—which were Bar Giora's?—but threw them straight into the fight for the upper city. The enemy, heavily outnumbered, wavered, then ran. One by one, the house of Ananias the High Priest, the palaces of the rich, the record office holding the moneylenders' bonds went up in flames, and a great cheer rose from the lower city. Like rats, the priests, the merchants, the wealthy stall holders of the Temple bolted for their last refuge—the walled palace on the western hill.

Now, the glint of victory shining on his armor, Eleazar switched his attack. In the full, glaring heat of the day—that glorious fifteenth of August—picked shock troops working under the skilled direction of a one-eyed ex-colonel of legions, Simon ben Eleazar by name, assaulted and finally took the Antonia fortress. As the last symbol of Roman domination over the Temple fell, and the Jewish flag with the emblem of the seven-candled menorah—the first truly national flag since the days of the Maccabees—fluttered out from the top of the Antonia battlements, the whole city went mad.

With the opposition soon mopped up, terrible things would now be done by Eleazar in the name of the revolution. He would not shrink from patricide and massacre: anything, however shameful, was justified in the cause of the people. Coldly, cruelly, his politically indoctrinated Temple Guard hunted down the nobles, the priests, pursued the merchants through the sewers and alleys of the old city. Finally, they cornered the High Priest and his brother, Hezekiah, near the Palace Canal and there they killed them.

But even worse was to come. At command headquarters, discussing the latest military position with Bar Giora and Simon ben Eleazar—a man to whom the guerrillas were increasingly turning for military guidance—Eleazar was startled to hear the sound of music and chanting from what now should have been a deserted Temple. Rushing through the great Nicanor Gates into the Court of Women, up the marbled semicircular steps that led into the Court of Israel, and from there into the Court of Priests, the three men came to a halt, amazed at what they saw.

Two lambs had just been sacrificed and the great altar of burnt offerings—a vast cubical slab of stone with four horns protruding from its corners—ran with blood while the whole area just outside the vast Sanctuary itself stank with heavy, rolling incense. A mass choir made up of Levites and young boys had been assembled, who, accompanied by an orchestra of harps and ten-stringed lyres, were slowly singing the holy Hallel service.

The men's eyes, however, were riveted on Menahem. He was clad in breeches that covered his thighs to the crotch, over which he had donned an ankle-length blue robe with golden bells and pomegranates attached to its tassels. In addition, he wore a breastplate of solid gold decorated with twelve kinds of precious stones, one for each of the twelve tribes of Israel, and on his head he wore a linen miter emblazoned with the four sacred letters *YHVH*. Arms outstretched to heaven, his patriarchal figure could be seen through the clouds of smoke and incense, outlined against the solid gold and silver plates of a door guarding the Sanctuary approaches, his great leonine head shaking with emotion, eyes burning with zeal as he intoned the solemn words "Let the shofar sound."

As the ram's horn blasted dramatically into the air, Menahem in a throbbing voice declaimed: "I will go before thee and make the crooked places straight: I will break in pieces the gates of bronze and cut in sunder the bars of iron; I will give thee the treasures of darkness, and hidden riches of secret places, that thou mayest know that I, the Lord, which call thee by name, am the God of Israel."

Eleazar took in the sacks of money, dazzling jewels, dull bars of gold heaped at Menahem's feet and in seconds realized what was happening: Menahem was proclaiming himself the Messiah, using an appropriately prophetic passage from Isaiah to allow him to distribute the Temple treasure among the common people. Such a message would be utterly irresistible. In minutes, the whole of Jerusalem could be applauding its Davidic savior—in days, it would be the entire country—and all Eleazar's political planning and scheming would have been wasted.

"Seize him," he shouted to the Temple guards.

His revolutionary officers, no respecters of holy places, grabbed Menahem and carried him away. Later, they would torture him to an agonizing death for his temerity in bidding for power over Eleazar's head.

But all this was nothing compared with the heroism of the tiny Jewish nation that had grabbed the Roman wolf by the throat and was holding on. When the first advance scouts for Cestius Gallus' forces reconnoitered the city, they were to find walls lined with thousands of armed men. They were not to know that the city was racked by internal quarrels, or that the sentries were mostly raw peasants likely to run away at the first sight of a Roman legion. They merely reported the position as they saw it: that Gallus had lost the race to be first into the city.

For Cestius Gallus, governor of Syria, lying on his couch in the command tent, ten miles away from the Jerusalem heights, nothing was either simple or clear-cut. The continuous pain from his ulcerated leg prevented clear thought. He wondered if the philosophers could understand this malaise, the inability to take action, the agony of indecision that always froze him when decisions were needed. With his leg on fire from the rub of his horse's flanks, he prepared, while his Negro slave boy dabbed the injured limb with ointment, to question his aide, a sprig of the patrician aristocracy who had just returned from a scouting mission.

"And how did your reconnaissance go?"

The aide, who bore the unbelievable label of Titus Pomponius Mamilianus Funisalanus Vettonianus and who still had smut marks mixed with the sweat on his face, answered proudly, "Well, we burned Bezetha, sire. No one can say we haven't taught them a lesson."

"And the walls?" Gallus said. "What chance of scaling the walls of the inner city?"

"We do not know how they are manned. The Jews made no sortie."

"Then their discipline must indeed be ferocious," Gallus said shrewdly. "You can just imagine the temptation to come out and attack a light force engaged in wrecking their homes, killing the old and infirm they had to leave behind. Yet none came."

The aide sucked his teeth. "Perhaps the thought of fighting Roman regulars has discouraged them?"

"Rubbish," Gallus exploded. "They have simply fortified their best positions and are content to wait, while out here our supply lines are menaced and the whole countryside waits like vultures to destroy us."

The aide said nothing, content to let the old fool prattle. Soon, with his connections, he would be back in Rome, the sunburned hero of the Judaean campaign, standing for the post of quaestor in the Senate, and this terrible nightmare would be past.

For a moment, Gallus reflected bitterly on his fate. Neither a clever nor an ambitious man, he watched earthshaking events on the move all around him, while he lay stretched on the rack of circumstance with nobody but this nitwit of an aristocrat to help him. "Well, let no one say we lack courage," he said eventually. "The legion will go on the attack at first light, but I must make it very plain that if success does not immediately crown our arms, we shall withdraw in good order to the north."

Six hours later, the legion struck camp. As it wound up the narrow defile at Beth-Horon that led to Jerusalem, the first rays of daylight could be seen glinting gold on the high spires of the Temple Sanctuary, lighting up that white rag with its crudely drawn emblem of the seven-candled menorah. The soldiers laughed at the sight. They were in good spirits; after so many days on the road—the auxiliaries having all the fun, burning the villages, raping the women—it would soon be their turn. No longer were they the iron reserve held back for all contingencies; they were going in to smash the Jews. So they marched at an easy, disciplined pace, singing as they went, their armor and helmets clanking with each step, men in the full flower of health, meat-fed, fined down to savage fighting animals who smelled of sweat and vinegar wine and now scented the sleek, exotic flesh of Jewish women.

Some died thinking of women—and so lived forever: the immense boulder, moving imperceptibly, hung for a second at an impossible angle at the edge of the cliff, then crashed onto the road below with a thunderous roar, sending up a gigantic cloud of dust. Yipping and screaming their strange, high war cries, the sunburned freedom-fighters from the south, from the Negev, the flower of Bar Giora's guerrilla force, came sliding down onto the cutoff baggage wagons. They were a motley crew, riding anything on four legs that could be persuaded to move—donkeys, mules, scrubby little ponies. In they came, stabbing with their lances. Caught in the still-dark defile by these murderous guerrillas who had appeared from nowhere, the screen of cavalry protecting the deeply laden baggage animals milled about in utter confusion, then fled. In minutes, Bar Giora, acting under the expert tactical advice of a certain ex-colonel, had detached the legion's whole food supply and was leading the mules away into the hills. As a victory, it did not compare to that of his ancestor, "the hammer of the Maccabees," over the Seleucids at the same spot over two hundred years earlier and celebrated in every Jewish home. It was no more than a successful skirmish by a few brigands against a legion's baggage train—but its effect on the future of the Jewish people would be incalculable.

Unaware, by reason of the narrow, winding road, of the carnage in its rear, the legion moved smoothly on. Marching through the still-burning ruins of Bezetha, it finally halted at the second Jerusalem wall and with much blowing of trumpets formed up for the attack.

At this fantastic sight—the massed, disciplined soldiers of a Roman legion of the line, the crested helmets of the officers, the eagles and standards held in perfect symmetry, the siege engines ready to be brought up—the Jews lost heart and fled the battlements. Nobody could blame them—peasant boys with blunt swords thrust into their hands and told to fight the power of Rome. Eleazar, watching them rush past him with terror on their faces, lashed at them with his cane, cursing them for cowards and traitors, but they took no notice, knocking him down in their haste to get away.

On the Roman side, Gallus' aide, sweating on his fine blood horse, galloped triumphantly up to Cestius Gallus, who had transferred to a litter to save his leg. "You have them, sire," he shouted, his eyes alive with enthusiasm. "They leave the walls."

"Have you not heard?" Gallus, to whom the news had just been brought, said wearily. "They detached our baggage train at Beth-Horon."

"What difference does it make?" said the aide. "Order the attack and you'll sweep the city."

"It's a trap. Surely you can see that?" Gallus said scornfully. "My dear Titus, Pomponius—whatever all your names are—the situation is obvious. They mean to lure my legion into the ruins, surround it so that we starve without our supplies, then pick us off one by one like the alley cats they are."

"Oh, I didn't realize," the aide said ruefully.

"I had hoped to provoke them into fighting us," Gallus said complacently, "but they were too clever. I, also, have shown myself not without a knowledge of military tactics and will not walk into the snare."

Confident that he had saved a Roman legion from destruction, Gallus, normally so indecisive, made his first real decision in a long time. He ordered his forces to withdraw.

And now the terrible time began: the Jews, treating his withdrawal as a miracle from God, recovered their morale and harried him without mercy. Every defensive move he made was anticipated with amazing foresight. The withdrawal became a retreat. Then, all siege equipment and artillery abandoned, the retreat turned into a rout.

When the legion reached the safety of Antipatris, it was no more than a tattered remnant, having lost over five thousand effectives. Such a major disaster would have to be reported at once to the Emperor Nero in Greece.

On board ship, the couriers had plenty of time to discuss in awed tones the Jew wearing a black eye patch, a Roman officer's cuirass and riding a white blood horse. He had been seen everywhere, directing the guerrillas' attacks. Those who had gotten near him and survived to tell the tale said that he bore the insignia and phalerae of a colonel of the line.

30

Vespasian sat in the Temple of Song at Actium, listening to Nero competing in the games. Watching would have been as good a word, because the corpulent Emperor, as well as being made up with kohl and rouge, was dressed in a brilliantly colored Greek robe with a scarf around his neck and wore neither belt nor shoes.

Accompanying himself on the lyre, the Emperor was singing interminable passages from a poem he had composed on the Trojan wars.

Even now, Vespasian could not work out what he was doing here in Greece as part of the Emperor's retinue; he had no wit, no sophistication, neither manners nor breeding. Also, at the age of fifty-seven he had a distinctly mediocre career to look back upon. Although he had done well enough in Britannia, he had antagonized the wrong people in Rome and his career had stagnated. He had, eventually, been lucky enough to receive the governorship of Africa, but even there had not learned the trick of lining his own pockets, and when they had disliked one of his judicial decisions, the people of Hadrumentum had even pelted him with turnips! Vespasian grinned ruefully at the thought and settled deeper in his seat. He folded his massive, peasant's forearms in front of him, his head falling on his chest. With Nero's appalling dirge, Vespasian, an unmusical man at best, found it difficult to keep awake. Once or twice the frantically shrill appreciation coming from a group of beringed, painted little boys jerked him sheepishly upright, but it was hard work just to keep his eyes open.

Eventually he dozed—and began to dream. One of those strange, disjointed dreams founded on the wildest of suppositions. For some reason he dreamed that his career would begin to prosper mightily if Nero should lose a tooth. Extraordinary, that. Really extraordinary. Vespasian smiled in his sleep and settled more comfortably in his chair.

So it was, at the most solemn moment of "The Trojan Wars," Nero's rolling bass voice was disturbed by a truly remarkable sound. Mellifluous, reverberating around the temple, the noise brought Nero's poem to an abrupt end amid shocked confusion—the contented sound of Vespasian's snores.

Nero, fury showing on his petulant face, ordered guards to remove Vespasian and hold him under close confinement. He stalked off the stage and retired to the villa that his Greek hosts had put at his disposal. Furiously he tugged at a bell-pull and, when a cringing slave appeared, ordered a flagon of his favorite ice water and also the presence of the boy Sporus.

279

Eventually, Nero lay down to sleep; the eunuch's comfortings had taken away some of his rage at Vespasian's cloddish snores, ruining his performance and almost certainly losing him the prize. Later he would have the man put to torture, and in "the ancient manner"—his head stuck in a fork and then beaten to death with sticks. The thought satisfied him. He turned his head to the wall and rested, but in only minutes there was a frantic knocking at the door.

"What is it?" he called irritably.

"Couriers from Judaea, sire," the captain of the guard called through the wall. "They crave immediate audience."

"All right, all right," said Nero irritably. "Let them come in."

The two men, dusty and sweaty, stamped into the room in their riding boots, drawing themselves to attention.

Nero had difficulty hiding a grin. He had just remembered the penchant that Galba, one of his governors, had for hot, sweaty men and how couriers, after racing through the day with urgent dispatches, had been made to strip and go to bed with him. Thank the gods I'm normal, he said to himself. "Gentlemen, you may stand at ease," he commanded. "Now what is this news from Judaea that is so urgent?"

In answer, they handed him a bulky dispatch from Cestius Gallus. The crippled governor had not attempted to cover up what had happened to the Twelfth Legion. Nor had he minimized the state of open war in the province. As Nero read on, fury grew on his spotty face, interplaying with amazement at the Jews' bravery.

He ordered the couriers from the room, then got up and strode backward and forward, thinking. Such was his state of perturbation that he tripped over his robe and pitched headfirst onto the marble floor, giving his mouth a nasty knock. The Emperor screamed for his slaves, almost in tears. If there were two things he was afraid of, they were revolt and personal injury, and in seconds he had suffered both.

Quickly, his personal attendants dressed his wound. "Get out," Nero said, "and fetch me Vespasian."

Brought from his cell, Vespasian was under no

illusions as to his probable fate. He entered the Emperor's chamber in a resigned frame of mind. He had braved death too often. He just hoped that his sons would be spared any suffering. The gods alone knew how poor the family was, without their being destroyed by their father's disgrace.

"Well?" Nero cursed. "What do you mean by ruining my performance?"

"I'm sorry, sire."

"What?" Nero screamed. "No moving speech, no emotional plea for mercy? Ah—I forgot! You're no greasy patrician, are you, Vespasian? Just a horny-handed son of the soil. I suppose that's it, and that's all the apology I'm going to get?"

"It won't happen again, sire," Vespasian said stolidly.

"You're quite right. It certainly won't."

Here it comes, thought Vespasian. The death sentence.

"And I'll tell you why," the Emperor stormed on, "because I'm sending you off to Syria as the new governor there, to put down the Jewish revolt. Draw as many legions as you want from Greece, Asia Minor or Egypt. Just put it down. Understand?"

Tough and unemotional as he was, Vespasian could not take it in. His head swam and his eyes streamed. Here he was approaching sixty, at the end of his career, being given the overlordship of the whole eastern Empire—a position of unbelievable power. Nero was playing a joke, he decided, but he would still have to be polite. "Thank you, sire," he said. "It is a great honor and I shall do my best."

"You know why I have chosen you, General?" Nero asked.

General—he was calling him General. Unbelievingly, Vespasian realized that the Emperor really meant it. "No, sire," he muttered shakily.

"So that I won't have to listen to your snoring, next time I sing."

"Yes, sire."

"Now would you like to hear the real reason?" Nero leaned forward.

"If you please, sire."

"I trust you," Nero said. "You're the only honest man in Rome."

Bowing out of the Emperor's presence, his mind still reeling, Vespasian bumped into one of Nero's personal slaves, carrying a bloodied handkerchief in his hand. "Sorry, sir, sorry, sir," the slave whispered.

"What's that?" Vespasian pointed.

"The Emperor's tooth," the slave replied.

Hours later, Vespasian sat behind a large table in the pleasant, airy villa that had been put at his disposal. It was amazing how every request he made had been immediately granted—how those courtiers of Nero's who had previously treated him with contempt now fawned on him. It did not take long for the word to go out as to which star was rising. The court had delicately attuned ears.

So much to do. His whole burly frame and thick bruiser's chin were hunched forward in determination. He had called for and received a precise staff report on the condition of the legions in the far-flung Empire of the East and now pored over innumerable half-folded maps that littered the table. So many problems. A whole staff structure to set up, officers, aides-de-camp, instructions to go out, legions to be provisioned—great armies must soon be on the move and allies would have to be treated firmly. A balancing trick would have to be performed, the requisitioning of large contingents of their men without disclosing any Roman need or weakness. So many things to decide. Which garrisons should be left undisturbed, how many legions he could afford to draw off into Judea. The Parthians—treacherous, powerful— lurked on Rome's eastern borders. Vespasian's head swam with the responsibility suddenly thrust upon him by his imperial master.

The scribes who sat in front of him, three rather effeminate Greek slaves, looked at this coarse, muscular peasant and yawned in bored contempt. To them, he looked both incompetent and barely literate. They were soon to change their minds. Quickly, crisply, he began to dictate. Requests went out, polite but firm, respectful but brooking no opposition—to Agrippa II of the Golan Heights, for his Roman trained regulars; to Soaemus and Antiochus, Syrian kings who had fleet cavalry and world-famous bowmen; to Malchus, king of Arabia, for more horse, even more bowmen. The formidable list grew longer. Now and again Vespasian would pause to allow his struggling scribes to catch up, tinkling a bell and demanding of his harassed aide, "Where's my son Titus?" Each time that the aide shook his head, real pain showed in Vespasian's eyes.

So the work went on—staff appointments to be made, stores to be accumulated—and slowly, as the picture unfolded, Vespasian came to the most important decisions of all. The massing of the legions. From the north, he himself would lead the Fifth Macedonia and Tenth Fretensis down through Asia Minor, and from Egypt, the Fifteenth Apollinaris would march north— there was an able commander there, Vespasian recalled, by the name of Trajan. In Syria, meanwhile, the battered Twelfth would retrain and bring up its numbers of effectives, and all of them, four elite legions, would rendezvous at Ptolemais. With these legions would assemble reserve cohorts of unattached regulars, uncountable thousands of auxiliaries and engineers. Slowly the scribes scratched away in their painstaking shorthand, the letters and dispatches taking shape that were soon to radiate across the Empire in a deadly web. Vespasian was taking the Jews seriously. "Has Titus come?" he barked again at his aide. Patiently, the aide regretted that Titus had not.

Vespasian bent back to the job in hand. He had already interviewed the two couriers from Judaea and had them make a written report containing profiles of the leaders of the Jewish revolt. Dismissing his scribes, Vespasian now began to study this report carefully. He read the cursory notes on the as yet little-known Silas the Babylonian and Niger of Peraea, who had brought in contingents from outer Judaea to help smash Cestius Gallus. With some amusement he studied the activities of John of Gishala, with less amusement the strength and toughness of Bar Giora and the political purpose of Eleazar. However, his face went set and grim when he came to the mass of notes surrounding the activities of a certain Jew wearing a black eye patch who affected a Roman colonel's cuirass and phalerae. Everywhere he had been seen in the forefront, directing maneuvers. Suspected of having kidnapped the High Priest's son in an audacious operation, he was rumored to have masterminded the incredible capture of Masada. Sitting on a white thoroughbred, he had been seen calmly directing the ruin of Cestius Gallus' iron Twelfth Legion. Vespasian's mouth set in a thin, obstinate line.

Putting the papers away from him, he sat back, muscular arms akimbo, and tried to relax. "Where's my son?" he asked for the sixth time, but there was no answer. His aide was diplomatically absent. I'm too old a man to have all this tension, Vespasian thought. I must plan my life more carefully—look after my health. A nap every afternoon with a comfortable woman would be the thing. No juicy little slave girl—he disliked the idea of using the body of a young girl as of right. One, perhaps two good healthy mistresses, able to cook country dishes and generally look after his wants. But not too expensive, he thought. For some years, since the death of his wife, he had done without the comfort of women because of their inordinate expense. But now, for his health's sake, a modest regime of female company could be tolerated by his purse. Vespasian's thoughts were interrupted by a knock.

"Come in," he called.

His son Titus entered and stood before his father, a faint, rather bored smile on his face. As always, Vespasian looked at him with mixed feelings. A peasant, he felt proud of this handsome, upstanding lad who bore himself with such graceful elegance. The fees that he had scraped together for Titus' education had resulted in a life of real hardship for Vespasian, but it had been worthwhile. The boy was a real patrician, a Roman noble. And handsome. A bit paunchy for his middle twenties perhaps, but that was only from good living. Yet the boy was being corrupted. Tales were told of debauches with Nero's cronies, that he even kept a troupe of dancing boys. Vespasian's nose twitched with displeasure not only at the immorality, but also the expense. Sow your wild oats, he thought, but not that. Have I sacrificed everything to rear a dissolute wastrel?

"Where have you been?" he demanded.

"I came as soon as I could, Father," Titus said sulkily.

Always a cheerful boy, he had become churlish and short with his father.

"I won't have this behavior," Vespasian said. "You're bringing discredit on me and your family."

"Family?" Titus said, lifting one eyebrow. "What family? Tax farmers, peasants who migrate to gather the harvest. You know what they call our family in Rome? Maggots from cow dung."

"Shut your mouth," Vespasian said angrily. He half rose, intending to strike the boy, but slumped wearily back in his chair. "You have heard of my new responsibilities?"

"Yes."

"Are you not pleased for your father?"

"Not while you treat me as a child to be lectured, a young boy to be punished."

Titus flinched as Vespasian levered his burly form away from his chair and advanced on him, fearing a blow, but now Vespasian did a surprising thing. He put his arms around Titus and said in a low voice, "Help me. In the name of all the gods—please help me." Titus, astonished, found his cheek was wet with his father's tears.

"What—what do you mean?" he responded awkwardly.

"I'm too old for all this work. It's come too late. Nero only gave me the job because he thinks I'm too stupid to be a traitor, but that's not the point. The task is enormous. It needs a far younger man."

"Then tell him," Titus grunted. "Not me."

"All my life," Vespasian said in a husky voice, "I've scrimped and saved for your education, your future. I'm not asking for thanks, but just want to point out that there is nothing you cannot now do better than any man in Rome. All I want is your help as a son."

"Father," Titus said, his defiance turning to bewilderment, "I don't understand."

"If I give you joint command, will you honor me, respect my advice?"

"Joint command?" Titus recoiled in amazement. "Are you serious?"

"Why not?" Vespasian demanded. "You are educated. You have the qualities valued by those eastern monarchs. You understand military matters. You sit a horse well and they say you can fight like twenty devils—and who else should I trust more than my own son?"

Titus looked at his father for a long time, but saw only pride—and love. Slowly he went down on his knees.

"Give me your hand, Father."

Vespasian did so.

Titus whispered, "I do not deserve a parent like you. I have been dissolute, rebellious and a spendthrift. Now that I know you need me, I shall be at your side."

"My son, my son," murmured Vespasian awkwardly. "Get off your knees."

"I shall dismiss my friends, sell my troupe of dancers. They were no more than an affectation anyway."

"I am glad to hear it."

"Now, Father, what is it you want of me?"

"Go to Egypt in my name. Tell Trajan to bring his legion. Organize the whole expeditionary force from the south."

"It shall be done."

The two men clasped hands, father and son, now friends and colleagues.

"First," Vespasian said, "sit down. I must tell you of something that weighs heavily on my heart and which, if I do not share it with another man, may drive me out of my mind. It concerns a former Roman soldier, a comrade of mine who now advises the Jews in their rebellion. The thought of fighting such a man frightens me. A Jew who rides a white horse and still affects a Roman cuirass and knows our tactics as well as any Roman general. His name is Simon ben Eleazar. I first met him when he saved my life at the games. He served under me in the Britannia campaign where he saved my life on two more occasions and we became—like blood brothers. When I was at my wit's end for funds, he sent me money. One favor I have managed to repay, but I still remain deep in debt to a dear friend."

"Steady, Father," Titus said, smiling. "A story such as this calls for a proper setting. Let us have some Falernian."

Vespasian, reaching for the bell on his table, said doubtfully, "An expensive vintage—are you sure we can afford—?" The two of them burst out laughing at this old problem that died hard.

And so, as the evening shadows lengthened into darkness, the two men drank and Vespasian told his son the story of his association with Simon and the bond, almost of love, that they had with each other.

All this happened at the turn of the year 66–67. It is worth noting that elected consul was a certain Gaius Suetonius Paulinus, a snappy, terrierlike ex-general who had defeated Boudicca. In this year, when the two men whom Simon most worshiped rose to positions of supreme prominence in the Roman Empire, he himself was poised to write a page in the history of the Jews that would live forever. All these men would soon reach the apogee of their careers, the lives of Simon and Vespasian intermingling and merging in climactic drama.

One other, Petilius Cerialis, was destined to render services to Vespasian that would provide him a place in history as important as the others'. But that is no part of events to be played out in Judaea, where fate would soon turn old friends into enemies.

31

The great Augustus chamber of Herod's palace on the western ridge of Jerusalem rang to the sounds of riotous orgy. The leaders of the insurgent armies had converged to discuss future policy and recount their exploits, but instead, the conference had turned into a monumentally drunken celebration.

For three days and nights the guerrillas roamed the palace, despoiling priceless paintings and sculptures, defecating like mountain goats on the superb carpets. Women had been brought in, the great hall resounding to the clash of cymbals and the playing of reed instruments as naked slave girls, sweat-covered belly dancers cavorted and gyrated, competing with the sleek-skinned women of the rich merchants who had been dragged from their hiding places, moaning and terrified, to please the guerrillas. Many fights had taken place before the guerrillas had finally drunk themselves into a state of insensibility, allowing an uneasy peace to descend on the banqueting hall.

Eleazar, clad in a plain, severe tunic, shunning the Jewish passion for ornament and jewelry, now strode in with a detachment of Temple Guard in full armor. Quickly, he had the leaders stripped of their weapons. He would have loved to kill them all, but needed these men to harry Romans in the countryside, while he trained the peasants in the facts of revolution. After a short recess, Eleazar reassembled the chiefs and proceeded to lecture them.

"You, who have liberated Jerusalem, now have it in your power to free the whole country." He began to outline the strategic situation in Judaea and Galilee, but the chiefs, interested enough to start with, soon became bored and started helping themselves once again to the wine.

At this, Eleazar became really annoyed. "Here you are," he screamed, "with a chance to build a great country, to raise the poor and starving from bondage, and all you want is loot and women. I tell you, you are filth—the spawn of cesspits."

"I'll not listen to this," roared John of Gishala suddenly, an ugly-looking *sica* appearing in his hand. "Come on," he shouted to his men, "back to the Galilee. We fight the Romans on our terms, not his." He shambled out of the hall, filthy, shaking from his excesses, his men swaggering after him in their dirty sheepskins.

Simon observed John's departure with a certain curiosity. For some reason John had ignored him, refusing to speak to Simon at all. His thoughts on the subject were distracted as Bar Giora walked over to him.

"Will you come?" Bar Giora said. "I go to my homeland in Judaea to beset the Romans coming up from the south. I will not fight under the orders of this turd." He glanced contemptuously at Eleazar. "I have need of your skills, Simon."

"I have returned to this country to fight Romans. I must first hear what the others decide."

"Well, you know where I am," said Bar Giora. "We had some fine times together and I hope we can soon be fighting side by side." They exchanged salutes and Bar Giora led his men from the hall.

Pleased at getting rid of the chief thorns in his flesh, but at the same time annoyed that he had, as yet, failed to dislodge Simon ben Eleazar from the city, Eleazar called the conference to order. With little effort, he managed to secure the minor guerrilla leaders' approval to a whole succession of decrees: the pliant Ananus, his brother, to be the new High Priest—a sop to any left in Jerusalem with religious convictions; the three remaining guerrilla leaders, Niger the Peraean, Silas the Babylonian and John the Essene, to be persuaded to lead their armies to bloody ruins against a trained Roman garrison on the plains of Ascalon. Only Simon, of the battered, mutilated face, the quiet voice and the one glowing gray-green eye, refused to be shifted. This man is dangerous, Eleazar thought. Perhaps the most dangerous of all. He reads my thoughts. He knows that I intend to train my army of peasants in the ways of revolution, and to make Jerusalem impregnable to attack, while the others perish in their thousands. Perhaps he will have to be killed.

The thoughts of Eleazar were disturbed by loud knocking. He signed to his guards to see who was causing the disturbance. Before they could get there, the doors burst open and a man sauntered in at the head of an escort of superbly armored and accoutered soldiers.

"Greetings," he said.

"Who are you?" Eleazar inquired.

Examining the stranger, Simon saw a sturdy, round-faced young man with wide, innocent eyes and a ready smile. He wore a toga patterned with notched bands and carrying ritual fringes, as though emphasizing that his education had been absorbed from both Roman and Hebrew cultures.

"I am Joseph ben Mathias," the man said. "I come in peace and with offers of help."

"What kind of help?" Eleazar said, fighting down a scowl. He knew this Joseph ben Mathias—there were few, indeed, who had not heard his name. The man was from one of the priestly aristocratic families and fabulously wealthy, owning vast tracts of the Galilee. Normally Eleazar would have no truck with him, but now an idea formed. "Nevermind." His manner quickly changed to the effusive. "You are welcome, and so is your help."

"I hear you have armor to spare," Joseph ben Mathias said. "Give it to me and I will mass an army to oppose the Romans when they enter Galilee."

"That is not impossible," Eleazar said. "I do not mean offense, but I must ask this: You have previously been a friend of Rome. Why have you changed sides?"

Joseph ben Mathias walked slowly around the table. Stretching out a hand, he helped himself to wine, adding water in precise half-and-half proportion, then drinking in slow, measured gulps. Simon noticed what soft hands he had, the rings on his fingers, all of precious stones, the gold ring of the Roman equestrian order. Everything that this man did, he decided, would be done only after the most considered thought, accompanied by a disarming smile of the purest innocence. "Oh, I am not offended," Joseph answered. "The question deserves a reply. None of us likes the Romans ruling our country. We are Jews after all. Some fight them. Others, like myself, have felt they could do better for their country by cooperating. You cannot deny that King Herod did great things for the Jews by such methods."

Receiving only the iciest of silence for his compliment to Herod the Great, Joseph went on, "Now, of course, things are much changed. We have the men, the armor, the treasure to fight a war. More important, with the Romans gone, we have been given time to mobilize and train."

Eleazar thought, you sit on the fence, let others do the fighting, then when it's safe, you stroll in here, your

290

Roman toga hung with the ritual fringes of a pious Jew, and ask for Temple money and Herod's armor. Forcing a smile, he said, "We shall help you all we can."

"You intend to take on four elite Roman legions in the field?" Simon asked.

"Why not? You may say that only guerrilla bands striking from the hills have any chance of success, but I'd remind you that Judas Maccabeus eventually formed an army that drove out the invader."

"How many could you raise and equip?" asked Eleazar.

"A hundred thousand or so," Joseph ben Mathias said carelessly. "You really would be amazed at the difference two months' training can make. In Rome, I have seen with my own eyes country bumpkins turned into legionaries within that time. Just let me have some of your spare weaponry."

"Of course," Eleazar said. "Of course." He went on, as if just struck by a brilliant thought, "And there is the very man here to help you. A former Roman colonel with immense military experience."

"I've heard of him," Joseph said blandly. "Who does not know of his exploits? I dared hope that you would be able to spare him."

"Oh, yes," Eleazar said, "I can spare him." He fought down a grin at the thought of Simon out of the way while he turned the already huge walls of Jerusalem into impregnable bastions. Win or lose, the Jews outside would perish while he sat in Jerusalem with the only cohesive strike force to support his revolutionary government. Turning to Simon, he asked, emotion in his voice, "Well, will you go and help Joseph ben Mathias build a Jewish army?"

"I have come here to fight Romans," Simon said slowly. "Naturally I must go where the biggest battles are likely to take place."

"Good, good," Joseph said, rubbing his white, manicured hands. "Between us we shall do great things."

"We shall do terrible things," Simon said with sudden harshness. "We celebrate the defeat of a Roman legion, but what is one mauled legion to an empire that can send thirty more?" He paused, then added soberly, "All we are doing is sending tens of thousands of Jewish boys to their deaths."

"We must persevere nonetheless," Joseph said. Even now, the smile had not left his face.

"And what do you care?" Simon sneered. "You are only in this for the sport. If you win, you become a great prince. If you lose, your many Roman friends will ensure that your life be spared. For you, when Jewish corpses choke our fields, when Jewish slaves are fed to the lions, it will have been just an amusing campaign."

Now, the eyes of Joseph ben Mathias opened wide in the look of an innocent suffering from outrageous injustice. "I hope, in time, I can persuade you to think better of me. Tomorrow morning—when I leave—you will come?"

"I will come," Simon said. He was sick of them all. The disorganized, drunken irregulars, the devious Eleazar, the polished, Romanized Joseph. Leaving the banqueting hall, he whispered under his breath, "Oh, yes, I will come, my friend, and I will watch you closer than a hawk, because at the first sign of trouble, you will be the first to change sides."

Walking along the great, arched aqueduct that spanned the Valley of the Cheese Makers and connected Herod's palace with the Temple, Simon was only vaguely conscious of the figure that passed him, clothed, like so many of the Am haarez—the common working folk—in a loose-fitting cloak of goat's hair, head swathed in a prayer shawl. When the figure turned to follow him, keeping the same distance whether he walked faster or slower, Simon suspected he had been marked for assassination by Eleazar. Stopping on the pretext of removing a stone from his sandal, Simon waited until the figure came close to him, then leaped, pantherlike, pinioning him to the ledge of the parapet, with a dizzy drop into the valley below only seconds away if the answers were unsatisfactory.

"Who are you?" he demanded. "Why are you following me?"

He eased the pressure of his arm to allow for a reply and was instantly rewarded by a girl's laugh. Impatiently, he ripped the pray shawl away. Delicious tawny hair came into view.

"Andrasta," he cried.

"Oh, Simon." She put her arms around him and they embraced with tears in their eyes.

"Only tomorrow I was coming to fetch you," he said. "Why did you leave Galilee? This town is not safe for a woman on her own."

"I was well disguised," Andrasta said. "Besides, I have a friend here on which you have taught me to rely." She glanced down at the dagger stuck in her waistband.

"Still, it was dangerous to come."

"Not as dangerous as staying with John of Gishala."

"What do you mean? He tried you?"

She nodded.

Simon shuddered. "I was a fool," he said. "I thought I could trust him."

"Oh, he did his best," said Andrasta, laughing, "but he's a brigand, you know, and used to taking anything he pleases. One must not blame him too much."

Simon, despite his fury, noted a subtle change in the girl's manner, almost as though her love for him had quenched her hatred for men. She had thrown off John's attack as a matter of no consequence and there was a softness and happiness about her that he had not seen before. "Nevertheless," he said, "I shall kill him."

Laughter danced in the girl's eyes again. Linking arms with Simon, she said, "Leave him. He did not hurt me. Tell me what you have been doing. I want to hear it all. Galilee talks of nothing but your exploits."

Simon told her of his exciting weeks in the Dead Sea valley and the subsequent relief of Jerusalem. "And now," he said at length, "we shall be like common tourists. I shall show you the holy city."

Together they explored Jerusalem. First, the vast Court of Gentiles, empty now of its lusty commercial splendor, with one drab booth replacing the hundreds of money changers' stalls and a roped-off stable area containing animals for sacrifice. Eleazar had expelled the speculators and imposed a "people's monopoly" on these lucrative revenues. With Andrasta, a Gentile, not being allowed into the inner courts—"ON PAIN OF DEATH" as the notices in Latin, Greek and Hebrew plainly said—they leaned against the *soreg* (the latticed fence) and from there Simon pointed out as best he could the glories of the Nicanor Gates, built entirely of burnished copper, the Corinthian Gates, made of stout, hammered plates of pure gold and silver, and how one passed through these gates into various courts until finally one reached the divine sanctuary where the Jewish God Himself dwelled, on whom the High Priest alone was allowed to look on the holy day of Yom Kippur. With wondering eyes, Andrasta followed Simon as he showed the awesome white marble columns of the sanctuary clawing the sky, capped with spires of pure gold.

Eventually, they wandered out of the Golden Gate, close by the Mount of Olives, and passed through the still-smoking new quarter of Bezetha and under the ramparts of the Antonia fortress, from which the tattered flag with its crude drawing of the seven-candled menorah still proudly flew. From there, turning south into the Valley of the Cheese Makers, they passed through gates let into two of Jerusalem's three defensive walls. These walls, explained Simon, had been built to formidable proportions by Herod Agrippa, who ruled Judaea for a short time as a reward for assistance given to Caligula and Claudius. Simon vividly remembered the visit from the bejeweled, bearded monarch and how it had been Herod Agrippa himself who had first prepared his young and impressionable mind to return one day and help the Jews in their struggle for independence.

"He must have been a strange man," Andrasta suggested. "A close friend of Claudius, yet fortifying Jerusalem behind his back with these enormous walls."

"An enigma," Simon said. "My opinion is that he thought he was the Messiah. He died suddenly before his plans could mature, and we shall never know."

Linked arm in arm, they continued to explore the city until that night, finding a comfortable inn, they slept in clean, soft linen.

As they lay in each other's arms, Andrasta, her mind elsewhere, allowed her slim fingers to roam down his body, only to draw them away as though they had been stung when they encountered his still-deformed genitalia. She would not have hurt his feelings for the world and knew she had made a dreadful mistake.

For Simon, with a terrible look on his mutilated features, began cursing Rome. Love, he knew, had finally made Andrasta conquer her fear of men. She was ready now to give herself to him, and he was impotent.

By stroking his forehead, massaging his thick hair with her fingers, she managed to lull him into restless sleep, although even in his dreams his voice could still be heard, full of hatred for Rome, which had destroyed first his family and then—if that was not enough—his manhood.

Next day, in the company of Joseph ben Mathias, they went to Galilee. They had two months before Vespasian's army, properly assembled and provisioned, would be in a position to take the field—possibly three, if the winter rains were heavy.

From now on, Simon and Joseph worked harder than they had ever worked in their lives, equipping and training legions of men in the Roman fashion.

All over Galilee, in quaint villages perched on top of rolling, fertile hills, and down in the great plain of Bersabe, the air was full of the sound of men drilling. From the Sea of Galilee, where fat carp swam the warm, sweet waters, to the stony heights of Golan, in fertile fields or on the snowy slopes of Mount Tabor, peasants learned the art of the Roman short sword, the Syrian bow, how to sit a cavalry horse. Nothing was spared in the teaching of military techniques. While Joseph organized the army's structure, deployment and provisioning, Simon held classes in making camp, marching in formation, following the standards, when to move to left or right, to wheel, retreat, the significance of trumpet signals, the deeper blast of the *cornu*.

Starting from nothing, a large and apparently first-class army took the field.

However, it lacked two things: the discipline of seasoned officers and actual battle experience.

This was sadly proved when Vespasian reached the Galilee early in AD 67 and, while waiting for his vast host to assemble, sent out a small force to reconnoiter the district. Confident of their newfound might, the Jews marched down into the plain to confront the Romans and were promptly cut to pieces by a mere six thousand foot and a thousand cavalry, under the command of an unusually able and inappropriately named tribune called Placidus. That this vast and expensively trained army should collapse so easily amazed even grizzled old Vespasian.

The only man who had seen it all happen before—who had personally watched a small, seasoned force of Roman regulars slaughter twenty times their number of brave, yet undisciplined Britons—was Simon. He had warned that the Jewish army would be decimated.

Curiously, with the Jewish force now reduced to guerrilla tactics, its effectiveness began to increase. Those contingents who had managed to escape the swords of Placidus locked themselves up in strategically important, walled cities and challenged the Romans to come and get them. The moment Vespasian realized how well-provisioned these cities were, how well-fortified, he knew he was in for a real fight and that heavy casualties would be inevitable. Until these towns were reduced, he could not advance through Samaria toward Jerusalem. From Gamala, perched on the other side of the Sea of Galilee, the regulars pointed a menacing finger at his supply lines. At Gishala, remote in the bleak Golan foothills, the wild piratical John, reinforced by thousands detached from the Jewish army, planned devastating swoops into the plain as soon as the legions had marched south. Vespasian knew all this: an experienced general, he would see that enough soldiers were left to withstand such forays. But one more town, with mighty walls capping a vicious, outcurving glacis of solid stone, straddled his main route to the south.

Jotapata.

This fortress would have to be reduced and the fight would be lengthy, costly, bloody. But Vespasian, far from being dismayed, could not believe his good luck. Information reached the burly Roman general that both Joseph ben Mathias and Simon ben Eleazar had ridden in to supervise Jotapata's defense. Hastily, he reinforced Placidus and ordered him to throw an iron ring around the town, imprisoning them. Sooner or later, whether it took months or years, he would have them: the supreme enemy commander, and Simon, the former Roman colonel, who had been the main architect and advisor of the Jewish insurrection.

Stroking his obstinate chin, Vespasian reflected on what he would do when he saw his old friend again. The strain between personal friendship and loyalty to his country would be terrible.

He found himself praying that he would not have to take Simon alive.

32

In the month of May, while spring flowers still carpeted the Galilee hills, Vespasian came to Jotapata.

The town, with precipices on three sides, was accessible only up a steep slope from the north. On this slope, in full view of the town, Vespasian deliberately deployed his vast array. At the front, countless contingents of auxiliary cavalry, Syrian bowmen looking indescribably evil in conical helmets and long flowing robes, and behind them, the mailed might of the legions. They made an awesome sight, these thousands of legionaries identically equipped in their articulated armor and steel helmets, javelins held rigidly at the regulation angle. The sun glittered on the golden eagles and standards, the colorful transverse crests of the centurions' helmets, the yard-long, silver trumpets held at the ready by the *tubicines* to sound the advance. From all over the Empire, row after row of sturdy veterans stood patiently in the heat, seasoned killers, beautifully dressed and paraded, disciplined and molded into one superb military machine, practically drawing breath as one man.

The Fifth Macedonia and Tenth Fretensis were there, having marched down through Asia Minor. The Fifteenth Apollinaris, hard, sun-bitten, skilled in desert warfare, had come up from Egypt with Titus and its own formidable commander, Trajan. In addition, the Twelfth—the old "Fulminata"—battered and bruised from its defeat under Cestius Gallus, had been reconstituted and now lusted to avenge the disgrace of losing an eagle to Bar Giora. If that were not enough, further cohorts had been drawn from two other legions garrisoning Syria—the Fourth Scythiae and the Sixth Ferrata—to make the numbers even more formidable. Lastly, behind the legions, stretching forever, came the artillery—the onagers, the mobile scorpions mounted on carts, and finally two massive siege engines in the use of which the Tenth and Fifteenth legions were particularly skilled.

To the defenders of Jotapata the sight was overwhelming and calculated by Vespasian to make them realize how useless it was to resist.

Vespasian, riding his favorite stallion, accompanied by aides carrying flags of truce, now rode boldly up to the walls.

"I wish to see Josephus." The voice came back, faint but clear in fluent patrician Latin.

"Your position is hopeless," Vespasian called. "Surrender and you will be given generous terms."

"I will consider," Josephus shouted.

Had there been hesitation there? Vespasian was sure that Josephus now knew the futility of resistance and waited for what he hoped would be a favorable answer. As he watched, the sun seemed to wink on a Roman cuirass worn by a man who advanced rapidly on Josephus. Was that Simon? Vespasian guiltily rubbed a grin off his sturdy, bruiser's features at the thought of seeing his old comrade again. The two figures seemed, in the distance, to grow close together, then merge, before springing apart again. He'll surrender, thought Vespasian—unless the Jew stiffens him.

"We fight," Josephus called down from the walls.

"Think again," shouted Vespasian. "You will all perish."

"I—I have no choice," Josephus called again. There seemed to be a world of emotion in his words.

There it was. There could be no doubt that the Jew had put new resolution into his commander's bones just when he had been tempted to yield the city. Very well. They would see. He was a patient man. Shrugging his broad, peasant shoulders, Vespasian rode away to plan his attack.

Next morning, he launched the assault. To his surprise, a well-equipped, disciplined army of Jews assembled in front of the wall, met, absorbed and finally threw back the seasoned legionaries. Vespasian, a smile on his stubborn face, now ordered similar attacks every day, not minding that the Jews fought every bit as well as the Romans.

In the evenings, at mess time, with the fastidious, Romanized Agrippa II watching his usual two-handed attack on a greasy meat bone, Vespasian would explain the tactics on both sides. "Once we are on the wall, they are doomed," he said. "Therefore they keep us from it while they can. It is an agonizing choice, nevertheless. Holding their ground is costing them heavy casualties, yet once they cede it, my siege rams can get to the wall."

"But you are suffering heavy casualties as well," observed Agrippa.

"Which I can replace," Vespasian said.

"And they cannot." Agrippa finished it for him.

"Exactly," Vespasian said, chewing noisily. "Exactly. It is a nice point which way they can last longer—preserve their men at the cost of the wall, or preserve the wall at the cost of their men."

"They are giving though," Trajan said, the flint-hard commander of the Fifteenth, which as the most experienced legion had been taking the brunt of the fighting. "I sense they will soon retreat." He paused. "I would like to know something of their leader. What manner of man is this Josephus?"

"An idle patrician," Vespasian said, stealing a shrewd glance at the upper-class sprigs of the nobility who inevitably did duty as tribunes in his legions. "I'm told he first experimented with the two Jewish forms of worship, the Pharisees' and the Sadducees', then, becoming bored with them both, sought other amusements in Rome. Finding nothing for him there, he then decided to assume the mantle of a national leader."

"You think that little of him?" Agrippa said casually. "A dilettante?"

"Exactly," said Vespasian, who was not quite sure what the word meant, "and in my opinion he will soon try to renew his association with Rome."

"You mean he will surrender?" Trajan cut in.

"Unfortunately, it is not he but his adviser who gives the orders," Vespasian said heavily. The conversation seemed to depress him, because, draining his wine quickly, he rose from the table and went to his bed.

Persevering with his tactics, Vespasian attacked again and again, shuttling the legions so that all his crack troops could have their chance at the enemy on the constricted front. Eventually, one day when the legions advanced, the Jews did not come out to fight.

Vespasian, quickly alerted, rode up again with his aides carrying flags of truce.

"Surrender," he shouted.

There was a moment of hesitation. "Never," Joseph answered.

Vespasian, looking closely, fancied he could see a figure in a Roman cuirass standing close behind Josephus. He was sure it was Simon.

"You have fought well. There is no disgrace in yielding the city now," he called again. "Lay down your arms and I will spare your lives."

"We fight on," Josephus shouted down.

Vespasian turned away and rode back down the hill.

"We have taken terrible losses," Joseph said desperately. "Surely you can see that it is of no avail? By now another commander might have marched away, but not Vespasian. He is stubborn. Once he sets his teeth in, he will not let go."

In his command room, Simon and his old friend Alityrus, the former actor, stood over Joseph, who was sitting, slumped, on his bed. The commander's face had lost its well-massaged look and his wide eyes were bloodshot with worry. "We have come to fight," Simon said, "and fight we will."

"Do you want children stuck on Roman swords? The

women raped? The men sold into slavery?" Joseph asked hoarsely. "I know this Vespasian. He will offer you terms once, twice—but after that he is merciless."

"Then this is a chance for your name to live in history," Simon said, sarcasm in his voice. "The Jews will always remember how Joseph ben Mathias held Jotapata against the Romans."

"You are mad," Joseph said, his voice cracking from the strain. "Because of you, I am as good as dead." All his patrician graces had deserted him and he was now talking with his hands like any Jewish merchant. He was young and the thought of execution by the Romans was too much for him. Throwing himself face downward on the couch, he gave way to racking sobs.

"Those who fight wars must sometimes be prepared to die," said Simon, his eye gleaming from his mutilated face. Stalking from the room, he went to prepare the next phase of the siege.

With the ground cleared up to the wall, Vespasian brought up his bowmen, slingers and mobile artillery and, with a spirited barrage to keep the Jews' heads down, began to erect screens to protect his engineers from the Jews' missiles. Denuding the hills of timber, Vespasian now constructed platforms for his heavy siege artillery.

Knowing that once the giant catapults were in position, the town would become indefensible, Simon now launched desperate sallies, sending suicide squads into the attack with blazing torches to fire the screens and hurdles the Romans had built to protect their working parties. For a time these tactics were successful, until Vespasian, by linking the screens into a solid line and concentrating his massive forces behind them, denied the Jews any further chance to penetrate.

The platforms grew inexorably higher. Simon's immediate reaction was to build his own wall higher, but the mobile artillery and lethal arrows made this impossible. Then Simon had the idea of constructing screens of animal hide, which had the elasticity to absorb the missiles hurled against his builders. At this, despondency hit the Romans.

Vespasian now withdrew his engineers from the

platforms and, with the weather growing very hot, decided to see if thirst could do to the Jews what his own men could not. He had managed to discover a secret path up the mountain on the other side of the town, along which Jews, camouflaged in animal skins, were hauling water at dead of night. Having blocked this supply, he now gave the Jews a couple of weeks to feel the effects, then rode up to the walls again.

"This is the last time I come to parley," he called. "Do you now wish to surrender?"

Joseph, marched out onto the battlements with the help of a sharp dagger pricking his ribs, managed to call hoarsely down. "We do not."

"I ask you once more to reconsider," Vespasian said, his accent becoming rustic and earthy with the gravity of the threat he was about to make. "Refuse and the town will be burned, your men enslaved, the women given to the soldiers and your children killed."

"We cannot surrender." Joseph had said "cannot" instead of "will not," with good reason. While in command of his own army, he had been kidnapped by brigands and forced to put up a front of heroism before his men. What had started out as an amusing dabble in military adventure had now turned into a grim struggle for survival.

"Then die of thirst," Vespasian said curtly.

As he turned to go, he was astonished to hear the sudden splashing of water. The Jewish soldiers had soaked their clothes and had hung them on the battlements so that the whole wall ran with water.

"What a flamboyant gesture," Agrippa II said at dinner that night. "And most destructive of my men's morale. I should like to meet the man able to give such an order."

"And what about the man who trained him?" Vespasian said, grinning broadly, a lamb bone held firmly in his large, work-stained hands. "The man behind him. Wouldn't you like to congratulate him as well? I can arrange it. He's a friend of mine."

Those who campaigned with Vespasian said that the better you got to know him, the more struck you were with his strange sense of humor.

302

* * *

When the sappers of the Tenth and Fifteenth finally managed to mount and site their giant siege pieces, Jotapata learned what hell could be like.

The population, shaking with terror, prayed. First the whistle—then the shattering crash as a giant boulder would knock down an entire house. After the cloud of dust and rubble had subsided came the groans of women and babies maimed by the stone shards that had exploded on impact. On top of the walls also, the quick-loaders and ballistae began to take a murderous toll, the heavy, javelin-type missiles frequently going through a whole file of defenders. It was from one of these direct hits that Alityrus, Simon's faithful friend, sadly perished.

To make matters worse, the two giant catapults, having knocked down the defenders' screens, switched targets and began to tear gaping holes through the thickness of the stone glacis.

With these breaches in the walls, Vespasian rode forward to survey the scene. No longer did he offer surrender terms. His face was grim with concentration and the need to conquer this obstinate city.

The orders he issued to his commanders were concise, typical of his strategy. He dismounted the pick of his horsemen, who were encased in armor from head to foot, and ranged them against the gaps in the walls with their long spears, so that when the gangways went down, they could force the first entry. Behind them, he placed the flower of his infantry. The rest of his cavalry he disposed to cut down any Jews who might try to escape. He stationed his archers, his slingers and artillerymen in a curving line that would bring a blinding covering fire to bear when he gave the order to attack.

Simon, watching these preparations, looked with sorrow at his own ragged defenders, matted and filthy, half-starved, tongues hanging out from thirst. This, he knew, would be the final attack. "They won't come silently," he told them. "They'll come with a battle cry from sixty thousand throats and a deafening fanfare of massed trumpets. This sound is something you won't

303

believe, until you find yourselves running from the battlements in terror. When it starts, stop your ears."

On the Roman side, Vespasian sat his stallion and asked his aides, "Is everything ready?"

"The cavalry is ready, sir."

"The artillery is ready, sir."

"They await your orders, sir," came the voice of the liaison officer for the Syrian bowmen and slingers.

"Ready, sir," yelped the young tribunes, one by one, on behalf of the assembled legions.

Down came Vespasian's arm. The peace of the summer morning was shattered by a huge blast from the massed trumpets of the legions, which in turn was drowned by the immense roar of the army's battle cry. For minutes, the very sun was darkened by the barrage of heavy and light missiles. Unbeatable, unstoppable, the Roman veterans, the flower of the imperial army, surged forward behind their golden eagles.

And incredibly—the Jews beat them back.

Patiently, and with little irritation apparent on his seamed face, Vespasian called off the assault. He now gave orders for more artillery platforms to be built and for every single platform to be lined with iron sheeting so that they could neither be pushed over nor set on fire by the desperate Jews.

When this was done, he was able to mount an artillery barrage so intense that the Jews could no longer stand on the walls. Satisfied that they were now unable to tell where and how he next intended to attack, he had his heavy siege engines switch their bombardment to the walls.

Day after day, the defenders of Jotapata endured a holocaust of missiles, boulders and javelins, until Vespasian decided that another attempt should be launched. He discussed the final details with his officers, then went off to bed.

He was half-asleep in his leather praetorium tent when the flap was pulled open and his son Titus came in, followed by the tribune Placidus. "Yes, what is it?" he asked, trying to keep the annoyance out of his voice. Many battles had been lost because men had been too frightened to wake their general.

"Placidus has a prisoner with important news, Father," said Titus. "He says the Jews are so worn out by their privations that they sleep into the small hours. For many nights past, you could have walked in and taken the city."

"It could be a trap," Vespasian said thoughtfully, "but I don't think so." By denying the Jewish sentries a view from the battlements, he had ensured that the defenders would need to remain in a perpetual state of stand-to. Exhaustion would now be the logical result.

"Do let me go, Father," Titus pleaded, his face tense with excitement. "I've done little in this battle so far." Seeing the look on Vespasian's face, he added, "Placidus will look after me."

"Very well," Vespasian said with pretended reluctance, suppressing a smile at his son's enthusiasm. "While I sleep, you may go and capture me a city."

And so, tragically for the Jews, it turned out.

In the pitch darkness before dawn, Titus, with picked men from the Fifteenth Legion, clambered silently up the walls to find the sentries fast alseep. With calmness and efficiency, Placidus now supervised the entry of the legion through the gaps torn in the wall and when, eventually, the Jews awoke, it was too late. The Romans were in. Fresh, well-fed, they tore the famished, weary defenders apart and Vespasian was roused at first light by the triumphant paeans of Roman trumpets blasting from Jotapata's battlements.

The Jews, many of whom had not eaten or slept for ten days, had been beaten not by the Roman legions, but by fatigue and hunger.

Vespasian, buckling on his uniform, hastened into the town. Passing the heaped bodies of the defenders, slaughtered to a man by the legionaires, Vespasian shook his head in sorrow. He hated unnecessary bloodshed, but the Jews had brought it on themselves. He had offered them surrender terms on three separate occasions and they had spurned them. Now, they must die. He strode on, until he found his staff officers standing in a knot, watching the citadel. "What's happening?" he demanded.

"See there, sir." A colonel pointed.

Vespasian followed the colonel's finger. The citadel

was built on the sheer, precipitous side of a mountain, and as Vespasian watched, one soldier after another threw himself off, his body turning over and over as he tumbled to the rocks below, preferring self-inflicted death to that meted out by Vespasian's legions.

"Any word of Simon ben Eleazar?"

"No, sir."

"I want the town scoured, the prisoners interrogated." Vespasian snapped. "I cannot rest until I know whether the Jew still lives."

An hour later, a breathless aide came to fetch him. A prisoner had information that Vespasian wanted.

This one, dragged from the citadel which the legions had now stormed, lay in a huge pool of blood and flies. His leg had been half severed by a ballista bolt and he had been unable to throw himself into oblivion like his comrades.

"Ah, Roman swine," he said, as Vespasian approached. "You must be the chief pig in the sty."

A trooper went to strike him, but Vespasian said, "Leave him. He is dying." He looked at the man with compassion and said, "You have news of your leader, Ben Eleazar?"

"Yes. O black turd of a misbegotten camel—"

Vespasian smiled, as if in appreciation of the man's flow of language. "Tell me then, because your time is not far off."

"He lives to fight again, Roman pig."

"That is not possible," Vespasian exclaimed.

"He took his chance—climbed down one side of the precipice with his woman. He said he had learned the art of climbing in your army."

Vespasian's face went thoughtful. Mountaineering was definitely one of the skills taught Roman soldiers and Simon had been a superb soldier. "You saw it?" he asked. "With your own eyes? The descent?"

"I did. He reached the bottom and waved to the others to follow. Many who tried did not know the secrets of the thing, lost their footing and died. Only a few escaped that way."

"There can be no mistake?"

"I wanted you to be told, O rotted-down dung of a

Roman manure heap"—the prisoner's grasp of Latin vernacular was phenomenal—"so that you would know what was in store for you."

"Very well," Vespasian said somberly. "Now tell me where he has gone."

In answer the prisoner hawked phlegm into his throat and spat contemptuously at Vespasian's feet.

Vespasian bent over and shook the man. "Where is he?" he roared. "Where did he go? I must be told!"

There was no answer. The prisoner had died.

The group of officers, watching Vespasian turn and walk away, began to mutter among themselves. No wonder the general hated Ben Eleazar, they thought, and wanted to see him killed. Not only had he held up the massed, armored might of Rome for seven incredible weeks, but the wolf had survived and was loose again on the rolling hills of Galilee. Yes, they agreed, it must be a bitter blow for Vespasian.

They could not have been more wrong: back in the privacy of his leather command tent, Vespasian lit an incense candle and, going down on his knees, said a solemn prayer of thanks to Jupiter Optimus Maximus for preserving his old comrade from death or injury.

Three days later, Joseph ben Mathias—or Josephus, as he was called by the Romans—was marched out of a cave by two Roman tribunes, Gallicus and Paulinus by name, and set down in front of Vespasian and Titus.

"Well?" Vespasian looked dubiously at the abject figure on the ground and turned to Titus. "He was a friend of yours. You decide what to do with him."

"Hardly a friend, Father," the boy protested. "Naturally we met in other people's houses. I never liked him and for my part you can kill him."

This impelled Josephus to catalog, in a quaking voice, a whole series of complaints against Simon ben Eleazar—how he had always wished to surrender and how he had been made to go on fighting to the end.

Vespasian, examining this smooth, bland Jew with innocent eyes that opened larger and larger the more persuasive he became, reached a decision. "He could be useful," he said thoughtfully. "The Jews still believe in

307

him. We'll have him address them in front of every city we besiege. He has a ready tongue and when they see he's alive, it might end the war more quickly."

"Very well, Father."

Josephus now advanced on Vespasian and, kissing him on his feet, said, "Imperator, I thank you."

Vespasian's forehead wrinkled with amusement. "Imperator? Now really, there's no need to overdo it," he said cynically. "I've already spared your life."

"Exactly," Josephus said, "and it is for that reason that I have waited until now to speak the truth. As a priest of Israel, I have a gift of foretelling the future. It is written that the next Emperor of Rome shall come out of the East—who else can it be except you?"

Vespasian got tò his feet and walked uncomfortably away. The honeyed tones of this devious fellow worried him. Prisoners recounted that Josephus had prophesied that the siege of Jotapata would last forty-seven days and he had been proved exactly right. The signs and portents of future greatness multiplied, but surely, he thought, at nearly sixty, it was absurd. Yet the Jews, as their biblical writings plainly showed, had always had the gift of prophetic insight.

He shrugged his burly shoulders and reached for a flagon of wine, laughing the matter off.

33

There was only one place where Simon could be. Save for the bandit's lair of John of Gishala in the north, no other pocket of resistance remained in the Galilee.

Gamala.

Set on the far side of the Sea of Galilee, the fortress sloped down a long, shaggy neck and then up and over a symmetrical hump, looking for all the world like the front half of a camel—from which, in fact, it derived its name. In an untidy cluster between the hump and the first rising of the neck lay the rickety houses of the town, built almost on top of each other, so tightly were they compressed. Where the camel's head should have been, there was a peak and here, predictably, was the citadel. On all sides the rocks fell away sheer, except from the far side of the hump's spine, where the going was reasonably good.

At this point—stabbing up the camel's rear, so to speak—Vespasian's legions besieged the stout town wall, while Agrippa II, whose territory it was, went forward to ask Gamala to surrender. However, the little king received such a crack on the elbow from a well-directed slinger's stone that he retired in tears to Vespasian's personal *medicus,* and from that moment the siege was on.

The general intended to conduct the operation very much as he had at Jotapata, giving the defenders no rest, while shuttling his ample forces. Then he would take the town. The inevitable progression. There was one difference from Jotapata: the town wall, although substantial, had no glacis of smooth, outthrusting stone. Accordingly it would be particularly susceptible to a lethal instrument of war—the ram.

With Titus sent off to subdue garrisons remaining at Tarichaeae and Mount Tabor, Vespasian now settled down to batter the wall to pieces. Each of the Fifth, Twelfth and Fifteenth legions manhandled up from their wagon trains a huge ship's mast capped by a heavy lump of iron cast in the shape of a ram's head and, with the wall swept clear of defenders by ballistae, rigged them on specially built cradles at strategic points. With a prize put up for the first of the three teams to knock a breach in the wall they bent, stripped to the waist, to the task of swinging the enormously long timber balks backward and forward with crushing, regular impact. Before long, large chunks of masonry began to fall.

Inside the town, Simon paced around his temporary headquarters, his face set in concentration as he considered how to contain Vespasian's relentless onslaught. Time was running short. Each thump of the ram hitting the wall made the ground tremble under his feet. He would, he knew, have to find an answer very soon. Suddenly, snapping his fingers, he said out loud, "I have it," then strode off to give sharp, concise orders to his commanders.

The Romans eventually smashed great holes in the town buttress and the Fifth Legion was quickly passed through, surging into the breaches like some huge sea, which, on meeting the densely packed houses, split into a thousand murderous rivulets of legionaries, each chasing its own section of screaming townsfolk through the dark, close alleys.

Simon, watching the reinforcements—the backup troops of the Twelfth Legion—come trotting down the hump, knew that nothing would ever stop their advance, so anxious were they to avenge their defeat. Events had played into his hands. With his whole face set in a lupine grin of triumph, he gave the order to counterattack.

For days he had kept his best men for this, husbanding them away from the killing ground of the fortress wall. Now, stripped of their armor for the sake of agility, they fell like so many savage alley cats on the surprised Romans. Out of their rigidly dressed fighting formations, the legionaries quickly became confused, then frightened. As they turned to flee, they collided with the Twelfth, rushing down the hill, eager for battle. Packed tightly between friend and foe, slowed by the weight of their heavy armor, the Fifth panicked. Caught in unfamiliar territory for a Roman legion, the soldiers were chased back through the tortuous streets and hacked to pieces. Those who climbed on top of the houses to escape their pursuers were picked off by archers stationed on higher ground. Simon ben Eleazar had indeed laid a dreadful trap for the Romans.

The measure of any general's greatness is his ability to respond to sudden crises, and Vespasian now took charge. Walking calmly into the thick of the fighting, much to the consternation of his staff, who could see what a brilliant target he made in his fine cloak and ornately crested helmet, he began talking to his soldiers. "Come on, lad," he said kindly to a junior centurion who was catching his breath against a wall, shivering with fear. "You know what to do. Go back in there and tell your boys to link shields—form testudos. They can't hurt you then. You know that." Arms akimbo, his bruiser's face set in a confident smile, he stood, legs straddled in the middle of a road, single-handedly stemming a mad rush of legionaries to the rear. "Right, you men," he called in mock sternness, "give us a marching song and, by the gods, you chaps of the Fifth know some filthy ones all right. Let's march quietly out of the town."

Bullneck pulsing with stubborn courage, chin out-thrust, the burly general walked amid a furious hail of slingshot, calling out orders in his distinctive peasant burr. "Right. Let's get out of here. Slow march, boys. Romans never retire at the double. Get those shields linked. It's time to be going home." The legionaries heard his confident voice, checked their stride; then, incredibly, turned about, walking shamefacedly past their commander to join their units, steadied, calmed by their revered Vespasian. Its courage restored, the legion remembered its training and retired in good order to the wall.

By taking his Fifth Legion literally by the scruff of the neck, Vespasian had saved a rout, prevented a massacre. Watching from his vantage point in the citadel, Simon knew that his old commander had been too good for him. By failing to win completely, the Jews had lost completely. The city was now doomed and would fall within days.

That night Vespasian addressed his massed legions. "In the same way we don't crow over victory," he said, "let us not moan about defeat. We're regulars and can take everything that Dame Fortune can hand out. Now rest, retrain, regroup—and don't think of anything but victory."

Simon, hearing the tremendous cheer which greeted Vespasian's speech, grinned in appreciation, having heard a few of them himself. Now he would have to do the same, walk among his men, a word of encouragement here, a word of praise there—but with no supplies, little food or water. Their position, in contrast to the Romans', was hopeless. That night, talking to the wounded, watching Andrasta direct the bandaging of hideous sword cuts, he did not hear one word of criticism, one curse at the awful fate he had brought down upon them. Fine men. Wonderful men. But part of a broken army—able to delay the Romans for a short time, but not defeat them. Seeing their cheerful, trusting faces and knowing what was in store, a lump rose in his throat and he had to walk away.

When Titus came back from moving a stubborn Jewish garrison off the slopes of Mount Tabor and heard about the reverse, he pretended to scold his father. "What?" he said. "You should have left it to me. Can't I rely on you for anything, Father?"

Vespasian cursed ruefully, aimed a mock blow at the boy and said, "I was outwitted, my son. By a Jewish colonel that I trained myself. He set the trap and I took the bait."

"Nevermind, Father," Titus said, grinning. "I'll finish it for you."

As Titus marched from the command tent, Vespasian's eyes dwelled approvingly on his son's short yet athletic figure, marvelous good looks, his thick tousled hair, his habit of looking at you with level gray eyes. He was glad this boy of his, whom he loved so much, was here to help him. Wearily, he returned to the mountain of paper work that always seemed to build up if he left the command tent for only a day.

Titus was as good as his word. With the same ability to infiltrate an enemy position that he had shown so brilliantly at Jotapata, he crawled through the lines of tired, starving Jews with a commando of picked men, opening a gap in the defenses through which the legions marched—but this time with discipline. What Simon had feared now happened. The Jews were unable to fight another battle and the town was quickly conquered. Simon, on his own, would have followed the others, some five thousand courageous fighters who, as at Jotapata, had hurled themselves from the citadel rather than surrender to the Romans, but, with Andrasta to consider, now made an agonizing decision. To surrender.

When Titus swaggered back to the command tent,

sweaty and triumphant, his sword still bloody, Vespasian said curtly, "What took you so long?" It wouldn't do any harm to take the boy down a peg.

"I have Simon ben Eleazar, Father," Titus said gently.

The color drained from Vespasian's face. The old look of strain came back to his features, that drawn, worried expression that had prompted Petilius Cerialis all those years ago to make that joke about "when you have finished relieving yourself." It was a long time since Vespasian had been drained of all confidence like this, not knowing whether he could stop himself from throwing his arms around the Jew and kissing him—an old friend who had saved his life. Yet many of his closest comrades had fallen at the Jew's hands, substantial detachments of the Roman army been ripped to bloody ruin because of him. What was he to do with this wolfish, one-eyed Simon ben Eleazar, who fought the might of Rome with training methods that he, Vespasian, had personally taught him? How should he treat this man who was more precious to him than a brother and yet not himself be considered a traitor to his country? There was no simple answer. Vespasian took the easy way out. By exercising delaying tactics.

"You must go to Upper Galilee," he said abruptly, changing the subject.

"What?" Titus was astonished.

"Take the Fifteenth and knock out John at Gishala," Vespasian rasped. "All Galilee is to be pacified before the autumn rains. You know that as well as I do."

"Very well, Father." Titus, mystified by his father's anger, turned to leave the tent."

"My son," Vespasian called after him.

"Yes, Father?"

"I want time to think," Vespasian said.

"Very well, Father."

Yes. That is the truth of it, Vespasian thought. Time to arrange my thoughts and then take the advice of my son. Did not the Jew send money to pay for Titus' very education? The boy will tell me what to do—help me come to a decision. When Titus returns, then I will see the Jew.

* * *

At Gishala, handsome young Titus stared up at the walls and shouted, "Surrender."

"On what terms?" John shouted back. He had seen the perfectly dressed ranks of a Roman legion, their huge engines ready to knock down his defenses, the thousands of auxiliary bowmen and cavalry, and knew he stood no chance.

"Surrender the town in exchange for your lives."

"My people prefer death to slavery," John called back.

Titus thought for a moment. It would take weeks of work and heavy casualties to reduce this place and the end of the campaigning season was at hand. It was a time to be generous. "Very well," he shouted. "All may go free—with the exception of yourself."

"Well, I'm inclined to accept your terms," John boomed. With his matted hair framing his dirty, ruddy face, his enormous, muscular, sheepskin-encased body outlined against the brilliant blue of the sky, he made a formidable figure. "We are, however, religious men and soon it will be our Sabbath. During this day we may engage in no activity other than worship." John, who had never said a prayer in his life, was hard put to fight back a snigger. "Will you pull your men back from the town during this time?"

"My father has taught me to respect other men's religions," Titus shouted back. "If I withdraw my legion from your walls, do you agree to surrender on the next day?"

"I alone will go on trial?"

"Yes. All the others will be freed."

"Very well," John shouted, "I accept." He added with grave dignity, "I am always happy to sacrifice myself for the sake of my people." Saluting, he left the battlements with a measured, dignified step.

Next morning, he slipped away. At dusk, when the Sabbath ended, Titus found he had the town but no John of Gishala, who, with a picked contingent of his army, already had a useful start toward the national redoubt of Jerusalem.

When Titus ruefully returned to camp and related this

314

to his father, Vespasian's mouth curled at the corners with amusement. Patting his son on the shoulder, he said, "Nevermind. Remember—you're only a beginner."

Sneaked out of custody by a guard sworn to silence, Simon came face to face with his old comrade, Vespasian.

Those who were privileged to watch, Andrasta and Titus, would never forget that night as long as they lived. How the two men silently embraced and went out into the darkness of the velvety Judaean night, yarning, reminiscing about the carefree days in Britannia, each one telling the other how he had fared in the long span of years since they had served together. At times, there was laughter—as when Vespasian described the people of Hadrumetum who had pelted him with turnips, and Simon, swapping tales, described Cerialis' extraordinary, knockabout affairs with women at Lincoln. When they remembered how one had saved the other's life, their voices seemed vibrant with the love each had for an old comrade.

A Judaean moon, brilliant and yellow, came over the horizon and they could be seen pacing one way, then back again, sometimes stopping to recall some unusually vivid recollection.

As the moon rose higher, the tone of the two men grew more intense. Now they talked not of old battles fought together, but—sad to relate—of those fought against each other.

On and on, the two of them paced, the bizarre sight of Vespasian, Rome's supreme commander in the East, master of the world's most powerful army, chatting on some distant frontier with an open rebel, an unkempt guerrilla who was a sworn enemy of his country. And so, all barriers of rank and country forgotten, the two men passed the night, a bond of staggering intensity between them, as if, by taking turns to save the other's life, they climbed together the highest pinnacles of the human soul.

As the moon began to set, the conversation of the two men turned anxious. Time was slipping away; they talked now in whispers, their faces pale and drawn.

Eventually, they walked back to the waiting An-

drasta and Titus, everything decided—Simon's life
spared against his own wishes and for the simple reason
that Vespasian flatly refused to kill him. In return,
Simon had sworn, reluctantly, to bury himself in the
seclusion of the monastery of Qumran, never to take up
arms while either Vespasian or Titus fought in Judaea.

Just before dawn, Simon and Andrasta departed,
dressed as nomadic shepherds driving a few pitiful
sheep. In the morning it would be let known that Titus
had personally taken the Wolf of Masada into the desert
and there executed him on his father's orders.

Unprotected and traveling alone, Simon and Andrasta would face danger, but nothing as terrible as
Vespasian and Titus now risked. By conspiring to free
an important rebel, a mortal enemy of Rome, they would,
if discovered, face the agonizing torture of a traitor's
death. To Vespasian, this was nothing. For a friend, a
debt repaid was more important.

34

That autumn, the roads of Judaea were thronged with
thousands of refugees and the marching and counter-
marching of armies. While Vespasian sent his forces
into winter quarters, satisfied to have subdued the
Galilee and broken the power of the rebels in the north,
the Jews writhed in the death agonies of their national
revolution, a stricken people.

As Simon and Andrasta walked slowly along the
Jerusalem road in the dust of a torrid autumn, they could
hear the sound of many armed men coming up fast
behind them. As it happened, they just managed to leave

316

the road as John of Gishala's horsemen came galloping into view. Fearing that Titus' furious legionaries would be in pursuit, John had led his men in headlong flight. His cavalry horses were in a distressed condition, sweat-stained, thirsty, many of them lame, as their riders flogged them toward the fortress of Jerusalem. As the big, ruddy-faced brigand swept past, he shouted, "Get those sheep."

In seconds, Simon and his wife found themselves sprawling in the dust, deprived of their small flock, the archrobber of the Galilee disappearing into the haze, not having recognized his former friends. Picking themselves up, the two set off wearily on their way, mixing with the other nomads and refugees.

Soon, as they came up to Jerusalem, the road choked with people leaving the city, Simon was able to learn for the first time of the tragedy that was being played out there.

Although Eleazar had built up the walls to formidable heights, he had been unable to keep Jerusalem for the "people's revolution." The city had been inundated by guerrillas, brigands, members of the Jewish army fleeing from the triumphant Romans, each group seizing a little bit of the city for themselves and setting up barriers against the other. The situation was starkly terrifying, each man fearing a knife in the back from his neighbor. With no one able to lead, anarchy gripped the city. For a time, the actual Temple was fought over while new power groups coalesced, some of Eleazar's revolutionaries joining a group of Zealots who had managed to seize the inner Courts, others joining the loot-hungry brigands of John of Gishala, waiting patiently outside the Temple like vultures, hoping to get their hands on the treasure. Simon could only shudder at the way that personal ambitions of power-hungry men had made a glorious revolution into a thing of shame.

Turning their backs on the golden-tipped spires of the temple, only recently so bravely won from the Romans, they descended into the Dead Sea valley.

Lower and lower they went, the fertile trees and fields changing in only a few short miles into a sun-blackened, stony wilderness, the heat becoming more furnacelike with every step. Eventually, desiccated, refined by the last heat of that climactic summer of 67 CE, they reached a place over one thousand feet below sea level, a place where no man in his right senses would want to live, a wilderness of soulless scrub. Here, where even in the spring grass grows no more than a thin green mold, already gone by the end of April and replaced by scree and tawny brown rock baking in the merciless sun, where crow fights hawk over any tiny creature that might by some miracle survive such lunar conditions, they traveled ever south. Almost buried beneath the crushing weight of heated air that filled this barren valley in the bowels of the earth, they picked their way through what moses in Dueteronomy called "a great and terrible wilderness"—a biblical country where great religions were spawned, where David fled from Saul, where vipers and scorpions crawl from holes in the rock to torment any traveler rash enough to lie down and rest while crossing the hellish terrain. To their left lay the haze-covered Dead Sea, cool-looking, beckoning the traveler with its shimmering blue waters flecked with white, until, lured to its shores, he found a deadly poisonous salt pan in which lumps of asphalt floated like so many dead fish.

At the end of their strength, despairing of taking one more step, they found a wizened old Bedouin woman, motionless, silent, watching them with brooding eyes, while two skinny goats, tethered nearby, quested the ground in search of fodder. She, knowing the only thing that could have brought these strangers was the need to bury themselves away from mankind, nodded understandingly and pointed along the valley with a dark, blackened finger. Proceeding in that direction for a mile or so farther, they came to the monastery of Qumran.

"Welcome," Jeremiah said.

The white-robed figure of the holy man Simon had taken to Judaea from Rome stood framed in the entrance of a stone hut. His face was thin, the shape of a bird of prey, with his eaglelike nose thrusting out from under his cowl, the flesh melted from his bones by a life of asceticism and unremitting toil in the fierce, dry heat. Only his eyes were alive, vibrant with the sureness of his faith. "Welcome."

Simon and Andrasta stepped inside, finding relief from the blinding heat. The floor was faced with stone pebbles, the walls were made of stone bricks and the roof was of reeds lying on cross timbers of felled palm trunks, the materials all chosen for their coolness and ventilation.

"Old man," Simon said. "You remember us? Of the boat?"

Jeremiah inspected each of them slowly before saying, "I remember you and am grateful."

"You will let us stay here?"

"The monastery is open to any Jew that comes, willing to pray and work."

"Then we will stay, if it pleases you."

"She is of Israel?" The old man peered doubtfully at the tawny-haired Andrasta.

"She is my wife."

At this, the old man went to a corner of the room and opened two great scrolls in turn, flicking the pages as if searching for something of wisdom hidden there. Eventually, he turned to them, eyes gleaming, "You must understand," he said, "since the death of the last patriarch, I am now the spiritual leader. There will be questions asked. Women are frowned upon here. They lead men into lust. A Gentile woman is doubly unwelcome."

"We will go," Simon said simply.

At this, the old man extended a featherlike hand. "Stay. I will find precedents in your marriage. There are many pointers in your favor. Have not many foreigners come to shelter under the wing of the Divine Presence? Were not first the Galileans and then, under John Hyrcanus, the Idumeans forcibly converted to Judaism? As it happens, Idumeans form many of my most zealous students of Torah." His fierce old eyes glowed with the thought of silencing any objections with such heavy ammunition. "Then, of course," he went on thoughtfully, "there are other precedents. Did not Esau marry a Hittite woman, Moses a Midianite? Even King David himself had a Calebite and an Aramean among his wives and as for Solomon, there were Moabites, Ammonites and many others in his harem, not to speak of Pharaoh's daughter. Of course—" he paused, "they

319

will say, with justification, that such marriages by kings were politically necessary and that mixed marriages by commoners only taint the purity of Israel's blood, and that is a good argument." He began walking slowly backward and forward, debating himself in a reedy voice, making points with his fingers only to knock them down again with others. "Explain," he said, finally, "how you came to marry."

As Simon recounted the history of his relationship with Andrasta, sudden triumph flared in the old man's eyes. "There is no problem then," he said, spreading his hands. "Deuteronomy twenty-one: ten to fourteen—an exception can be made for any woman captured in war. In due course, I shall conduct a ceremony welcoming her into Israel." The old man rubbed his skinny hands with pleasure at surmounting what had looked like a difficult hurdle.

As for Simon, he could only nod in admiration at the wicked pleasure Jeremiah obviously derived from marshaling his vast knowledge of the Bible to suit whatever course might please him at the time. "I am grateful" was all he could say.

"You flee from the Kittim—the Romans?" the old man asked.

"In a way," Simon said. "It is important that all Israel should think me dead."

"Your secret will be safe here."

"I fight no more," Simon said.

"That is good," the old man said. "For Israel, the way to greatness is not through battle, but through the worship of God."

"I wish also—if it is permitted—to learn something of the history of my people."

"Work hard," Jeremiah intoned. "Respect our rules and I myself will instruct you in our traditions. Your wife must also learn much of the ways of a Jewish wife. That"—he pointed to Andrasta's beautiful hair—"must be shorn. 'Her adornments are tainted with corruption.'"

"It cannot be done," Simon said. He eyed the tawny, sinuous coils of the girl's plaits. "You would destroy in a minute what has taken a lifetime to grow?"

"A Jewish woman must wear a wig. You know that.

She must not tempt other men." He threw his eyes heavenward and exclaimed, "'The sins within her skirts are many; her garments are the murk of twilight. Her bed is a couch of defilement. Her lodgings beds of gloom.'" Looking at Simon again, he said, "I have nothing personal against this woman, but this is a holy house of God devoted to meditation. With her bold glances she will make fools of the virtuous."

"We will move on," Simon said.

The old man spread his hands. "Where else will you go? Stay—in return for helping me here from the house of the Kittim, but you may never be initiated into the degrees of our order. Never can you be anything other than the most menial servants of God. Six months you may stay here. Until the winter is over and no more. By then your secret should be safe, forgotten."

"And my wife? Her hair?"

Again he spread his hands, putting his ancient face on one side, half cunning, half resigned. "Hide it. As you are menials here, I exempt you from such requirements." He went to a corner of the anteroom and rummaged in a chest, muttering to himself, before coming up with two cowled, white linen robes. "Wear these." Moving to another cupboard, he produced simple clay plates and a mattock for each of them.

"What is this for?" Simon asked.

"Cleanliness is important above all. With so little water, disposal of our body waste becomes a problem. It is the custom to walk into the land, do what is necessary, then bury it deeply under the surface."

Simon nodded. "I understand. While we are here we will observe your rules and work hard for our keep."

Work hard they did. There was a bewildering amount to do. For the whole of October, Simon toiled with the other men, replastering the cracks caused by the hot summer sun in the catchment cisterns. With such tremendous emphasis on cleanliness and purification rituals, not to speak of serving the needs of over two hundred souls in such a dry climate, the loss of the tiny rainfall would be a catastrophe. When this was done, there were new reeds to be laid across the roofs, especially over the room where the brethren labored day after day in silence, writing the holy scrolls, preparing

321

their own religious works. For many of the initiates, work would become less menial as they were admitted into the lower ranks of the community—perhaps the baking of bread, the cooking of simple foods. But Simon and Andrasta were given the dirtiest jobs, emptying the latrines the privileged scribes used, cleaning the cesspits, stripping the carcasses of the newly slaughtered animals so that their skins could be dried and sewn together for use by the industrious writers. Even at quiet times, there was always the weaving of flax, the herding of goats and sheep. The days were hard and exacting. Assembling at first light, with morning prayers, they worked all day with a meal at noon—when no talking was permitted. At dusk, back to the simple tent allocated to them by the side of a cave into which they could move, should there be a dust storm or exceptionally wet weather.

For them it would be the happiest time, for once not fighting, not facing imminent death. At night they would lie together, exhausted, sleeping in each other's arms or just listening to the ritual chanting of the Hasidim as they gave thanks to God for the chance to serve Him yet one more day. Slowly, with their whereabouts kept secret, the legend of the Wolf of Masada faded from the lips of the people of Israel, and the tale told by the Romans, that he was dead, became generally believed.

As the winter wore on, Jeremiah, as a reward for their industry, would call them into his cell once a week and tell them things, wonderful things, about the history of the Jewish people. There had been a great empire, he said, under King David, but God had punished the Jews for straying into wickedness and the Temple of Solomon had been destroyed and the Jews oppressed thereafter by one foreign ruler after another. Then in 165 BCE Jewish rebels under the leadership of the Maccabees had revolted against Antiochus Epiphanes and after a series of brilliant victories had rededicated a cleansed Temple in Jerusalem, throwing out the heathen altars placed by their enemies. Had the Kingdom of God returned? No, it had not, Jeremiah declared. The Maccabeans, or the Hasmoneans, as the royal house they founded came to be called, had usurped the office of the high priesthood of

Israel. Where before, Antiochus had sold the office to the highest bidder, the sacred rites were now celebrated by the bloody hands of warrior chieftains. In despair at the blasphemies perpetrated by their own people against the Lord, at their lack of repentance, holy men had gone off into the desert to pray, somehow to keep the sacred essence of true Judaism alive. As they could see, Jeremiah declared, they were still there. Nothing had changed. Foreign conquerors came and went, the divine office of the high priesthood a polluted thing, a sinecure to be sold for profit. Now, he said, his scribes were occupied with writing of the latest wickednesses that had taken place in Jerusalem, murder of the holy Menahem by Eleazar the so-called people's revolutionary, the Temple profaned by looting brigands. God was punishing the Jews, he said. Soon they would be scattered to the ends of the earth, their Temple destroyed once again.

Andrasta had listened to each lesson, becoming more and more enthralled with the stories Jeremiah told. As time went on, Simon, a man of action, had grown impatient, sometimes obviously so, with the old man's theological rantings. But to Andrasta the history of this stiff-necked, subborn race to whom her husband belonged was a revelation. Looking at the girl sitting there, bright-eyed, fascinated, as he wove for her countless tales of biblical folklore, a smile came into the rheumy old eyes of Jeremiah. It was often the same with converts. They were apt to become more Jewish than the Jews themselves!

And was there anything, Andrasta had finally asked him, that the Jews could do? Anything to preserve their wonderful heritage and bring them back to their true faith, after breaking the divine covenant Moses had made with God?

At this, Jeremiah had pondered deeply before making his reply. The Almighty had not sent them to his house by accident. The Romans intended to exterminate the Jews from the face of the earth. They were an efficient race, he knew that. He also knew that God was merciful, that He had sent this couple to him for refinement in the crucible of Judaism. That He had a mission for them. When the words of his answer came out, Jeremiah was conscious that they were not his words, that they came from a higher source. For many days afterward he would pray in undiminished ecstasy for this divine intercession.

"Yes," he found himself saying slowly, "the Jews can be saved, but only by such an outstanding act of faith as will live in their minds through two thousand years of dispersal—an act that will light their way like a torch until they come together once more, as a people."

Why two thousand years? he asked himself. Why did I say that? It was all very strange. Muttering to himself, he went off to give thanks to God for guiding his mind. There was, he thought, something strange, almost unreal, about that couple. Clearly, God had chosen them for some great task.

In March 68 CE, with a new campaigning season approaching, the peace of the Qumran monastery was rudely disturbed by the sudden arrival of Bar Giora, the young Lion of Wrath himself, mounted with his commanders on fine horses, a large force of infantry bringing up the rear.

After leaving Jerusalem in disgust, a year before, Bar Giora had gone south to Masada, joining a certain Eleazar ben Yair, Menahem's relative and successor, who now held the place for the Zealots. The two groups, who had cooperated originally in taking the fortress, made natural allies. Down there, unhindered by Romans, who had not yet penetrated the south, Bar Giora had carved out a vast territory.

Now he had come to Qumran for a reason. He was about to advance in force to Jerusalem on a very important mission and for this he required Jeremiah's blessing.

"And why do you go to Jerusalem?" Jeremiah asked. Since the death of Menahem, the mantle of spiritual shepherd had fallen on him, and he was determined to assert his authority.

"Rival armies are destroying the city." The handsome, dusky young man, sitting on the stone bench in the old man's cell, toying with a glass of water—all that passed for hospitality in this ascetic's retreat—added, "It is said that John of Gishala intends to plunder the Temple."

"This is grave news," Jeremiah said. "And you wish to save the treasure?"

"I do," Bar Giora answered.

Inevitably, as he spoke, he happened to cross glances with Simon. Even under the white cowl, the drooping lips, the telltale eyepatch could not be fully hidden. Leaping toward him in amazement, Bar Giora ripped off Simon's robe, exclaiming, "But you are dead! They said you were *dead!*"

"Leave me alone, in peace. Tell no one."

"But how can I do that?" Bar Giora said, laughing. "Even now, my soldiers gape in shock. Old friend, it is good to see you. Come with me to Jerusalem. With your help, when it is known that the Wolf of Masada is back from the dead, how can we fail to take the city?"

"I fight no more. I gave my word to the Romans."

"Not fight? The Wolf of Masada not fight? I cannot believe my ears."

"Nevertheless it is true."

"Well, no man would ever dare call you a coward," Bar Giora said. "But I do not understand it, all the same. You are not debarred from a mission of mercy. Save Jerusalem from destruction and help rescue the sacred treasure at the same time." White teeth showed in his sensitive face. "You and I together. Just like the old times."

Simon looked at Jeremiah, hoping for guidance.

"Go with him, my son," the old man said, his voice beginning to tremble as though he were suddenly gripped by some terrible emotion. "The Almighty in His mercy has spoken to me. All Israel will soon be scattered to the four winds as just punishment for its sins, but to you has been given a great task, the making of a legend on to which our people may hold through many years of dispersal—like a great tree in a storm—until future generations find our country once again. Go with him."

"I will go," Simon murmured. He felt transported by a sense of purpose, indefinable, but very strong, very real. Like his old friend Vespasian, he sensed an uncanny feeling in his bones that told him his life was surging toward a magnificent climax.

Before they left, in a simple, moving ceremony, Jeremiah married Simon and Andrasta according to the laws of Israel.

* * *

Simon was glad to be with the dusky boy again, the leader from the south who reminded him so much of his youth. His eye dwelled appreciatively on his slimness, sensitivity of feature and the strength of his biceps. Yet there was something—some change in Bar Giora which disturbed him. An insistence on being addressed as "General" that had not been there before—a strange tendency to describe himself as "we." He now carried himself in an aura of regal isolation. Perhaps it is his rank, thought Simon. It has gone to his head. He'll soon be cut down to size when he sees how badly Herodian armor stands up to a Roman legion.

Winding down toward Jerusalem from Jericho, the road passed close by the Mount of Olives and the Garden of Gethsemane, then approached the magnificent, gold-plated Shushan Gate on the northeastern ramparts of the Temple.

As they came closer, Simon was shocked to see the smoke pall hanging over the city, the battering the Temple Sanctuary had already taken from the civil war.

Because of the great power of his army, Bar Giora was able to impose a truce on John of Gishala's brigands, besieging the Temple, and the rump of Eleazar's revolutionaries, defending the inner Courts.

"Fellow Jews." Bar Giora was quick to address the rival factions. "Let me remind you of something. It is springtime." He paused, then roared out, "In case you do not know what that means, I will tell you. The Romans are coming." Eyes blazing, he went on, "Why do we try and destroy each other when the Romans mean to kill us all? Let us unite and face the enemy. Even now, he marches down from Galilee. When we have defeated him—when Rome flees, that is the time to decide who governs Judaea."

A great roar went up from the fighting men in Jerusalem when these words were heard and relayed through the city. Old enemies threw down their arms and fraternized, drinking together, swearing friendship.

Quickly, a new army was forged with Bar Giora as overall commander. He would, he told them, prefer henceforth to be addressed as "General of Israel."

Profiting from the temporary peace that now hung over the city, Simon proceeded to organize the collection of the Temple treasure. Peace, he knew, had been achieved only by the use of the supreme threat.

The Romans—Bar Giora had told them—were coming.

The Romans did not appear to be in any hurry.

All through the winter and early spring of AD 68, Vespasian sat in winter quarters, steadfastly ignoring the pleas of his officers to attack the capital while its defenders decimated each other in civil war. The old general had folded his arms and said with the usual obstinate smile, "They are doing my work for me."

However, when good campaigning weather arrived, Vespasian felt the dark presence of the Emperor over his shoulder. He took his army in a sweep from north to south on the eastern side of the holy city, rolling up the nests of guerrillas in the Jordan Valley, cutting off the doomed defenders of Jerusalem from outside help.

One thing Vespasian needed to know was the whereabouts of Bar Giora. He had heard about the Lion of Wrath and his army and did not want it falling on his unprotected flanks without warning. In fact the two had missed each other by only a couple of days and when Vespasian reached Jericho he finally closed a steel trap on all the forces massed in Jerusalem. But Vespasian was not to know that. For the moment, he needed intelligence—and reconnaissance. Accordingly, he detached a small force on an independent foray to the western shores of the Dead Sea.

The commanding officer was the redoubtable tribune Placidus, and directly in his path lay the monastery of Qumran.

Placidus left camp full of hate for Vespasian, planning his downfall. In spite of his great triumphs, he had been refused promotion. If he had stopped to think, he would have known it was for two reasons. First, he wore scent, and, second, he was a man who enjoyed cruelty. One vice Vespasian might have tolerated, but the other he learned about only when first arriving at the northern shores of the Dead Sea. Interested in its salinity, he had idly asked Placidus to find out how easy it was to float without swimming. Placidus had at once bound the hands of several prisoners and thrown them into the water. The prisoners suffered terrible agony from the salt in their eyes. Vespasian, anxious to be rid of the man's presence, sent him on this reconnaissance mission.

One thing had been nagging Placidus for some time: the end of the Wolf of Masada. Titus had apparently executed him, but Placidus had never been able to find a soldier who had been on the mission and the whole affair had been hushed up. He had almost forgotten about the matter until the episode of the old woman. They had found her shepherding a few goats, and after killing and dining well on the animals, his men had strung the old woman up over the fire and begun roasting her as much for amusement as for any information she might have to give. Perhaps they might have spared her life, but the old woman had endured silently until near death, then had started cursing the Romans, calling down upon them the wrath of the Wolf of Masada, who even now, she said, was resting and praying, regathering his strength in the holy monastery of Qumran.

That was all Placidus needed to know. It had long been rumored that the Wolf had served with Vespasian in Britannia and that they were friends. If the Jew still lived, it was proof that Vespasian and Titus had plotted to save his life. And that was high treason. He would send a message to the Emperor. On the day Vespasian and Titus were executed, Placidus would receive his coveted promotion.

Placidus set out for Qumran at high speed. From the monastery watchtower, a sentry saw the Romans coming and hastened to tell Jeremiah. The old patriarch moved quickly. This, he knew, meant final destruction. He had the sacred scrolls hidden in caves set in a cliff nearby and all the brethren of the monastery young enough to travel sent to the safety of Masada. Only ten old men were left. He and nine others. Just enough to form a minyan—a convocation for holy worship. Their life was over and they would die happily here, at this peaceful, desolate place heavy with the spirit of God. As the Romans approached, they went out to meet them.

Placidus had the old men stripped of their clothes and

pegged them down in the grilling sun. His instructions to them were quite simple: "Talk—and your lives will be spared."

When there was no answer, he strode off, giving them neither food nor water for the whole day. To his amazement, as dusk came, Jeremiah began saying evening service, the other nine men giving the rolling responses and chanting hymns with joy in their voices. Next morning he strode among them, asking if any had changed their minds, but Jeremiah, by way of answer, struck up the morning service in a strong, vibrant voice that belied his frailness, the others joining in, saying the Hallel. That evening, after two days without food or water, two men died. It was a miracle that any still lived at all, but they were accustomed to hardship and poor food, and nourishment had always been less important than prayer.

With only eight left, Jeremiah no longer had his minyan. Accordingly, each man now prayed separately to God, morning and evening.

"What are they saying?" Placidus asked impatiently of a soldier who knew a little of the religion.

"The Kaddish for the souls of the dead."

"And those near death? I notice they repeat a certain phrase over and over again."

"'Hear O Israel, the Lord our God, the Lord is one,'" the soldier said. "It is their holiest prayer."

"Their God doesn't seem to be doing much for them now," Placidus said carlessly. He hawked dust from his throat, spat idly into the ground and strolled off into the shade of the monastery.

Now the elders began to die quickly, and by the third day only Jeremiah still lived.

Placidus, incredulous that no one would give him the information he wanted about the Wolf of Masada, strode up to Jeremiah, stirring him with the point of his thonged boot. The old man had wasted away to little more than transparent flesh, almost invisible now, against the brown, oven-hot rock. "Speak," Placidus said, "and you may still be saved."

The old man by a great effort managed to shake his head. Although his body was at its last gasp, his brain was clear: he hoped he had taught Simon ben Eleazar

329

well, that the Wolf of Masada had grasped his message—that the Jews were doomed—that fighting against the Romans, however courageous, was useless, that only by some imperishable gesture of matchless courage and dedication would the Jews create a legend capable of keeping their race intact through the long years of dispersal until they returned once again, to claim their homeland. The man was rash and impatient, he knew. But the woman understood. Even now, she had assured him in a moment of confidence, her mother had created a legend in the far-off mists of Britannia which would sustain and carry that island race to future greatness. Yes. He had taught them well. He could do no more. Now he would die, happy and contented, in the bosom of Israel. Somehow, summoning up his reserves of strength, he started praying in a strangely powerful voice: "The Lord reigneth; the Lord hath reigned; the Lord shall reign for ever and ever," he intoned solemnly.

"Blessed be His name, whose glorious Kingdom is for ever," he said three times.

Seven times in succession he cried out in a great voice, "The Lord He is God," to the amusement of Placidus, who stood watching him.

Tears streaming down his cheeks, the old man finally declaimed: *"Shema Yisroael, Adonoi Elohenu, Adonoi Ehud.* Hear O Israel, the Lord our God, the Lord is one."

Then he died.

On his way back to rejoin Vespasian, Placidus ran into a few of the general's scouts.

"Have you heard?" shouted a young tribune. "Bar Giora is shut up in Jerusalem and the Wolf of Masada is with him."

So it was true, after all! Vespasian had secretly spared the Jew. If the general's adoring soldiers were too loyal to report the matter to the Emperor, he certainly was not. The general would strip him of his rank and throw him into prison once he knew of the atrocities perpetrated at Qumran, but that would not matter. When the Emperor learned the true position, his promotion would soon be rapid enough.

Meanwhile, he outranked the fresh-faced young tribune sitting his horse in front of him. "Wait," he commanded.

Procuring ink and papyrus from his saddlebag, leaning against his horse's flank for support, he penned an incisive note to the Emperor, telling him of Vespasian's treachery and the plotting that was going on with the Jews. He then detailed the young tribune to gallop straight for the coast and catch the first ship for Rome. He had no doubt that this dispatch would reach the right quarters. His father was a senator and, like most aristocrats, never too well disposed toward Vespasian. He, personally, could be depended upon to take it before the Emperor.

As he went to make his report to the general, Placidus could not help grinning. Vespasian's days were numbered and so were those of his handsome, charming son. If there was one man who always believed every allegation of treason, who never failed to take immediate and savage countermeasures against those suspected of plotting against him, it was the Emperor.

Nero.

35

Slowly, Nero performed the ballet around his sleeping couch. He could not dance at proper pace or in correct rhythm because his strong, muscled legs, once his best feature, were now just slabs of fat. Wearing the face mask of his beloved Poppaea, he could feel her presence flood into him. For a moment, while he danced, there was peace and he could forget that he had kicked her to death when she was pregnant.

Soon he would have his eunuch Sporus summoned and he would make love to him. Sporus had the slim build of his beloved Poppaea, the same white skin and amber hair. Again, for a little while, he could imagine that she still lived, that he had not murdered her as he had his mother and so many others. As he pranced around in his best muslin-and-lace tunic, terrible sins weighed heavily on the Emperor.

For a long time now, he had lived in an unreal world, his mind unhinged by extravagance, perversion and orgy; only his sense of self-preservation remained acute. For over a year he had disported himself in Greece, entering their four national games one after the other, the dates being specially altered so that he could compete, and he had come back in January to an enormous triumph, the crowd cheering him as he rode down the Via Sacra in a gilded chariot with his trophies for singing, dancing and lyre playing. Yes, the mob loved him. But for the upper classes who hated him, there had been only terror.

As he danced, corpulent and panting, Nero smirked at the thought of his secret police. Under Nymphidius Sabinus, a ferocious bastard of the deranged Caligula, and the evil, moustachioed Tigellinus, all Rome quaked in terror. The spy, the informer, the torture chamber—his two commanders knew only too well how to use them. Nero giggled at the senators, the aristocrats who had conspired against him again and again and now lay dead. Even Seneca—the wily statesman who had led a charmed life for so long—had not been spared, and what a fuss his former tutor had made over the simple act of killing himself! So austere and ascetic had the old hypocrite become that the blood simply had not run from his lean, spare old body after the veins had been severed. Even poison hadn't worked! In the end, they had had to carry the old fool into a vapor bath and suffocate him. Yet he had gone—while he, Nero, was indestructible. What had the crowd shouted as he had made his proud way toward the Forum? "Hail victor of Olympia!" "Nero Apollo, Nero Hercules!" These were the cries of the common people of Rome, who still adored him. While he had their love he would reign forever. True, the governor of Lugdunum, one Vindex, had revolted, naming Galba as Emperor, but the rebellion had been put down with ease. Now in AD 68 all seemed quiet and Nero had come

332

to Rome for a quick conference with Sabinus prior to retiring to Naples for the summer.

When Sabinus was announced, Nero went out to meet him. Tall, rawboned and nearly bald, Sabinus had inherited Caligula's murderous propensities, but Nero greeted him in a happy, almost carefree mood. Gaily, he made Sabinus follow him around the fabulous Domus Transitoria while he demonstrated the many ingenious contrivances he had installed there. Nero was proud of the fantastic palace he had built on the site of the rickety old tenements so conveniently destroyed by the great fire, and could never resist the opportunity of showing off the great organs run by hydraulic power, baths with golden taps carrying both salt and sulfurous water, and his ultimate masterpiece—a banqueting hall that revolved day and night like a bizarre merry-go-round. His grief for Poppaea forgotten, Nero ran through the palace like a depraved, floppy-cheeked child, stalked in turn by Sabinus, who was waiting his chance to give Nero grave news.

"Your Majesty," he said, when they had returned to Nero's private apartments, "I must tell you that Rubrius Gallus, your commander of the army in northern Italy, has revolted in favour of Galba."

For long seconds there was silence, then Nero put his face to one side and started weeping loudly. "That Vindex was responsible for all this," he sobbed. "I can forgive disloyalty, I can even forgive him his rebellion, but do you know what that unspeakable fellow said about me? He said that I play the lyre badly. That is untrue, unforgivable." He looked imploringly at Sabinus. "You know how well I play, don't you?"

"Yes, Majesty," Sabinus said. Under his bland exterior, his mind was a whirlpool of thoughts. He was beginning to realize how mad Nero really was. "You are an excellent musician," he assured the Emperor.

"Nobody can ever depose me," Nero said grandly. "Not while the people of Rome love me." He waddled over to the balcony, throwing his arms out wide, in an extravagant gesture to the mob always waiting below.

To his amazement, instead of the usual cheers, he was greeted by a storm of boos. A brick narrowly missed his head, taking a large chip out of a Corinthian column. Shielding his face with his forearm, Nero ducked back inside, retreating from the storm of hostile shouts, catcalls and insults. "Why?" he asked in a dazed voice. "Why?"

"There is a shortage of grain," Sabinus said. "You know how Rome feels about that."

"Who's responsible?" Nero shouted. "I'll have his head."

"It is nobody's fault," Sabinus said in a toneless voice. "Shipping is scarce because of the demands made by the Jewish war. Matters came to a head this morning, when the mob, hearing a grain ship had arrived at Ostia, found it full of sand for the arena."

"Do something," Nero screamed savagely. His face had become flushed and red, like that of an old strumpet dressing down some serving maid. "Call out the Praetorian Guard. I'll teach them to insult me like that."

"Yes, sire," said Sabinus, bowing himself out.

Sabinus did not go straight to the Praetorian Guard. He went to his friend Tigellinus, temporarily confined to his bed through illness. For hours they discussed the situation. Both men were born survivors, and if Nero went, they had no intention of going with him. Eventually, they came to a decision, typical in its murderous treachery. The best possible way to survive would be to hasten Nero's going.

Accordingly, Sabinus went off to see the commander of the Praetorian Guard but with a set of requests very different from those Nero might have imagined.

That night, Nero lay caressing Sporus. Only the smooth-skinned eunuch knew how to send him into transports of dreamless ecstasy that would blot out his fears and his guilts.

He was disturbed by a hammering at the door. Spiculus the gladiator, his personal bodyguard, entered sheepishly, holding a papyrus dispatch. "Sorry, master, for disturbing you," he said, "but this was brought personally by a senator of Rome who demanded it be taken to you at once."

Nero snatched the message from the gladiator and impatiently unrolled it. His face paled as he read the

334

grave accusations of the tribune Placidus. Burying his head on Sporus' silky shoulder, he started to weep again, his doughy body shaking convulsively. "Not Vespasian as well," he said. "I never thought he had the mind for treachery. He always seemed far too stupid."

Quickly he dismissed the gladiator and the eunuch, and taking quill and papyrus, he wrote out a peremptory order for the immediate recall of Vespasian and Titus and their subsequent execution. "Guard," he screamed again at the top of his voice, but no golden-greaved soldier rushed in to crash his javelin butt down hard on the floor and snap to rigid attention. Nero, panicking, rushed out of his rooms, crying, "Soldiers, where are you?" but only the sounds of his desperate running feet echoed back to him along the miles of deserted corridors.

Now he managed to get a grip on himself and sent to his friends messages carried by Spiculus and Sporus, but sensing that the Emperor's end was at hand, not one of them answered him.

About midnight, Nero and his two faithful servants fled the palace, but the Praetorian Guard, bribed by Sabinus to transfer their allegiance to Galba, kept on his trail.

Eventually the Emperor realized that he could run no longer, and as he sheltered from a heavy summer rainstorm in a cave, debated whether to surrender himself to his pursuers or commit suicide. When Spiculus came rushing in and related that he had heard the Praetorian Guard intended to kill him in "ancient style," Nero went white with terror. This was the death where they trapped your head in the fork of two upright sticks and beat you slowly until your heart stopped. He could not contemplate that, could not bear the thought of such agony. Crying, "What a loss to the arts I shall be!" Nero stabbed himself with two daggers.

And so, on a rainy night in June AD 68, they hauled his body onto a cart and took it back to Rome. As they did so, the papyrus documents condemning Vespasian and his son to death for high treason fell from the tunic of the dead Emperor. The rain lashed down on them and soon the ink began to run and the papyrus began to curl. Before long, the documents sank gently to the bottom of a rain puddle, no more than illegible pulp.

The lucky star that guided the career of General Vespasian had still not failed him.

For days, Simon labored, hiding the fabulous treasure as best he could. With his work in the Temple approaching a climax Simon now walked up the twelve steps leading to the Sanctuary, conscious of the solemnity of the moment. This place, sacred to his people, would soon be razed to the ground by the avenging Romans. He could almost sense the suffering of generation after generation of Jews dispersed all over an unfriendly world, the yearning they would put into their prayers, the nostalgia they would keep in their hearts for this wonderful edifice erected to the glory of God, but polluted by their wickedness and soon to be destroyed as a punishment for their sins. It was indeed a solemn moment—as though he were, literally, writing history.

Simon came up to the gloriously embroidered Babylonian tapestry showing a sacred map of the heavens and against which he had seen the patriarch Menahem outlined before being dragged away by Eleazar for execution. From here on, this was holy ground and only priests might venture farther, but Simon had been given a specific task by Jeremiah. Parting the great curtain, he muttered in astonishment at the burnished golden plate of the double door leading into the *heikhal*, or holy place, the sculpted vines from which hung clusters of grapes made of solid gold, in glittering profusion. Superstitious, his heart thumping in awe, Simon unlocked the great doors. Inside the chamber there was little ornament—only items of priceless value and holiness. The golden Table of the Shewbread, the two long, silver trumpets used for sounding the sacred teruoth and tekioth, the calls to worship on High Holy Days and the fantastic, golden menorah, the symbol of the Jewish faith. His eyes were riveted on that solid mass of gold—its worth must be inestimable. How many would it take to remove such weight? Yet removed it must be, or the Romans would have it. Snapping orders, he called in his men. Shaking with fear, the soldiers rigged a block and tackle.

The Wolf of Masada now advanced farther down the chamber until he came to a simple curtain. Beyond that curtain was the Holy of Holies. A place of infinite mystery, deserving of the most awesome respect. The Almighty, the God of the Jews, dwelled there. No one was entitled to pass beyond those curtains except the High Priest. To do so was to gaze on the face of Jehovah and for this one would suffer certain death. Had not Pompey, the Roman general, strutted arrogantly into the Holy of Holies, only to die a short time thereafter? Only the High Priest might see the face of God and then only on Yom Kippur. As these thoughts passed through Simon's mind, he was disturbed by a hand on his shoulder. Turning, he saw Bar Giora.

"Well," Bar Giora said, his eyes burning, staring straight ahead, "you may not go in there. You know that?"

"I do."

"But we may," Bar Giora said with infinite condescension. "We may."

"And why is that?" Simon forced himself to ask. With sinking heart he knew the answer before Bar Giora, referring to himself as "we," gave it. Here it was again—the curse, the old Jewish curse, back to plague the sanity of their leaders, just at the moment when their wit and courage were needed.

"But surely you must know?" Bar Giora said, wide-eyed, blinking his long lashes. "It is written that God shall send not only a religious teacher, but also a lay Messiah, a mighty warrior, to lead his people back to their former greatness. Obviously we must be he. It is plain that God has marked us for that purpose."

Simon tried smiling at his old friend, expecting, with the boy's quick mind and sense of humor, a smile in return, but to his amazement he realized that the Jewish leader was deadly serious. Bar Giora wore that faraway look Simon had first noticed at Qumran, an expression of transfixed mysticism, a face that bore witness to a strange ecstasy of spirit. "We shall go in," Bar Giora announced. "God has no secrets from his chosen Messiah." Parting the curtains with one impulsive gesture, he marched through, while Simon and the soldiers shrank back, turned to the walls, not daring to look upon the face of the Almighty.

337

In a few minutes, Bar Giora returned, carefully closing the curtains behind him. "There is nothing to see," he said. "Nothing at all. The room is empty."

Simon's work in Jerusalem was done; he was conscious now of a false calm, a dangerous tranquility, hanging over the city. The truce between the opposing factions was about to break at any moment. Jewish unity was coming apart with the passing of every day on which the Romans inexplicably did nothing. The next outbreak of civil war, Simon knew, would be far more terrible than the last, with Bar Giora's well-armed but undisciplined soldiers joining the fray.

It was time to go—and quickly.

All that remained was to honor his pledge to Jeremiah and take the most holy of the treasures, the symbols identified with the emotional heart of the Jewish faith: the Table of the Shewbread, the ceremonial silver trumpets, the great, golden seven-branched menorah, to be hidden at Qumran.

Simon, seeing no Romans, assumed that they had returned to their base in Caesarea. In fact they were still here, blocking the route to the south, as he was soon to find out—in tragic circumstances.

But why, during the year 68–69, the Romans had sat tight and done nothing would soon become a matter of common knowledge.

36

Gaius Licinius Mucianus, governor of Syria, was as much a credit to Rome as his predecessor, Cestius

Gallus, had been a disgrace. Rich, aristocratic, he was a tall, charming old soldier who had earned his decorations serving against the redoubtable Parthians. He ruled Syria well but firmly, a soldier's man more than a politician's, and with no ambition other than to serve his country.

It was precisely the state of his country that was occupying the mind of the spare, blue-eyed nobleman as he took to his couch on an unseasonably hot day in the early spring of the year 69. Surely, he thought, after the death of the madman Nero, one might have expected someone a little better to try and rescue Rome from the chaos in which it had been left. Nero had been superseded by Galba, a half-senile, raving pederast, only to be overthrown by Otho, a splayfooted, bandy-legged, perfumed effeminate who had only risen to public prominence as compensation for Nero's taking his wife, Poppaea, as Empress. Hardly the right kind of qualifications for the strong man that was needed to hold Rome's conquests and possessions! Mucianus was a patriot. The situation had become intolerable. In Rome, yet a third Emperor ruled—Vitellius, perhaps even a greater roué, a greater pervert, a greater glutton than any of those who had preceded him.

Something must be done, but what? And how? As Mucianus lay preoccupied with his thoughts, a footman came through the door and announced that Titus had arrived and wished to see him.

A smile lit up the blue eyes of the patrician when he heard the news. The young man was certainly coming to Antioch with unusual frequency these days, but the old soldier knew perfectly well that it was not just to see him.

In the course of his trip to Rome to pledge his father's allegiance to Galba, Titus had met a famous and beautiful woman—Berenice. Poised, self-assured, almond-eyed, full-lipped, with the glossy, cosseted skin one would expect of a Semitic queen, her impact on the young man had been immense. His thoughts filled with the elusive scent of her provocative body. She had first enticed him and then denied him. He was glad, learning of Galba's death, to turn back home for instructions. That would justify more time at Antioch before returning to the rigors of active service, and Antioch meant only one thing—Berenice. The relationship flowered, with the worldly Berenice amused by the young man twelve years her junior, and Titus, in turn, madly infatuated with her.

Curiously, Vespasian had never seemed to mind, even when his son made excuse after excuse to return to Antioch. The old general's mouth did compress into an even firmer line than usual and the old look of strain crept back onto his face, but it was hard to say what his feelings on the subject really were—rage, annoyance, perhaps, at his son's shirking military service; pride even, that his own flesh and blood was able to mix on equal terms with royalty. In any case, he had always let him go. The courtesy visits that the young man was always careful to pay to the governor's mansion had become a close personal relationship with Mucianus himself.

For that reason, the smile on Mucianus' face as he rose to greet Titus was a genuine smile of pleasure. With no children of his own, he was coming to think of this young fellow who could ride, sing, wrestle—turn his hand to everything with casual ease—as his own son.

"Welcome," he said, "welcome. I am glad to see you here. Do you stay long?"

"As long as I can," Titus said with a smile.

"Ah, what it must be like to be young," said Mucianus, the mass of wrinkles around his eyes meshing and crinkling pleasantly at the thought. "I do not flatter myself that you have come here to spend your time with an old soldier living on his memories." Although there was pain in Mucianus' voice, it was not the Pain of jealousy. Mucianus was no homosexual.

"My father sends his compliments," Titus said.

"How is he?" asked Mucianus. "What news do you have from Judaea?"

Titus shrugged. "We are all confused," he said. "With new Emperors changing so quickly, Father does not really know what policy to adopt."

"Why doesn't he take Jerusalem?" Mucianus asked curiously. "There is little to stop him."

"Most of the time the Jews fight each other and destroy themselves for us. Although they have a temporary truce, Father says it will not last long."

Mucianus chuckled. "Your father is a sentimental old humanitarian," he said. "He seizes on the chaos in Rome not to sack such an ancient and historical city."

"Perhaps you are right," Titus said, smiling. "To tell you the truth, I think he is tired of war."

As wine was brought in, they chatted about the appalling situation. Inevitably, friends though they were, a certain strain crept into the conversation. Neither man wanted to be heard expressing open disloyalty to Vitellius, without first knowing the other's feelings.

"You know," Mucianus said casually, very casually, "we out here in the East could make our presence felt in Rome, perhaps even dictate the situation there—if we worked together."

"What do you mean?" Titus said, interested.

"Well, I have three legions, you and your father command elements of four more. A master of an army that size might well be listened to—"

"I hadn't thought of it that way."

There was silence, each man certain of the other's disloyalty, but not daring to make the first move. Eventually, Titus, younger than the other, more rash, blurted out, "Just supposing the Emperor were deposed—who would you wish to put in his place?"

Mucianus sipped his wine, filled with a great peace. Now that the young man had come into the open, his relief was enormous.

"Well," he said, leaning back on his couch, "let us consider. Such a man should be one under whom our eastern armies would feel able to unite—beyond reproach, a patriot, a man able to lead, to bring Rome back to its accustomed greatness. Fair in all things. Just. Hardworking. Do you agree?"

"Of course," Titus said enthusiastically, "and you would have the vote of both my father and myself. Truly I know of no one whom the description fits better."

"Me?" Mucianus said in astonishment. "You think that was what I meant? No, I did not intend to put myself forward."

"And why not? The choice would be ideal."

"You are kind," Mucianus said heavily. "Your sentiment is much appreciated but I am the wrong man

341

for the job. You see, the succession must be assured. There must be sons to take over the burden from an aging father. I have none and therefore I would not do."

"Then who can you have in mind?" Titus said wonderingly.

"Someone," Mucianus said, "whom the soldiers love as one of their own. A simple man, straightforward and down-to-earth, neither licentious nor overholy, careful with money but without being mean. A man to put the country on its feet—a man whom we can all trust. I refer, of course, to your father, Vespasian."

"Has he gone mad?" Vespasian said jokingly. "What's Mucianus trying to do—get us all killed?" He lifted up the bottle of cheap local wine and, disdaining a glass, drank peasant-style, straight from the bottle, the Adam's apple in his thick, seamed neck throbbing rhythmically.

They were sitting in Vespasian's simple, tented command headquarters deep in the Judaean desert, and Titus was recounting his conversation with Licinius Mucianus.

"You have never been afraid of death, Father, in a good cause."

"Maybe not," Vespasian said, "but I know my place all right. What qualifications does a fellow like me have for such an exalted position?"

"The soldiers love you."

"Now don't flatter me, son."

"You know it's true."

"Mucianus is also popular with his men. In addition, he has influence at court and comes from a great patrician family. If he proclaims himself Emperor, I'll throw my legions behind him. Tell him that. Now go and enjoy yourself at his court in Antioch and leave me in peace to fight the Jews."

"Father," said Titus quietly, "Mucianus has no sons and you have. This, he says, makes you the natural choice. You must not shirk your duty."

Vespasian folded his burly arms in front of him and glared at Titus. "Who are you to tell me my duty?" he bellowed. Then he began to think. All his life he had starved, scrimped, penny-pinched for the sake of his boys. Could he afford now to deprive them of this chance, the ultimate pinnacle of success? He stole a quick glance at Titus. If ever there was an Emperor in the making, it was Titus, and perhaps, dare he think it, young Domitian after him? A whole Flavian dynasty. What rubbish. How stupid even to think of such a thing—yet had there not been omens? Prophecies? He remembered that human hand the dog had brought in and deposited under his table. The hand of destiny, so his friends had called it, and hadn't that priest Josephus, a renegade, it was true, but with all the prophetic power of a Jewish holy man, called him "Imperator," years before the current troubles had begun? Vespasian, so level-headed in other ways, happened to be superstitious. He thumped a large, meaty hand on the table. "I'll tell you what I'll do," he said. "I'll come, just to please you, but on one condition only."

"What is that, Father?"

"We consult the oracle on Mount Carmel. It is considered most sound."

"Very well, Father."

The welcome Mucianus prepared for Vespasian was splendid with rows of legionaries in full parade dress lining his route. At the banquet later that evening, however, Mucianus outdid himself.

The party was as small as it was exclusive, with couches arranged around a horseshoe-shaped table occupied only by senior army commanders and royalty drawn from the states linked by treaty obligations to Rome.

Mucianus had placed Vespasian, as guest of honor, on his right side and Queen Berenice on his left, with the adoring Titus on the far side of her. Uneasy and hot in his full dress uniform, Vespasian sat, perspiring and unhappy, through the proceedings. He noticed that Titus, like the other guests, was reclining at nonchalant ease in a cool, highly ornamented, colored robe, talking to the poised, almond-eyed queen, and a pang of envy momentarily touched him. Lacking the social graces, he would have looked a fool, he knew, in such clothes. Engaged in conversation with such an elegant creature as Berenice, he would have been exposed as stupid and boorish. As it was, he could only admire from a distance the slim, expressive naked shoulders of the queen and the easy charm of his son Titus.

Mulishly, his face red and strained, Vespasian gave his attention to the food. It was superb—a welcome change from an army field kitchen. From the moment the hors d'oeuvres were brought in, it was obvious that Mucianus had spent a fortune. Instead of the usual eggs, tuna and vegetables, there were pike livers, pheasant brains, flamingo tongues and lamprey milt, delicacies brought from every corner of the Empire by naval triremes.

"Do you like the prawns?" gushed a corps commander's wife Mucianus had thought it politic to seat next to Vespasian. "I'm told they are towed alive to the coast in special underwater nets."

"Really," grunted Vespasian, crushing the delicacy between his strong teeth and spitting out the shells. Lusty, deprived of women for months, he was annoyed that Mucianus had not seated him next to some prospective bed companion—a normal enough courtesy provided for generals of his rank—but obviously his host had thought the occasion too important. He drank heavily of the wine laced with honey that accompanied these tidbits, morose and ill at ease. He sat through the next course of succulent lobsters, endless dishes of baked sole and mullet, his mind going back to the visit he had paid to the oracle at Mount Carmel on his way to Antioch. Hoping at least for some cryptic message which would have enabled him to ridicule the plans for high office everybody seemed to be making for him, he had been staggered when the priest, Basilides, had walked out through a cloud of billowing incense and pronounced an incredible prophecy. "Know you, Vespasian," he had said, "that a mighty seat is given you,—limitless borders and a multitude of men." Cutting short the interview, Vespasian had paid him and gone on his way. Sixtyish, with a hatred for the pomp and opulence of high rank, Vespasian wanted nothing better than to settle down to happy retirement, farming some small-holding with a couple of good, strong peasant women to serve him, but the whole world was conspiring to throw undreamed-of prospects in his path. Stolidly, he waded into the loaded trays of meat which slaves had just brought in, staggering under their sheer weight. There were peacocks, served with their spread tails skewered into the roasted flesh, succulent young lambs imported alive from the Alban hills and as a pièce de résistance Mucianus' chef had proudly produced his own delicacy—pigs' livers from animals fed only on figs and honeyed wine, a taste so delicate that even Vespasian marveled.

Vespasian was a trencherman and could eat and drink most people under the table. Helping himself regularly to the endless supply of Tusculum and Falernian wine that the attentive slaves kept placing in front of him, the general glanced idly at Titus and Berenice, only to note with surprise the look of annoyance that his son now wore.

After watching the queen's behavior for a little while, Vespasian soon discovered the reason. Bored with her youthful admirer, the queen was setting her cap for the elderly but charming governor of Syria, Mucianus himself. Slim, elegant, her flesh smoothed by the attentive fingers of her slave women, Berenice was one of those women whose attractions reach their peak at the age of forty. She had long, black, glossy hair and her silk *stola matronalis* had been slashed to the waist with sensational boldness to reveal more than a hint of hard, tight, purple nipples and, if that were not enough, the queen had painted her lips the same color. Now, with her dress also cunningly cut to display her satiny shoulders, she had turned away from Titus, gold ornaments shimmering against her exposed cleavage under the embarrassed gaze of Mucianus.

Titus, usually self-composed and cheerful, was furious. Vespasian could see that. As the meal progressed through a lengthy entertainment and reached the final course of one enormous pyramidal cake four feet high, surrounded by fresh and dried fruits, the queen continued blatantly to ignore her young lover. Vespasian could not help grinning. It was good to see Titus taken down a peg, and he wondered what his son was going to do.

He was soon to know. Scowling, Titus suddenly grabbed Berenice by the nape of her neck and on the

345

fleshy part of her thigh, and hoisted her urgently over his shoulder. Without asking either Vespasian's or Mucianus' permission to leave the banquet, the muscular young man stalked arrogantly off, the queen screaming with rage from her humiliating position.

There was a buzz of consternation, but Mucianus leaned indolently across his couch and engaged Vespasian in conversation with an easy smile, and taking his cue, the rest of the guests relaxed and pretended to ignore the incident.

"It was lucky," Mucianus said, in his patrician drawl, "that owing to the intimacy of this occasion, we excluded bodyguards. There might otherwise have been an ugly incident."

"Titus can look after himself," Vespasian growled. Having come all this way at Mucianus' insistence, he was not going to feel guilty for his son's behavior.

"No, no." Mucianus smiled charmingly. "Do not misunderstand me. It is only that the queen is important to our plans."

"An ally is an ally," Vespasian said, his mouth full of cake. "They will do our bidding whatever it may be."

"She is a woman of great importance," observed Mucianus. "Her brother is Agrippa the Second, whom I believe you know. Under various Emperors he has been rewarded for his loyalty with ever-increasing territory. He now holds all of Trachonitis and Peraea, as well as the lands of Golan. By permission of his sister Berenice, he also rules her kingdom of Chalcis. At the moment, he is in Rome, acting as our eyes and ears."

Vespasian could only marvel at the energy of the talkative little monarch who was doing so well under Rome's protection. "You said she was of great importance?"

"Why, my dear Vespasian," said Mucianus, "do you not know? She may have ceded her kingdom but, like most women, knew how to hang on to the contents of the treasury. You have seen her jewelry—the gods alone know what it's worth. She is a woman of fabulous wealth—perhaps the richest of all the monarchs in the eastern Empire."

"Why should you care?" Vespasian asked, knitting the thick eyebrows of his seamed face. "I would not have thought money would impress a man such as you."

Mucianus nodded his head gracefully at the compliment, then said softly, very softly, "But that kind of money, Vespasian, is needed to finance military campaigns."

Mucianus brought Vespasian back to the miseries and cares of his own position. He nodded curtly, then sat back on his couch, burly arms folded, as he waited for the speeches to begin.

"My dress," she said. "Don't tear my dress." Her voice was now pleading.

Titus had deposited her on a couch in the anteroom and his muscular hands were already reaching for her clothes. Impatiently, he allowed her to unclothe. Eyeing him almost fearfully, the queen was amazed to see the pulse beating madly in Titus' neck. Suddenly, she found her legs forced open wide and, paralyzed, for some reason unable to struggle, felt the young man lower his heavy, sweaty thews on top of her, penetrating with incredible force and thrusting with all his massive strength.

"Ill-mannered, peasant pig" was all she had time to snarl before a hand clamped over her mouth, reducing her curses to an impotent, spluttering whisper. The young man's force was truly incredible. She was literally pinned to the couch, her delicate limbs forced wide and high in the air, creaking from such unaccustomed and humiliating violation.

She felt herself begin to shiver. "By Jehovah's bones," she blasphemed. It was building now—the fire, the desire. The chain reaction, the fury, yet the need for sexual submission. No one had ever dared treat her like this before. In her own kingdom she would have ordered such a man executed, but these plundering Romans were another matter. What had happened to that fawning, adoring boy she had taunted and teased for so long? Who had hardly dared touch her? She had provoked him too far and was now paying the penalty in a way she had no possibility of controlling. Her ribs bruised, hardly able to breathe from the force of the young man's lust, she let her thigh muscles go soft in acceptance at the same time that her belly exploded in red, sweaty heat.

347

With her arms raised high above her head, fragile wrists pinned bruisingly to the couch by Titus' hand, the black kohl painted so strikingly across her face began to run from her eyes. Raking his sweaty shoulders with her fingernails, she began to match his crude assault with an even more urgent warmth.

Moaning in their terrible ecstasy, they writhed and twisted, oblivious to the weighty speeches now being delivered in the banqueting room.

Mucianus could wait for Titus and Queen Berenice no longer. Time was running out for all of them. Rising to his feet, he delivered a speech of welcome which, by its charm and elegance, had the guests' attention riveted. Vespasian could not help but admire the patrician governor who possessed those rare qualities of patriotism and honesty.

"Vespasian." Mucianus turned suddenly toward him. Taken by surprise, the general went red-faced with embarrassment. "Vespasian. I, Mucianus, and all of us here invite you to be Emperor. Three Emperors have we had in Rome in the course of one year, each one worse than the last. Even now, Vitellius dissipates his powers in drunken revelry while all Rome holds its breath. Can you now refuse the crown? Your men love you and we need you. You, Vespasian, have seven whole legions, not to speak of fleets, of cavalry, of auxiliaries. Also remember one thing—we who have deliberated about rebellion have already rebelled." Mucianus sat down to enthusiastic applause.

Vespasian stood up. Lacking the grace to make a speech, he preferred to engage Mucianus in an open discussion. "So we've burned our boats, have we?" he growled.

"I think so. Yes." Mucianus smiled.

"And where are those seven legions?"

"Your four. The Fifth, Twelfth, Fifteenth and Tenth. My three will pledge themselves to your service."

"Cavalry? Auxiliaries?"

In answer, Mucianus smiled at a swarthy man reclining on the far side of the table.

The man stood up. "I am King Soaemus of Commagene. My bowmen and cavalry are known throughout the Empire. Vespasian, I give them to you." With

Mucianus leading the applause, the king sat down.

"Also," Mucianus went on smoothly, "Agrippa the Second pledges his army, and from Rome, an old friend of yours, Petilius Cerialis, sends greetings and promises his loyalty."

Vespasian smiled a little at the thought of the gangling womanizer whom he had known in those far-off days of the Britannia campaign.

"Money," he demanded. "How do we finance such an undertaking? The cost is going to be enormous."

For several minutes there was absolute silence. Even for their favorite commander, the legions would not march unless they were paid. The sum needed would be colossal.

"I will pay your bill." A woman's voice rang out, cool and clear from the back of the room.

Gasping their surprise, the guests turned and found to their amazement Berenice, accompanied by Titus, standing at one of the entrances. "Five million sesterces, ten million? What does it matter?" she called. Gazing softly at Titus, eyes brimming with love, with desire slaked, she went on, "For these Flavians, no cost is too high."

There was a loud sigh from the assembled guests. Not many people could pledge such an enormous sum so casually. Carried away by their emotions, the allies and corps commanders rose to their feet, cheering and clapping, while Vespasian looked back at them in trapped desperation.

"Listen to me," he roared, banging a great meaty hand on the table. "The key is neither money nor men. The key is Egypt. Whoever holds the granary holds Rome. Only when Tiberius Alexander and his army swear allegiance will I take this post you press on me. Only then," he went on, thumping the table, "not before."

Now, with Vespasian's conditions made known, the banquet continued more soberly, breaking up earlier than it might have. All were conscious that they had plotted treason. If Tiberius Alexander did not declare for Vespasian, the eastern armies might well change their mind—and they could all find themselves executed within the year.

As for the rugged old peasant who had banged the

table and informed the guests of his conditions, he could not wait to get back to the simple life with his troops. Journeying into the bleak Judaean desert, he could only wonder why they persisted in trying to load such a stubborn old fool with honors and pray that they would now leave him in peace.

Simon left the doomed city of Jerusalem just as civil war broke out again, but only to fall under the interested gaze of one Vipstanus Tampianus, a *tesserarius* in rank, of the Tenth Fretensis, commanding a small sentry post camped out in the hills.

With Bar Giora needing every man he could find, Simon, once clear of Jerusalem, had been left with a mere five soldiers as protection against robbers, and these were soon overwhelmed by Tampianus' heavily armored legionaries.

The leering soldiers assembled in a group around the prisoners and their mule-drawn cart. Sweating in the burning sun, they soon stripped away the heavy bags of flax hiding the treasure until, inevitably, the beautiful golden Table of the Shewbread, the seven-candled menorah, the glittering silver trumpets were exposed to view.

Tampianus was furious. A few bags of coins he could have taken for himself—a share for the scum serving with him would have ensured their silence—but this would have to be reported to headquarters. Finally, he gave orders for the cart and the prisoners to be moved back to his outpost in the hills, where he could amuse himself with them at leisure and find out if they had other treasure hidden.

Once there, he summoned the Jewish leader before him—a man with a mutilated face and one eye. Fitting across one of his hands the dreadful, leather-studded cestus with which the Romans boxed, he said coarsely. "Where have you hidden the rest of your treasure?"

"There is nothing else," Simon said.

Tampianus struck Simon a terrible blow across the face, ripping skin and bone, making blood spurt onto the dusty ground. "Jew," he said, showing his stumps of teeth, "you cannot mean that."

"There is nothing."

The *tesserarius* struck him again. As the dull thump of the blow came to Andrasta, gathered outside with the others, she could stand it no longer. Because she was dressed in a capacious Arab robe, with her tawny hair hidden from view, the Romans had not yet realized that they had a beautiful woman among their captives. But now, flinging off the robe, she revealed herself for the first time. Rushing forward, she screamed, "Stop it. Leave him alone."

When the first vulgar oaths and catcalls of the legionaires had died down, Tampianus said, "Come here."

At the sight of this tall, lithe female advancing toward him and at the thought of what he was going to do to her, the membranes of Tampianus' throat became so thick that he had to hawk twice on the ground before he could speak. "Your name?"

"Andrasta."

He pointed to Simon. "You are his woman?"

"Yes."

"You are my woman now. Go to my tent."

Andrasta stood her ground.

"You can take me," she said in a low voice, "use me as you want—I cannot prevent it—but what if I were to devote myself willingly to your pleasure?" Eyes half closed, her wide mouth curling silkily, lazily, she went on, "Have you any idea of the ecstasy a woman trained for pleasure can give? Of the arts of the temple girls in lands far to the east of here? The soft touches of the trained houris of Arabian harems? All these things was I taught before I was rescued from slavery. Now I can be your slave, willing, adoring, using my long fingers"— she showed her slender hands in a delicate flutter—"to massage you through the long watches of the night, to fan your body into a white flame of burning fire—all this I will do for you, in exchange for one thing."

Tampianus, accustomed to the slack thighs of cheap Caesarea whores, breathed heavily from the sheer sensuality of this tawny-haired beauty he had discovered so miraculously in the stony Judaean desert. He said hoarsely, "And what is that?"

"This man's life." She pointed to Simon.

Tampianus laughed. It would not do any harm if he

left the man alive for a few days and it would ensure that the girl was cooperative. "All right," he said. "He lives only while you continue to please me. As for the others"—he turned to his men—"kill them."

Tied to a pole near the Roman's tent, Simon now knew real agony. The sound of Andrasta's gasps, sighs, the occasional cry of pain, the rustle of bodies, came to him clearly. He shuddered at what she must be enduring in the darkness of that tent so that he might live a few days longer. Slowly, he raised his suffering head to the stars and wept.

Each morning, Andrasta brought him food and water, and as the bruises grew on her skin and deep circles became dark and livid under her eyes, a temporary madness gripped the soul of the Wolf of Masada. Howling at the top of his voice, he would pray to the Almighty for mercy, and it was during this time that his hair began to turn gray.

On the sixth day, Tampianus marched among the blackening corpses of the Jewish soldiers, called to his own men and said, "The girl bores me. Tonight she's yours."

"What about him?" One of the legionaries pointed to Simon.

"Crucify him."

37

The rope bit into his chest, holding him hard against the cross. The soldier with the sledgehammer put the long copper nail in his mouth so that he might more easily prize open Simon's clenched fingers. "Don't struggle," he said, almost kindly. "They say it hurts less that way."

The fingers, already mutilated by the pancratiast, parted easily. In went the nail, driven home with a mighty blow. A surging wave of pain rose inside him, exploding into a scream. Somehow, in the way that separates a brave man from a coward, he bit it back stillborn, so that although he still jerked like a gaffed fish, only a groan escaped his lips.

As they held his other hand outstretched and ready for the nail, the soldier rested the sledgehammer and said craftily, "All right, Jew. You're the leader. Tell us where the treasure is. We can help you—we know the vital spots—we can send you to paradise or to hell. A nail an inch too much to one side and the blood leaps from you and you're gone in minutes." He paused to see that Tampianus was not watching, then went on, "We can show mercy, you know. Even if we miss—there are other ways, a spear in the side, no peg supporting your crotch so that the life drains from you in hours, while we make you drunk as a pig on vinegar wine." He hefted the sledgehammer, an expert at his job, and waited for an answer. "Well, Jew, how about it?"

Simon spat in the man's face. The soldier nodded, not angry. He had crucified countless men before—some were frightened, others were brave. It was all the same to him. He felt no personal involvement. There was just no reason now why he should trouble himself to show mercy. Resting the nail against Simon's other palm, he drew the hammer sharply back—

The clatter of hooves came suddenly to his ears. Resting his hammer again, he turned to see a troop of soldiers riding in. From their glittering, polished cuirasses worn over vivid red tunics, the golden greaves and ornate helmets, the purple cloaks that denoted staff rank, this could only be the general's personal escort.

"By the priapus of Hercules," Vespasian swore pungently, "what is going on here?"

Drugged, remembering little of the awful, jolting journey that followed, Simon came to, lying in a hospital bed in the leave center of Caesarea Philippi on the shores of the River Jordan.

Here, the air was cool, scented by the lush vegetation,

pleasant with the tang of cork and eucalyptus. For several days he was made to stay there, while a *medicus* treated his injured hand. From the orderly, always a rich source of gossip, he learned that there was going to be a court of inquiry. Yes, Simon thought, a court was inevitable. The Wolf of Masada, sworn by Vespasian to be dead, killed by his own son, Titus, had turned up in the Judaean desert with the priceless emblems of the Jewish faith! As if that was not enough, had the General permitted his crucifixion? He had not. Instead, he had ordered Simon cut down.

There was no doubt: for the sake of his old friend, Vespasian had finally brought about his own ruin. As for himself, Simon had no illusions. The treatment he was receiving was due to the last of the general's patronage and he would be nailed back on the cross within minutes of the judicial decision.

He did not mind the prospect of dying. But the thought that Vespasian might himself face death for treason depressed him beyond belief. In sheer misery, he turned his face to the pillow.

He was awakened by a soft hand on his forehead. Andrasta stood by his bed.

"You are feeling better?" she asked in a small voice.

She stroked his hair, running the newly gray strands through her fingers. "How you have suffered," she said.

Simon pulled himself upright. "Look at what you endured at the hands of that Roman to save my life."

She smiled gently at his mutilated face, that drooping, almost sinister lip caused by the Greek wrestler's nail gouge when he fought for her in the arena.

This was a different Andrasta, no longer hating, resentful, thirsting for revenge, but tranquil, her face in repose. Even now, Simon could not quite believe the way she had taken Tampianus' sexual abuse as a thing of no consequence. It was as if her stay at Qumran and instruction at the hands of Jeremiah had instilled in her some revelation—a message about the inner meaning of life.

He felt love for her surge through him. "I'm sorry," he said. "All I have brought you is torture, rape and the fear of death. In these last few years, I have had no time for you, ignored your very existence. I do not deserve your love any longer. Leave me now—perhaps I can arrange through Vespasian for you to go free. He does not war on women."

She stroked his head again. "Ssh." She soothed him. "Lie still. Get better."

"For what? For death?"

"Our time is not yet. First, Jeremiah has a great task for us."

"You believe that?"

"I am sure of it." Her face changed. There was now a look of determination, of unshakable purpose.

Simon silently watched her go. Buoyed with hope by her inner strength, the Wolf of Masada recovered quickly and in days was well enough to see Vespasian.

He was shocked to see the change that had come over his old commander. While Andrasta had found some strange radiance, Vespasian, eyes haggard, shoulders slumped, sat somberly in the shade, ignoring the hoarse sounds of soldiers bathing in the river.

"You broke your oath." Vespasian's peasant voice sounded cold.

"That is untrue," Simon said. "I was escorting Jewish treasure to safety. That is not fighting."

"It is, when it can be melted down to provide weapons and armor," said the general.

"You do not understand," Simon insisted hotly. "It was to be hidden for safekeeping at Qumran. Jeremiah insisted that the treasure should not be polluted by being used for war. Otherwise I should never have done it."

For minutes there was silence in the darkened room, then Vespasian said wearily, "Very well. I suppose I must accept your word." Somehow he had managed to hide the icy chill that had gripped his heart at the mention of the word Qumran. So Simon did not know yet of Placidus' terrible deed. He was glad, at least, of that. Vespasian still felt the odium of his soldiers' savage destruction of the monastery. Everywhere his troops murdered and raped, but that was the way of war—yet how could he explain the appalling torture and massacre in such terms to an old friend who had just had a six inch nail driven clean through his hand? He said, "By leaving Qumran you exposed yourself to capture and thereby brought shame on me and my family."

Simon hung his head. "The mission was forced on me," he said.

"And so was the necessity for my men to torture Jews," Vespasian said abruptly. He bent back to his papers in the gloom of the darkened room, and Simon, realizing the interview was ended, quietly left.

Vespasian watched him go with brooding eyes. Even now, he loved the gaunt, mutilated fighter as his own brother, respected him for his bravery, thanked him for sparing his life to enjoy an illustrious career, even if it were to be ended now. Yet war had a habit of turning friends into enemies and the two could never be close again.

His thoughts turned to the court of inquiry that had already been dragging on day after day. Although he had ordered the investigation—the act of a man who had nothing to fear—he had been too proud to lie in order to defend his name and the verdict was a foregone conclusion. It would mean humiliation, disaster. The court had judicial immunity from military action on his part and could be relied on, made up as it was of patrician officers, aristocratic governors' aides, to smash the career of this upstart peasant. He could see it all now. Mucianus would be called down from Syria to take over the legions. Condemned as a traitor, Vespasian would be lynched by his men before the death sentence could be officially carried out. His thin lips compressed in that familiar expression of strain. He had scrimped and saved, hoping for high things for Titus, and death would be the reward for both of them—because he had to pay off a debt to the Jew.

Head bowed on his folded arms, Vespasian waited for the verdict. It was to be delivered that morning and could not be long delayed.

Suddenly, he heard cheering—not just one burst, but a steady sound coming nearer all the time. Yes, he thought bitterly, it had happened enough times before—men turning against their general. Louder still came the cheers. They reminded Vespasian of the baying of hounds closing in for the kill. He got up from the table, squaring his shoulders. Chin outthrust, he turned to face the mob.

He opened the door and the noise hit him like a hot

blast, *cornua* blaring, *tubicines* grunting out enormous paeans of sound. "Imperator," the soldiers cried. "Imperator Vespasian Caesar, Vespasian Augustus—Imperator, Imperator!" An unbelieving look on his face, he allowed himself to be borne shoulder-high around the camp. Seeing an officer in the crush, he managed to grab him for an instant. "What's happening?" he demanded. "What's going on?"

"Do you not know, sire?" the flushed tribune shouted. "In Egypt, Tiberius Alexander and his legions have taken the oath to you as Emperor. In Syria, Mucianus has promised to follow suit. Do you not understand, sire? You are Emperor of Rome."

For Vespasian, things that had seemed impossible quickly became possible.

To the Jew and the tawny-haired woman standing before him, he said curtly, "As an act of *clementia* to mark my accession, I am freeing all Jewish prisoners of war here at Caesarea Philippi. Your lives are spared. You may leave when you wish."

"You owe us nothing. We do not ask for your mercy," said Simon.

The Emperor inclined his head. He said coldly, "Perhaps I have paid off the principal, so let us call this the interest."

The men eyed each other silently. Simon said, "I wish you good luck, Vespasian, although my country fights yours. You will make a fine Emperor. Perhaps the greatest Rome has ever seen."

"Good-bye," Vespasian said, the frost still in his voice.

"Good-bye." Simon turned on his heel.

"Simon." The Emperor came swiftly around his desk and the men embraced. For seconds they stayed like that, bearhugging the warmth from the other's body. Then they parted, knowing they would never see each other again.

At Masada, Ben Yair welcomed Simon and Andrasta to the fortress, although, in their poor robes, dirty and tired from the journey, he could not believe at first who they were.

"May you stay?" Ben Yair said, astonishment in his

voice. "You, who are known as the Wolf of Masada—who captured this rock from the Romans in the first place? We are honored to have you. We shall elect you our leader and you shall put our defenses in order."

Simon cut short Ben Yair's enthusiasm. "I cannot fight," he said quietly. "My wife and I ask only to be allowed to live here in peace."

"I have heard this rumor," Ben Yair said, wrinkling his brow, "but did not believe it true that you fight the Kittim no more. There must be some strange secret here."

"You are entitled to an explanation," said Simon. "I am an old comrade of Vespasian's. Many years ago, when we were both young and carefree, we fought Rome's battles together in Britannia."

Ben Yair's eyes sparkled. A religious man, he was also a fighter. He had an underslung jaw that jutted out, with flat lips and a flat nose, giving an impression of strength and purpose. This was the face of a man brave in battle, and Simon could not help liking him at once. "It is true there is no bond like that of old comrades," Ben Yair said thoughtfully. "Vespasian is a good man. I understand now why he would not kill you."

"And you will fight here," Simon asked, "when the Romans come?"

Ben Yair wrinkled his sunburned forehead. "You think they will not leave us alone?"

"The Romans cannot leave Masada to the Jews. While Masada lives, it is a beacon, a rallying point to our people."

"Then we will fight them." Ben Yair shrugged. "Although our numbers are small and there are many women and children, we are not afraid to die. When will they come?"

"After Jerusalem falls, they will come for Masada."

"But the walls are strong and our army great in numbers inside the city. Will not Jerusalem hold?"

"Even now, while they should be preparing their defenses, siting their artillery, our people fight among themselves," Simon said, pain in his voice. "When Titus comes, they will unite and fight bravely—but too late. The capital will not last a year."

"Then we must not make the same mistake," Ben

Yair said resolutely. "I shall give orders for the walls to be strengthened, weapons to be prepared, ammunition and food accumulated. It is God's will that we defend this place with courage."

"It is God's will," Simon said.

"And you?" Ben Yair asked heavily. "How will you occupy yourself in these days to come?"

Simon said, "Lend me two stout men and a scribe learned in the art of writing upon copper."

As Simon explained his wish that an imperishable record of the Temple treasure be left at Qumran, Ben Yair threw open his muscular, sunburned arms and gazed across the pale-blue Dead Sea to the distant, haze-smudged mountains of Moab. "Yes," he said, "these are great tasks, well worth doing. What can be better than to preserve the sacred heritage of our people?"

38

With Mucianus drawing off elements of the Fifth, Tenth, Twelfth and Fifteenth legions to campaign in Europe, the net around Jerusalem temporarily loosened. Simon and his companions were able to move back to Qumran. They arrived there in the autumn of the year 69 CE, just as the summer heat had begun to dissipate.

In a whole year, the sun, fierce hawks, voracious insects had removed most of the flesh from the tortured bones of the martyrs that the tribune Placidus had killed, but enough remained to tell of their awful agony. The first task was to bury the old patriarchs in the simple manner of their orthodox sect, feet pointing toward the north—and the Temple—hands crossed over the pelvis, in the little cemetery adjoining the monastery. That done, and a short prayer said for their souls, the next duty was to make an inventory of all the treasure with a coded description of each hiding place.

The young scribe they had brought with them sat at a desk in the cool, whitewashed scriptorium of the monastery and began the laborious job of cutting the Hebrew letters on thin rolls of copper which would record for all time the sites of the treasure hoards. Named Saul, the scribe was tall and strongly built with square shoulders and the ready smile one would expect of a boy of twenty. Nearer Andrasta's age than Simon's, he soon found himself more interested in the tawny-haired beauty than in his work.

One day, thoroughly bored with the eternal monotony, he had playfully grabbed her as she brought him food and, sitting her on his knee, kissed her. At first she had fought savagely, but the boy had said something funny and made her laugh. To her subsequent burning shame, admiring this gay, six-foot Adonis who moved with all the grace of youth that Simon no longer possessed, she kissed him back. Simon, returning early from his day's work, caught them.

That night he would not sleep beside her and she wept continuously. Deprived, with Simon, of any form of physical love, she had succumbed for a few moments to the kisses of this handsome boy—and her husband had seen it. She hated herself. Distractedly, wringing her hands, she went to Saul and explained about Simon's terrible injury—why he could not make love, his impotence caused solely because he had wanted to protect her from the horrors of Roman slavery.

When Saul learned the truth, he too wept. By nature open and generous, the gesture he made was typical of the boy. Kneeling before Simon, he bared his throat and offered the Wolf of Masada his favorite dagger. "Kill me," he said. "Because to you, a man I should worship, I have done a terrible wrong."

"In what way did you abuse my wife?" asked Simon quietly.

"I swear to God I only stole a kiss," the boy wept, "but does that matter, knowing the price you paid for her love?"

"But you were only paying tribute to her beauty," Simon said, the lines of grief that had etched his eye vanishing one by one. "Even I, ancient as I am, can still remember my youth. You are not forgiven because, now that you have confessed, I find there is nothing to forgive."

"A penance, a punishment," the boy begged.

Simon grinned, his drooping lower lip curling in thought. "When I am dead, look after my wife."

"That is no penance. It is a privilege."

"I am serious," Simon warned. "I hold you to it."

"I promise," the boy pledged, "to protect her. Honor her. Even as you have done."

"Get off your knees," said Simon. "You are my friend."

That night the Wolf of Masada slept again in Andrasta's arms, but the incident had a strange effect on him. He would spend his secret moments praying in the silent, deserted synagogue, that he be made a man again—for a miracle—for the right to seal his love with Andrasta with a baby. Such a miracle, he knew, was impossible.

But still, as a Jew, one of His chosen people, he had a right to ask.

Eventually, the work was finished and in a cave high in the cliff face, near the monastery—a secret place close to where Jeremiah had stored the accumulated writings of his holy sect—Simon gently laid two scrolls of copper to rest.

This was the only record in existence of the fabulous Temple treasure. "Will it ever be found?" Saul asked doubtfully.

It was Andrasta who answered him. More than ever, she seemed charged with the will to carry out Jeremiah's prophecy. She stood there, a tall figure of beauty, her skin tanned an even gold by the sun. "It will be found someday," she said. Awed, silenced by the certainty of her voice, the inner radiance she seemed to have found, the little group made the difficult journey back to the stronghold of Masada.

Within months, an extraordinary thing occurred. As if in direct response to his prayers, the ever-merciful hand of the Almighty touched the loins of Simon ben

361

Eleazar, and Andrasta found herself with child.

At the bris Ben Yair himself performed the ritual circumcision. After it was over, Andrasta sat under the stars, looking proudly at her squalling baby, while the others, forming two rings—the men facing the women—did a joyous folk dance. With much drinking of the rose-colored Judaean wine, the celebration went on well into the cool autumn night. Ben Yair motioned Simon to one side.

"Now we must talk seriously," he said. They walked to a quiet spot, close by the wall where it plunged fifteen hundred feet into the valley below.

"You have news?" Simon asked.

"Bad, I'm afraid," Ben Yair said. "Jerusalem has fallen and the Temple burned to the ground. It is just as you predicted. If our men had not fought each other before engaging the Romans, it might have been different."

"The leaders? What of them?"

"Eleazar dead. John of Gishala and Bar Giora both taken."

Simon still could not bring himself to hate that dirty, ruddy-faced bandit with whom he had lived those first few months in the Galilee. As for Bar Giora, he had been brave, a good friend and a fine soldier—before he had become Messianic. He wondered how the Romans would kill them. Crucifixion? The wild beasts? Their deaths would not be easy.

"I am sorry to hear that," he said at length.

"I have other news," Ben Yair said. "Titus leaves to join his father in Rome."

Simon nodded.

"My courier is a reliable man," Ben Yair went on. "My information is that we will be left in peace while Vespasian sets his Empire in order. There is a revolt in Gaul, chaos in Rome. As for Judaea, a new procurator is being sent out to clear up the wreckage."

"How long before he comes?" Simon asked.

Ben Yair shrugged. He took a drink of wine and passed the clay jug to Simon. "Your guess is as good as mine," he said. "A year—perhaps eighteen months. You must use the time well."

"Me?"

"With Titus gone, your oath is canceled. Will you now fight for Masada?"

"I will fight, said Simon.

39

In Rome, there had never been six months like it. After the darkness, there was light. A burly, stubborn-faced peasant descended from a family of Sabine laborers had come to the capital, determined to put his imperial house in order.

Laws were passed in bewildering succession. Nothing was too difficult for the Emperor to tackle. A program of public building to clear the ruins of the recent fighting, an increased panel of judges to deal with the backlog of lawsuits. Punishment for those who deserved it, mercy for those who had merely backed the wrong horse in the civil wars. In one way, however, the Emperor, with a deserved reputation for meanness, behaved in a fashion bordering on sharp practice.

The country was bankrupt; years of Nero's mad extravagance followed by civil war had emptied the treasury. Somehow the currency must be stabilized, the economy put right. Vespasian set out to do it. He would stop at nothing, it seemed—selling favors, taking bribes, even going into business himself and cornering the market in pepper! Nothing mattered as long as the money came in and financial confidence was restored.

Some of his sayings were destined to be famous. "How much will my funeral cost?" he demanded of one astounded civil servant. "Ten million sesterces," the man had replied after considerable thought. "I'll take a hundred thousand now and you can throw me into the

Tiber," Vespasian said, his seamed face cracking in a smile.

Then there was the time a courier rushed to inform him that the Senate had just voted him a statue worth a million sesterces. Vespasian had immediately held out his cupped hands for the money. "Right. Let this be the base."

Such was the consistency of his blunt humor that his advisers were disappointed if there was not each day yet another peasant joke to relate around aristocratic dinner tables with amused disbelief.

As good an Emperor as he was a general, Vespasian possessed the rare ability to inspire utter loyalty. Petilius Cerialis had not only headed the crazy cavalry charge into Rome that had taken the city for his old comrade, but was now in the north, disposing of the rebellious tribes. Only later would Vespasian learn what a threat this rebellion had been and how narrowly the gangling aristocrat had triumphed.

Now, in the spring of 71, the news was all good. Titus was coming back, bringing thousands of prisoners, enormous treasure.

"There must be a triumph, sire," murmured one of his advisers.

"Oh, yes," joined in the others, "the biggest ever, for you and Titus Caesar."

"Think of the money it'll cost."

"We will raise the funds privately," they said. "A thanks to you, sire, for all the benefits you have brought."

"Very well," Vespasian said, "but only as long as it does not cost me a penny."

Choosing his moment, the Emperor's aide now stepped forward. "I have news of your son, sire. He will be home within the week."

Vespasian sank back on his cushion with a sigh of relief. All this work was killing him and Titus could take over some of it. Besides, Titus would be sure to have news of the Jew.

On the day of the triumph, while Rome gathered strength in the cool of the morning for the joyous celebrations to come, Vespasian and Titus dressed early.

Wreathed in bay and wearing the traditional crimson robes, they held an informal audience near the Temple of Isis.

Both were eager to see face to face the legendary Jewish commanders who had resisted the might of the Empire for so long. Titus himself had put off such a moment in Judaea, so that he might share it with his father.

Loaded with chains, battered, filthy, John of Gishala and Bar Giora were dragged forward and thrown before them. Bar Giora immediately held his hand high toward heaven and began declaiming, mixing passages from the Scriptures with his own personal message to mankind. John, in contrast, squatted calmly on the ground, a glint of merriment in his blue eyes. By nature a man of the mountains, accustomed to living hard in the high, cold air of the Galilee, the rigors of prison had hardly touched him. His single earring glinting brilliantly in the morning sun, he looked fearlessly up at the Emperor.

"And the Lord decreed that a leader should come unto the children of Israel," cried Bar Giora, dusky face alight with fervor. "There shall arise among you one different from all the others, strong as a lion, mighty in war—" His speech was terminated by a heavy, thonged boot crashing into his belly. The guard drew back his foot for another kick, but Bar Giora now sat gazing mutely at the sky.

"He is no longer with us," observed Vespasian.

"Withdrawn into his own private world," agreed Titus. "Madness has indeed touched him."

"Yet he quotes from the holy writings of the Jews," Vespasian said. "Is there not a continuous history of these false Messiahs?"

Titus, curly-headed, tanned, chuckled. "They tend to bestow the mantle lightly. Consequently, many are tempted to wear it."

"Yet it has caused us much trouble," Vespasian said, frowning. He turned to John. "Well, fellow, what do you have to say for yourself?"

John, not in the least disturbed by the importance of the Emperor and his son, perhaps the most powerful men in the world, struggled to his feet and let out a great, gusty laugh. Even with shoulders bent by the weight of his chains, he was a formidable figure. "Listen to me, Farmer Vespasian," he said. "I'm not ashamed to die. I've had a good life and a merry one, and by all accounts you've had your share too."

The guards, aghast, ran to beat this man who had dared address the Emperor in such familiar tones, but Vespasian motioned them away. "Yes," he said, his voice going rich with peasant dialect, "I like my drink and women, I'll admit, but I don't go looting and killing to get them."

At this, John threw back his head and roared a great booming laugh that came strangely from a half-starved prisoner facing death. "You're wrong, my friend," he said. "Your legions have perfected what I, in the hills of Galilee, have only imitated."

A silence fell over the escort. Surely by that remark the prisoner had now made certain an agonizing death.

Vespasian, the lips of his stubborn face tightly compressed, pointed suddenly to Bar Giora. "Kill that one," he said. "Put him out of his misery."

"But, Father," exclaimed Titus in surprise. "He is plainly mad. Surely the other is more dangerous?"

"Ah," said Vespasian, his face a picture of peasant cunning. "You miss the point. The first one is mad enough to be dangerous, whereas a brigand will never be more than a brigand. Besides," he added stubbornly, "the bandit showed courage."

The guards dragged the Jewish leaders away. Later, they would both be made to march in procession for the amusement of the Roman mob and, at the end of the triumph, one freed, the other executed.

The almighty, through Vespasian, visited the supreme penalty on Bar Giora for gazing on His presence in the Holy of Holies.

The triumph made the one accorded Claudius for the conquest of Britannia seem puny in comparison.

First came the Senate, gorgeously robed, followed by the band of harshly blaring war trumpets, guaranteed to set the crowd on edge; then came carts bearing spoils of war, the fabulous riches of Judaea, heaped mounds of coins, ornaments and jewelry that sparkled and glittered in the sun. Then came priceless hangings stripped from the houses of the merchants of Jerusalem, even the Babylonian curtain from the Temple itself, escorted by attendants clad in fabulous robes of crimson dye.

When the golden Table of the Shewbread came into sight, its great weight requiring a specially strengthened wagon all to itself, the crowd exploded into oohs and aahs, marveling at the delicate, soaring fingers of the seven-candled menorah mounted on its top and the sacred silver trumpets lying by its side. Now, with the crowd in a happy mood, came huge floats, some three stories high and of a size that staggered even the jaded mob, portraying graphically walls of enormous size thrown down by siege engines, whole formations of men put to the sword, cities stormed, armies surrendering, the Jewish Temple flaming into final destruction. Prisoners of war, sweating and straining in their yoked harnesses, pulled the stupendous floats out of view.

After the priests leading the sacred white bulls destined for sacrifice, to the accompaniment of softly playing flutes, the crowd thrilled at the sight of Jewish war captives. Specially selected by Titus for their exceptional strength and physique, to heighten the achievement of his legions in defeating them, they walked as proud and straight as their chains would allow, indifferent to the catcalls and insults of the gloating Romans.

The cheers now reached fever pitch. The Emperor was coming.

Preceded by the huge blond Germans of the Imperial Bodyguard, their bear skins draped flamboyantly over their gilded cuirasses, the Emperor's carriage rumbled into view, Titus in another carriage behind him and Domitian cavorting on a bold white charger at his brother's side. Thousands of adoring Romans rose to their feet, craned out of windows, stood on the tips of their toes to scream a paean of adulation—"Imperator—Imperator—Imperator." For Vespasian, after so many years of hardship, it was a proud moment, especially with his sons sharing his glory. But the intensity of the crowd's screams somehow frightened him and he began to feel uncomfortable. "What an old fool I was to have this triumph," he found himself muttering under his breath, "what stupidity, what expense."

But now came what the Romans really craved. Power.

Raw, naked, overwhelming power. Exchanging the rotten fruit which they had brought to shower on the captives for beautiful wreaths and garlands of flowers, they awaited the coming of the iron men who had made them the most privileged people in the world. Down the procession route the legions stamped, a massive display of armored might in their oiled and polished cuirasses, the rich crimson of their tunics merging with the purple of the officers in a riot of color. At the noise of their thonged boots biting with a harsh crash of exact sound on the route leading to the Capitoline Hill, seeing the massed eagles, the leopard skins of the standard bearers, the high crested helmets of the colonels of regiments, the crowd roared with pride and excitement. One after another the massed ranks of the legionaries swept past, contingents from every unit that had served in Judaea or campaigned across the length and breadth of Europe to place Vespasian on the throne. The Syrian legions, the Egyptian levies sent by Tiberius Alexander, those from Moesia, Pannonia, Dalmatia, the iron Fifth, Tenth and Fifteenth, fresh from the blood-glut of Jerusalem. All were represented except the Twelfth. For its disgrace under Cestius Gallus it was banished to lonely outpost duty on the Euphrates. And so, with the strangely dressed auxiliaries of Agrippa and King Soaemus bringing up the rear, their skirtlike garments, fish-scale armor and conical helmets always a curious sight to the Romans, the soldiers marched away, leaving only the dwarfs and clowns to guy the famous personalities that had just passed.

Now Vespasian waited at the Temple of Jupiter Capitolinus, while to the ruffle of drums the Jewish captives marked for death were executed in the Forum one by one.

Hearing an enormous shout from the crowd, Vespasian turned to his aide and said, "Which one was that?"

"Bar Giora, sire."

Vespasian's eyes became red and moist.

"So it's true then," remarked Cerialis casually, huge beside the diminutive monarch Agrippa II, "he really does weep when men are killed by his orders."

"He weeps not for that Jew," said Agrippa shrewdly. "He weeps for one yet to die."

The strain of months of hard work culminating in the triumph itself had taken its toll on Vespasian. Now, with Titus there to help, at last he was able to relax at a simple banquet with his old comrades.

Feeling in distinctly good form, he addressed himself to Cerialis, sprawling on the next couch. "I want you to tell us your adventures," he said. "I hear women have nearly been the death of you."

The big cavalryman laughed easily. "It happens to be so, sire. I was in Treves at the time, heavily involved with this rather delightful creature, when the alarm sounded. In seconds, the town seemed to be full of Germans. I can tell you I was out of that bed in a flash. It wasn't the first time I've had to fight in my underpants."

Everyone chortled, including Vespasian. Beaming, helping himself to wine, he said, "There was another story, I believe?"

"Oh, that." Cerialis grinned. "Well, once a week I got into the habit of sailing up the Rhine by barge to inspect the garrison at Bonn. While the soldiers camped on the riverbank, I used to entertain a certain Ubian beauty, Claudia Sacrata by name. Gentlemen, she had skin like kissed honey, delicious, absolutely delicious." There was laughter at Cerialis' reminiscenses as, all white teeth and tanned vitality, he waited for the sound to die down before continuing. "Well, this swine, Civilis, the enemy chief, had been observing my movements without my knowing. He descended on that barge on the precise night I should have been entertaining the lady and burned it to a cinder."

"Where were you then?" Vespasian asked.

"At a nearby inn, luckily." Cerialis grinned. "She complained the rocking of the barge made her sick."

There was a roar of mirth at Cerialis' vulgarity. Even Vespasian's face parted in a broad smile. "I've heard your lovemaking was disturbed once before," he said. For some reason Vespasian seemed unusually interested in hearing the details of Cerialis' encounters with the opposite sex.

"Ah, that was the time of the Boudiccan rebellion. A dark-haired princess, she was. A regular hellcat. It was at Lincoln, as I recall. The whole army of the Brigantes suddenly arrived from nowhere and massed on a hill opposite the city. I had a young tribune on my staff at the time, quite inexperienced. He burst into my private quarters without knocking and caught me stark naked with the princess. I've always had it in for that tribe ever since."

"Well, now you may have your revenge," Vespasian said smoothly. "The Brigantes are in revolt. Go and quiet them down, will you? I hereby appoint you governor of Britannia."

For a moment there was complete silence, then the small gathering of generals and members of the Emperor's family rose to their feet and burst into spontaneous applause. The posting was one of great prestige. The honor, immense. A sign of imperial gratitude and imperial trust. The career of Cerialis, as well as Vespasian, was about to reach its zenith.

"Now, gentlemen," Vespasian said, standing, lifting his cup of wine, "let us all drink to the health of old comrades."

They rose to their feet and drank as one man.

For a moment, Cerialis could not help thinking of those who had served with him in Britannia. "We have all come a long way, sire, since the old days," he said. "I wonder whatever became of that Jew you had on your staff? Simon something or other? If anyone should have gotten to the top of his profession, I should have thought he would."

There was a sudden, awkward silence. Everyone in Rome knew about Vespasian's problem with the Jew, except, it seemed, Cerialis, who had only just returned from his campaigns.

With great effort, Vespasian managed a normal tone of voice and said, "I am pleased that we brought the golden Shewbread Table and seven-branched menorah here for all to see. Rome must not be allowed to forget my son's victories. I will build a triumphal arch immediately and these symbols—yes, and the sacred silver trumpets of the Jews too—shall be depicted on it." He turned to Titus, then kissed him on both cheeks. "It shall be known," he said proudly, "as the Arch of Titus."

Now, Vespasian, pleading the accumulated fatigue of

the last few weeks, made his excuses and went to his bed. Only Titus, listening to the respectfully murmured good-byes as the gathering stood to watch the Emperor going, knew what a struggle it had been for his father not to break down completely at Cerialis' casual remark. By right, Titus knew, Simon should be sitting with his old comrades, loaded with honors, instead of peering out from the top of a distant arid plateau as he waited for the Roman legionaries to come and kill him.

PART
V

MASADA—WHERE IT PASSED INTO HISTORY

(70–73 CE)

"Masada shall not fall again."

—Oath taken by recruits of crack Israeli units on the heights of Masada

40

In the year 72 CE, as the hot summer gave way to the more agreeable heat of autumn, a dust haze hung over the northern end of the Dead Sea valley, edging nearer with each passing day. It soon became apparent to the defenders of Masada that the Romans were building a road down which they could pour supplies, men and ammunition. It was plain that at any moment a Roman legion would appear over the horizon.

Ben Yair and Simon, the first in overall authority, the second in military command, now undertook a final inspection of the work they had carried out in the two years they had been left in peace.

The accomplishment had been formidable. The huge casemated walls built by Herod the Great, twenty-eight feet high and eight feet broad, lined with towers reaching to a height of seventy feet or more, had been carefully repaired. Supplies of timber had been laboriously carried to the high plateau so that any breach in the walls could be quickly filled. At the top of the snake path large round boulders had been piled, ready to roll down on any detachment crazy enough to assault the narrow defile.

Secretly, in exchange for their silver shekels bearing the glorious message "JERUSALEM THE HOLY" and dated from the year "ONE" of the Jewish rebellion, Simon's agents had gone far afield to buy Syrian bows—lethal, lightweight, wood-and-bone death dealers that were the best of their kind in the world. Now for every able-bodied man and woman on Masada there was a bow and an adequate supply of arrows. In addition, hundreds of small pieces of silvered scale armor had been found in the old Herodian storerooms and the women had been kept busy day and night, sewing these to the rough cloth tunics of their men. When they had finished, the Jews could produce a suicide squad of a hundred and fifty well-built, well-protected men to beat back any group of legionaries who might, by some miracle, gain the walls. Of this squad Saul, the muscular young boy who had acted as a scribe and shown some promise as a swordsman, was given command.

Quietly, the leaders made their rounds; one stocky, flatnosed, with an outpointing, thrust-forward jaw and eyes that burned with the love of God—a man who would fight for his religion as well as pray; his comrade, in contrast lean and lithe, his figure retaining much of the strength of youth despite his battered, mutilated face and hair that had turned an iron gray. Together they inspected the storehouses bulging to the brim with food that would not deteriorate with time—pulse, corn, dates, fruit from the nearby oasis of EinGedi, oil, wine in good quantity. Carefully, they leaned over the casemated walls and checked the line of water channels running from every corner of the great fortress into the catchment cellars hewn out of live rock by Herod's workmen. Here they had seen for themselves how the flash flood from just one thunderstorm would be channeled into these reservoirs, providing water not only for drinking and washing, but also for the vegetable garden they had started on the plateau.

For months, perhaps for years, the Jews would be self-sufficient. Everything that could be done had been done.

The men stood idly on the casemate, looking toward the north with the view of the Dead Sea and, on the far side, the dust-hazed mountains of Moab, stretching away into the arid wilderness of Arabia. Sensing from their quiet laughter that the tour of inspection was over, Andrasta came to join them, Saul, as always, close by her side.

In the fullness of time, God had rewarded Andrasta with yet another child and she held the squalling Jeremiah tenderly in her arms—the baby named in

376

memory of the heroic old sage of Qumran. Saul, whenever his military duties allowed, never seemed to be far from Andrasta's side. No longer did he try to snatch kisses, but he followed the superb-looking, straight-backed woman around with devotion, almost as though his behavior required a perpetual display of contrition. Now, the four of them stood there looking across the great vault toward the north, each of them with the same thought.

Eventually it was Saul who uttered the words. "When will they come?"

"As soon as their supply line is ready," said Simon. "It can be at any moment. Anytime."

"And who will win?"

"The position, from a military point of view, is finely balanced," Simon said coolly. "We are only a few hundred men and women against thousands of seasoned Roman soldiers, yet the fortress is almost untakable."

"Almost?" Saul echoed curiously. He turned to face Simon, making the little silvered plaques of his old Herodian armor sparkle brilliantly in the strong Judaean sun. "In order to conquer Masada they must first reach its walls, and surely that's impossible?"

"You do not know Roman engineers," Simon said. "They can run rivers through deserts, turn valleys into mountains. Yes, they can reach the walls if they have the patience—and, more important, if they have the time."

Ben Yair wrinkled his brow. "Please explain that," he said. "I do not understand." Military tactics had always worried him.

"In the summer heat, the valley below becomes a deathtrap where nobody can live. The Romans must take Masada by the spring, or leave us in peace for another year—and that, they dare not do."

"Why?"

"Their prestige would suffer. We are the last outpost of the Jewish state. The last bastion of freedom. If they do not subdue us quickly, the whole of Judaea might well rise again." Simon paused, then smiled. "If I were the Roman general, I would be prodigal with my men, disregard casualties. They can replace soldiers easily enough, while for us every one of our effectives lost is a disaster."

"Yes," Ben Yair murmured, "you have given us the answers to many questions, yet whether we are victorious or not will surely depend entirely on another factor that you have ignored."

All of them—Simon, Andrasta, Saul—looked at the stocky, fighting Zealot who stood, legs astraddle, like a rock on the top of the casemated wall.

"The will of God," Ben Yair said, his fierce underslung jaw cracking in a strangely gentle smile. "For the future of our people, perhaps it is necessary that we perish well, rather than survive badly."

It was a strange remark and the others did not understand, but Andrasta, looking at him, felt the warmth rise within her, permeating her belly, her breasts, her lungs, filling her brain with the certainty of her knowledge. Jeremiah had known and had passed God's message on to her. Now, Andrasta was sure of one thing. Ben Yair knew it too. A message involving a mission, a magnificent gesture intended to light the Jews' way through two thousand years of dispersal.

The iron men of Legio X Fretensis came swinging along the narrow road the engineers had constructed along the western shore of the Dead Sea, and as their boots crashed down on the packed stone and scree, they sang. The legion was happy. Its record was good and its tradition impressive. Hardened against frost and cold, sun and heat, under the ferocious discipline of General Corbulo, it had come to be known as the flower of the Roman army. It had acquitted itself well through the rigors of the Jewish war, never panicking before the crazy guerrillas who had descended from the Galilean hills, never retreating in the face of the desperate, starving freedom-fighters of Jotapata, Gamala or Jerusalem. They sang because as soon as they had accounted for a handful of Jews perched on top of some arid mountain, they would get their medals, their torques and golden spears, their back pay and well-earned leave. There was just this one small campaign— no more than a rest cure, they had been told. They would amuse themselves watching the death agonies of a few

378

hundred stray rebels and then—there would be women. After the sack of so many towns, few of the legionaires had not acquired the taste for screaming, kicking, wild-eyed Jewesses.

There were no Jewish effectives left—so one was told—but this was the Roman army and one took no chances. Accordingly they marched in good order, by the book. In front, a screen of auxiliaries and Syrian bowmen able to move fast, to reconnoiter suspicious wadis, gullies, defiles suitable for an ambush; then a stiffening of legionaires, followed by the engineering corps responsible for road making and campsites. The personal baggage of the senior officers followed, protected by a detachment of cavalry, and then the commanding officer himself, Legate Flavius Silva and his staff, splendid in their purple cloaks and crested helmets, escorted by the colorful, beautifully accoutered horsemen, always a hundred and twenty to each legion, their sleek, groomed animals in magnificent contrast to the lean, rangy mounts of the auxiliary. Heads down against the dust cloud raised by the well-shod cavalry, urged on by dry-mouthed teamsters, came the mules pulling the creaking artillery wagons, onagers, ballistae, carts full of traveling cranes and the specialized siege equipment that Silva had been careful to bring.

Next, in all their gleaming pomp, came the standard bearers with the regimental colors, the portrait of Vespasian, the Aquilifer in leopard skins and bearing the great golden eagle of the Tenth Fretensis, the *cornicines, tubicines,* trumpets hooded against the terrible scouring action of the windblown sand.

Now, marching six abreast, came the fighting men, the iron, pulsing heart of the legion. Before you saw them, you could almost smell them—with their sweat-soaked leather jerkins on which jingled their articulated armor and the stale odor of vinegar wine. In front of each cohort were mounted tribunes, wearing elegant muscle cuirasses paid for at enormous expense by the proud patrician families from which they came; then a line of centurions—grizzled veterans these, but with bodies as hard as jerked meat, able to fight and march along with the youngsters, clutching their swagger sticks, their gaily crested helmets turned transversely to those of the soldiers so as to identify their rank. Line after line marched the hard, cruel veterans of the Tenth Legion, five thousand in all, the elite mailed fist that had cost a fortune to produce, arm and train. Behind them, stretching to infinity, cooks, orderlies, camp followers, carts laden with soldiers' baggage; then, awful to behold, thousand upon thousand of filthy, dusty Jewish prisoners, manacled together, stumbling along with their heads down, kept moving only by the cruel, metal-tipped scourges of their mounted escort.

Glancing in front and behind him, Flavius Silva was sure he had forgotten nothing. Above all, Silva was a careful man. That was why he had been chosen to take Masada. Better generals than he, men with far more flair and vision, after one look at the huge towering fortress of Masada would have thrown up their hands in amused frustration and left the Jews to rot in their torrid hell. A place like Masada was a spoiler of reputations. If you failed to take it, you were disgraced. Even if you succeeded, nobody would shower you with congratulations. An elite legion of the line was not expected to fail against a few hundred untrained men accompanied by their women and children. But Silva was not interested either in disgrace or in triumph. He was by nature a plodder, reliable, phlegmatic and, above all, patient. Certain to do his duty. Coming from the Sabine region eighty miles away from Rome as did his patron, Vespasian, he shared the peasant upbringing, the burred speech, and although he would never have the flair and rough charm of the Emperor, he could be depended on to do a sound job. Picked over the heads of many men with superior talent and intellectual ability for the governorship of Judaea, he had in reality been chosen for this one vital task, the eradication of this last remnant of Jewish resistance, this last defiant symbol of national revolt which, under the military command of the legendary Wolf of Masada, laughed at mighty Rome.

The orders burned in Silva's pocket; they had come from Titus, sharp, peremptory. Take Masada—and quickly. That gave him, before the burning heat of the following summer, no more than six months—seven at the most. If he were unsuccessful, he would have to march his force away from this scorching valley of death, only to bring it back in the autumn, by which time the Jews would be reinforced, rearmed, resupplied. That was why Silva had taken along such sophisticated siege equipment, such an enormous labor force of Jewish prisoners, redirected from the spectacle their fate would have provided in Roman amphitheaters.

As he called his army to a halt on the few miles of coastal plain that lie between Masada and the Dead Sea, Silva felt like wincing, perhaps cursing, at the dark, formidable ramparts falling almost sheer from a height approaching fifteen hundred feet. Instead, he kept a grim, determined expression on his face. Short—no more than five feet—squat, Silva was conscious that the troops tended to laugh behind his back. If his lack of height were not handicap enough, Silva had a problem with his hair. For Silva was a truly hairy man. It bushed out over the top of his muscle cuirass, it cloaked the back of his hands and forearms in a thick pelt, it curled blackly out of his ears and nostrils. The last burden that he had to bear was that, despite his appearance of apelike masculinity, he had a voice that tended to crack at moments of stress. Hence his need, most of the time, to appear braver than the brave, more noble than the noble.

While his army rested, Silva, accompanied by his staff officers, made a complete circuit of the fortress, the horses picking their way with difficulty over and around the boulders and rocks at the foot of the stronghold. Finally, he went half the way around again until he was facing the middle of the plateau's western escarpment. "Gentlemen," he said, keeping his voice down nicely, "here we shall build a ramp."

Amazed, his staff pointed out, one after another, the enormous labor involved, the time factor. At least four months would be needed to move any appreciable amount of earth.

To their surprise, the hairy little general laughed. "What does it matter?" he said. "Put the prisoners on double shifts and if it kills them, we will get more. The work can even take six months, but I do not care, because when our siege engines are level with their battlements, we will have them—in days."

It was a silent and chastened staff that accompanied

Silva back to the main army. They had come prepared to laugh at the hairy little fellow, but were beginning to realize for the first time why he had been given command.

There was more to Legate Flavius Silva than met the eye.

From his headquarters in Herod's main palace on the northwest corner of the rock, Simon watched the progress of the Roman works with inner fatalism and a show of confidence which, he knew, was unwarranted.

Right from the start he had restrained the Jews from capering on the battlements, cursing the Romans as they waved their weapons. He had kept them back. Out of sight. Silva must not be allowed to learn how pitifully few they were. When the time for a counterattack came, it would have to be a complete surprise in order to minimize casualties.

On their side the Romans had not tried to force the path. Although willing to accept losses, Silva realized the impregnability of the position and kept his soldiers busy in other ways. A complete wall was built around Masada. Within a month, Silva had effectively sealed off the fortress from all contact with the outside world. As for the ramp, it grew imperceptibly day after day, a foot at a time, the steep incline of its newly thrown earth edging nearer and nearer the casemated wall on the western edge.

Simon and Ben Yair could only stand and impotently watch the flash of thousands of spades in the sun as Jewish prisoners of war worked feverishly to build up the great mound of earth. Soon, the perpetual clink of spades, the crack of whips lashing the bent backs of their countrymen increasingly took toll. "Let us do something—anything," Ben Yair raved.

"What do you suggest?" the Wolf of Masada said, looking almost scornfully at the group's spiritual leader. "Certainly, from our superior height we can reach their construction works with our few ballistae, but we will kill more Jews than Romans, besides giving away the strength of our arms."

"And we will waste ammunition too," added Saul. As

leader of the Palmah—the highly trained assault team waiting to go into action—his advice could not be ignored.

Ben Yair went off to pray. In the little synagogue on the western cliff, with its view of the Judaean mountains framed between its delicate pillars and porticoes, Ben Yair would pass the time in countless services, roaring out a portion of the Torah every Sabbath morning in a great voice that echoed in all directions, chanting the Hallel and invoking the wrath of God on the evil Kittim who lay below.

For the first three months, there was no exchange of fire. True, the Romans had begun swaying up a heavy onager on a high mountain close to the southern tip of Masada, but had been careful to site it out of range of Jewish artillery. As the year turned, the ramp, although steep and very narrow, finally reached the foot of the casemated wall. Well up the slope, the Romans now began building immense wooden siege towers from which, when they had mounted their onagers, they would be able to sweep the defenses. Remembering how their wooden structures at Jotapata had been put to the torch, the Romans lined these with iron plating.

"Attack them. Knock them down," pleaded Ben Yair. Simon shook his head.

"At least fire on them. Make their work difficult," he implored.

"And kill our own people?"

"It is a necessary sacrifice."

"I have just one hundred and fifty young men trained and wearing armor," Simon said evenly. "Against the Romans that is nothing. They will be blown away like a speck of dust in the breeze. I will pick the time to attack."

Ben Yair glared aggressively at Simon. "Will there ever be such a time?" he challenged. "Perhaps you fight for Vespasian now, a traitor to the Jews."

Simon's one eye glowed gray-green, but he made no reply. Ben Yair, realizing the terrible thing he had said, hugged Simon, begging forgiveness.

Returning his embrace, Simon felt no ill will. "You must trust me. I know what I am doing. I promise you there will soon be fighting enough."

* * *

Down below, General Silva was not misled. He did not take the inactivity of the Jews as lack of heart. The Wolf of Masada was doing just what he, Silva, would have done in his place—husbanding his resources and hoping for the element of surprise when the time came for desperate measures.

He now began to work on their morale, hoping to gauge something of the Jews' strength and eagerness for battle. At dawn each morning, a tribune selected for his strength of voice would shout a message to the Jews immediately after the *cornua* had blasted out the shrill notes of reveille.

In the still desert air, every word came clearly to the defenders.

"Listen to me," the tribune would shout. "My commander is a reasonable man. Surrender now and he will let you disperse to your villages. Every day we come closer. Can you not see that you are doomed? Jews—think of your women and children—don't you want to save their lives?" He would go on in the same way, rational, reasonable, then suddenly one morning change his whole tone, aiming to create terror in the Jewish defenders. "Our men grow impatient," he would roar menacingly. "While you keep them here, they lack comforts. Surrender now and let them go back to base, or expect the worst—your wives raped to death, your children spitted on their swords like so many chickens, your mothers crucified for the hawks to gouge out their eyes. Is that what you want? If so, you are going about it the right way."

To this and similar messages the Jews made no reply.

Stroking his hair, which had rapidly grown into a luxuriant black beard, the little general nodded his head grimly at their silence. It was proof that a highly disciplined force existed on the plateau—one that would fight like all the fiends of hell when the time came. Breakfasted, Silva would stump off on his short legs to watch the progress of the sweating prisoners on the ramp where they were building the artillery towers.

In this strange, unnatural peace, Simon and Andrasta grew even closer together. Each morning when

384

the military conference was over, they would go hand in hand to their special place, descending through the hidden passage to the marvelous summer palace of Herod the Great. On the lower terrace, carved as if by magic out of the precipitous northern prow of the boat-shaped plateau, they would spend their time in contemplation of its sheer majestic beauty. At times they would make tender love. Shielded from the dry southerly wind and perpetual, brilliant sun, they would lie in this superbly engineered paradise closeted in each other's arms. Both their bodies had been violated, subjected to every cruelty that the Romans had been able to devise, but here, suspended in time and space, God smiled at them, restoring a miraculous vitality to their abused flesh.

The place was truly one where miracles might happen. Even Herod had gained tranquility of mind by gazing at the wondrous view northward to EinGedi and beyond, and eastward across the Dead Sea, with the whole sweep of the Judaean hills to the west. One hazy, dreamy afternoon, Andrasta was so moved by the superb mosaics, the rows of delicately grooved and plastered stone pillars capped by gold-plated Corinthian capitals, the elegant marbled and painted walls, that she had gripped Simon fiercely and cried, "Let me die here. Yes. This is where I shall die."

Simon, surprised, had merely shaken his head and squeezed her hand. Yet the thought dragged him back to reality, knowing as he did that death might soon be upon them. He did not take her there again.

It could not last—the false peace. The eerie quietness that lay like a gray shroud over the beleaguered fortress.

One day, without warning, with massed Syrian bowmen unleashing covering fire to keep the Jews' heads down, the Romans began swaying their huge catapults up the two armor-plated towers they had built. Now the Tenth Fretensis were renowned for the incredible size of their ordnance, even the great walls of Jerusalem proving no match for the missiles their onagers threw, each one weighing more than half a hundredweight. Once those siege engines started firing, the stout walls of Masada would shatter in a day. To survive, the Jews would have to smash those towers.

That night, Saul assembled the Palmah. Pointing at the great iron-plated structures that menaced them, brilliantly lit by flares to keep off night attacks, Saul split his force in two groups, giving them careful instructions.

When the moon waned over the stark Judaean hills, his men began pushing into place the big boulders that had been kept handy, close by the wall. With one last heave the boulders went over, tumbling and crashing down on the detachment of legionaries that Silva had detailed to guard the towers. With the line of soldiers swept away by the crushing impact, the Palmah charged home, prizing off the iron plating with crowbars and igniting the tinder-dry wood underneath with the Romans' own flares. The Jews made good targets for the Syrian archers, silhouetted as they were against the bright flames. By the time the survivors reached their own lines again, a priceless fifty men of the Palmah were either dead or badly wounded.

As for General Silva, his staff had expected him to scream with rage or show some sign of displeasure at the setback, but in this they were disappointed. Silva had merely stroked his beard, smiled and ordered the towers built up again. "Gentlemen," he said philosophically, "you can have anything in this world if you are prepared to pay the price. You may find the Jews have overpaid."

For the Wolf of Masada, as well as for Silva, the battle had become an absorbing problem based on the passing of time; when the Romans raised their towers again, the Jews must attack them or perish, and in such an attack they would certainly lose another significant proportion of their best men. How many times could the Romans raise their towers before summer came? How many times would the Jews have sufficient strength to demolish them?

Now it was March. Springtime. The sun was getting uncomfortably hot, yet within only fourteen days Silva, with unlimited supplies of timber, iron plating and slave labor, had rebuilt his artillery platforms.

With heavy heart, Simon ordered the Palmah forward once again. Surging down the slope, they pressed their attack with incredible heroism against a withering fire from the archers Silva had deployed, clinging to the narrow platforms around the base of the towers. For a second time the structures went up in a blaze of incandescent fire, but before the Jews retired to the casemated wall, they had left many more of their comrades to eternal sleep in the dust of their homeland.

Now, small lines of strain began to show around the eyes of General Silva. However, his voice remained quiet and confident as he ordered the towers rebuilt yet again, his labor force of prisoners to be worked literally to death until this was done.

While Silva sat alone in his praetorium tent an aide informed him of the arrival of a Roman, an important man, judging from the number of his slaves and the opulence of his litter. Isolated in the wilderness on a tough and inglorious mission, Silva needed all the influential friends he could get. Hurrying to meet the visitor he found—Josephus.

A lot of things had happened to the former Jewish general since Vespasian had spared his life at Jotapata. All of them good—for Josephus. Turning renegade, he had demonstrated his newfound loyalty to the Romans by pleading with Jewish soldiers manning the walls of Jerusalem to surrender. Vespasian also remembered how the captured Jewish commander had openly addressed him as "Imperator" when they had met at Jotapata and confidently prophesied that Vespasian would soon mount the throne. Superstitious, Vespasian had now heaped honors upon him. Prosperous, opulently robed in a toga of the Roman equestrian order, sure of his niche in Roman society, Josephus advanced confidently to shake hands with General Silva. "My dear general," he purred, "what a pleasure it is to meet you. This is indeed a hellish part of my country. How unfortunate you are in drawing such a campaign and how well you seem to be coping."

Fawning upon the Jew, Silva gave orders that he and his entourage be given every possible comfort and invited Josephus to share food with him in his command tent.

Later, having banqueted on fresh provisions brought specially from the oasis of Ein Gedi, the orderlies dismissed from the praetorium, the men, alone at last, sipped wine and talked.

"What are you called now?" Silva asked the Jew curiously.

"Flavius Josephus—and you are called Flavius Silva?"

"That is so."

They smiled at each other. In adopting Vespasian's family name, both of them were plainly the Emperor's men but Josephus had the stronger patronage and Silva bore this well in mind. "May I ask what brings you here?" he inquired, his face a mask of courtesy.

"I have some small reputation as a writer," Josephus said. "In view of my particular—advantages—the Emperor has commissioned me to write a history of the Jewish war. Your campaign, being the final one, seemed important to study."

"I see," Silva said. "Then let me outline the progress of the siege to date." He launched into a description of what had happened so far, with Josephus listening intently. Knowing that the Jew had it in his power to make or break his career, Silva, after emphasizing how success or failure was now balanced on a knife edge, ended formally. "Permit me to offer you every possible facility for observing the battle, and needless to say, your advice at any time would be greatly valued."

"That is kind of you," said Josephus.

Silva was not fooled by Josephus' air of wide-eyed innocence, while Josephus in his turn thought the hairy general looked more like a monkey than the commander of a Roman legion.

In the heat, the exhausted prisoners worked more slowly and it was nearly April before the towers were rebuilt.

This time Silva himself strode out, straddled his cuirassed, armored body on two short legs and called up to the fortress.

"I have news for Simon ben Eleazar," he shouted.

At this, the need for secrecy no longer important, Simon shouted back, "I am here. What is your news?"

"The Emperor guarantees the life and freedom of every single person in your fort, if you surrender now."

"Give your master my greetings," Simon shouted back. "We shall win or die, as the case may be."

"Your cause is hopeless. In days we shall break your wall into bits."

"It is early summer, Roman," Simon shouted mockingly. "Up here it is cool, but in the valley your men will soon perish like flies. Do not leave it too late."

Now, for the first time in his career, Silva's facade of confidence cracked wide. For months he had bottled up his frustrations at being handed this dead-end campaign, concerned for his own welfare if he did not take Masada soon. The Jew was openly baiting him, and under his beard the Roman general reddened with rage. "By the gods, you will die then," he shouted. "All of you, down to the smallest infant, will be put to the sword." The threat was meant to be delivered in a warlike tone, but the general had forgotten how his voice cracked in times of stress, and he sounded like a hysterical schoolgirl.

Trying to maintain some semblance of dignity in front of the massed legionaries, whom he knew were sniggering behind his back, the little general stumped off, giving incisive orders for immediate execution.

In precisely one hour the huge artillery piece that had in the past few months been quietly swaying up the mountain to the south of Masada would commence firing. Under cover of the bombardment and the confusion it would cause, the great metal-tipped battering ram of the Legio X Fretensis would be hauled up the ramp to confront the western wall.

Hairy little General Silva knew his job.

The first intimation that the Jews had of the readiness of the huge artillery piece was at their conference next morning. There was a short *wheeuw,* followed by an explosive crash as a half-hundredweight boulder came hurtling out of the sky, smashing into the ground with enormous impact. Simon and Ben Yair went out to watch. On the north face of the adjoining mountain, the Romans could be plainly seen, heaving at the skeins of twisted rope, winding the onager up for another launch. A man was detailed to observe the operation and every five minutes or so he would yell, "The stone cometh." The whole garrison—men, women and children—would take cover. The Romans, realizing that the shock value

389

of the bombardment was fading, now erected screens around the onager so that the moment of launch could not be observed. But the sharp-eyed lookout could see the white stone clearly in the bright sun and was able to give warning. The Romans finally hit upon the idea of painting the stone black, and now the Jews suffered. No longer able to go on the alert, they labored, slept, fought under the death-dealing bombardment. In a few days most of the storehouses had gaping cracks which would ensure the ruin of their supplies when the next flash storm came. In places the casemated walls began to crumble, baring any defender to a shower of arrows and quick-firing ballistae if he so much as showed his head.

Covered with dust and stone splinters, the Jews came to resemble burrowing animals that spent their lives under the desert rocks. Somehow they held on. They endured, staying watchful and in good heart, nursing their weapons and ammunition.

Now, for the third time, in full and open view of the Jews, the Romans began swaying up their artillery into a commanding position on the towers. In twenty-four hours the job was complete and the Jews had done nothing.

"Will he attack us again?" Silva asked Josephus over dinner that evening. "I would be grateful for your opinion. You knew Ben Eleazar, did you not?"

Josephus picked the pork clean from his plate. It was amazing how a man who had once been a Pharisee priest could forswear his religion when expediency called. He had chosen pork as if to emphasize his allegiance to his new country at the expense of his old. Decisively, he answered, "Ben Eleazar wins his battles with boldness, not with caution. If he does not pull down your towers, it is because he no longer has the capacity."

"That is my view also," said Silva. "He must now be desperately short of men."

Silva was right. The cost of storming the siege engines had become unacceptable. Simon now had to husband his small numbers so that a force, however tiny, still existed to throw the Romans back when they breached the wall. The battle had entered its final phase.

Next morning Roman firepower reached total intensity. A combined barrage of ballistae and onagers forced the defenders into deep cover, while a gang of sweating legionaries smashed down piece after piece of the wall with their battering ram, until the buttress was broken all along the edge of the steeply inclined ramp.

Now, as the *cornua* blasted their frenzied, imperative call to charge, the Tenth Fretensis in close formation came trotting up the slope. Heavily armored and carrying a great weight of metal, the heat quickly tired them, and by the time they bent into the testudos, the strength had left their legs. With the Romans' barrage lifting for fear of killing their own men, the defenders quickly emerged from their burrows in the shattered casemates and broke the testudos by rolling a heavy boulder down the hill. Their own small number of precious ballistae now came into play, flinging heavily weighted pila with sufficient impulsion to pluck whole files of legionaries off the slope as if by a giant hand, sending a spray of broken bodies spinning and reeling to their deaths.

Eventually the Romans retired down the slope and both sides paused to count the cost. Great heaps of Roman dead littered the steep ramp, but so intense had been the fighting and so cunningly had Silva placed Syrian sharpshooters in his towers that many Jews also lay with their enemies. As Simon had expected, Silva was prodigal in his expenditure of men because of the desperately few days that were left before summer.

Now, secretly, the Wolf of Masada called every single man in the garrison to work through the night on a second wall built behind the ruins of the first. Fashioned to Simon's own design, it consisted only of loose sand and stone, packed into a framework of stout timber. In the morning, the Romans laughed at the contraption, but their laughter soon stopped when they found their battering ram merely compacted the wall, making it stronger. Also, its incredible powers of absorption appeared to cope equally well with the huge boulders the onagers kept crashing down upon it.

All that day, the heat grew, the sun arching across the heavens toward the Judaean hills like a ball of searing fire, shining impartially on Jew and Roman alike—but the Jews, protected by shade, did not have to clamber up a precipitous slope in full armor. Pacing his praetorium tent, Silva waited until just before dusk, then ordered a surprise attack by lightly armored, expendable auxiliaries, preceded by a swift, deadly barrage of bolts and arrows. The Jews were waiting and the charge ended in bloody failure.

That afternoon, it had become impossible to fight, to think, even to live in such stupefying heat. Silva knew he would have to triumph in the next forty-eight hours—or admit defeat. Early next morning, before the sun rose, he stumped on short legs to the *auguratorium* whence the priests of the camp determined the omens by watching the birds and the stars. The priests seemed quietly optimistic. Heartened, Silva sacrificed, a solitary figure at the legion's altar, then called together his commanders to give orders for the final assault, which was to be a particularly terrifying maneuver he had conceived during deliberations.

Judging the wind to be right, blowing from west to east into the defenders' faces, the Romans armed their catapults with burning lumps of Greek fire. Although their apparatus soon took flame, they managed to drop enough of it on the wooden supports of the wall to start them burning fiercely. The *cornua* sounded again and the Romans charged. The defenders, coughing, choking, blinded, could do nothing to stop them, and the triumphant Romans, cheering hoarsely, surged over the wall. Just as it seemed Masada must surely be overwhelmed, the wind completely reversed direction, as it sometimes will in hot desert climates, blowing back into the Romans' faces, singeing them to inglorious flight.

Screaming their thanks to God, their savior, their redeemer, the Jews moved back onto their wall, but incredibly the wind shifted once again and the Romans, taking heart in their turn, counterattacked. By nightfall they held the smoldering ruins of the wooden wall, and only a deep ditch, lined with a thicket of sharp palisades sticking out of the ground, lay between the Romans and the open plateau. Once across that simple ditch, they would fan out and the massacre would commence.

For the Jews, there was only gloom. While the Romans swigged *posca,* or vinegar wine, in the *contubernia* and swore to avenge their comrades, the defenders prepared for the end.

By the light of a guttering candle, the leaders held a conference.

"How long do we have?" asked Ben Yair.

"Tomorrow. Perhaps the day after. That is all," said Simon.

"They will have to cross the ditch," Saul said.

"If necessary, they will walk across the bodies of their own dead."

There was silence as each man faced the hopelessness of the position.

"The fenugreek is ready," said Ben Yair.

"And the olive oil." Saul smiled.

"Gentlemen, let us return to our positions, because they will soon be coming," said Simon.

The men dispersed. It was no time for emotion, for rhetoric. It was merely a matter now of fighting to the end, living for the next day.

Just before dawn, they came: the first cohort of the Tenth Fretensis, the sharp, steel-hard cutting edge of the legion specially held back for the final assault. Up the ramp and over the wall they trotted, deeply tanned veterans, tough as teak. Contemptuous of the flight of arrows the Jews unleashed, they bayed wolfishly to keep up their courage and thought of the soft-skinned women, theirs for the taking on the other side of that ditch.

Down went the gangways with a crash, then with a roar of trumpets two huge standard bearers led the way across. Such was the enormous, armored impact that the Jews were literally swept away, but rising from where they were hidden at the bottom of the ditch, three Jewish volunteers reached up and calmly threw a bucket of fenugreek across each of the planks the Romans were using as bridges.

Cut down by enraged legionaries, the Jews died in their own blood as they fell back into the ditch, but they had done their job—made the gangways as slippery as ice. Cursing in their rage, Roman after Roman poured onto the gangways only to lose his footing and fall, one after another, upon the sharpened stakes, writhing in agony until Jewish arrows put him out of his misery.

Still the Romans came. They were brave. Inhumanly disciplined, stepping on the mounting corpses of their dead comrades, they waded through the bloody ditch and came clambering out on the far side, short swords at the ready—to be doused by screaming women carrying buckets of boiling olive oil. Howling, clutching at their tightly fastened *loricae segmentatae* as the hot oil seeped through the open metal bars of their armor, the Romans danced a macabre death waltz. They were literally fried alive. The smell of their blistering flesh was revolting even to the Jews. Sobbing out their agony, the first cohort, for the first time in their history, retreated.

That night, the air became hideous with the threats of the Romans. In broken Hebrew, the surviving veterans of the first cohort informed the Jews in starkly obscene detail exactly how they intended to violate their women and children and, as punishment for the boiling oil, how they would crucify them afterward.

"You hear that?" Ben Yair said. "They will crucify even our women and children. What can we do, Simon?"

"Forestall them."

"There are many of us still left," Ben Yair said, wringing his hands. "We cannot kill our own people against their will. Mass suicide on such a scale needs agreement, needs discussion, and we do not have the time."

"I will give you time," said Simon. He turned to Saul, in the darkness. "Tomorrow I shall take over command of the Palmah."

"But why?" Saul cried.

"Grant me the privilege of dying in battle," the Wolf of Masada said. "Now, I hold you to your promise. Guard and protect Andrasta and the children. Do what is necessary to save her from the Romans."

"I shall."

For minutes the men sat in silence. Then Ben Yair said quietly, "It is over?"

"It is over," Simon said. "The Palmah is gutted. We have only twenty young men to resist the Romans. That is all. Otherwise there are only women, children and the aged."

"Then we must do as you say," Ben Yair said soberly. "You have done well. No one else could have held them off as long. All of us thank you for our extra days of liberty."

Saul nodded. "The Wolf of Masada will not be forgotten," he said.

There was silence again; each man embraced the other and went to his post.

Tomorrow would bring only death.

41

Later that night Simon and Andrasta lay together, clutched in each other's arms. As the first pale glimmerings of dawn stole over the mountains of Moab they knew they did not have long. Beside them, the children whimpered restlessly in their sleep. Softly, unemotionally, the two of them talked. All their lives they had known cruelty and destruction. Even death itself was familiar. Like the coming of an old friend.

"Have I been a good wife to you?"

"Precious beyond words. And I? Have I deserved praise as a husband?"

"The best in the world."

"Not true," Simon said. "For I am a coward. Because I cannot bear to put you to the sword, I must die the easy way, in battle, leaving another to do my work."

"You will weave your legend," Andrasta said easily, "and we will weave ours."

"You really believe that?"

"I do," Andrasta said. She kissed him lightly on the cheek and asked, "Will you pray?"

"I am not a praying man, but if you wish, you may listen to this. "'A woman of worth,'" he sang, "'who can find? For her price is far above rubies. The heart of her husband trusteth in her; and he shall have no lack of gain. She doeth him good not evil all the days of her life.'"

Andrasta had never heard her husband sing before,

and at the sound of his voice in the darkness, she imagined that he was a young man once again, serenading her, wooing her. Quietly, so as not to interfere with his beautiful song, she wept.

"'*Rubowse, bonowse, osew, hoel*—many daughters have done worthily,'" Simon sang on, "'but thou excellest them all.'"

"That was beautiful," Andrasta said. "Now will you pray?"

"In truth, I have sinned much," said the Wolf of Masada, "and I do not know how."

"Then I will pray for us both," said Andrasta. In crystal-clear tones, she recited the beautiful Twenty-third Psalm of King David. "'The Lord is my shepherd: I shall not want. He maketh me to lie down in green pastures: He leadeth me beside the still waters. He restoreth my soul: He guideth me in the paths of righteousness for His name's sake. Yea, though I walk through the valley of the shadow of death, I will fear no evil; for Thou art with me: Thy rod and Thy staff they comfort me.'"

Simon waited until she had finished, then kissed the children and began buckling on his armor. He did not wish her to see his tears. He embraced her for the last time, then strode off.

"You will see," she cried after him fiercely. "What we have done here will not be forgotten. It will be as a lamp to your people over thousands of years of darkness. One day they will come back—in their hundreds and in their thousands—and they will remember."

The Legio X Fretensis would not let go, unaccustomed either to defeat or heavy losses: the obliteration of this defiant pack of Jews had now become a matter of honor. Despite the insufferable heat, they needed no urging by General Silva to finish the job.

At dawn, as predictable as sunrise itself, they came again. Walking up the steep ramp to conserve their strength, climbing the shattered wall. Formed into disciplined maniples, they plunged once more into the body-filled ditch and stormed across the other side.

This time they were ready for the screaming women and their pots of boiling olive oil. In seconds, the women were spitted by the arrows of specially positioned Syrian bowmen. On the far side of the ditch, the Romans assembled in close ranks. At a sharp command, they locked shields and broke into a jog trot. The famous Roman armored assault was about to sweep across the heart of Masada.

Then the Palmah hit them. A phalanx of twenty desperate survivors smashed into the Romans with unbelievable impact, their Herodian armor clashing against that of the Romans. At their head was the lean, grizzled, one-eyed Wolf of Masada, teeth bared in a snarl, his sword thrusting with murderous efficiency. The legionaries recognized a suicide mission when they saw one; men determined to die do not behave according to any military manual. They have the strength of madness—a fury that understands neither retreat nor superiority of numbers. All one can do against it is to give way and wait. No ordinary combat will defeat them.

The Roman line split into two groups. The Palmah tumbled one group back into the ditch in a welter of blood, then turned to deal with the other. Again, the Romans retreated, but the urgent braying of trumpets and the hoarse-voiced centurions soon brought them to order and the threat of discipline began to equal their fear of suicidal madmen. As reinforcements surged over the wall, the tiny Jewish force was slowly beaten back. Even heroes weaken. One by one the men of the Palmah died, the silvered scales of their Herodian armor tinkling with a strangely gentle sound at the bloody impact of each body upon the harsh Masada soil.

Simon was still the relentless death machine. Using all of the black arts learned so long ago in gladiatorial school, his sword flicked in and out, faster than a snake's tongue. Slowly, a pile of dead legionaries grew around him, and even the Romans marveled at the insane purpose of this legendary Jew with his one gray-green eye. No sword, it seemed, could cut him down, but as the Romans shrank before him, he offered, for a moment, a clear target to a Syrian bowman.

As the sharpshooter's arrow lanced deep into Simon's throat, a great gout of blood burst from his neck. He knew immediately that he was done for. He stood there swaying. Legs apart, he bellowed his fury at the

Romans, challenging them to come and finish him off.

He began to stagger drunkenly around the high plateau, and now a hush settled over the legionaries. They grounded their arms and silently watched him. In seconds, the whole of Simon's life seemed to slip by with monstrous speed. The horror of the arena—those carefree, arrogant days of youth when women had been more important than a solemn oath to his father—that strangely deep friendship he had formed with Vespasian, now Rome's mighty Emperor. All these things he thought of, while the drumming grew in his ears and the brown mountains of Judaea began to swim and turn black before his gaze. He staggered, then collapsed in the dust. He found himself thanking the brown-eyed woman for all those years of contentment. That was good—to have been given time to remember her. Finally, he thought of Andrasta and her magnificent, uncomplaining courage, her clear skin burned to a dark brown by the Judaean sun, those cornflower-blue eyes, the long tawny hair, close-plaited and tumbling down her slim shoulders. At this, the madness faded from his mutilated features and the glare of his eye seemed to soften before, flicking upward, it froze suddenly, finally, into the permanent fixed stare of death.

The Wolf of Masada was no more and the Jews broken. The Romans lifted their helmets from their heads and cheered. They made ready to celebrate their victory in an avenging orgy of rape and violence, but the sudden, deep braying of the *cornua* sounding the retreat could not be disobeyed. Sullen at this inexplicable order, the Romans retired. Tomorrow, Silva would give them the women they craved, but first he intended to marshal the prisoners in an orderly manner, have the woman Andrasta identified and then taken into custody with her children. Neither Silva nor Josephus was going to overlook the chance of doing such an enormous favor for the grieving Vespasian.

As the soldiers melted down the slope, a great calm descended over the battlefield, a silence that held strangely through the rest of the day and into the night. Both sides knew that with the sacrifice of the Palmah and the death of the Wolf of Masada, the battle was ended.

Tomorrow, marching up the slope behind their eagle standards, the Romans would come.

In the ruins of the palace, the Jews assembled. No one manned the walls. There was no need. No possibility of further defense. Of the people on Masada, only a handful of able-bodied men were left.

"Jews of Masada," Ben Yair called, "tomorrow, when the Romans arrive, you will be taken prisoner and then executed. Let us deny them this pleasure and make an end to our own lives before morning."

At this, the old men and women began to mutter. "We're no use as slaves. Perhaps they'll let us go. They won't want us."

Ben Yair said, "Don't you realize they'll kill us all? Didn't you hear their threats to crucify young and old alike? Can you not understand that we, who have mown down the flower of their legion, will assuredly find our deaths made hideous?"

Still they murmured, debating among themselves. The Romans were a civilized people. Their general, by reputation, a fair man. Surely he would not condemn old women to the slow torture of the cross or beat old men to death. The young women and children must take their chances, but surely they at least would survive.

Eyes blazing, Ben Yair screamed at them, "Have you lost all courage? All the nobility you displayed in this siege? I tell you now that it is God's will that we should die. Did He not turn back the wind into our faces? It was a sign to us that we must perish and if we die, let us go tonight, with self-respect, rather than tomorrow for the Romans' amusement. Let us lay down our lives for the Almighty so that in thousands of years to come it will be remembered as a magnificent gesture, rather than a shameful massacre. Jews"—he held out his hands to them—"do what God asks. Create a legend. A story of bravery for Jews scattered all over the world to tell their families. We who with our half-trained women and children have inflicted such terrible injury on a Roman legion—are we then to go to our deaths as meekly as lambs? You fought like soldiers, now I ask you to die like soldiers."

The breathtaking horror of what Ben Yair proposed— the mass suicide of everybody on Masada—was still too much for the Jews to contemplate and they sat silently, shaking their heads.

Suddenly, Andrasta stepped forward and began addressing the meeting in a bold, clear voice. Content to stay in her husband's shadow while he was alive, this tall, fine-boned woman, with her plaited tawny hair flowing in the wind, would now startle the Jews with the strength of her personality. "Surely you are not afraid to die?" she asked scornfully. Throwing back her head, she laughed. "Come now. It is no great thing. I alone among you might find my life spared by Vespasian, yet I choose to go first. I will show you the way."

"You?" Ben Yair cried. "Why should you, born a Gentile, show us our duty?"

"For many months I stayed at Qumran with the great sage Jeremiah," Andrasta replied. Her face, ravaged with grief from Simon's death, now seemed to take on some inner light. Eyes shining, she paused, weighing her words carefully before she went on. "One day he took me aside and told me that I had been chosen to help in some great task. My husband, Simon, was a warrior—a fighter, he said, and would not understand. Of the two of us, I alone would be given this mission and it would be vital for the history of the Jewish people."

"This mission—what was it?" asked Ben Yair loudly, so that everyone could hear.

"To see that we create a legend when we die that will be a message to our descendants. To light a torch that will guide their steps through the years of darkness."

"This is my wish also," Ben Yair added solemnly.

Andrasta turned to Saul and said imperiously, "Come on then. Let us get it over with. There is no time like the present and death is no difficult matter." Tall and straight, with all the queenly bearing she had inherited from her mother, she swept out of the meeting with her two children.

Saul followed her. It was his sworn duty to help her. Interpret her wishes. If she wished to die cleanly, painlessly, rather than be taken by the Romans, he would not stand in her way. They went down the steps that led through Herod's villa on the northern tip of the plateau, until they reached the beautiful paradise of the lower terrace where she had spent so many happy hours with Simon. "Here," she said. "This is where I shall die. Will you please do it now?"

"And the children?"

"Them also."

"How shall I do it?"

"In truth, I do not care, as long as you are quick." There were tears in her eyes. She walked into the adjoining bathhouse so that the children would not have to watch. "Now. Get it over with."

"May I at least kiss you good-bye? I have loved you always. You know that."

Smilingly, the girl came toward him, offering her cheek. Saul pulled out his dagger and drove it hard under her rib cage, piercing her heart, so that she died instantly. So quickly and cleanly did she perish that not even the faintest glint of surprise came into her blue eyes as she fell forward into his arms. The warrior placed her reverently on the floor, then went back for the older boy. Showing the same merciful speed, he quickly killed him, laying him down beside his mother. Returning to do the same to the little toddler squalling miserably on the stone floor, he suddenly stopped and said, "It is enough. This one shall live to continue the line of Simon ben Eleazar." He lifted the baby to his shoulder and mounted the steps, wondering who could look after the boy. As luck would have it, he discovered two elderly kinswomen who had not gone to the meeting with the others. Quickly, he hid them, together with the child, in a cave set into the cliff of the plateau, telling them to stay under cover until he returned. Then he went back to the meeting which was still in progress.

"It is over, then?" asked Ben Yair.

"Yes," Saul replied, "she is dead."

At this, a great groan seemed to rise from the assembled crowd. Shamed by the girl's example, they now found the courage that had deserted them and begged to be the next to die. An old rabbi stood up. "It is plain that the Almighty wishes this deed to be done," he said in a quavering voice. "I shall be next." Another stood and shouted, "I have precedence over him and it is for me to set the example." The meeting quickly turned into tumult as a mass of elders clustered around Ben Yair, each of them pleading that for one reason or

401

another, he had the right to kill himself before the others.

"Sit down," Ben Yair roared. He was still their leader and the noise died as they hastened to obey him. "My children," his voice went soft, "do not fight among yourselves. We will elect ten to do the deed for us. Men who will be swift and merciful."

This idea was immediately agreed upon and ten men chosen, with Ben Yair and Saul among them.

"Now go to your quarters," said Ben Yair. "Each man must lie down with his family, placing his arms across his wife and children to steady them, baring their necks so that they are offered cleanly to the sword. My comrades, do not be sad. Go with happiness in your hearts because this is a great thing that you do for your people."

The meeting ended, each man making his own farewell to his family, preparing them for the sword. They waited until, hearing the soft step of the executioner, they shut their eyes, said the *Shema*—the last prayer to God before death—then whispered quietly that they were ready. No one struggled as the sword came down. With patient, cold-blooded courage, old men, women and children lay prone on the ground, waiting for their turn.

Within hours it was done. Now the ten met again, their swords red with blood. "Well," said Ben Yair, "since we are a minyan, we may say a last prayer before choosing him who will kill the rest of us."

The men marched to the synagogue and Ben Yair defiantly read the portion from the Torah appropriate for that week, after which they roared out the Hallel, concluding with a mighty Kaddish that echoed off the Judaean mountains. When it was over, one of them, who was called Jonathan, asked, "Shall we now draw lots?"

Ben Yair nodded. Sending for the little shards of pottery with their names painted on them—in other days, identification chits for the drawing of rations—he had them all placed in a narrow-necked wine jar. He shook the jar vigorously and, averting his face, reached in with a hand and picked—Saul.

"Very well, I will do it," said Saul. He was content

402

because the two women and the baby would now be safe. He would be the last man alive on the plateau before the Romans came.

"One thing we must do," said Ben Yair. "We must burn everything. One storehouse however we shall leave intact for the Romans, and in there they will find our bodies and know we died deliberately and did not perish by fire."

The men accepted the wisdom of his remarks and, with the sky already lightening from the east, sped off to carry out the task. Soon, the whole of Masada was ablaze, quickly becoming, in the dry climate, a vast, roaring holocaust. The Romans, lying in their *contubernia,* could only wonder at the loud cracking of the tinder-dry wood and the sparks exploding hundreds of feet into the air.

Their job done, the men adjourned to the storehouse that had been left intact. Standing at the far corner of the plateau, it would remain untouched by flame and provide stark evidence of what the defenders of Masada had done. Quickly—there was no time now, even for a handshake—the nine men sat down and bared their necks for the sword. Saul was young and strong. His sharp blade cut cleanly into flesh and bone and one after another the men died stolidly, courageously.

Now, even as the eastern sky was alight, Saul ran back to join the two women and the child he had hidden in the cave. Finding parchment, he sat down and wrote in his beautiful scribe's hand, "Romans. These women guard the son of Simon ben Eleazar. I, Saul the scribe, ask the Emperor to spare his life in memory of our great leader."

He tied the parchment with ribbon, rolled it tight and sealed it, to give the appearance of formality. He handed it to the women, hugged them, patted the cheeks of the baby and, as the Roman trumpets shrilled the reveille, descended the hidden staircase to the little bathhouse where Andrasta lay dead with her child.

With the aid of some stones, he wedged his sword securely in a crack running along the floor. He unbuckled his armor until he was bare at the waist.

He looked toward the north, toward the ruins of

Jerusalem and the Temple, then, speaking in a loud, firm voice, said, "Hear, O Israel, the Lord our God, the Lord is one."

He fell forward on his sword.

By some mischance, the onager crew on the adjoining mountain had received no change of orders. Accordingly, they started their bombardment again at dawn.

The first boulder missed completely, but the second, at maximum range, soared high over the whole length of the plateau, then arched down almost vertically on Herod's villa built on the northern terrace.

The whole lower level collapsed with a great crash of masonry, entombing the three bodies.

42

"Is it not a fine piece of work?" Vespasian said to Josephus. The two of them stood admiring the newly finished Arch of Titus, white and glistening in the sunshine. The sculptor had surpassed himself, the captured menorah, the trumpets of silver, the heavy golden Table of the Shewbread depicted as being borne with intolerable strain on the backs of the Jewish prisoners.

"Truly excellent, sire," said Josephus.

"And such events must be recorded as a lesson for all those tempted to rebel against Rome," Vespasian said. Then, peasant's eyes glinting shrewdly, he added with heavy formality, "I therefore confirm my commission that you write an official history of the Jewish war, for the benefit of the whole Roman people." By this move he had neatly shifted the burden of paying Josephus from the imperial treasury to the Senate. Vespasian's seamed face broke into a smile at the thought.

"It shall be as you command, sire," Josephus said.

"Good," Vespasian grunted. He said nothing more, but instead started a slow walk. "He died well, eh, Josephus?" he demanded without warning. "The Jew— Ben Eleazar?"

"Magnificently, sire, by all accounts."

"Then away and begin your history," Vespasian said heavily.

"Sire." Josephus turned to leave.

"Wait," Vespasian said suddenly, "I haven't finished." He paused for a second, gathering his thoughts. "Look here," the Emperor went on, his voice awkward with embarrassment, "the fact is, this is difficult for me to put into words. I don't have a gift for fine phrases like you, Josephus, but I want you to do something for the Jews as well. Mention their bravery, their fighting qualities—just for the sake of my old comrade. Do you see what I mean?"

"I see," said Josephus. He saw a great deal. Suddenly, he could envisage a whole new life of dedication stretching ahead of him. It was as though a curtain had opened, letting in bright light on his dark thoughts of self-hatred. Now, at last, he could cleanse his conscience, purge the heavy load of guilt he felt in abandoning his own people. Yes, he would write a story, superb in its style, magnificent in its turn of phrase, but that would not be all. It would be a story with two messages: on the surface, a paean of Roman victory for the common mob, yet hidden underneath there would be another, far stronger, far more enduring; its true meaning only understandable with the passage of tens of centuries. Only he, Josephus, had the skill and the knowledge to write such a history. Only he had the burning need to make amends.

And what a story it would be! What a tale of suicidal rebellion against the iron cruelty of Roman rule! A saga of Jewish heroism, of how a small tribe of fighting men took on the whole might of the Roman nation, hurling back first one legion, then another, a tale culminating in a gesture of the human spirit which would have no equal

405

in the treasurehouse of the human soul. And because he, Josephus, would be their historian, the guardian of their fate, the recounter of their bravery, perhaps the Jews would not disappear from history like countless other nations—the Hittites, the Philistines, the Assyrians, the Moabites, the Samnites, the Chatti, the Cherusci, the Silures, the Brigantes, the Sumerians, the Phoenicians—the list was endless. Perhaps this small tribe, scattered to the four winds, deprived of a homeland, herded into ghettos, ridiculed, tortured, massacred at the whim of the countries where they had been given shelter, would remember the story of Masada and take heart. One day, Josephus thought, because of him, the Jews would remember their military tradition and, if the spur of imminent extinction became sharp, would stream back to Israel and say to their enemies: This is our country. Here we are and here we stay, and as at Masada, you will not drive us out or take us prisoner, because we shall either win or die. And with God's grace, they would refound a mighty nation, small in numbers but great in valor.

"I will do as you say, sire," Josephus said to Vespasian. Quietly he bowed himself out of the Emperor's presence. He wanted to be alone now, to think, to plan. Lions, he thought. I shall make them as lions in the wilderness, unconquerable, untamable. Because of me they will remember their past. They will remember Masada—and one day, long in the future, they will write such a story of military courage as will make their enemies acknowledge them as the finest fighting men in the world.

Only the patronage of Vespasian has given me this great opportunity, thought Josephus.

And this patronage had arisen because of a strange and enduring friendship between a Roman Emperor and an obscure Galilean.

EPILOGUE

ON MARCH 14, 1952 A COPPER SCROLL CONTAINING AN inventory of the great Temple treasure was discovered in a wadi near the monastery of Qumran. Much work has already been done in deciphering the descriptions of the likely hiding places—but that is another story in itself.

With the writings of Josephus as the only existing source of information, Masada was excavated in 1965 by the eminent general and archaeologist Yigal Yadin. On July 7, 1969, twenty-seven bodies of men, women and children were buried by the Israeli Army with full military honors and the site has now become a military and historical shrine revered by the Jewish people.

Perhaps the most exciting of all the discoveries made there were the skeletons of a young woman and a small child, lying close to a warrior clad in old-fashioned armor, in a corner of Herod's villa on the northern terrace. Preserved miraculously over two thousand years, the hair of the young woman was arranged in two long, beautiful, tawny-brown plaits.

THE BIG BESTSELLERS
ARE AVON BOOKS

☐ Birdy William Wharton   47282 $2.50
☐ The Second Son Charles Sailor   45567 $2.75
☐ People of the Lake Richard E. Leakey &
    Roger Lewin   45575 $2.75
☐ "The Life": Memoirs of a French Hooker
    Jeanne Cordelier   45609 $2.75
☐ Adjacent Lives Ellen Schwamm   45211 $2.50
☐ A Woman of Independent Means
    Elizabeth Forsythe Hailey   42390 $2.50
☐ The Human Factor Graham Greene   41491 $2.50
☐ The Train Robbers Piers Paul Read   42945 $2.75
☐ The Brendan Voyage Tim Severin   43711 $2.75
☐ The Insiders Rosemary Rogers   40576 $2.50
☐ The Prince of Eden Marilyn Harris   41905 $2.50
☐ The Thorn Birds Colleen McCullough   35741 $2.50
☐ Chinaman's Chance Ross Thomas   41517 $2.25
☐ The Trail of the Fox David Irving   40022 $2.50
☐ The Bermuda Triangle Charles Berlitz   38315 $2.25
☐ Lancelot Walker Percy   36582 $2.25
☐ Snowblind Robert Sabbag   44008 $2.50
☐ Fletch's Fortune Gregory Mcdonald   37978 $1.95
☐ Voyage Sterling Hayden   37200 $2.50
☐ Humboldt's Gift Saul Bellow   38810 $2.25
☐ Mindbridge Joe Haldeman   33605 $1.95
☐ The Monkey Wrench Gang
    Edward Abbey   46755 $2.50
☐ Jonathan Livingston Seagull
    Richard Bach   44099 $1.95
☐ Working Studs Terkel   34660 $2.50
☐ Shardik Richard Adams   43752 $2.75
☐ Watership Down Richard Adams   39586 $2.50

Available at better bookstores everywhere, or order direct from the publisher.